2004

Country Splendor

by

Helen Marie Fias

authorHOUSE

1663 LIBERTY DRIVE, SUITE 200
BLOOMINGTON, INDIANA 47403
(800) 839-8640
www.authorhouse.com

This book is a work of fiction. Places, events, and situations in this story are purely fictional and any resemblance to actual persons, living or dead, is coincidental.

© 2004 Helen Marie Fias
All Rights Reserved.

No part of this book may be reproduced, stored in a retrieval system, or transmitted by any means without the written permission of the author.

First published by AuthorHouse 04/28/04

ISBN: 1-4184-0903-0 (e)
ISBN: 1-4184-0902-2 (sc)

Library of Congress Number: 2004091969

Printed in the United States of America
Bloomington, Indiana

This book is printed on acid-free paper.

CHAPTER ONE

Picture yourself relaxing on a soft bed of grass, on a warm, sunny day, beside a gently flowing stream, listening to the softly, rippling water as it plays over the rocks. A gentle breeze stirs your hair, leaving you feeling as if a fairy just passed by. You rise up on one elbow, just enough to allow your eyes to wander across the grassy field nearby. A slight movement catches your attention. A white, furry rabbit sits nibbling on the clover at the edge of the clearing. A meadowlark breaks forth in song from her nest on the far side of the field, where the wild grass grows. You lay back, savoring the tranquility of the moment. Memories begin to surface, of days long past. How far back does your memories take you?

My first coherent memories were of life on a dairy farm in Wisconsin. This was the second farm I was to live on, I was told. I just turned three years old in March of 1940, when my parents moved us there. My younger brother, Robert, nicknamed Bob, was an infant, two years younger than me. When I was old enough to understand that the farm we lived on was referred to as "The Robert's Place," I naively thought it was named for my brother. It was some years later that I learned that all the farms in that area were known by the first people who established them, i.e., the Robert's family established this one.

We were a family of seven at the time, consisting of mother and dad, two older brothers, Ronald and Roy, my older sister, Mary Eileen, then me and my younger brother, Bob.

This farm, as most of the dairy farms in that part of the state, consisted of two hundred acres of gently rolling hills worked into fields of corn, oats, barley, and hay. There was a patch of land left for the cattle to graze on as well as a wooded area at the back of the property. Large oaks, a few evergreen trees, apple, chokecherry, hazel nut, and a large orchard of sugar maple made up the wooded area. This particular farm had a handy creek running through it as well. The creek was considered a real bonus for children who loved to go hunting tadpoles and polliwogs in the early spring, and frogs and crawfish in the summer.

The house, barn and sheds of this farm, were built close to a graveled, country road. Our large, two-story, white farmhouse set on a knoll facing the road and in view of the two neighbors who owned their farms across the road from us. Behind the house a large red barn could be seen, with its majestic silo extending into the sky. A smattering of smaller buildings were arranged where they were most useful for their specific purposes. The granary and chicken coup were in close proximity to the barn. The milk house was positioned between the barn and the driveway to make it assessable to the delivery trucks from the Creamery in town. Behind the barn was the pigsty, with the straw from the grain piled high above it, to lend warmth for the pigs through the long winters, and to help keep it a bit cooler through the heat of the summer. Along the gravel driveway that was located to the right of the house, were sheds filled with the equipment it took to work the fields and bring in the harvest. Everything from plows, discs, cultivators, manure spreaders, wagons and hay mowers were found there. The closest shed to the house held daddy's prized Chevy. The driveway itself passed by the house, then the sheds, to turn to the left close by the milk shed and barn, and then continued in a wide curve to pass by the back door of the house, connecting again to the main part of the driveway, just past the house.

Helen Marie Fias

The most often used path from the back door of the farmhouse, ended up at the three-holed outhouse, all built of wood, and painted red as all of the outer buildings were. Some called this building a privy, others called it the toilet, but we called it the outhouse. I often called it a nightmare. A bench ran the length of the inside, with two high holes cut in it for the longer limbed people to sit over, while a lower level was provided at the end for shorter legs. Half moon cutouts high on the end walls provided a little light, as well as a place for the fragrance to escape through.

This was where my first education of controlling bodily functions came into play. Whenever I felt the 'urge,' I had to 'high tail' it up that path – in whatever weather – regardless of rain, snow or sleet, to wrench open that heavy door, to swiftly pull up my dress, lower my bloomers and hope I had time to position myself over the shortest and smallest hole. Ignoring how cold it felt and how precarious it was, teetering on the brink of that dark cold pit, I struggled to relax enough to get the job done. To me the winters were pure torture, as Wisconsin winters can be bitterly cold, and they seemed to last forever. And if the cold wasn't bad enough, all you had to tidy yourself with was a page from the mail-order-catalog, hung on a nail, used for that purpose. On the upside though, it gave me something to look at if I had to sit there for a while.

Once done, it was a race to see if I could pull my clothes back in place before reaching the kitchen door. Opening the door, I would plunge into the comfort of mom's warm kitchen, where I would warm my cold hands at the large kitchen range. As a result of this torture I would try to put off responding to the 'call of nature' for as long as was humanly possible.

The summer times were more pleasant. The suns warmth lasted throughout the night, and light lingered longer at the end of the day. I loved listening to the soft chirpings of the sparrows and starlings that made their nests, and raised their young in the rafters above our heads. I didn't mind their droppings all over the place; it was just one more factor of country living one put up with. I usually cleaned the spot I wanted to use, with paper from that handy Sears and Roebuck

Country Splendor

Catalog. Often, I would leave the door swinging open, so I could hear the cows softly mooing for their calves out in the pasture. If I were truly lucky, I would be serenaded by the sweet-throated meadowlarks, heralding the spring, as they sang to their young from their nests in the high grass of the pasture. "Prettiest sound in the whole world," I would say to the spider making its web in the corner.

    I dreaded the winter calls of nature though. Especially when the sun was sitting low on the horizon, and darkness was creeping around every corner. I had to brave all the scary things that emerged from my fertile mind. They were more terrifying to deal with than mom's spankings, if I waited too long and wet myself.

    The harshest lesson concerning that subject came my first winter of using the grown up facilities. It was extremely cold out. The snow was piled high on either side of the path, where my brothers had shoveled it, making the pathway easier to manage and easier to find. But this particular night was very dark. The moon had just started making it's way across the sky, casting shadows everywhere. The wind whispered spookily from around the corners of the house, and with my highly imaginative mind, I could envision all kinds of things, just waiting along that path to grab me, or worse, hiding around the designated building I was heading for. Or even worse, perhaps they were already inside, just waiting to grab me as I opened the door, and groped my way in the darkness to the shortest spot to sit.

    I had put off answering the call of nature as long as I dared, but finally, when I knew that I could wait no longer, I grabbed my coat and slipped my arms into the sleeves, as I ran from the house, tearing up that slippery path as fast as I could run. Suddenly I slipped on a patch of frozen snow, lost my footing, and fell hard on my back, loosing control of my bladder as I hit the ground. "Oh no!" I cried, knowing I was in big trouble now. Mama warned me plenty of times about waiting too long, and she had little patience for a disobedient child. I tried to think of ways of hiding what had happened, but no solution would come to me. I had no choice but to go back and own up to what had happened.

Helen Marie Fias

I was crying great sobs by the time I entered the kitchen. Mother met me with a concerned look on her face, but when she realized I wasn't hurt, but scared of another whipping, she stifled a grin and decided to teach me a lesson I would not soon forget.

The only means of heat in the living room was a round metal parlor furnace, that was kept hot, to warm as much of the house as possible. Mother taught us children, at a very young age, to have respect for the dangers it held for careless hands.

Mother removed my coat, lifted my dress to expose my wet, winter underwear. She unbuttoned the seat flap, and let it fall against my stocking covered legs. She then turned my exposed backside towards the furnace, telling me to stand still, and to remain there until my under things dried.

I stood, and I stood, and I stood, until I became bored with standing. I kept wondering if there wasn't a faster way to get this drying done. 'What if I got closer to the stove and bent over to better expose the wet material?' As this thought took place, so did my actions, only I miscalculated how close I had gotten to the source of all that drying heat. As I bent over, my bare bottom became planted squarely against the hot metal stove. Seconds later my screams began. Daddy jumped up from his comfortably upholstered chair, dropping the book he had been reading. It fell to the floor with a thump, as he reached out and grabbed me away from the stove, leaving some of my delicate skin clinging to the hot metal. He yelled for mother, who was already on her way from the kitchen. She took in the situation with one quick glance, turned and went for her medical bag. Because no one went to doctors, or hospitals in those days, except in critical cases, the regimen of home medical practice began. I don't know which was more painful – the healing balm that was slathered all over my raw wounds, that seemed to lock in the pain, or all of the bandages wrapped around me to cover the wounds. I gratefully forget how long the torturous pain continued, or how long it took before I could sleep in spite of the pain, but I definitely remember the screaming pain I endured, each time my wrappings had to be changed. Everything made me hurt, the unwrapping, the cleaning and then swabbing of more ointment, and the rewrapping. It was especially painful to eliminate those things from my body that nature demanded from time to time. To say that 'my lesson' continued for sometime is an understatement. I've heard it said that the amount of pain suffered in the teaching of a lesson, is in direct proportion with how well that lesson is learned, and of how well it is remembered. There must be some truth to that statement, as that was one mistake that I never repeated, nor ever forgot!

CHAPTER TWO

Spring came, my wounds had healed, and I could not wait to go barefoot again. We children took our shoes off as soon as there were patches of grass showing through the snow, and never put them on again until school started in the fall. Running barefoot everywhere, was so liberating. How wonderful the freshly turned earth felt between our toes, as we followed at a distance behind daddy and his plow, which was being pulled by one of daddy's prized workhorses. I often carried with me an empty can, to fill with all the wiggly, fat earthworms that had suddenly been exposed to the open air with the turning of the sod. The earthworms were used as bate, when the boys went fishing in a nearby lake.

Without shoes on I never had to worry about getting them wet, when the warm spring rains would thoughtfully leave fat puddles for me to splash through. It seemed like overnight the earth would begin to bloom with all sorts of new life. The golden dandelions were the first flowers to show their faces, and how I would love to pick great bunches of them to proudly present to mama. Tiny May flowers would spring up everywhere, followed by violets, pink beauties and majestic trilliums. The lilac trees would burst forth with their lovely purple blooms, and the apple and plum trees would preen in their springtime white and pink finery.

During that time of year, I felt there was no better place on earth to live, than on our wonderful farm, so full of new life. We had new calves cavorting around their mothers in the pasture. Tiny pink piglets could be seen shoving and nuzzling for a tit to feed from, as their mother sow relaxed on her side. Downy, little, yellow chicks followed their mothers around; as the hens scratched in the dirt for the corn and grains we threw to them.

    I loved slipping out of my bed early in the morning, tiptoeing from the room so I wouldn't wake my sister. It would be barely daybreak, but the feeding of the cows and the milking would have already begun. I would dress quickly; grab my little tin cup as I passed through the kitchen, head out the back door and run to the barn. My feet would get wet from the dew, as I crossed the grassy center area, which was surrounded by the driveway. The gravel of the driveway would stick to my wet feet, which I brushed off on the concrete floor of the barn, as I entered the milking area where daddy and my two older brothers would be.

    I walked down the concrete aisle, behind the stationed cows, checking around each one, looking for my father. When I found him, he was sitting straddled on a three-legged stool, with his head resting against the cows' softly heaving side. He reached beneath her to extract the milk from her teats. The milk made a swish-swoosh sound as it hit the insides of the galvanized, milk pail, that daddy held securely between his knees. The strong muscles of his arms would move, as his strong, broad hands worked rhythmically, first the one pulling on a teat, then the other.

    I called cheerfully, "Morning daddy!" He turned to look at me. His sky-blue eyes lit up and a playful smile tugged at the corners of his mouth, when he saw me standing there, with my little tin cup held out towards him. He wished me a good morning, as he reached out to take the cup.

    "Vell, angel, aren't you up a little early?" he said, as he directed the stream of milk from the teat into my cup. When it was brimming full of the frothy, warm milk, he would hand it to me.

    "It's not early daddy, it's morning. See, the sun is up," I would declare, as I pointed to the window, where the first yellowing rays of the sun could be seen. He would laugh, as he watched me drink my milk, licking the foam from around my lips. "Daddy, have you seen Ginger this morning?" I asked. Ginger was our big orange cat that hung out in the barn to catch the field mice that came in to snatch at the hay and grain.

"No, I haven't seen her yet this morning. Why don't you take a look around and see if you can find her. She is usually out here by now."

"Okay, daddy," I said, as I took off on my quest, walking as quickly as I could without spilling my precious milk. Further down the row of cows I saw first one of my brothers, and then the other, busy milking as well. I threw them each a "Good morning" in a wave as I passed by. They both returned my wave and turned back to their work.

Dad had a herd of twenty-some prized Guernsey and Jersey milk cows. They each were named according to their color or disposition. Black Bess was named for her dark coloring, and her grown daughter was named Betsy. There were Amber and Pansy, named for the color of their eyes. Buttercup, Daisy and Honey were named for their light coloring, Sugar and Blessing for their sweet dispositions, and on the names went. I called out each of their names, as I proceeded through the barn, giving them a wave and a good morning smile. Once in while, one of them would turn their head to look at me, and reward me with an accompanied long, low, "Moooo."

Milking the cows twice a day, plowing, planting, cultivating, and harvesting all the food for the animals, as well as for us, was hard, backbreaking work. It was up to everyone in the family to help out in anyway they could.

Before daybreak, dad and the two older boys began the barn chores. In the winter months the cows were contained in the barn, where they would stay warm and protected. Before each milking, the boys would throw down hay from the loft, and spread it out for each cow to eat. Then they would add a special ration of dry feed or silage to their hay, to improve the milk quantity. Once the milking was finished, the barn was mucked out, and fresh straw was brought in, and spread out for them to lie down on.

Country Splendor

In the warmer weather, the cows were kept in the barn overnight only. After being milked the following morning, they were released to wander in the pasture, grazing on the summer grasses. While in the barn, the cows stood, lined up in a row with their heads through stanchions, to keep them in their place. There was a metal cup at one side of the stanchion where the thirsty cow would push her nose against a metal ring, releasing water into her cup, where she would drink her fill. That was a great time saving device that was just being implemented in most of the barns. Water was pumped from the well into a large holding tank in the top part of the haymow, where it would be gravity fed through long tubes to each stanchion's cup.

The milking was done by hand, into buckets, which, when full, would be poured into tall metal, sterilized and filtered milk cans. After the milking was completed, the cans would be moved to the cool, milk house, and placed in deep vats of cold water. There they would stay fresh, until the creamery trucks would pick them up, later that day.

After the morning milking was done, the cleaning of the barn began. There were long trenches, called gutters, which ran behind the cows and caught most of their droppings and urine. Large metal vats, called manure carriers, hung from a long track that ran the length of the barn, and could be pushed or pulled along the track as needed. The vat was open at the top, so that shovels full of manure could be lifted up, and deposited in the vat. The bedding straw would be shoveled in the vats as well. Once the cleaning was done, the full manure carrier would be pushed out of the barn, to the end of its track, and by pulling a chain, the vat would release, roll upside down and deposit it's load onto a pile.

Every couple of weeks, a manure spreader would be pulled up close to the pile, and the manure would have to be forked into the bed of the spreader. A team of horses would be used to pull the spreader, while the driver would sit high on a seat at the front of the spreader, holding the reigns and guiding the horses. As the team pulled the spreader across the field to be fertilized, a foot controlled lever would open panels on the bottom of the spreader, allowing the manure to fall into wide paddles, that would spread it out evenly across the ground. Later these fields would be plowed, disked, leveled off and planted.

It was true that a lot of backbreaking work went into running the farm, but it also produced strong backs, arms and legs. My father, at five foot eight inches tall, was broad shouldered, full chested, and slim hipped. His arms and legs were muscular and strong. My brothers at twelve and fourteen years of age that summer, were well on their way to having the same fine physic as their father.

I couldn't find Ginger, the cat, in the milking area, so I went into the haymow, looking for her. I heard a mewing sound coming from a secluded place behind the door that opens into the horse barn. Creeping carefully towards the sound, I peered around the half opened door, and there was Ginger, nursing and cleaning four tiny new babies, all comfortable in their bedding of hay! I was so delighted that I gave a screech of joy, bringing a nervous glance from Ginger along with a warning meow. Wow! Four babies! I ran as fast as my legs could carry me to tell my brothers and daddy about my discovery.

My brother's were not impressed. They knew she was pregnant and ready to have her litter any day, so it was no surprise to them. Daddy reacted surprised, whether he was or not, and said in his slightly German accent, "Vell, vell, vell. Guess you should bring Ginger here so I can feed her some milk. She will be needing extra nourishment now."

"Okay!" I said as I took off. I didn't need to be told twice. I hurried to where Ginger was, picked her up and carried her back to where daddy was milking.

"Put her down, child," Daddy ordered. I placed her on the walk behind the cow daddy was milking. To my surprise, a stream of milk hit Ginger in the mouth. She acted as if she expected it, the way she caught the stream and drank it down. But it was my first time to witness such a thing, and I was so tickled, I couldn't stop laughing. Daddy would press the teat just right again, sending more milk her way, and she would catch it in her mouth, drinking it and then licking at her lips until the next stream came. Once she had her fill, she sat back on her haunches, and began licking her paws and cleaning her face. It

Country Splendor

was the funniest sight I had ever seen. As soon as Ginger headed back towards her babies, I took off for the house to let mama and my big sister in on the exciting news.

They were both in the kitchen, frying up a large and wholesome breakfast. One large frying pan was full of fresh peeled and sliced potatoes, and another was full of fragrantly smoked and frying bacon. Mary Eileen, called Eileen by the family, had the table set with plates, glasses of milk and silverware. The fresh churned butter and yesterday's baked bread was in the middle of the table. A tall pot of coffee was made and set at the back of the stove to keep warm. There was a bowl of mothers' home canned applesauce and a jar of her home made strawberry preserves on the table as well.

It all smelled and looked so good that my tummy started rumbling. I almost forgot what had brought me running to the house, but mother noticed that I was wound up about something, so she turned to me and asked, "And what have you been up to this early?"

"Oh, yes," I said as I remembered what brought me running to her. "I watched daddy feeding Ginger milk right from the cow! It was so funny watching her grab at it with her paws and drinking it from the air! You should have seen it, mama, it was so funny!" And I began laughing again as the picture replayed through my mind. Eileen nodded her head in agreement; as she remembered how she felt the first time she had seen that same scene.

"Well now, why would daddy be feeding Ginger?" Mother wondered.

"Oh, I know!" I exclaimed, all excited to have even more information to tell mama.

"I'll bet she's had her kittens," Eileen stated.

"How did you know? I wanted to be the one to tell!" I complained.

"Hey you two, that's enough. Helen, how many are there?" Mama said, trying to return me to my first feelings of importance of having special news to share.

Helen Marie Fias

Eileen had been teaching me to count and usually I could, but in my excitement I just held up one finger for each kitten. "This many," I said.

"Four of them? That's good. We can use more mouse catchers around here," Mama said.

"What do they look like?" asked Eileen.

"Tiny kittens, what else?" I answered, sarcastically.

"No, I mean, what color are they? I saw a black tom cat around here some time back and I was wondering if he might be the father," Eileen explained.

"Oh, well, lets see. Mostly they were orange like Ginger, but I think there was one that was darker. It was kind of hard to see them, they were hidden behind the horse barn door in the dark." Turning my attention to mama, I asked, "Mama, may I have one for my pet? Please, mama? I've never had a pet of my own." I was dancing from one foot to the other in anticipation of having my very own pet.

"Mom, if she gets to have one as a pet, I want one too. I've never been able to have a pet of my own," complained Eileen.

"Just a minute you two. A pet requires a lot of work, especially if it is an indoor pet. Now if you want to call one of them your own, and promise to keep it outside or in the barn, that's another matter. But we have enough work to do in this house without adding an animal in here." When mother talked with that kind of conviction in her voice, we knew that there was no arguing with her. She had her mind made up and it would be impossible to change it.

"Helen," my sister said softly, close to my ear, so mother would not hear, "I get first choice cause I'm the oldest. Okay?"

"Okay, do you want to come see them now?" I whispered back.

I mustn't have been as quiet as I thought, because mother spoke up, "No, not now, the men will be in to eat any time now and we need to have it ready. Once breakfast is over, and you two have cleaned the kitchen, then you can go play with the kittens for a while. Eileen, you take over here at the stove while I go change your baby brother, and bring him in for his pablum. Helen, you put the chairs up to the table and pour the milk. Be careful not to spill it." With that warning ringing in the air, she proceeded out of the kitchen. I stepped to the door of the front room, watching as mother approached Bobby's bed.

He was sitting up, chewing on his fingers, when mother reached him. "Hello, my little man, how are you this morning?" She asked, with pride in her voice as she marveled at how beautiful her baby was.

Bobby started wiggling and gurgling at the attention he was getting. He reached his arms up to mother as if to say, "Please pick me up." And she did, kissing his soft blond curls as she held him close against her chest.

I watched with envy, wondering if she held me that way when I was a baby. There were times I wished I was a baby again. I got all the attention until Bobby came along. After that, it seemed that daddy was the only one who showed me affection. Eileen was five years older than me, and she would play with me some times, when she wasn't too busy, or preoccupied with her own pursuits. She seemed to enjoy teaching me to read and count, and I loved having her read to me from her storybooks. I envied her being able to go to a place called school, all through the winter. She would tell me about the friends she had made, and the games they would play during recess. It all sounded so wonderful to me. It could get very lonely on the farm with the older kids in school. But I had the barn cats, and then there was always Chaser, the dog that dad brought home for the boys. He was a hound dog that seemed more interested in chasing things through the woods, than playing with me though. I usually found ways to entertain myself, but there were times that I missed having children my own age to interact with.

I turned away from watching mother with Bobby, and completed the tasks mother gave me to do. A few minutes later, dad and the boys came into the kitchen, first, stomping the dirt from their feet at the stoop, and then going to the washbasin to wash their hands. "Something smells good!" Dad exclaimed, as he always did when he came in to eat. Eileen moved the bowls of food from the warming oven to the table, and placed them in front of dad's plate. He waited for everyone to come to the table, and then took a portion of food from

Helen Marie Fias

each bowl before passing it to his left. The next person in line helped himself to a portion, and passed it on. I would watch the boys heap their plates high, and I wondered how they managed to put so much food into their stomachs.

At first, there was only the sound of people eating, and asking for someone to pass them something, but eventually conversation began to circulate around the table. At breakfast, it was usual to discuss what had to be done that day, and who would do what. Once that was settled the real conversation would start. This is where I learned many things. If I sat quietly and just listened, things were discussed that was sometimes beyond my years of understanding, but I would remember everything, and what I didn't understand, I would ask my sister about later. She was able to explain most everything, in a way that helped me understand it.

I learned why dad would have a heifer taken over to a certain farmers place, leave her there for a few days, and then return her to our pasture. Eileen explained to me that the heifer was at the right age to start having babies, so daddy took her to have her introduced to a prize bull the neighbor had. She explained to me that it took a mama and a daddy to produce a baby. That sounded logical to me and I accepted that answer, without wondering why, yet. Having excepted that concept, I then understood why Eileen was wondering about the black, male cat that came around our Ginger. He must have been the daddy. But if there needed to be a daddy and a mama, why didn't they live together like my daddy and mama did? There must be something more to this than I knew yet. If I asked Eileen too many questions though, she would just shrug her shoulders, and answer that I was too young to know all the answers yet. I would have to be satisfied with that answer for the time being, but I was determined that one day I would understand everything.

I learned how to walk within hearing range of adult conversations, being quiet not to draw attention to myself, and just listened. I learned a lot of interesting facts that it would take me a few more years to totally understand, but eventually it would all fit together.

CHAPTER THREE

After the men left the table to begin their next chores, Eileen and I washed and dried the dishes and put them away. Next Eileen washed the tabletop, while I tried to sweep the floor. I wanted to help as much as I could, so we could go look at the kittens again. Mother was still busy with Bobby, as we slipped out of the house and ran giggling to the barn. Eileen wondered if she might get in trouble, slipping away without asking mother if there was anything else she was to do first. "No," I answered. "Remember how she said that after breakfast we could go see the kittens? We did all our chores didn't we?"

"Yes, all we knew to do, but mama might have needed some other help before we left."

"Well, it's too late now, we are in the barn. Come on, they are in the hayloft, behind the horse barn door."

As we neared the family of kittens, we heard the mother cat meowing and hissing, like something was wrong. We hurried to see what was bothering her. There was our dog, Chaser, looking them over, a little closer than Ginger felt comfortable with. He wasn't being aggressive, just curious, but Ginger still insisted on him going away. We came up to him, grabbed his collar and walked him to the outside door of the haymow. Once escorted out, he sniffed the air and took off with a run towards some interesting scent. We returned to Ginger and her family, to take a closer look at the kittens.

Country Splendor

Ginger was settled back down in her nest of hay, with her four babies nursing contentedly, once more. She watched us warily, as we both reached for a kitten, but she did not protest. We held the ones we picked up to the light where we could get a good look at them. Mine was the color of Ginger, but with stripes on its tail.

"Let's name this one Ring Tail, Eileen. Look at the stripes that go around its tail like rings."

"Why don't we decide which one we want as our own pet, first? That way we can each name our own kitten. Then we can name the other two, okay?" Eileen reasoned.

"Eileen, do you think that Ronald and Roy might like a pet kitten too?" I asked, thoughtfully.

"I doubt it. Neither one of them are big on cats. Now, if it were puppies we had here, that would be a different story. And Bobby is way too young to even know what a pet is, so I think we can safely name these ourselves."

"The one you are holding is a lighter orange, isn't it? I think I'll put mine back and see what the other two look like," I said. "Oh, look, there is the dark one, it is black. I like it, can I have it for my own?"

"Remember, I am suppose to pick first. I kind of like that one too, but let me see what the fourth one looks like," Eileen said, as she reached for the last kitten. "It's almost a smoky color. I think I'll take this one, and that will be its name, Smokey."

"Then can I have the black one? I'll name it Blacky."

"Oh that's original!" Eileen said, with a smirk.

"Sure is," I said, not understanding what she meant. "We have named our own so can the ring-tailed one be Ring Tail?"

"That's a stupid name," answered Eileen. "How about Ringo?"

"Ringo? That's a stupid name!" I echoed.

"You have a better idea?" She asked.

"No, I guess that would be all right. How about Honey for the light orange one?"

"I like that, believe it or not. That is a good name for that one. So now we have them all named and our own picked out, I think we should put them back with their mother and leave them be. They are so young yet; their eyes aren't even opened. We probably shouldn't play with them much, until they are a little stronger."

"Okay, what should we do now? Do you think mama would let us go see the Olson girls for a while? I really love playing with them," I coaxed.

"Well, it wouldn't hurt to ask, I guess, let's go find out." She headed out the side door of the haymow and started at a fast clip, across the road. She crossed the center grassy area, then the driveway on the other side, and up the porch to the back door.

"Wait up, you are going too fast," I cried, as I struggled to keep up.

By the time I had reached the kitchen, she was already beside mother in the front room, and had already asked her the question. Mother said, "You have been working hard, helping me all week. Why don't you and Helen go on over to Olson's for a couple of hours? I could use some help with the noon meal though, so try to be back by then."

"Come on Eileen, let's go, let's go," I begged, as I danced around her. Mama smiled at my excited reaction.

"Just a minute, I need to brush my hair first, and it wouldn't hurt you to brush the tangles out of yours as well. You have hay hanging from your head."

"Okay, okay, but hurry up. I'm so excited I could fart!"

"What did you say, Helen?" Mother asked indignantly. "Where did you hear such a thing?"

"The boys were talking about seeing a girl at the movies when they went last Saturday with dad. Roy said that she was the prettiest girl he had ever seen, and Ronald was talking about how he got so excited when she said hello to him, that he farted," I replied.

I noticed mother was holding her hand over her mouth, and her eyes seemed to be dancing. Eileen was bent over with laughter.

Mother cleared her throat and said, "Helen, that is not something a lady would say. You must not repeat everything you hear your brothers say. Don't repeat that again, you understand?"

Country Splendor

I wasn't sure why it was a bad thing to say, the boys seemed to think it was really funny, and Eileen sure laughed. But when mother gave an order, I knew that I must mind her.

"Okay, mama, I won't say it again," I said, as Eileen attacked my hair with her brush. "Owe, take it easy, I won't have any hair left if you pull it all out!"

"At least then you wouldn't have to worry about having it brushed. Okay, I think that will do. Let's get going or we won't have much time to play," she remarked, as she lay the brush down and headed for the door.

"Bye mama," I called, as I followed Eileen out the door.

"Bye now, and remember to be home by noon." I heard her final orders as I rushed to catch up with Eileen.

We walked down the road until we passed the Zobel farm, cut through the ditch, and crawled through the barbed wire fence. We were now standing on Olson property, but we still had to follow the path through the woods to reach the large two-story farmhouse they lived in. We hurried as fast as we could, with Eileen in the lead by several yards, and me trying valiantly to catch up. My side was hurting by the time we crossed the cow pasture, rounded the barn, and caught sight of the girls playing in the yard, between the barn and the house. Eileen called to them and they came running to meet us.

Betty was the oldest of the Olson girls, but a couple of years younger than Eileen. She was the first to reach Eileen, and started talking excitedly, "Hi! Have you come to play or are you here to baby sit?" Although Eileen was only nine, she was mature for her age, and was called upon to take care of the Olson girls when their parents went into town.

"Just came over to see you for a while," Eileen answered.

Carol was my age and Lillian was a year younger, and they came running up to me, and walked with me back to where the older girls had settled down to talk. We all sat in a semicircle on the lawn, and chatted about all that had happened since the last time we were together. The morning went much too quickly. Eileen took a look at the sun. "Oh, oh, it's close to noon. We have to go now, Helen."

I looked up, squinting against the sun's bright glare. "How can you tell?"

"When the sun is directly above our heads it is noon. If you look carefully, you can see that it is almost there."

For the next few seconds, all eyes were looking at the sun, digesting that bit of information. "Come on now, if you look long enough you can go blind. Just take my word for it, it's time we left." With that settled, Eileen rose up and pulled me up with her. The other's stood up also, and shouted their goodbyes, as Eileen pulled me behind her, waving with her free hand.

We followed the path we had taken to get to their home, walking around the barn, and across the cleared area to the woods. The girls had followed us around the barn, and stood waving goodbye, as we disappeared into the woods.

I dawdled down the path, watching for squirrels. The creek we had to wade through, had pools of tadpoles, and I played at catching them. I would squeal with pleasure as they wiggled through my fingers and fell back into the water. Eileen had stopped in a small clearing ahead of me, picking a bouquet of spring flowers for mother.

"Helen, come on, we are going to be late," she called. As I ran to catch up with her, I tripped over a tree root that stretched across the path in front of me. I cried out as my knee hit the hard ground. Eileen came back to me, and helped me to my feet, inspecting my bloody knee. "You're going to live, stop sniveling. We'll clean it when we get home."

She grabbed my hand and hurried me across the road, and up the bank. By the time we reached the house, the boys and dad were already sitting down to eat, and the glare that mother directed at us, as we entered the room, told us that she was mad. She didn't say a thing though, but dad got up and headed our way.

He must have known that we were supposed to be home in time to help prepare the meal, and we weren't. He headed towards Eileen, shaking his fist at her with a threatening air. "Why weren't you here to help your mother? She has had to deal with a cranky baby, as well

Country Splendor

as prepare this meal all by herself! She told you to be back in time to help her, and I expect you to mind her!"

Eileen wasn't very tall, but she stood her ground in a defiant way. I cringed and tried to hide behind her. Daddy frightened me. I had never seen him really mad, and I didn't like the tone of his voice, or the anger in his face. She tried to tell him that my falling held us up, but he wouldn't listen.

"Young lady, you are in big trouble! You know you were supposed to be home to help your mother, and I don't want to hear any lame excuses! I have a good mind to whip you right now!" he shouted at her. She just stood there, looking up at him, not giving an inch. I thought to myself, 'Eileen is so much like dad; strong willed and defiant. She is going to be in real trouble if she's not careful.'

He didn't hit her, but he looked like he wanted to. "Eileen, you are grounded for the rest of the summer. You stay close and help mother with all of her chores. Do you understand?" She still did not respond, but at least she did not talk back. She just stood looking at him. He clinched his fist as he turned and headed out of the kitchen door, calling back to the boys, "You two get a move on and get back to work!"

I had been hungry before we got home, but now I was only upset, and my tummy hurt. I forgot all about my scraped knee. I crept back out of the house, going through the front room door, sneaking around the house, and out to the barn. I hurried into the haymow and curled up in front of Ginger and her babies. I picked up my kitten and held it against me as I started to cry. I just felt so awful, that I had to let it out. "If I hadn't played in the creek, and if I hadn't fell down, this probably would not have happened." The thoughts tormented me. Ginger got up and came to me, brushing against my head, as if she was trying to comfort me. I lay there a long time, falling asleep with my black kitten in my arms.

Someone was shaking me awake, "Hey, lazy bones, wake up. It's almost milking time and mom is worried about you, you've been gone a long time," my brother Roy said. "What is wrong? You aren't the one dad yelled at."

"I know, but he was mad and it was more my fault than Eileen's. I was so scared, I was sure that Eileen was going to get beat, and all because I took too long, following her home."

"It wouldn't have been the first time dad hit Eileen, and it probably wouldn't be the last, given her strong stubbornness. That is what really makes dad mad. She shouldn't defy him like that. You know, when he gets mad he just goes crazy sometimes. I've just about had it with his temper, myself. I really don't think I will hang around here any longer than I have to," he stated, sounding very serious.

"Roy, why does daddy get so mad some times?" I asked.

"I don't really know. Listen squirt, mama said for me to find you and bring you in, it's almost supper time." He looked at what I was holding. "Hey, is that one of the kitten's? Pretty small isn't it? Looks like a fuzzy mouse!" He laughed when he saw how indignant I became.

"Don't neither!" I retorted.

He laughed again. "Better be careful, you know how old Chaser likes to dig up moles and eat them. He may mistake this one for a mole!"

Roy enjoyed teasing me about anything, and everything. It seemed to please him if he could get me mad. He especially found it funny, if he could get me upset to the point of me stomping my foot, while putting my hands on my hips, in defiance, which I was doing right then. I said, "That dumb dog of yours had better be good and leave my kittens alone or else!" I stomped my foot again for emphasis. Sure enough, he started laughing again, and reached out a hand to ruffle my disheveled hair.

"Come on now, pumpkin, you need to go to the house and let mother know you are alright. Now git," he said, as he gave me a shove in the direction of the door.

"I started walking, slowly, towards the house, when I realized that I needed to stop by the outhouse first. Then it became urgent, and I broke into a run towards the closed door, grabbing the handle and wrenching it open. My startled, eldest brother, sat there with his pants

Country Splendor

down around his ankles, and the catalog in his hands. "What is this?" he exclaimed, covering himself with the catalog.

"Sorry, Ron, but I got to go, really badly! Please!" I begged.

"Well, shut that door and I will be out as soon as I can."

I stood outside the door, crossing my legs, gritting my teeth like that would help, and becoming more impatient with each passing minute.

"Hurry up Ron!" I shouted, just as he opened the door and stepped out. I ran past him and headed for the short-seated end, pulling my bloomers down, as I went, not even caring that the door was standing open.

When I was finally in place, and everything began to work the way it should, I looked up to see Ron standing there in the same place, grinning at me. "You were really desperate weren't you? You really should not wait so long to head out here. Remember what happened last winter? You don't want to go through anything like that again, do you?"

"Well, I didn't do it on purpose. I fell asleep in the barn and just woke up," I explained.

"What happened to your leg, it's all bloody?" he asked.

"I fell down over a root and skinned it, cause we were trying to hurry home."

"Well, hurry up and come in, supper's about ready," he said, as he turned and headed for the house. "I'll let mom know where you are, and that your knee needs some tending to. Hurry now, you don't want to make mama mad again."

I continued sitting there for a few minutes more, thinking about my brothers. Ron was the eldest, and ten years older than me. He was the tallest of the men in our family and slender, with dark hair like mamas'. He was a quiet sort, who liked to read a lot, and did whenever he found the time.

Roy, on the other hand, was two years younger than Ron, shorter like dad; in fact he looked the most like dad of the two boys. He had dad's square jaw, light colored eyes, more gray green than blue though, and wavy hair. He was only twelve years old, but already his shoulders were broad, and he could do as much work as his older brother did, when he had a mind to. But he resented having to work long hours, instead of being able to chase and have fun with his friends.

I especially liked the times when Roy would clown around to make me laugh. He had built up his strength and balance, to the point of being able to walk on his hands, with his feet in the air, for quite a distance at one try. Eileen said that he was just showing off, because he liked being the center of attention.

Of the two boys, dad seemed to favor Roy the most, even though Roy did the loudest complaining and resented dad for pushing him so hard.

Ron, though he might have resented the hard work, seldom voiced a complaint. He seemed to have more endurance, as far as working long hours was concerned. I never heard him defy dad or mother. In fact, I think he was more aware of the pain that dad suffered, when dad's bad kidney acted up, and was trying to pass another kidney stone. At least, that is what Eileen explained was happening, whenever dad took to his bed in the middle of the day. I loved my big brothers, but of the two, I felt a little more protected with Ron than with Roy.

Remembering Ron's parting warning mentioning mothers temper, I thought about how quickly mama could get mad, and how swiftly that backhand of hers would catch me by surprise. Usually, it knocked me across the room, or at least flat on my butt. I loved my mother dearly, though. I respected her and knew better than to openly defy her. So, reluctantly, I pulled up my bloomers and followed my brother to the house.

After supper we were relaxing in the front room, when Roy walked to the window and looked across at the neighbors' farm on the other side of the road. The Zoble's had two children close to my older siblings age, named Herbert and Gertrude. Ron, Roy and Eileen would get together with them whenever they could, to do whatever they did for fun. Because I was so much younger, I seldom accompanied them, so I really did not know what they did while together, but that they all liked each other was obvious.

Country Splendor

In fact, I think Roy liked Gertrude a lot, because Eileen said he had a crush on her, whatever that was. I noticed that he looked longingly over there, quite often. "Hey!" he yelled, "Dad come look! I think the Zobel's chimney is on fire!"

"What?" Was the exclamation that erupted from all corners of the room, as everyone jumped up, and ran towards the windows and the front door, to get a good look.

"Yep, sure is!" Dad concurred, from his vantage point on the front stoop. "Bet they don't even know it, but the fire is shooting pretty high already, and it could start their roof on fire. Roy, head over there and tell Emil that their chimney is on fire. Tell them that we are on our way with extra buckets and ladders! Ron and Eileen, head for the shed, and grab all the buckets you can carry, and head over there. I am going to run by the Foss place to round up more help. It will take more than the few of us to have an effective water line, running to the house, from their pump and up onto the roof."

"Dad can I go too? I can help pass water buckets or something," I begged.

"No, Helen," Mother answered for dad. "I need you to stay with Bobby so I can go help. You can watch from the front stoop, but stay close to the house, so you can hear if Bobby wakes up and needs you. Do you understand?"

"Yes, mama. I understand." I was disappointed that I couldn't go with the others, but I consoled myself with the fact that at least I could watch what was happening from the front stoop. I stepped out onto the front porch and stared at the strange scene. I had never seen such a fire! It was red-hot coming out of the chimney, with black smoke billowing high into the sky above it. As I concentrated on the fire, I could see black and red cinders landing all over the roof. Roy was already rounding the Zobel's house, heading for the kitchen door, which was out of my sight. Mother was almost to the road, when I heard Ron and Eileen calling that they were coming. They rounded our house and headed across the yard, using it as a short cut. The large buckets they carried in each hand, bumped against their legs as they ran.

By the time mother was out of my sight, Eileen and Ron were crossing the road. Then I saw Roy and mother, leading the Zobel family, around the side of the house, to where they could get a look at the chimney. Eileen and Ron joined them.

There seemed to be a lot of lively conversation going on, as well as a lot of finger pointing. Mr. Zobel and the boys soon headed for the hand pump in the back yard. I couldn't see them at this point, but I could imagine what was going on. Someone would have grabbed the pump handle by this time and another would have placed a bucket under the spigot.

The women and girls followed the men to the back of the house, and probably were helping form the bucket line to hand the full buckets of water along to the person designated to carry it up a ladder.

I was glad that our house sat high on a knoll. With their house at a much lower level, I had a clear view of everything that went on, on the roof at least.

I watched as Mr. Zobel appeared on the roof. A ladder must have been placed against the house on the backside. He was motioning wildly and yelling, but I could not make out what he was saying.

Dad and the three Foss men were running down the road towards the Zobel farm. They didn't take the time to run for the driveway, which was several yards on the other side of the house, but jumped the ditch and headed across the lawn, and around the house, vanishing from my sight.

Now Mr. Zobel was reaching for a bucket that appeared above the roofline of the house and within his reach. He made his way as close to the chimney as he dared, and threw the water towards it. Sparks flew even higher.

Dad appeared on the roof just then, and I could see him pointing around him to the roof itself, and I wondered if the roof was beginning to burn. It hadn't rained for a couple of months and the weather had been summer hot, so it probably was dry. He talked to Mr. Zobel and then went to the side of the roof and I could hear him shouting orders. Before long, there were two sets of buckets, appearing at two different places, with Mr. Zobel throwing water at the chimney and dad sloshing water across the roof. Where dad had thrown the water, a small puff of smoke could be seen, curling towards the twilight blue skies.

This activity lasted past dark. The darker it got, the easier it was to see where small flickering fires were licking at the roof, at places that dad had not wet down, yet. This continued on for some time, and I began wondering if they would ever get it under control.

Bobby began to fuss. I expected that he needed his diaper changed by this time, or perhaps he was hungry, as it had been some time since mother had nursed him. I was never allowed to change him, though, because the cloth diapers had to be fastened with large safety pins. Mother was afraid that I would stick Bobby with them. Bobby was so active that Eileen had me hold him still, while she did the job. Mother had a time doing it herself, sometimes. Now what should I do? I couldn't leave him alone long enough to run over to the neighbors to get mama.

I decided to give him a bottle of milk. Mother kept a couple of baby bottles and nipples around in case of emergency, and I decided that this was one. I pulled a chair from the table to the tall shelf she kept the bottles on, climbed up and managed to reach one. Luckily it had a nipple already pulled on it, so I didn't have to search for that. I went to the icebox and brought out the pitcher of milk. I pulled the nipple from the baby bottle and poured in some milk, spilling only a few drops. But then, I had to pull the nipple back over the lip of the baby bottle. I had never tried it before, and it felt like my fingers were all thumbs. I struggled with the rubber nipple. It looked easy when Eileen did it.

Bobby's cries had now risen to a very loud wail, and I was getting more nervous by the minute. The harder I tried, the more impossible it seemed. Listening to his cries, I became more determined than ever, to accomplish this feat. I sat down, put the bottle between my legs to hold it upright, and used both hands to pull the nipple open enough to slip over the small neck of the bottle. Just as I thought the nipple was going to go on, the bottom of the bottle slipped backwards, causing the top to fall forwards. The milk spilled down my legs and onto the floor.

I sat there, watching the milk spread a cross mother's clean linoleum floor, and I cried. What was I going to do now? I had used up most of the milk. I wondered why mother or Eileen hadn't come home? They must have known that Bobby needed more care than I could give him. I couldn't change his diaper and I couldn't give him a bottle. Then I remembered a trick Eileen used once, when even a bottle wouldn't satisfy the baby. She found a clean cloth, laid it out on the table, put a pile of sugar in the middle, and then pulled the cloth together above the sugar. She twisted the cloth to keep it together, dipped it in milk and let Bobby suck on it. He quieted right down. What did she call it? Oh yes, a sugar titty.

Okay, I could do that, I decided, as I wiped away my tears. Even though the front of my clothes were wet with milk, I ignored the discomfort, as I set about to make a sugar titty for Bobby to suck on. It really wasn't that hard, and I was proud of myself, as I stuck the small cloth filled lump into some of the spilled milk on the table.

Hurrying to Bobby, I pulled him out of his crib. He was heavy and I almost dropped him, but managed to hold him against myself, as I lowered him to the floor. He was walking some now, which made it easier to get him to the rocking chair mother used, while holding him and nursing him. I sat down and helped him crawl upon my lap. I put the milk soaked, sugar titty, in his mouth, and he settled down against me, sucking on it. At least he was quiet, even though I could feel that he was very wet. Well, so was I, but I wasn't going to worry about that right then.

We must have fallen asleep, because the next thing I was aware of was a weight being lifted out of my arms. I came awake with a start, struggling to comprehend where I was and what was happening. "It's alright, Helen," Mothers' soft voice said, "I'm home now so you can go to bed."

"Mama, what happened? Is the fire out?" I asked, as the fire was still uppermost in my mind.

"Yes, it's out. The men are soaking the house down so no possible hot spot can flare up, but I'm sure it will be okay now. Their house filled up with smoke, and they are trying to air it out. It must have

Country Splendor

backed down the chimney when they flooded it with water, but it will be okay. Looks like you had some excitement here as well. The kitchen floor is all wet and sticky with milk, and I can't tell which of you is the wettest. You need to take those clothes off. I will sponge you down with soap and water before you put your nighty on."

"He was crying so hard, mama, and I tried to make a bottle for him, but I couldn't get the nipple on. I'm sorry I made such a mess."

"I figured it out, honey, but I don't blame you. You tried the best you could. Where did you learn to make a sugar titty? Bobby still had it in his mouth when I picked him up."

"I remembered Eileen making one for him once, when nothing else would satisfy him, and it seemed to work, so I thought I would try it. He took it right away, mama."

"Okay, it's late and everyone will be home soon. They will want to wash up and get to bed, too. So make your potty run, and when you get back in I will have the water warmed to bathe you. Now hurry! I'll light the lantern on the back porch to help you see your way to the outhouse." She pulled me to my feet and walked me to the back door.

Once I was back in the kitchen, mother washed me off with a cloth dipped in warm water, and bandaged my knee. She slipped my nighty over my head, letting it fall to my ankles. She kissed me on the top of my head and sent me up the stairs, with a reminder to say my prayers. I patted my hair where her lips had touched, and thought, 'She loves me.'

Shortly after I crawled into the bed I shared with my sister, she crawled in too. She was still so wound up by all of the excitement of the fire that she couldn't fall asleep right away, so she shook me to see if I was awake. I rolled towards her and listened, with rapt attention, as she told me her side of the story. Nothing this exciting had ever happened to us before, and we talked into the wee hours of the night. Succumbing to exhaustion, we finally drifted into a deep, dream filled sleep.

CHAPTER FOUR

At breakfast the next morning, the main topic was the fire the night before. Dad had been up early and went over to the Zobel's to make sure all was okay. When he returned and joined us at the table, he told mother that Mrs. Zobel seemed to be having some difficulty breathing. Emil told dad that the smoke activated an attack of asthma that she suffered from, periodically.

Mother decided to take her an old remedy that she had found effective with breathing problems. She told us of how I had almost died of pneumonia when I was one year old, and she had pulled me through using it. She said that she had also saved Eileen with the same remedy, when she was very young, after the doctor had actually admitted that there was nothing more he could do for her. It was hot, fried onion, mixed with Vicks Vaporub and used as a poultice, placed on a cloth, which was laid against the chest. There was also a mixture of herbs in hot tea, with lemon, that mother prepared and had one drink, that helped clear up mucus and opened air passages.

She assembled the ingredients as Eileen and I began washing the dishes. Before mother left the house, loaded with her supplies, she reminded us to sweep the floor and take care of Bobby. He was still asleep in his crib. "Mother, we will take care of everything until you get back. I hope you can help Audrey, she's such a nice lady," Eileen said. We hurried through the chores, anticipating the leisure time we

Country Splendor

would have until her return. Eileen had promised to read to me while we waited.

Before we could curl up in a couple of chairs, though, Bobby woke up. He pulled himself upright, and began to shout and shake his crib for attention. Eileen lay down the book she had brought to the chair with her, and went to Bobby, lifting him out of his crib. "Helen, you make him a bowl of cereal while I change his diaper." Twenty minutes later, we returned to the front room, sitting Bobby down on the floor, and returned to the chairs. Eileen opened up her book and began to read aloud to me about Little Red Riding Hood.

As I listened, I watched Bobby playing with some toys on the floor. When bored with them, he began finding ways to move himself around. He would pull himself into a standing position against dads' over stuffed chair and then head across the room, sometimes taking several steps before landing on his padded behind. He would howl for a minute, but when we refused to pay any attention to him, he would stop. Then he would scoot across the floor on his bottom, pulling himself along by reaching out with his legs, as far as they would go, and then pulling them towards himself. I couldn't help laughing at the funny way he moved himself around.

Eileen watched him a few minutes, finding it amusing also. "Kind of reminds me of a crab I saw once," she giggled. But when I continued to be distracted by Bobby's cute moves, she shut her book and headed up to our room. I watched her go, then shrugged my shoulders and sat down beside him. I picked up his ball and rolled it to him. "Get the ball Bobby," I said as it rolled past him. He scooted after the ball, picked it up and threw it randomly around the room. I was kept busy, chasing the ball for him. I kept him entertained for some time, until he started rubbing his eyes and yawning. I figured he was ready for a nap. I managed to pick him up and push him over the railings, into his crib. He didn't like falling and put up a howl, which brought Eileen running down the stairs yelling, "What happened?"

"He was sleepy, so I put him in his crib, that's all," I explained.

"Next time he needs to be put in his crib you let me do that. If he fell wrong he could break his neck," she scolded.

I turned away from her frowny face and left the house for the barn. I wanted to see my kitten. At least it wouldn't be yelling at me for trying to do something for it! As I stepped off the porch, I noticed daddy had backed the Chevy out of its shed and was lifting the hood. "Whatch ya doing daddy? Going somewhere?" I asked as I walked up beside him.

"Not if I can't get this thing running right. Something is making a grinding sound every time I try to back it up. Got to fix it so if we need to go somewhere in a hurry, we will be able to take the car." He reached for a tool, then asked, "Is mom back yet?"

"No she's not, and I'm going out to see Blacky. He's got his eyes open already, and I want him to know me. So I got to play with him everyday," I explained.

"What makes you think your kitten is a boy?" Dad asked, waiting to see what answer I would come up with. He seemed to be amused a lot by my imaginative logic.

"Well, he's like Roy, always picking on the girls."

"What girls does he pick on?" he asked.

"Well, he likes to pick on me and sometimes Eileen, and sometimes Gertrude too," I answered.

"The cat picks on you and Eileen and Gertrude?" Daddy asked incredulously.

"No, Roy does, daddy, that's silly!"

He broke out laughing, and how I loved hearing daddy laugh. It was a deep rumbling laugh that made others who heard him laugh too. With a trace of amusement still in his voice, he asked, "And how do you know which kittens are girls?"

"Well, the light colored ones are girls and the darker ones are boys, that's just logical," I replied, with that confident air I had when I repeated a big word I heard someone else use.

Then he really did laugh, and it sounded as if it came all the way from his belly, which made me laugh too. He placed his hand over his mouth as if that would help him gain control. I laughed until I was afraid I would wet my pants. "Gotta go daddy," I called as I dashed for the outhouse.

Country Splendor

After tending to natures call, I headed straight for the barn and to the kittens' nest. Only they weren't there. I couldn't imagine where they had gone, they were right there yesterday. I ran back to daddy, "My kittens are gone!" I cried.

"What do you mean – gone?" Daddy asked.

"I mean they are not in their nest behind the horse barn door! They were there yesterday."

"Has anything happened to disturb them lately?"

"Well, a couple days ago Chaser was in there looking at them. I chased him out. You don't think he would have eaten them, do you?" I asked, almost in tears.

"No, of course not, but he might have bothered them again, and the mama cat decided to find them a new home. I'll bet if you go in there and search real good, you'll find them in a new hideaway."

"Okay, daddy. I'll go look, and I'll tell you if I find them, okay?" I repeated. He nodded as he turned back to his working on the car.

Off I dashed, back to the haymow and my search for the kittens. It took quite a while; searching in every place I thought they might be. I had about given up hope, until I ventured into the calf barn. There was one calf pen that was full of fresh straw and hadn't been used for a while. Behind an extra pen door that had been stored, leaning up against the back wall, I heard a slight scuffling sound. The right side of the door was tight up against the sidewall, but on the left side the lower edge stood out away from the wall, far enough that I could peek around it. There in a snug bed of straw were the kittens. "Your momma must be out hunting some food." I reached in to find my kitten among the mass of kittens, playing together.

I played with Blacky for some time, until Ginger came running back to her babies. She complained as if she wanted him back with the rest, so I placed him back into the nest. I said goodbye and told Ginger that I would see her later. I headed back out to let daddy know where I found them.

As I approached the car, I found that daddy was half under the car, with tools lying all around him. He was speaking out loud, sounding very angry. The longer I stood listening, the stronger his language became, and I heard words that I had never heard before. He said them with so much emotion that I was sure that they must be very special words!

Those words came from him, again and again, and sounded more important every time he said them. I thought 'he really likes hearing them to be using them so much.' I was always picking up new and important sounding words so I thought; 'I'll go in and share them with mama.'

Into the kitchen I went, in search of my mother, and there she was, standing on the opposite side of the table from me. Her sleeves were rolled up, and she was kneading fresh bread dough, with flour reaching all the way up to her elbows. I closed the door and turned to her, looking right at her I repeated the new words, just the way daddy had said them. "God damn you!" I said, as I was thinking of how impressed she would be.

But the look that came on her face was not one of pleasure or delight. She stared at me, as she rounded that table, like something was on fire. Whap! My face was burning from mom's backhand, and I was looking up at her, with my seat on the floor and my back against the door. My eyes were brimming with big tears of disappointment and hurt, and the tears spilled over, rolling down across the hand that was holding the smarting cheek she had connected with. She walked purposefully back around the table, stopped on the other side, and began kneading the dough again. She looked at me, saying very forcefully, as she pronounced every word carefully, so I would never forget it, "Don't you ever say anything like that again!"

At first I sat there stunned and confused at mother's reaction. 'But daddy said that' I thought to myself, as if that should make it all right to repeat it. But my cheek was smarting, and the back of my head, where it hit the door, wasn't feeling very good either. I finally came to the conclusion that, even though daddy said those things, for some reason, I wasn't supposed to. I made a promise, then and there, that I would be careful not to repeat daddy's 'sometimes words,' especially those that he said the loudest!

Country Splendor

The spring rains hit forcefully and lasted several days. Dad came into the kitchen, wiping his feet on the mat as he entered, and shaking the water from his curly hair. "See, mother, why I was in such a hurry to get the spring planting done? The fields are saturated with water, and it's still coming down! Whew, I pity the farmers that still have their planting to do. They won't be able to get into the fields for days, even if the rains stop soon."

"Have you checked on the pigs? That's kind of a low spot they are in, I would hate to loose any of them now." Mother sounded worried as she stared out the window.

"The boys are suppose to be feeding them now." The words were barely out of dad's mouth when Roy came running through the door, all upset.

"Dad, come quick, the pig pen is flooded and I'm afraid that the mother sow will drown her babies!"

Dad rushed out after Roy, pulling his rain slicker back on. A few minutes later he was back with a muddy piglet in his arms. "Here, mother, clean this baby up. It was wedged under the mother and almost drowned. We will move the pigs to one of the calf pens inside the barn, until this rain stops and the ground dries out." He handed the baby pig to mother's outstretched arms, and headed back out the door.

"Helen, run and bring some of those old towels we use for cleaning, and tell Eileen to come down stairs and take care of her crying brother."

By the time I delivered the message to Eileen, rounded up the towels and reached mother's side again, she had the baby pig washed clean. "Sit down, Helen, spread out that largest towel," she ordered, as I hurried to obey. She brought the baby pig around to me and laid it on the towel, helping me dry it off. It was so tiny and pink, with its cute little snout and curly tail, that I was immediately captivated by it. Mother picked up the piglet, towel and all, and laid it on the open oven door, where the heat from the stove would warm it up. Our kitchen range was a large, wood-burning stove, with four stove lids on the cooking surface, and a large oven beneath the firebox. It was almost always warm, as mother was either baking or cooking on it, a great deal of the time. She instructed me on how to hold the piglet so it would not fall off the oven door, and told me to stay with it until it was good and warm. I happily took charge, watching it closely and petting its back. Eileen walked into the kitchen and over to check out my charge.

"Little thing isn't it? Must be the runt of the litter," she said.

"Runt? What's runt?" I inquired, always interested in new words.

"Runt means the tiniest of the litter." Eileen explained. "Its getting warmed up, look how pink its skin is." She reached out and petted it, as it began to wiggle and move around.

"Mama, can I hold it now? Its all warmed up," I said.

"Yes, but hang onto it carefully, so it won't fall from your lap." She reached over me and picked the piglet up from the oven door and placed it on my lap, closing the oven door as she raised up.

It wiggled and started pushing at me with its little snout. I began giggling and exclaimed, "I think its looking for a titty, mama!"

"Just hang on a minute, I'm warming it a bottle of milk," she said.

"I want to give it its bottle," stated Eileen.

"U-ungh," I mumbled as I pulled it close to me. "Its my piggy, I feed it!"

"What do you mean, your piggy? You're always wanting everything for yourself!" Eileen exclaimed.

"Do not!" I insisted, rather loudly, which brought a howl from Bobby.

"Eileen, go take care of your brother and leave Helen alone. She's doing just fine by herself. You can hold the piglet later," Mother stated emphatically.

"How come I've got to take care of Bobby all the time? It's not fair!" Eileen said, as she headed for the front room.

"Mama, can I have this piggy for my pet, please, pretty please, with sugar and ice cream on it?" I begged, piling up all the good things on it I could think of to make the request sweeter.

"Helen," Mother began in her very practical, down to earth, no nonsense voice. "You know that we don't make pets of anything we will eventually sell, or eat."

"What? Eat piggy? We can't eat piggy, mama. She's so tiny, and besides, there are plenty of other pigs to eat," I cried.

"She might be tiny now, but she will grow up. If you had your way, everything on this farm would be your pet, and we wouldn't have any meat in our pantry. You must understand that some things can be pets, and other things must be for food. Pigs are for food. That's just the way it is. Now put the piglet in this basket I have fixed for it. We will give her back to her mother as soon as she is settled in the barn."

When mother used that tone of voice with me, I knew she meant what she said, and there was no further talking about it. "Yes, mama," I conceded, as I took the now empty bottle out of the piglet's mouth, and placed her in the blanket lined basket.

Dad and the boys came in for their afternoon lunch and announced that the sow and her litter were comfortably settled into their stall in the calf barn. They would be taking the baby back to its mother when they went out to milk. I sat beside the basket, stroking the small, pigs' back and talking softly to her. I assured her, that I would see to it, that she was comfortable in the straw bed in the barn, and that I wouldn't let anyone eat her, ever. I was certain I could keep that promise, if I just let daddy know how much I loved her. He would understand.

CHAPTER FIVE

Spring turned into summer, and with it the heat hit. Summers can be very hot in Wisconsin, and the nights are almost as warm as the days. Because of this 24-hour a day heat, the gardens and fields flourished with bountiful results. There was always something to do. From the first berries that ripened in early summer, to the last berries and fruits in the fall, we made jam and pie filling. As the vegetables matured, we had to pick them, wash and prepare them for canning. Most of the canning was done in large, water filled canners, placed over the heat of our kitchen stove. Each canner would hold two full rows of jars, usually twelve to a canner. Water would cover the closed jars, and have to be kept at a slow boil for several hours, the amount of time depending on what was being canned.

Mother used three sizes of jars. Pint jars were used for some of the vegetables that mother used for soups or stews and for the last of the jams or jellies. The quart sized jars were used for the largest percentage of canned goods, which included vegetables, fruits and meats. They were the best size to feed our family. The two-quart jars were filled with the special foods that were used when we had company, or when we had to feed the harvesters. Slowly, through the summer, the many shelves in the root cellar would fill with jars of colorful foods. There were enough canned goods in the cellar, to feed our family, for two years, at least. Mother wanted to be ready for any eventuality that might occur.

Country Splendor

Everyone, who was big enough to do anything, was enlisted in the efforts. That included from the tilling of the ground, to the planting, hoeing, weeding, harvesting and canning.

In contrast, the Wisconsin winters seemed to last forever, so everyone looked forward to the warmth of spring. It was a relief when the ground was ready for plowing. The boys were actually looking forward to hitching a horse to the plow and guiding it up and down the field, just to have a reason to be outdoors. Eileen and I would take turns, riding the horse, to help guide it.

I enjoyed helping put the seeds into the ground as soon as the fields had been harrowed smooth. I walked behind daddy as he used the potato planter to plant the pieces of potatoes that he had cut up, making sure there was a sprouted eye on every piece he was going to plant. The hand held planter had a long container secured to the back of the handle that held the pieces of potatoes. It had a sharp end that daddy would push into the ground, then by stepping on a lever the lower section would open up, allowing a piece of a potato to roll into the hole. As he pulled it up, the lever would move back closing the hole the potatoes came out of. Then as dad moved it forward to plant another piece, he would drag his foot over the first earth hole covering the potato piece with the rich earth. In one afternoon he would have planted a very large patch of potatoes. It had to yield a large enough crop to not only feed a large family for another year, but enough left over to plant another crop the following spring. Actually, there was always enough to feed some of them to the pigs as well. They loved potatoes, as well as all the other vegetables that we grew in abundance.

Daddy would cultivate the garden soil until it would sift through his fingers. Then it's planting was left up to mother and the children. The boys would use a spade to make an incision in the soil deep enough to plant the various vegetable seeds and plants. Mother and Eileen would do the seeding and planting, and I would come behind and smooth the soil back over, or around them. By helping with the planting I took a personal interest in the garden. I would run out daily, to check on the growth of the tiny sprouts, as they poked above the ground, and then matured to full blown plants. I would spend part of every day in the garden with mother and Eileen, as they pulled weeds, and worked the hand cultivator between the rows. Bobby was placed in a basket or on a blanket under a shade tree nearby, and my primary job was to keep an eye on him.

When the vegetables were ready for harvest, I would be the first to pull off a pea pod, peeling back the green shell and eating the row of fat, little, sweet peas. The first of the long carrots I pulled from the warm earth, I readily cleaned by the sweep of my hand, and ate it with relish. It tasted so good. A Ripe tomato right from the vine was like nectar to me.

The men had all the fields to prepare, plant and cultivate, as well as harvesting the crops as they matured. This was in addition to the daily milking and care of the farm animals. Dad and the boys would be up before dawn each day, to begin a very long day, working into the dark many evenings.

The younger children had the chores of feeding the pigs and chickens, carrying in the wood for the stoves, keeping the water containers filled, the eggs gathered and whatever help they could be in other ways.

Once the morning milking was done, the men would come in the house for a hot and hearty breakfast, usually around six o'clock. By nine or ten they were back in for a lunch of sandwiches, coffee and dessert. At twelve o'clock noon, the large meal of the day was served, thus called dinner. There would be plenty of meat and potatoes, vegetables, fresh baked bread, milk or coffee to drink and something sweet for dessert. By three in the afternoon we would have another lunch prepared for the men, and once the milking was done in the evening, we had supper ready. Supper usually consisted of leftovers warmed up or at least a lighter fare than dinner. Many nights there would be a light lunch before bedtime as well. This food fueled the energy that was spent out in the barns and fields. Because everyone worked so hard, physically, rarely was anyone over weight.

Country Splendor

Because Eileen had been grounded from visiting the neighbors, I seldom saw anyone other than our own family, or the occasional visit from friends or other family members.

I kept busy most of the time, but on those rare occasions when the immediate chores were done, and there was time for other pursuits, I longed to visit Betty, Carol and Lillian Olson.

It was one of those rare afternoons that I had time on my hands that I grew restless. Mother had laid down with Bobby for an afternoon nap. Eileen was reading a book and didn't want to be bothered. I remember sitting under the oak tree in the front yard, playing with my kitten, Blacky. It had been a long time since I had visited my friends and I longed to go see them. Why couldn't I go? Why should I have to stay home just because my sister was grounded to home for the summer? "Blacky, would you like to see my friends? They are so nice and I know they would like you too. Wish I could go over there. It's really not that far and I know the way. I bet I could go over there and see them, and be back without anyone even knowing I had left. But I think I'll leave you home this time, maybe you can go next time, okay?" The kitten continued batting at a butterfly and seemed content to wait there for me.

Off I ran on excited feet, flying over the hard packed dirt road, crawling carefully through the wire fence, and following the winding path across the creek and through the woods to the Olson barn. I almost lost my nerve at that point, wondering if Mrs. Olson might be mad if I came at a time when her girls might have chores to do. But here I was, and I heard laughter coming from the other side of the barn. It was the girls! I ran around the barn and there they were, having a water fight, using buckets of water and dippers to throw water at each other. Their laughter was contagious and I stood laughing at them, unnoticed, until Betty came around the corner of the house and saw me standing there.

"Hey, Carol, Lillian! Look who came to see you!"

"Hey, Helen!" they chorused, as they came running up to me with full dippers that they immediately swung at me. The water caught

Helen Marie Fias

the side of my hair, dripping down my arms, feeling cool against my heated skin, and sending gales of laughter through all of us.

"That feels good! Got another dipper?" I asked. We played and laughed and the time flew. Before I knew it, Mrs. Olson came out to call the girls in for supper and saw me there.

"Helen, I didn't know you were here? Have you been here long?" she asked.

"Just a little while. Guess I had better go. Can Carol and Lillian come over to see me sometime?" I asked wistfully.

"Maybe, one of these days, but I really think you had better get home now. Your mother will want you home in time for supper." She turned and went back into the house.

"Bye Carol, bye Lillian, bye Betty. See you," I said, as I took off for home. I ran all the way, as I knew it was later than I should have stayed. I kept hoping that no one missed me, and that I would be able to slip in unnoticed. I had barely crawled through the fence and stepped onto the road when I saw Eileen running towards me, calling my name softly. I thought, that was kind of strange, she usually yelled at the top of her voice at me.

She reached me and said, "Get in the ditch, hide. Mama is mad, has us all out looking for you. If you don't want to get a licking you had better go back to the Olson's. Mom and dad will come get you after supper and they won't spank you in front of their friends."

I stood there dumb struck, not moving, and not knowing what to do. I knew I didn't want to go back to the Olson's after Mrs. Olson told me to go home. I delayed action a minute too long and my brother, Roy, spotted me from the top of the hill. "There she is," he called to my oldest brother, who was just coming from the creek. "There she is down on the road by Olson's woods."

The jig was up, and Eileen had no choice but to grab me, and act as if she had just found me. Seeing our brothers coming after me, I realized that this was a far more serious thing than I had imagined. They grabbed me and hauled me off, over the hill and to the house, with me screaming all the way. They were not hurting me, but I was pretty sure I knew someone who was going to, as soon as I got home.

Country Splendor

Sure enough, mom heard us coming and she met us on the porch. I was small for my four years and she was country wife strong! She picked me up by one arm, clear off the floor, and whipped me with daddy's strap, right there in the air. By the time she let go of me, I knew I had been whupped good, and I knew why, and I knew that I should never repeat that same offense, ever again!

CHAPTER SIX

The summer days waxed hot and humid. Because the heat was relentless day and night, the days began to run together all as one. It was difficult to fall asleep at night, and when one finally did, it was hard to wake up in the morning. I noticed fuzziness in my head. I asked my mother about it, as she worked at the stove, preparing breakfast. "Mama, my head feels full of thick fuzz this morning. Why?"

"In this heat, no one sleeps real well, so it leaves us all a little sluggish feeling. That is that fuzzy, headed, feeling you have. And that is why I get up early to have fresh coffee ready for dad and the boys. That seems to help them get started," she explained.

"Can I have some coffee too?" I asked.

"You are kind of young to start your day with coffee, but maybe a little in your milk might help." She reached for the coffee pot and poured a little in my cup.

"Thanks mom, I feel better now," I stated after a couple of sips.

"Wow, works fast on you doesn't it?" she laughed.

"What's so funny?" Eileen asked as she entered the kitchen with a hungry Bobby in her arms.

"Mama let me drink coffee and it helped me wake up," I stated triumphantly, feeling more like a grown up because I had some coffee.

"She did not! You're fibbing again!" Eileen said.

"Am not!" I shouted back.

Country Splendor

"Girls, that's enough of that. Eileen, I just put a little in her milk, it was just enough to taste a bit. Put Bobby in his chair. Helen can make his pablum for him while you have a little coffee in your milk too." Mother was good at placating us children. She tried to treat us all alike, not wanting to show favor to one over the other.

I pulled my chair over to the cupboard, climbed up on the chair and reached into the cupboard for the box of dry, baby food cereal. As I was stepping down from the chair, the door burst open and Roy came rushing into the kitchen, shouting, "Mom, old Black Joe is dead!"

I was startled and dropped the box I was holding. "Oh no!" I exclaimed, as I saw the cereal fly from the opened lid of the box and land on the floor. "Oh, No" I repeated, as Roy's news penetrated my consciousness.

"Helen, for goodness sake, clean up that mess. What happened Roy?" Mother asked.

"I don't know. I went to feed the horses and found him dead in his stall. Dad thinks his heart just quit, because he is so old," Roy explained.

"Boy, if it isn't one thing around here, its another!" Mother sighed. "Has dad said what he wants to do with Black Joe's remains?"

"I didn't wait around to talk to him. When I took him to see Old Joe, he just stared for a minute, and then told me to run and tell you. He said that he and Ron would be in, in a minute."

"Okay, sit down, you are white as a sheet! Helen, get that baby's food fixed and feed Bobby. We don't want him crying when dad gets in here. Eileen, stop that sniveling. That isn't going to help a thing."

"But he was my favorite horse! He was so gentle, and I loved riding him, and guiding him down the field for daddy as he plowed." Eileen tried to stifle her sobs, as she turned to mother. "Can I go see him?"

"Yes, I guess it won't hurt. Tell dad that breakfast is ready too, if he still feels up to eating." She watched as Eileen disappeared out of the back door, leaving it swinging open, as she hurried across the cleared area to the barn. Mother crossed to the door and began to close it, then thought better of it, as she said, "Maybe if we leave it open we might catch a passing breeze. It is so hot in here."

I turned to look at her and worried at how red her face looked, and at the same time, so pale. As I studied her, she seemed to wilt a bit, walked slowly to a kitchen chair, pulled it from the table and sat heavily down upon it. Then she dropped her head into her hands, with her arms resting on the table.

"Mom, are you alright?" Roy and I inquired as one voice, with Bobby echoing his version of the same question, "Mum wite?"

"I'll be all right. Just need a minute to get hold of the situation." Mother sighed deeply.

"Helen, get mother some water," Roy ordered, and for once I did not answer with a smart retort, but got up and did as he asked.

"Thanks," Mom said, as she grasped the glass in one strong, browned hand, and brought it to her lips, drinking deeply. "That's better."

A slight breeze drifted through the room, and you could hear an audible sigh follow it, as each one us was touched by its passing.

I had just finished giving Bobby the last spoonful of his milk-covered pablum, when daddy stepped through the door. Right behind him followed Ron, with Eileen bringing up the rear. They all found a chair to pull out from the table and sat down. Eileen was still wiping tears from her reddened eyes when dad spoke. "Vell, vell, vell. What a bunch of gloomy faces we have here. I know that you all loved Old Black Joe," he stated, with a slight sigh. "But what is, is, and now we must decide how to make the best of it."

"Eileen, fetch dad a fresh cup of coffee. Are you up to eating some breakfast, Hubie?" Mother asked, using her pet name for him, instead of his given name of Hubert.

"Just some coffee for now, but you boys should eat. You've already put in half a days work, and there will be plenty more to do later." Dad sounded concerned for them, and apologetic at the same time.

They both got up; taking their plates to the stove with them, where the hot food waited in the lidded, hot, caste-iron pans. For once they didn't just sit at the table waiting to be served by either mom or Eileen,

Country Splendor

which was their usual custom. I followed with a plate for myself, but as I stood there, waiting behind my brother, Roy, I turned and looked back at the table. Eileen had her head dropped in her folded arms, and mother and daddy were studying each other's faces. They looked into each other's eyes as if to read in them, the others thoughts and feelings. Daddy smiled at mother, and reached out a weather-browned hand that he placed over hers, which had been resting on the table in front of her. "It's going to be alright, Verna, we'll get through this. The good Lord will get us through this, just as He has through all the other trials we've faced."

It was the first time I had heard daddy refer to 'the Lord,' in that way. It was usually what mother would have said.

She managed a somewhat waveringly smile back at him, "I know Hubie, I know."

"Just got a thought, how about I go over and talk to Emil. He lost a horse some time ago. Maybe he can tell me how best to dispose of ours."

"Yeah, dad, that's a good idea," Ron interjected, as he placed his plate of food on the table and sat down. "Herbert said his dad sold their dead horse to some kind of place that buys them. Got more for him dead, than he could have sold him for. He was an old horse too."

"Vell, that settles that, then," Dad said. "Now I'm ready for some food." I was just beginning to fill my plate. I turned to dad, offering to fill my plate for him, and then getting another one for myself. "That's wonderful, princess," he said, as he rewarded my offer with a smile that always lit up my heart.

"How come you never offer to fill up a plate for me?" Roy asked, as he finished filling his and started for the table.

"Cause you're big enough to do it yourself!" I snapped.

"And dad isn't?" he retorted with a sneer.

"Dad's special and you are just an old lazy boy!" I shot back.

"Okay you two, enough of that," Mother scolded.

Eileen had listened to this exchange, and put in her two cents worth, "Because, I always have to do it for you, big lazy bones!" she shot at Roy. "I'm surprised you know how to lift the lid off the skillet without burning yourself!"

Somehow this tickled dad, bringing a chortle from him.

Roy didn't appreciate someone getting one up on him, but he decided he was more hungry than upset, so he filled his mouth with food instead of more words.

Eileen, feeling vindicated a wee bit, got up from the table and offered to bring mother a plate of food. "Just a bit, I'm still not hungry," Mother answered. "Helen, on your way to the table, would you please give Bobby a piece of toast to chew on? He's cutting teeth and needs to have something solid to chew on."

"Okay, mama," I answered, reaching into the warming oven for a second piece of toast. It was just high enough that I had to stand on tiptoes to reach it, but I made it without spilling any of the food on my plate. As I passed the baby, I handed him the toast, tipping my plate ever so slightly, but just enough for my own piece of toast to fall to the floor. It had barely touched the floor, when our dog grabbed it and retreated to the spot beside Bobby's chair, where he always laid, in hopes of catching whatever Bobby might drop. I let out a wail, almost dropping my plate, trying to retrieve the toast.

"Helen, let the dog be, put your plate on the table before you drop it too. Then you can get yourself another piece of toast. We can always make more if we need to."

"Okay mama, but that dumb dog should be kept outside!"

"Mom, Helen said damn!" Eileen said, as she set mother's plate of food on the table in front of her.

"Did not!" I argued. "I said dumb!"

"Yes, she did say dumb," agreed Ron, as he pushed back his empty plate, pushed his chair back and got up, and headed for the kitchen door.

"Children, we have enough on our minds with out any haggling this morning. Let's have some peace and quiet now," Mother stated in a no-nonsense voice. We all fell quiet and finished our breakfast in silence, each thinking our own thoughts. I was wondering why anyone would want to buy an old, dead horse.

Country Splendor

The rest of the morning went fast as we all began our daily chores, and waited for dad to return from Emil Zobel's place.

By lunch time dad was back, and as we gathered around the table for our mid-morning snack, we anxiously waited for dad to tell us what Old Black Joe's fate was going to be.

"Well, Verna," Dad began. "There is good news and not so good news. The good news is, that there is a place just past Barron that buys dead horse carcasses. Guess there is quite a lot they can salvage from them. They cut them up and sell parts to other factories. Some buy the hoofs to make glue. Some use the hair for stuffing couches and chairs; the rest is used for dog food and even fertilizer, I guess. Anyway, we are going to go to town right after lunch and talk to them. Emil says that they will send a truck out, yet this afternoon, to pick up the carcass. They will pay us by how much Old Joe weighs. That will help us buy another horse."

"That sounds good to me," Mother agreed. "So what's the bad news?"

"Well, it might take us a while to buy another horse. You know there's a war on and although we haven't gotten into it yet, I guess the government has put a lid on how much metal the factories can use to make tractors and such. That has driven up the price of tractors, as well as other farm machinery. Everybody is hanging on to their horses now, so that also drives up their prices."

"What will we do, dad? King is a strong horse but we will need more than just him to bring in the harvest this summer," Ron stated.

"Vell, Emil said we can borrow his horses when he isn't using them. All the farmers around here are planning on helping each other, with the main harvesting. Maybe, with their help, we will be able to get it done. Meantime, I am going to ask them to keep an ear and eye out for another good work horse, that someone might be willing to sell."

After lunch, Dad started up the Chevy; drove over to Emil's to pick him up, and headed into Barron to the plant that would buy Old Black Joe.

Helen Marie Fias

The boys were reminded of what they were to do while dad was gone. Mother had Eileen and I, haul in buckets of water to fill up the canners, placed on the stove. This wasn't in preparation of canning however, it was washday, and the water would be used for that. Keeping the kitchen stove hot, long enough to heat up this water, added to the heat in the house. We decided it was cooler to keep Bobby outside, in the shade, where we could catch an occasional breeze, than in the front room. Eileen brought out her storybook of fairy tales, and proceeded to read to Bobby and me. Mother was busy setting up the wash and rinse tubs, as well as sorting the clothes in the need-to–be washed first pile, and so on, until they were all sorted.

Mother filled the washtub with warm water and soap, and put in the first of the colored clothes to be washed. The rinse tub was filled with cold water. The large canners on the stove were filled with the white clothes, which needed to be boiled. Bobby's diapers, bedding, and some of his nightclothes, and the underwear, were placed in one tub, and the white shirts, towels, and sheets were in the second tub. Left to boil on the stove, the act of boiling as well as the heat, cleaned the clothes, but the stove had to be replenished with wood, to keep it burning, and the heat made the kitchen almost unbearable. Mother had set up the washtub and rinse tub outside, held off the ground by placing them on dad's sawhorses. She then put the washboard inside the washtub, and one by one, she scrubbed the dirt out of the clothes that were soaking in the warm water. When clean, she wrung out as much of the water as she could, then put the clothes into the cool, rinse water, swishing them around with a clean, broom handle, that dad had salvaged from a ratty old broom. Once the soap was rinsed out, the clothes were wrung out by hand again, and put into a straw basket. It would be up to Eileen and I, to hang them on the clothesline. Eileen had to do the hanging, as I wasn't tall enough to reach the clothesline yet. But I would take the clothes out of the basket, shake them smooth and hand them to her. She draped them on the line and secured them with wooden pins. The breeze, blowing gently against the clothes, along with the suns hot rays, dried them.

Country Splendor

Of course, we had to keep one eye on Bobby, because he could toddle out of our line of vision faster than a cat with its tail on fire. At least that is what Eileen would tell me. I had never seen a cat with its tail on fire, but with my imagination, I could see it, and it might have been funny to some, but to me it was a pitiful sight.

I looked at Blacky, Ringo, Smokey and Honey, now almost grown, chasing butterflies around the yard. Bobby followed after them, trying to catch first one and then the other. He would reach out to grab a tail, stumble and land on his tummy, laughing as he pushed himself back up on his feet, and then take off after another kitten. 'Catch the kitten by its tail,' I would think to myself, 'but to set that tail on fire? No way!'

Bobby was such a good baby. I could never remember him actually shedding tears. He would make unhappy sounds when he needed his diaper changed, was hungry, or just wanted some attention, but to actually cry tears, no. I had never thought of it as strange, back then, only that he was a happy baby. It would be years before we found out that he had no tear ducts.

Dinnertime came and went without dad. Mother had prepared some cold salads that morning, and with sandwiches to round out our meal, we all ate our fill and went back to our chores.

When dad's car turned into our driveway, followed by a big truck, we were all aware of it, and everyone was running towards the back yard. I had grabbed up Bobby, to keep him safe on the back porch, as we watched the vehicles come to a stop, and the drivers exit. Dad had pulled his car up to the house, giving the truck room to stop close to the barn. He walked back to the truck, and stood talking to the two men, who had driven the truck. Emil stopped by the back porch to say a few words to mother, and then extended a raised hand in farewell to the rest of us, as he left for home.

The men walked into the barn, and maybe it was just because I was so interested to see what would happen next, that it seemed like a long time before they returned to their truck. The driver got in and maneuvered the truck around, backing it towards the door that Old Joe would be pulled through. The second man jumped up on the bed of the truck and worked the crank handle of the winch, unwinding the rope and handing dad the hooked end of it. Dad and Ron pulled the rope into the barn. Roy ran between the barn and the truck, delivering messages from one group to the other. Once all was in place, the crank was turned to wind the rope back up and around the cylinder. As we watched the laborious process, we could see a black mound move slowly from the barn, and towards the back of the truck. The back of the truck had been dropped down, forming a ramp for the body to be pulled up onto the truck. Slowly, we could make out Old Black Joe's hind hoofs caught up in the rope, as it began to lift him up from the ground. I was so caught up in the process, that I forgot to be sad about the horse. Once he was on the bed of the truck, the winch was secured, the tail of the truck lifted, and secured back into place. There was more talking between the men. Finally, dad shook hands with the men, who then turned, climbed back into the cab and drove off.

The deed was done, and Old Black Joe would soon be spread among many useful products. I thought a long time on that. At least he would be serving a purpose, and not just rotting in some deep grave, like my sister told me we would do after we died.

CHAPTER SEVEN

Sundays were usually a special day. Unless it was a dire emergency of some kind, only the necessary work was performed on that day. Often it was a fried, chicken dinner day, with company coming to share it with us.

This Sunday morning, I heard the chickens squawking their displeasure, with something, or someone disturbing them. It was early yet; the men had not come in from milking. I guessed that mother was out, rounding up our dinner already. I dressed hurriedly and took off for the chicken coop. 'Oh, oh, company is coming' I said to myself as I met mother on the path with a pullet in each hand. They were young chickens, not fattened up yet, and just beginning to lay eggs. Mother told me once, that they were the most tender for frying and therefore company meat. "Who's coming to dinner, mama?" I asked, as she approached.

"And how do you know we are going to have company?" Mother inquired.

"Cause you have two chickens today, and if it's just for us there would be only one. Also, these are pullet's."

"Well, little miss smarty, we actually will have three chickens for dinner, because the Espeseths and the Frisingers will be here today."

"You mean Norman and Sally Frisinger, and their kids, Shirley and Russell, Eileen and Norma?"

Country Splendor

"Yes, them and Andrew and Cora Espeseth with Carlton, Irvin and Alan."

"Why do we have to have all those boys here? They just like to pick on us girls!" I complained.

"They probably will run off to the creek with Roy and Ronald, and you won't even see them, most of the time," Mother stated, matter-of-factly.

"Well, I hope so! Does Eileen know they are coming?" I asked.

"Yes, I told her yesterday. Dad met the men in town at the feed store, and asked them if they would like to come over. It's been quite a while since we have all gotten together. You and Shirley will have a great time together. You can show her your kittens."

"How soon will they be here?" I asked, getting more excited by the minute.

"Probably right after church. They usually attend church in Barron on Sundays."

"Why don't we attend church, mama? We go sometimes at Christmas, and once we went at Easter, but how come they go every Sunday?"

"Lot's of people go every Sunday, and I would like to, but dad would rather do some fishing, or just plain resting on that day. He works hard all week long and needs to have a day of rest," she explained.

"Don't Andrew and Norman work hard all week too?" I asked.

"Actually, Norman is a truck driver for the creamery and works only five days a week. Someone else drives his truck on the weekends"

"What's weekends?" I asked.

" Well, weekend is the last two days of the week. Saturday and Sunday."

"Does Andrew drive truck too?"

"No, he's a dairy farmer, just like your daddy, but he has three boys to help him with all the chores, and besides that, he doesn't have the bad kidney like your daddy has," she explained.

"Why does daddy have a bad kidney? And what is a kidney?" I probed.

"You are just too full of questions, young lady, and I've work to get done. I'll explain it to you later, okay?"

"Yes mama," I said, hoping she wouldn't forget to tell me, because I would just think and think on these questions until I knew the answers. It was hard being so small, and not knowing all the things the bigger and older people did.

"Now Helen, run to the house and tell Eileen to put a big pan of water on to boil, so we can clean these chickens," she instructed.

I took off for the house, as she headed for the woodshed, where she would chop off the chicken's heads, and go get another. I burst through the kitchen door, letting the screen door slam behind me, yelling Eileen's name.

"I'm right here," she said, from across the room, "You don't have to yell, you'd wake up the dead with that voice of yours."

"Would not! You can't wake up the dead. Ron said so! He said dead is dead and nothing can wake them up!"

"Big deal! I just meant that you are too loud! Listen to Bobby, you woke him up, and now I'll have to change and feed him. I was hoping to sit here at the table for a few minutes, before I had to get busy," she complained.

"Well, mama says you should put on a big kettle of water to boil, as she is fixing the company chickens," I said importantly.

"Oh yes, she did say that we are having company today. I haven't seen Norma or Eileen in a long time. It will be good to have someone my own age to talk to for a change, as long as you and Shirley will leave us alone," she finished disdainfully.

"Don't worry, I have the kittens to show her, and we will have lots of fun without you big, old girls, bothering us!" I declared.

"You haven't fetched any water yet this morning. Go pump the water and I'll help you bring it in. Right now I need to tend to Bobby."

"Okay," I agreed, as I grabbed the two buckets that sat by the back door, and pushed through the door, letting the screen door slam again. Mother was heading my way, with three headless chickens hanging from her hands, blood dripping from their raw necks. "Eileen is

Country Splendor

waiting for this water mom, she said for me to pump these buckets full, and she would help me carry them in, but she is changing Bobby first," I said in one long breath.

"Helen, I will lay these chickens here on this bench next to the house, while we get some water boiling. I need to gather some more firewood so we can singe them once we have them plucked. Keep an eye on them for me."

"I will, mama," I replied, as I sat one bucket under the waterspout and the other one beside it. I went around to the pump handle and began to bring it up as high as I could, and then pull it down, push it up and pull it down. Once the water was running freely into the bucket, I would have to put all my weight on it to bring it all the way down. I had the first bucket full and was pulling it to one side, to make room for the second bucket to fit under the spout, when I caught a flash of dark brown run past me to the house. I almost turned the bucket over in my haste to turn towards the house. There was Chaser, headed for the dead chickens. I yelled at him, and took off running after him, but he had a long head start and was much faster than me. He grabbed the first chicken he came to, and headed across the back yard, towards the pasture. I ran after him, yelling for mama with all the lungpower I could muster, while still moving after that dog.

He plunged over the fence with all the ease of a long legged, muscular canine, but I had to slow down long enough to part the wires, and try to fit myself through them. Moving as quickly as I could, I let the top wire loose before my last leg was all the way through. The wire barb caught me right behind the upper, fleshy part of my leg, below the knee. Although I felt skin rip, I wasn't about to stop to see how bad it was. I had one thought in mind, and that was to catch that dang dog before it had a chance to eat mama's dinner meat. She trusted me to keep it safe, and I didn't want to let her down. Roy, who had been at the back of the barn and heard my cries, saw Chaser racing across the field with the chicken in his mouth. He started out after him, way ahead of me. Eight years older than me, and with much more powerful legs, he was able to head across the field and tackle Chaser, just as he slowed at a blackberry thicket.

He ordered the dog to drop his prize, and Chaser obeyed, looking rather chagrined, I thought. He hung his head in shame, as Roy chastised him. Roy picked up the chicken, stuck it in front of Chaser's nose and scolded, "Bad dog, bad dog!" As I approached, Roy held the chicken out to me, and told me to take it back to mom. As I turned to walk away, he noticed blood running down the back of my leg. "Helen, wait!" he ordered.

I stopped and asked, "What?"

"You're bleeding, your leg is bleeding. You must have cut yourself on that barbed wire! Here, let me tie my handkerchief around it until you get home. Have mom take care of it right away. You don't want to get infection in it, and have your leg fall off!" He said it very seriously, but with a tell tale twinkle in his eye.

"Oh, it won't either! You're just saying that!" I chided him, as he tied his make shift bandage in place.

He laughed, and said, "Well, it could get infected and that's not good, so get now and take care of it. Tell mom not to leave those chickens where Chaser can get to them. All that fresh, blood smell, is too much for a hunter like him."

Mother was relieved to see her chicken returned in good enough shape to still be used for dinner. "We'll cut off the part the dog had his teeth into," she said, as she took it from me. "What's the bandage for?" She had seen Roy tackle the dog, and my return walk, but she wasn't aware that I had been hurt.

The fence grabbed me as I crawled through," I explained, as I held my hand over my wound.

"Here, let me see that," she said, as she turned me around, unwound the handkerchief, and inspected the damage. "Let's get you into the house and pour some Iodine on it." By this time it was throbbing, but the pain I was going to be in, when she poured that red medicine on it, was something I did not look forward to.

It burned so badly that I started to cry. "It needs to burn the bad bugs out of it, so infection won't set in," she explained. Somehow that didn't alleviate the pain at all, but it did stop hurting in a few minutes. She wrapped my leg in some white cloth she kept for bandages, tore

Country Splendor

the end of it into two pieces and securely tied it around my leg. "There, that should take care of it."

"You're such a baby," Eileen chided, as I wiped the last of the tears from my eyes. "If you had been watching like you were suppose to, Chaser wouldn't have gotten the chicken in the first place."

"I can't watch everything and pump your old water for you at the same time! I don't have eyes all around my head. You should have been helping me!" I demanded.

"Come on girls, let's get these chickens plucked and ready, the water is boiling." Mother took one chicken at a time, and by hanging onto the neck, she dipped it in the boiling water, then pulling it out, she would turn it around, hanging onto the feet and dip it again. When she tested the feathers and they pulled out easily, she laid that one on a long pan, and dipped the next one.

We sat on the back stoop, pulling the feathers from the chickens until they were plucked clean, down to the soft down next to the skin. Once that was done, we called Mother from the kitchen. She looked the chickens over, and then placed some crumpled paper into an outdoor, fire pit. She struck a match against a stone and set the paper on fire. Holding the chicken by its feet with one hand, and by its neck with the other, she held the chicken over the fire, rotating it slowly, while burning off the soft down. Then, in clean, warm water, we scrubbed the smoke from the chicken and laid it on the counter, ready to be cut up. Eileen and I gathered all the feathers into a garbage pail, while Mother proceeded to gut the chicken, and dropped the entrails into the pail as well.

Next, we cleaned the vegetables to be cooked for dinner, adding the potato peelings, carrot tops, and other leftovers, to the pail as well. Once the pail was full, we carried it to the pigpen and dumped it in the trough for the pigs to eat.

We had barely returned to the house, when the men filed in for breakfast. Mother had prepared it while Eileen and I were plucking the feathers off the chickens. It was waiting in covered pans, on the back of the stove. Eileen handed me the plates from the cupboard, and I handed them to the men, who helped themselves to the food. We then sat silverware at each place, and filled their cups with coffee. Fresh cut bread and freshly churned butter had been placed on the table for all to help themselves. Once the men were eating, Eileen, mother and myself, filled our plates and sat down to eat as well.

Dad emptied his plate and then finished off his cup of coffee. "That was good, Verna. Helen, could you see if there is any coffee left?" he asked. I hurried to the stove, and using a heavy hot pad, carefully took the half empty coffee pot from the stove, and carried it to dad's side. When he noticed me struggling with it, he took it from me and poured his cup, and then offered it to mother. "So, I understand you had an exciting morning," he directed at me. "Roy said you had quite a gash on the back of your leg, how does it feel now?"

"Once the iodine stopped hurting, it was fine," I said, slyly sneaking a look at mother to make sure I hadn't offended her in some way.

She just laughed and handed the coffee pot back to me. I returned it to the stove, and sat back down at my place. For some reason, I felt unusually hungry that morning. I asked mom if I could have some coffee, with a piece of bread and butter, to finish up my breakfast. "Coffee?" Dad asked. "What are you trying to do? Stunt your growth? You're no bigger than a pea pod now."

The boys both laughed, and I became indignant, but for once was speechless. How could I contradict my father? So I sat with my head down, pouting. Mother leaned over to dad and whispered in his ear. Dad looked my way and said, "Vell, little one, I guess it wouldn't hurt if you had a little coffee with lots of cream in it, and maybe a spoon of sugar as well, how's that?"

I looked at dad to see if he was joking with me. I thought I could tell by the soft look in his sky blue eyes, that he meant it. Then he smiled and nodded, and I knew for certain, that it was okay. I grinned and went to prepare my special treat. How good that tasted to me, and how I loved my daddy.

The rest of the morning went rushing by. We hurried through our chores, giving the front room an extra thorough cleaning. Mother had us help with the preparations of the tables, putting extra leaves in the already large kitchen table, and setting it with the best dishes and

Country Splendor

silverware. An extra table was set up in the front room, for the older children to sit at.

Eileen took special care with her hair and dress, and then she brushed my hair free of tangles. At four years old, I wasn't really concerned about how I looked. But I was beside myself with excitement, waiting for our company to come.

Just before one o'clock, they followed one another into the driveway and around to the back, where they parked. Both were four door sedans, but the Frisinger's was a dark blue Packard and the Espeseth's car was a black Ford. We watched from the porch, as the doors opened and kids as well as grownups, started piling out of the cars. The women held covered dishes in their hands, which they presented to mother. Cora brought a large chocolate covered cake, and Sally brought a fruit salad.

The men also came bearing gifts. Andrew brought a bag full of the first pickings of their early, ripe, sweet corn, and Norman had a container of his wonderful, smoked fish. These Scandinavian men had big hearts and even bigger frames. They had grown up on adjoining farms to my father's. The three of them had literally known each other all of their lives. They even attended the same country schoolhouse, which my brother's and sister attended. Their children were growing up as friends with us, as well.

The boys raced to join Ronald and Roy, while Norma and Eileen moved to meet my sister, Eileen, on the porch. I stood by the Frisingers' car to welcome Shirley, as soon as she could alight from their car. The men welcomed each other with handshakes, and the ladies headed right for the kitchen, to talk. I wanted to take Shirley to the barn to see the kittens, right away, but mother intervened and let us know that we needed to eat first. "There will be plenty of time to see the kittens later," she assured us.

Dinner went well, with everyone eating their fill, and sharing many animated stories. Laughter and good-natured jesting added to the reverie. Shirley and I sat at the table in the front room, with the older girls. They accused the boys, of finding room around the kitchen table, so they would be closer to the food. We all laughingly agreed.

Once everyone's appetites were satiated, groups began breaking up and walking outside. The men headed for the barn, while the boys took off for the creek, just like Mother had predicted. The ladies shooed the girls out of the kitchen, telling them to go have fun, and the women would clean up.

Off to the haymow, Shirley and I went, in search of the kittens. They had left their nest in the calf barn some time ago, and roamed around at will. They were good mousers and kept fat and healthy. We found Blacky and Smokey tight-rope-walking the high beam, while Honey and Ringo slept in the hay. We coaxed Blacky and Smokey down to where we were, then gathered Honey, Ringo and their mother, Ginger, up together. We played with each one, looking them over, and comparing them with one another. Then I shared with Shirley how daddy fed the kittens with milk. She had never heard of such a thing, and laughed when I explained how they would bat at the milk, with their paws, and then lick them off, as well as washing their faces. "Sometimes even washing each other's faces," I said, eliciting laughter at the thought.

We heard the men talking in the cow barn, and dropped our voices to a whisper. We stepped closer to the door, so we could hear what they were saying. We giggled, when we heard them talking about what heifers were ready to be impregnated. We didn't know what that meant, for sure, but guessed it meant that they were to become mommies soon. We felt a bit guilty, eve's dropping on them, but at the same time, we were being very adventurous. We laughed behind our hands, and made funny remarks that made us laugh even harder, which we tried to stifle, so they wouldn't hear us.

Then Andrew asked dad how his kidneys were. I shushed Shirley, so I could hear every word. I had been trying to find out what was wrong with daddy from mother, but she was always putting me off. At last, I might learn something.

"The one that was damaged, when I fell from the hayloft onto that wagon tongue, gives me real trouble. It develops stones in it, and it is so painful when they pass, that I can hardly bear I," Dad confessed.

Country Splendor

"Was that the fall you took in 1935, when you were working for my brother, Arthur?" Norman asked.

"Yes, the very one. Should have gone to the hospital then, I guess, but there was so much work to do, and Arthur wanted it done, right then. He didn't know what he would do if I didn't stay and help. You know how it is." Dad finished, lamely, not wanting to hurt Norman's feelings, I'm sure.

"Why haven't you had something done for it, Hubert? You really should you know," remarked Andrew. "There is a good doctor in Madison that you should go see."

"I can't afford to take time away from the farm to go to a doctor. I've lived this long with the pain, and anyway, there just is not enough money for doctors, and you know how they are, always wanting to operate. What if something went wrong, and I never came through it? What would Verna and the kids do without me? I just don't want to take that chance." Dad's voice wavered a bit, as he stepped out of the back door. I leaned closer trying to hear, but their voices faded, as they moved away from the barn

We moved back into the roominess of the haymow and I picked up Blacky, rubbing my face into his silky fur. Shirley kept talking about things in her life, and I tried to concentrate on what she was saying, but I kept hearing dad talk about his injury. I thought to myself, 'What if something happened that he wouldn't come back to us?' I couldn't understand how something like that would happen, but there was something in his voice that frightened me. I couldn't imagine living without my father with us. The fun had gone out of the day for me. All I could think of was that I had to talk to my mother, as soon as I could. Selfishly, I wanted everyone to leave. I needed to talk to my mama.

CHAPTER EIGHT

Our company left before the evening milking began. It had been a long day, only because I had this pressing need to talk to mama about daddy, and I knew it would have to wait until I could be alone with her. My opportunity came while Eileen and I were helping prepare the evening meal. Bobby became fussy, and Eileen was told to take him into the front room and change him. Grabbing the moment, I went and stood beside mother, as she stirred the soup.

"Mama, I need to ask you something."

"What is it?" she inquired, in a voice that suggested that she was willing to hear my question, and maybe even answer it this time.

"Shirley and I were in the haymow today, and we heard daddy talking to Norman and Andrew. He talked about his bad kidney and he sounded sad. Andrew said he needed an operation. What is a kidney and what is an operation?"

She looked at me for a long moment. I began to wonder if she was going to answer me, but then she nodded as if she had answered her own question. "First, a kidney is an organ in our body that helps purify our blood. That means, it takes the bad things from our blood and leaves the good. The bad stuff is passed out of the body when you go to the outhouse. Understand?" she asked, and I nodded. "We actually have two kidney's, one on the right side of our body, and one on the left. The kidney of daddy's that was hurt is on the right side. You heard him talk about the fall that caused the injury? Where he landed across

Country Splendor

the tongue of the hay wagon?" I nodded again. "Ever since then, that kidney hasn't been good. Little hard stones form in it, and when they try to pass out of the body, it creates a lot of pain. Sometimes a doctor can open the body up, and remove what is bad, or correct the problem, so the kidney will work right. That is what is called an operation."

"But won't that hurt really bad? Daddy talked like he could die from that operation. Mama, I don't want daddy to die!" I cried.

"Neither do I, but sometimes people die if something is wrong in their body and they don't get it fixed. And by the way, before they cut anybody open, the doctors put them to sleep, so they don't feel a thing." After patiently explaining this to me, she asked, "What else did you hear them say?"

"Well, Andrew said there was a doctor in Madison that could help dad, and that he should think about seeing him. Where's Madison?"

"Madison is a large city Southeast of here, probably several hours drive away. Did he say the doctor's name?"

"I don't know, because they walked out of the barn, and I couldn't hear anything else."

"Helen, I want you to set the table now and get it ready for supper. Put out the soup bowls, with the bigger spoons for the men, get a loaf of bread from the pantry for me to cut up, and then get the butter from the ice box. Think you can do all that for me?'

"Course I can mother, I'm getting pretty big," I stated importantly.

"Sure you are," she agreed, with a grin she tried to hide by turning her head back to the soup kettle.

That evening, after supper, I noticed Eileen heading out to the outhouse and I accompanied her. For a change she seemed to welcome my company, instead of being annoyed. In fact, she seemed happier than I had seen her in a long time. "You have a good time with Eileen and Norma?" I asked.

She smiled a little, as if she were savoring something very special. "Yes, I did," she answered.

"Where did you go? Shirley and I went out to see the kittens, and afterwards we were looking for the rest of you, but we couldn't find you. All the boys seemed to be gone too. Where were you?" I asked again.

"You promise you won't tell?" I nodded my head in agreement. "We were down by the creek, you know, that spot where the low part spreads out the widest? We waded after small fish, and then got into a water fight with the boys when they came to see where we had gone. We got so wet, that we had to lie on the warm grass, until we dried out. The boys teased us and told us tall stories of some of the things they had done. You know, just boys bragging about themselves to try and impress us girls. Course, we only believed half of it, but it was fun just the same." She hesitated a moment, then lowered her voice as she confided, "But the one thing that worried me a bit, is what Roy was bragging about doing."

"Well, what was that?" I asked, after she paused so long that I was afraid she wasn't going to tell me more. By this time we were seated, leaving the door slightly ajar, because of the heat inside. The flies buzzed around, lighting on us from time to time, and we would swish them away impatiently.

"Listen, I think he was just talking to impress the girls, but I don't want you to tell anyone, because he could get into trouble." She sounded serious and genuinely concerned.

"I told you I wouldn't tell. Now what did he say?"

"Well, he was telling of how he is tired of all the work he and Ron have to do everyday. He thinks that dad is too hard on them. He says that he has a mind to just get on his bike and ride away from here, and never come back."

"Could he do that? Where would he go? He's not old enough to get a job, is he? And what would daddy do, you know that daddy is sick don't you?" I asked Eileen.

"One question at a time. I don't know what Roy would do, if he did try to leave. He's only twelve, and that's not old enough to get a full time job. He hasn't finished school yet. I know some boys stop school before they finish high school, to work full time on their father's farm. Maybe there are farm people who would give him a place to sleep, and food to eat to work for them, but he says he doesn't want to do

Country Splendor

farm work all his life." She seemed to be talking more to herself than to me. She sounded wishful, as if she would like to do something like that herself.

"Eileen, I heard daddy talk about his bad kidney. Andrew is trying to get daddy to see a doctor in Madison. Him and Norman said daddy should have an operation, but daddy doesn't want one. He was afraid it might make him die," I said with an air of importance in having something to tell Eileen that she didn't know.

"Really? Maybe an operation is what he needs. I've seen him lying on his bed, when that kidney was hurting him, and he seemed to be in so much pain. I think sometimes, that that is what makes daddy so mean, why he gets so mad and whips the boys when they are caught goofing off, instead of working," she said. "Mama says that he gets upset when he can't work, and he gets worried, because if the work doesn't get done, we won't have what we need to get through the next long winter. I get tired too. I wish sometimes that we lived in town, and dad had a job like Norman, or some of the other men do."

"Suppose we could live in a nice big house like some of our cousins do? They even have running water in their houses, and lights," I stated, wishfully. "Think of that, inside toilets. Remember when we visited grandma and grandpa in Rice Lake? It would be so nice not to have to run through the cold like we do. Are we poor?" I asked.

"What makes you ask that? Who said we were poor?" she asked indignantly.

"Shirley said that people who live in town, and have lights and toilets inside their houses, are rich. Farm people are poor cause they don't have those things. We don't, so we must be poor."

"I really never thought about it that way. We always have plenty to eat, and we have new shoes and nice clothes for school. Daddy even has a car. I think we are not poor or rich, I just think we live a different kind of life, here in the country. Some of our city cousins come out here, and think we have it better because we have so many animals, and we have horses and large gardens. We have fields to run in; a creek to play in, and they seem to want that. So I don't think we are poor," she said, as she summed up all the different ways of looking at things. "Besides, it is kind of nice being able to sit out here in the summertime, with the sweet smell of the honeysuckle growing all over this outhouse, and the butterflies looking for nectar in their blossoms. It's peaceful, don't you think?"

"Hey, you two, it's not going to be so peaceful if you don't hurry, and let someone else use that thing!" Roy yelled, as he hit the door with a clod of dirt.

"Alright, alright, we will be right out." We yelled at him, as we pulled our clothes back in place, and shoved the door wide, stepping out into the twilight evening.

"Eileen, look, the lightening bugs are out!" I yelled, as I dashed after some of the glowing bugs, which were flitting among the flowers along our path. If we caught them while their tails were lit, and pinched them off, we could spread the stuff on our arms, and it would stay lit for several minutes. But I liked to get an empty fruit jar and put the bugs inside. Then I could watch them blink off and on all evening. Mother would have me set them free before I went to bed though, telling me that then I could catch them another night. If I kept them in the jar they would die. I had learned what dead meant, when I saw Old Black Joe. I didn't want that to happen to my lightening bugs, or my daddy.

A few days later, I glanced out the barn door, to see Andrew Espeseth drive in, and pull up to the kitchen door. Dad had a bag with him, as he left the house, got in the car, and rode away in it. "Where's daddy going?" I asked mother, as I ran into the house from the barn. She had tears in her eyes as she picked Bobby up from the kitchen floor, and carried him into the front room, where she sat down in her rocker, cradling Bobby against her.

"Dad is going to Madison, to see the doctor Andrew told him about," she said.

"Is he going to have an operation?" I asked, feeling a little frightened, remembering how he said he could die.

"We won't know until the doctor has a chance to check him out, but it is possible."

"What does 'possible' mean?" I wanted that clarified.

Country Splendor

"It means that if the doctor thinks it will help, then dad will be operated on."

"Will he be coming home tonight?" I asked hopefully.

"If they operate on him, he won't be home for a while. They will keep him in the hospital until he is able to come home. Even if they don't operate, he wouldn't be home until tomorrow," Mother explained.

"But what is a hospital?" I asked, ever wanting to understand everything.

"A hospital is a place where very sick people go to be cared for until they get well. They will take good care of dad, don't you worry," Mother stated, with a finality to her voice. I knew that meant that she was through answering my seemingly, endless questions, but I just had to venture one more.

"Mama, how will daddy get home? Will Andrew stay there to bring daddy home?"

"Tell you what, Helen, if dad stays there for awhile, Andrew will come by and let us know. He will also tell us when daddy will be able to come home. Now, if you will go help your sister prepare lunch for the boys, and let me be, I will let you ride along when we go down to get dad. Would you like that?"

"Oh yes! Yes! Yes!" I cried as I ran for the kitchen. A ride in a car, all the way to Madison, to get daddy! What an exciting prospect. I dashed into the kitchen, just as Eileen came in from the milk house, with a fresh pitcher of milk.

She carried it to the table, and turning to me, she said, "Helen, help me make some sandwiches, and then I want you to run to the field where the boys are cultivating, and call them in for lunch." Sometimes she seemed much older than her nine years. She seemed to take charge when the folks were not around, or when mother wasn't feeling well. I was to learn that farm children grew up much quicker than their city cousins. They had chores to do from the time they were small, and they were given responsibilities that many people thought were too much for them. However, as one of the children involved, I was confident I could do the chores entrusted to me. We proved more than once, that we were capable of doing a lot more than other's thought possible. I guess we just grew up a lot faster than our city cousins, because we were taught, and trusted to do more than they were, at a much younger age. To us it was a normal way of life.

Without dad's help, the chores were even a heavier load for the boys to handle. Mother tried to lighten the load by helping with the milking, or having Eileen help them. But I could tell that they resented the extra burden placed upon them. When they came in for a meal, or had a chance to relax after the evening chores were done, they would inquire about how dad was doing, and asked how soon he would be home.

Andrew or Norman would get to a phone in town as often as they could and call the hospital in Madison, to see how their life-long friend was doing. Then they would make it a point to stop by long enough to convey the latest information to mother, who would then relay it to us children.

"The operation was performed and the doctor's were comfortable with dad's progress," she said. "They even gave a tentative date when he should be released to come home."

We were glad to hear the positive reports, but mother cautioned that even though dad would be coming home soon, he would not be able to take over his workload for some time. Both Ron and Roy groaned about that, because the grains were setting on, and the harvesting would be beginning soon. Mother reassured them that the neighbors would come and help with the harvesting, but there was the issue of getting the winter wood supply in. "You two need to go to the woods, and begin cutting down the trees for that."

"But dad picks out the trees to be taken down, to thin the woods so the young trees can grow straight and tall. He will have a fit if it's not done right," Ronald stated, with Roy nodding in agreement.

Mother answered their worries, with the assurance that she was sure that they had seen their father do it enough that they could make the right choices, without him, this time.

Country Splendor

Cutting the wood was no small chore, nor without its dangers, if done wrong. Mother talked to Emil Zobel, and asked if he would over-see the boys falling the trees, so no one would get hurt.

He told mother, "I would be honored to help out. I owe you, Hubert and your children so much, for helping save our house, that it is the least I can do."

After milking the next day, Emil and Herbert arrived with their horses in tow. Not only would they help with the cutting down of the trees and limbing them, but also they would use his horses to pull the logs out of the woods, and up to the wood shed. There they would be allowed to age. The logs pulled up the previous year, would be split and chopped into firewood, for this coming winter.

Seeing that they had help, Ron and Roy were much more willing to get to work, and agreed to do so as soon as breakfast was finished. Mother invited Emil and Herbert to sit down and have something to eat as well. They accepted a cup of coffee and a piece of French toast, covered in mother's homemade maple syrup.

Mother sat down across from Emil, with a fresh cup of coffee for herself. "How is Audrey doing?" she asked Emil. Mother had a sixth sense when it came to trouble, and she sensed something was not right with Audrey.

"Well, Mrs., she's been poorly ever since the chimney fire. I've had her to the doctor in Barron, but he just gave her something to build up her blood. He thought she was anemic, I think he called it. She just doesn't have the strength she used to have. She needs to take a nap twice a day now. I don't mean to badmouth her at all, you understand? I am really concerned about her."

"Yes, I do understand, Emil. Would it be all right if I go over after a bit and see her? Sometimes us women can get to the bottom of a problem, better than these doctor's can."

"I would much appreciate it, if you don't mind. Gertrude is with her and does most of the work, so Audrey can rest."

"I made several blueberry pies yesterday, think I'll take one along. I know she really enjoys blueberries," Mother added.

Emil nodded in agreement. "Much obliged for the coffee and toast too. That maple syrup of yours is very tasty. We should get to work, and get as much done before the heat hits the hardest. How about it boys?" Emil asked, addressing all three boys. They all got up and headed out the door in answer.

"Eileen, would you and Helen like to go over to the Zobel's with me? I need to talk to Audrey alone, so you girls could talk to Gertrude, while watching Bobby play outside."

"Sure, I'll change Bobby and we'll be ready to go," Eileen said happily, looking forward to a change in her everyday routine.

We walked across the road, Eileen and I hanging on to Bobby's hands between us, and propelling his little legs faster than he normally could walk. We followed mother as she crossed the road ahead of us, carrying a blueberry pie in one hand, and an unopened jar of her home made Maple syrup in the other.

We crossed the ditch and walked across the freshly mowed lawn to the front steps. Mother waited for us to catch up to her. "Eileen, knock on the door for me, my hands are full," she said, just as the door opened, revealing a delighted Gertrude welcoming us in.

"I brought you all some pie and syrup. Got more than I know what to do with. Is your mother around?"

"She's in her bedroom, I'll let her know you are here," Gertrude said, as she disappeared through a half opened door, that led to her parents bedroom. Presently, she reappeared, beckoning to mother. "Mrs. Ruprecht, mother would like you to come in to the bedroom. I'll take the things you brought into the kitchen. Eileen, do you and the kids want to come into the kitchen with me?" she asked imploringly, as she handled the gifts carefully. You could tell that she needed to talk to someone, too.

I thought that Bobby and me might be in the way, so I offered to take him outside and show him the baby goats. I had seen them when they were tiny, and I wanted to see how much they had grown since then, anyway.

The girls were evidently relieved to have some time alone, together, and voiced a definite yes to my offer. Bobby and I made our way out

Country Splendor

the kitchen door, and across the backyard to the pen, where the goats were kept. I was surprised how much they had grown in two months. "Look Bobby, look at the goats."

"Goes," he repeated. He didn't talk very much, so it surprised me when he tried to say something.

"Goats." I pronounced it carefully, as I stooped down in front of him so he could see my lips. He tried saying it again, but it still came out, "goes." But I was delighted that he was trying to talk.

We stood watching the goats play together, and Bobby would clap his hands, saying, "Goes, goes."

Next, I walked Bobby to the pigpen, and again was amazed to see how big the babies had become, since I had seen them in the spring. They were rooting around in the mud, looking for roots, and snorting in disappointment. Bobby was delighted with everything he saw. "Goes, goes," he said.

"Not goats, Bobby, these are pigs. Pigs," I repeated slowly.

"Pis, pis," he said, clapping his hands together. I couldn't help laughing at his pronunciation of the words.

We continued to the pasture, where we could see the cows eating grass as they lazily moved about, swishing their tails at the flies that buzzed around them. The young calves were half as large as their mother's now, and cavorting around their mothers, kicking their back legs in the air, as they played like happy children.

"Cows, Bobby, cows," I pronounced carefully.

"Cows," he said.

"Yes! That's correct. Cows," I replied.

"Helen," Mother called.

"Here," I called back.

"Come on, we have to get back and get lunch and dinner ready for the men."

"Coming," I shouted, as I grabbed Bobby's hand and pulled him away from the cow scene. I headed him towards the house and mother, who was waiting on the porch for us.

As I approached her, I noticed her furrowed brow. I had the sense of her being deeply troubled about something. However, when I asked her what was wrong, she only shook her head and said, "Come on, we've got work to do."

Eileen said goodbye to Gertrude, as she came out of the house and joined us. It was a silent group, walking home together, with each of us thinking our own thoughts.

CHAPTER NINE

Two weeks later we received word that dad was doing fine and would soon be able to come home. Andrew offered to drive us down to get him. Mother asked him, if he would mind if Bobby and I rode along, as she had promised me that I could go. Of course he wouldn't mind, and we would leave early Friday morning.

Mother anticipated the offer, and had already talked to Eileen about it. She told her that she had promised that I could go along and that Bobby would be going with us, as well. She then asked Eileen if she would mind staying home, as there was only so much room in the car? Mother told her that if she would agree to stay home, that she would be able to go to the movies the next time dad planned on going.

Eileen said that she really didn't want to go on that long a trip anyway. She would stay home, prepare a meal for the boys, and catch up on some things she wanted to do.

I was so excited, that I didn't think I would be able to sleep much the night before going, and I told Eileen so.

"Tell you what, Helen, I will ask mom if we can have a lamp in our room tonight, and I will read you to sleep."

"Okay, I like it when you read to me. But I'm sorry you won't be going along with us tomorrow," I stated wistfully.

"Actually, I am glad I don't have to go. If I went I would have to take care of you and Bobby. If I stay home, I only have to make the boys a meal, and I can have all the rest of the time to myself. I can do

Country Splendor

anything I want! I am looking forward to that! And also, I get to go to a movie!" she sounded very happy about the whole thing.

"What's a movie like?" I asked, never having gone to one myself.

"The movie theater is a large building, full of rows of seats for people to sit on. Up in front is a big sheet hung on the wall. Pictures that move are shown on that sheet, and the pictures tell a story. You have to buy a ticket to go in, and see it of course. Maybe, when you get a little older, you will get to go to a movie with me. It's hard to describe to someone who has never seen one," she stated. "What story would you like me to read to you?"

"How about, you just tell me a story, cause I can go to sleep better if it's dark." I must have dropped right off to sleep, because I do not remember the story Eileen told me. It was still dark when Mama gently shook me awake.

"Come on, Helen," she was whispering, "Let Eileen sleep. I have your clothes ready for you down stairs." I got up and followed her down the stairs. An oil lamp was burning in the front room; mother was already dressed and Bobby was dressed to go, although he was still sleeping. "Hurry and dress now, Andrew will be here soon. We need to get an early start, because it is a long trip, and we want to be home before dark tonight," she explained.

I was dressed, and just putting on my last shoe, when Andrew drove up to the back door. Mother hurriedly tied my shoes and told me to grab the paper sack lunch she had prepared to take along. As I headed for the kitchen, she crossed to Bobby's bed and picked him up, keeping a light blanket wrapped around him. She stepped into her bedroom and grabbed a couple of pillows to take as well. We left through the kitchen door, climbed into Andrews's car, with mother in the front seat, and Bobby and me in the back. He sprawled out against the pillows mother placed there, and continued to sleep, with a thumb stuck contentedly in his mouth, making soft little suckling sounds.

I was so excited; I couldn't sleep, although it was still dark out. We were going to get my daddy! It seemed like such a long time since he had left. I stared out the window, although there wasn't much to see yet, only an occasional light in the farmhouses we passed. Then I noticed that the sky was turning a lighter color of gray. I watched as it grew lighter and lighter, until a yellow caste crept across it. The sun was peeking over the horizon on its way up, and there were only a few wispy clouds along the edge of the sky. Then the sky and clouds took on a bright orange glow, with a bright yellow lining. I sat awed by the beauty of it. I could make out shapes of things we were passing. There were cows moving around in one pasture, and horses standing quietly beneath a tree in another. As it grew lighter out, the orange and yellow colors paled, as the sun moved higher, and the sky took on a clearer blue.

A small dog like animal crossed the road, and when I pointed it out to mother, she told me it was a fox. A fox! I had only seen pictures of them, but now I had seen the real thing. I was interested in everything I saw, and I kept pointing at first one thing, then another, asking mother what it was. She patiently explained to me, what each thing was. I especially liked going through the towns along the way, as there was so much to see that was new to me.

When we went through Cameron, the first town on our route, it was still dark out. A few lights were coming on in various homes and buildings. Most everything was in deep shadow.

Miles further on we went through Chetek. There was just enough light by then, to make out the shapes of the buildings. It was a larger town than Cameron. Passing out of Chetek, we were again passing miles of farmland, and scattered buildings. Next, we came to a town with a name, which struck me as quite funny. When mother told me it was Bloomer, I started laughing. "Really? Like the bloomers I wear?" I asked, between giggles.

"Yes, that's it's name," Mother confirmed, and Andrew made some comment to mother I didn't catch, but she laughed right out loud, and he chuckled.

"In fact, Helen, this is where Daddy's sister Della and her husband, Charlie Black, have their farm. You were there once, but maybe you were too young to remember."

"Could we go there again one day? I would love to see it," I said.

Country Splendor

"We are suppose to go there for Thanksgiving this year, but we will have to see how your daddy is by then." She sounded doubtful, and I took that as a very unlikely happening.

The next long miles past quickly, as it became lighter and easier to make out the homes and fields we passed by. Soon we were entering another town. "This is Chippewa Falls," Mother said. It was light enough to see clearly now and I was fascinated by the beautiful buildings.

"Chip-pe-wa Falls," I pronounced slowly. "I like that name. What is falls?" I asked mother.

"That's usually a place in a river where the ground falls away, and the water has a long way to drop to the next level. That is called a falls," she explained.

"Is there one here we can see?' I asked. "I would love to seen one."

"There is a falls close by, but it is off to the East, and it would take us out of our way to go there," Andrew explained. "We really do not have the time now."

I understood his reasoning, and I was anxious to see my daddy, anyway.

Finally, the almost white, bright sun was in full view, and the sky brightened up until I could see long distances. It was the first time I had ever watched the night sky turn into morning, and I found it fascinating as well.

The next town we pulled into was called Eau Claire. It was really big. Mother told me that this place was called a city, as it was so much bigger than the other towns we had went through. Andrew asked us to help him find the street sign that pointed us to Hwy 94. That would be the hiway we would travel on, the rest of the way to Madison.

"Is it much further?" I asked. It seemed that we had already come a long way.

"We are not even half way yet," Andrew answered.

"Are you getting hungry, Helen?" Mother asked.

"Actually I am a little hungry and thirsty too," I answered.

Andrew said, "I am going to watch for a gas station. This would be a good place to fill up my gas tank. There should be one open here somewhere." Just ahead, at the next corner I spotted a filling station, and pointed it out to him. "Yes, I see it, thanks," He said. "We could get the gas, and maybe some pop there, then we can pull over somewhere, and eat a bite."

"That sounds good to me," Mother said. I nodded my head in agreement as well. As we pulled into the filling station, Bobby woke up, and sat up, looking around. I imagined that he was quite confused at first, falling asleep in his bed, and waking up in a car.

The gas station attendant was beside the car before Andrew could roll down his window. "Fill it up, please," he said. "And would you check that rear tire of mine? It seems to be a little soft."

"Sure thing," the attendant said, as he motioned to another young man, and instructed him to check the tires, while he proceeded to put in the gas. When that was done, he checked the oil, the water, and washed all the windows. Andrew followed the first attendant into the station, where he paid for the gas, and bought us each a bottle of orange soda.

Andrew opened his door, and passed the soda's into mother. He proceeded to crawl in, and reached for the key again, as he said to mother, "they told me about a nice park just on past the main part of the city. It will be a lovely place to stretch our legs and have something to eat. There are picnic tables, as well as public toilets there."

"Sounds perfect to me," Mother responded, with a smile. I was excited by everything and had a hard time not annoying mother with my questions.

The large buildings fascinated me. I wanted to know what each one was. There were so many and they were so tall. It was early enough that there were few people on the streets yet, but many of the buildings were lit up inside. Large lit windows, in some of the buildings, advertised clothing, shoes, furniture, and hardware. I was totally absorbed, trying to see everything. 'I will have so much to tell my sister when we get home,' I thought to myself. The large buildings gave way to smaller buildings, and a few blocks further on, we saw

Country Splendor

a beautiful park, quite large it seemed. There was short green grass as far as the eye could see, with tall trees of several varieties, smaller bushes, and lots of flower beds placed along the paths. A large water fountain was in the middle of the park. I could hardly wait for Andrew to park the car in the adjacent parking area, and bring it to a stop, so I could hop out.

"Helen, you wait for us to tell you, you can get out. You could get hurt! Now take Bobby's hands, and help him out. You keep hold of him, I don't want him running off and getting lost." Mother said, as she gathered up the lunch sacks she had brought, and climbed from the car, shutting the door with her foot. Andrew was already out, with the soda bottles in his hands. He motioned for us to follow, and he led us down a flower-lined path, to a picnic table within view of the fountain.

I couldn't contain my excitement anymore, and I took off at a run towards the fountain. I gasped at the sight of that water shooting into the sky, reflecting the suns' bright colors as it fell back into the lower basin. I ran back to the picnic table and asked, "Mama, can I take Bobby closer to the fountain, please? Just for a minute?"

"Well," she looked at Andrew and he nodded his head, "Okay, but just for a few minutes. We need to eat and get on our way."

"Thank you, thank you," I shouted, as I pulled Bobby across the intervening path. His little legs had to move fast to keep up with my longer legs, but he didn't fall. We reached the fountain, and saw that there were coins lying in the depths of the water. "Mama, there is money in here," I shouted. I tried to reach one, but got hit by falling water, and pulled back.

"That's all right, Helen. People throw coins in, and then make a wish on them," she explained.

"Why?" I asked.

"Because they think their wishes will come true."

"Can I do that mama? Make a wish on a coin, and through it in there, too? Please?" I asked, as I walked back to the table, with Bobby still attached to my left hand.

"Sure Helen," Andrew answered, as he fished in his pants pocket for a coin. He pulled out two bright pennies, giving one to me and one to Bobby.

We hurried back to the fountain. I held my penny in my right fist, squeezing it real hard, as I whispered a wish. Then I opened up my hand, and dropped the coin into the water, watching it fall among the other coins. I turned to Bobby, and he had his penny in his mouth. "Hey, you aren't supposed to eat that. You are suppose to make a wish and put it in the water."

"No!" he said, as I tried to extract the coin from his mouth. He grabbed it in his little fist and wouldn't let go.

"Your wish won't come true if you don't put your penny in that fountain," I tried to reason with him.

"No, no!" he repeated.

"Okay, then. Be that way," I said; as I led him back to the picnic table. "Mama, Bobby still has his penny, and he keeps putting it in his mouth."

"Well, we can't have him swallowing it. Here Bobby, give me the penny," Mother coaxed.

"No, mine!" he said, as he took off running with it.

"Helen, get that boy and bring him back here. I have half a mind to paddle him!"

I ran him down, grabbed his arm, and pulled him back to mother. She took him from me, and forced the penny from his mouth. "There now, you've lost your penny," she said, as he puckered up his face, and threw himself down on the ground. "Listen here, little man! That will only get you a spanking." She raised him to his feet. "You must not put pennies into your mouth. You will swallow them. Do you understand?"

I don't think he understood what she was saying completely, but he understood the tone of her voice, and he stopped throwing his fit. Instead, he crawled upon the bench, and reached for a cookie that mother had put there for him. She gave him a sip from her pop bottle, and he grabbed it with both hands, trying to keep her from taking it

Country Splendor

away from him. He drank several good swallows before she could wrench it away.

Mother shook her head at Andrew saying, "I didn't think he was that strong!"

"When it comes to something they really like, they have a lot of determination," he laughed. Andrew being the father of three big boys, and now another baby boy, he thoroughly understood them.

We sat around the table, eating our sandwich, and drinking our soda. The sun was warm against our skin, and the scenery was pleasing to the eye, both colorful and serene. A variety of birds could be seen, flitting from tree to tree, and brightly colored butterflies played among the flowers. A friendly gray squirrel approached our table, as if hoping for a hand out. Andrew threw a small crust of bread down on the ground, where the squirrel could see it. He ran to it, picked it up, and examined it, while sitting back on his haunches. Then he put it in his mouth, and ran up a big oak tree. We all laughed as we watched him go, his large, full tail being the last thing we saw, as he disappeared among the leaves.

"Come on children. I know you are enjoying it here, but we must be on our way. I will take Bobby and change his diaper, while you make a trip to that toilet over yonder, Helen."

Once we each had taken a turn in the toilet, and had picked up our things from the table, we climbed back into Andrews Chevy, and continued on our way. Bobby stood on his feet, watching out the back window, until mother turned around, and pulled him down to a sitting position. "You sit there now," she commanded.

He tried to roll over and get back to his knees, but she reached back and swatted him on his behind, and turned him back around. "I said for you to sit down. Sit down! Do you understand?" He looked at her with his big bright eyes, and toppled over to a prone position. I handed him his bottle. He took it and held it against his chest, while sticking the thumb of his other hand into his mouth.

On down the road we went. Country scenes of fields and farms, pasture lands and ponds. Farm animals of all kinds, were scattered among the rolling hills. There were small towns along the way. Foster,

Osseo, Northfield, Hixton, Black River Falls, Millston and Tomah. Mother would tell me the name of each one as we passed through. On we traveled, through Douglas, then Hustler, Mauston and Lyndon Station. Now we were in hill country and heavier growth of trees. It was a welcome relief, from all the rolling hills we had passed over. Just past Lake Dalton, we passed a ski resort. "We have to watch for Hwy 39 now," Andrew instructed. "We are only about 65 miles from Madison."

I know that he was trying to encourage us, but 65 miles still sounded like a long way.

Although I enjoyed the scenery, and found it very interesting, it seemed like that five- plus hours they said it would take, was taking forever. I kept thinking of my dad, and I just wanted to see him again so badly!

We turned south on Hwy 39, and passed The Devil's Hill Ski Lodge. The huge log buildings looked inviting, sitting on the banks of Blue River and Crystal Lake. The scenery was some of the wildest I had ever seen, and I glued myself to the window, not wanting to miss one thing. At each turn the road took, another beautiful sight would present itself. We even saw a family of three deer, grazing in a grassy meadow.

Eventually, we entered an area of houses and businesses that lined the streets, and stretched out as far as the eye could see. "Mama, is this Madison?" I asked excitedly, for I had never seen such a big city.

Andrew answered for her, "Yes it is, now we just have to find the hospital. I would like to fill up with gas before we head home, so I'll find a gas station now, and they should be able to tell us the easiest way to the hospital from there." We pulled into a gas station, stopping by the pumps. The gas pumps with the big round colorful tops on them fascinated me. I loved watching the gas run through the tops, before flowing down the hose, and into the gas tank.

We were barely stopped, when three attendants surrounded the car. Andrew rolled down his window, as one of them approached his side of the car. He told him to fill it up. One of the other young men washed all the windows, as the third one checked the tires. Andrew

Country Splendor

got out of the car, and talked to the one who was handling the hose that was filling up the car with gas. "Can you tell me how to find the hospital?"

"Sure can, continue down this street to the big Sears and Roebuck department store, turn right just past it, and its right down that street a piece. You can't miss it."

By the time Andrew returned to the car, the fellow who had checked the tires had also checked the oil, and the water in the radiator. Andrew thanked them all, and handed the gas attendant two dollars, and told him to keep the change.

True to the directions he gave us, we found the hospital without any trouble, although the Sears and Roebuck store was further down the road than we anticipated.

Once stopped at the hospital, mother came to the back, opened up my door, and had me wait outside while she reached in, laid Bobby on his back and changed his diaper again. I danced with excitement, and impatience, to get started into the hospital. It seemed so huge, by far the biggest building I had ever seen. I wondered how we would ever find my daddy in there.

Mother picked Bobby up in her arms, and instructed me to stay beside her, as Andrew walked on mother's other side, taking her arm and helping her up the long flight of stairs. He opened the door, letting mother and I in first. We walked up to a counter, where a lady dressed in white, waited behind it, watching us approach. "Can I help you?" she asked.

Andrew spoke first, telling her that we were there to take Hubert Ruprecht home. She wanted to know what he was there for, and mother told her he had, had an operation.

"He should be on the second floor then. Wait just a moment and I will have an orderly take you to him," she said. She summoned a young man, also dressed in white, and told him whom we were there to see.

"This way," he said, as he led us down a long corridor to a flight of steps. Once on the second floor, he took us to another counter, and asked the lady sitting behind it, what room Mr. Ruprecht was in. She looked on a chart and directed us to his room, letting us know that we could take him home, after the doctor had checked him over, and given mother the directions she must follow, once he was home.

The smell of the hospital bothered me; it was a strong smell that stung my nose. I followed mother into the room the lady had indicated with her hand, as she pushed it slightly open and stepped back, so we could enter first. It took me a moment to realize that the pale, and helpless looking man, in the white covered bed, was indeed my daddy. His eyes fell on mother's face, first. His eyes lit up, and a rather weak smile played around his lips, as if they would rather cry. Mother placed Bobby on the floor, as she approached the side of father's bed, and grasped his hand tightly in hers. I couldn't see her face, but when she spoke, her voice was quivery, as if full of tears. She bent down and touched his forehead with her lips, whispering, "Oh Hubie, I have missed you so much! How are you doing?"

When she rose up enough that I could see daddy's face, I noticed his big, blue eyes, were glistening with tears that he was fighting to control. But one wayward tear spilled over and left a wet trail, as it rolled down his cheek. He swiped at it, and blinked the rest back into submission.

"I'm ready to go home. This hospital food would do better being given to the pigs!" he tried to joke. Andrew and mother responded the way they knew would please my daddy, and they laughed heartedly. That eased the tension in the room. "Vell, Andrew, how are things going? Has the harvesting started yet? The corn must be about ripe enough to take in by now."

It was more of a statement than a question, but Andrew replied, "Yes, the tassels are brown and the ears are full, so we will be getting it cut and put in the corn bins any day now. We have been watching it, and it's fine. In fact, me and my sons, and some of your neighbors, plan on getting to it Friday. We should be able to finish it all in one day. The second hay cutting has been done, and that's already in the mow. You've got enough for the winter. Heard that your boys, and the Zobel's, got the wood cut and stacked also, so you see, everything is

Country Splendor

done that needs to be done. You just concentrate on getting yourself well." He finished with a no-nonsense air, reassuring dad.

I had been easing myself closer to the bed, although mother and Andrew took up the room. Andrew noticed me, and stepped back to give me room to get closer to daddy.

"Hey, there's my little angel!" daddy exclaimed, as he reached an arm out to me, encouraging me to come closer.

I grabbed at his hand, and he pulled me close enough to give him a hug. He moaned slightly, as I pressed against his side. Mother pulled me back with a jerk, "Helen, you are hurting daddy's side!" she said, a bit harshly.

I pulled away and started to cry. I didn't mean to hurt him; I just wanted to be close. He reached out for my hand, and moved me closer to the head of his bed, where he pulled my arm around his neck, and managed to plant a kiss on my cheek. "It's alright, angel, I know you did not mean to hurt me. Now don't cry, I'm going to be fine, honest." Dad said soothingly, as he petted my head. I pulled away, giving him a teary smile.

"I missed you so much, daddy," I told him.

"And I missed you too, little one," he assured me.

The door opened and the doctor walked in. He was about dad's height but a lot leaner, giving him a look of being taller, especially in his white smock. He had white hair and a kind looking face. He introduced himself, and then asked us to leave, so he could give dad a last good look before discharging him. Mother asked if she could stay, as she needed to ask questions on how to take care of dad. He said that would be okay, but he really felt the rest of us should wait in the waiting room. Andrew took over, picking Bobby up in his arms, and taking me by my hand, he walked us out of the door, and into the waiting room.

The waiting room was a square cubicle that had a smattering of rather hard chairs lined up along the walls. In the corner was a table with a few catalogs, and books made up entirely of pictures. Andrew said they were comic books. I had never seen a comic book before, and found them very interesting. Even though I could not read the writing,

I found the pictures fascinating. Bobby grabbed one and started pulling at the pages, until one ripped. "No, no Bobby," I scolded. "You mustn't tear them up." I took it away from him. He started to fuss at me, and threw himself on the floor, kicking his feet in the air, to let me know that he was mad at me.

"Hey, young man, come here and I will bounce you on my knee," Andrew said, as he reached for Bobby and pulled him up on his leg. He proceeded to hold Bobby's hands, and he let him ride his leg, as he moved it up and down. Bobby responded with glee, laughing, and forgetting all about the picture books.

After what seemed to me, to be a long time, but probably was only a few minutes, the door opened to dad's room and the doctor came out, followed by mother. He told her that he would send a nurse in to get Hubert dressed, and then we could take him home.

"Just remember what I told you, about applying the ointment and changing the bandages. The bandages will need to be boiled between uses, so as to sterilize them. Infection is still a possibility until he is completely healed. He should not do anything that could pull at his stitches. He could tear the incision open. Also, give him some of this medicine. I will have the nurse send some home with you. It will help alleviate some of the pain and make him more comfortable. I will have the nurse give him a dose before you leave to help him on that long ride home. He might be more comfortable if he could lie down in the backseat.

"We brought some pillows along to help cushion him some," Mother replied.

"Good, and one more thing. Have him drink plenty of water, especially water from boiled potatoes. That should help his kidney stay clean and free from stones."

He shook hands with mother, and with Andrew, then tussled my hair, saying, "Take care of that daddy of yours. Okay?"

I felt very important to be noticed by the doctor, and to be given a job to do. I grinned shyly at him from around mother's back. He grinned back, then said to mother, "The nurse will let you know when Hubert is dressed and ready to go."

Country Splendor

She thanked him as he nodded his reply, and left the room.

Once dad was made as comfortable as possible, in the back seat, mother had me sit in the front, between Andrew and her, as she held Bobby on her lap. We headed home, and I noticed Andrew drove a bit slower, than when we drove down, and he seemed to take each corner a little more carefully.

Mother tried to watch dad for any sign of discomfort, and she reached her hand back to grasp his, every once in a while. "Are you alright, Hubie?" she would ask.

Finally, after answering that same question a number of times, he stated, "Honey, I'm fine. Please stop worrying. I'm going home and that's what matters."

"Did they treat you okay?" she asked. "Was the operation very long?"

"I would just as soon not talk about the operation right now. The nurses were very nice, and tried to make me as comfortable as possible, though the food wasn't your good cooking. I am looking forward to some decent food. They don't know how to flavor anything there!" he stated, with definite exclamation.

The ride home seemed even longer than the ride down. I had to sit still, and that was very hard for me. I've always had a lot of energy, and some part of me wants to be moving all the time. I squirmed and tried to move. Mother warned, that if I didn't hold still, she would make me walk home. One time, I got so antsy that I managed to turn enough to get my legs under me, and face the back seat. For once mother didn't keep her word, and put me out of the car. I hung over the back of the seat, and talked to daddy, until mother made me turn back around, and leave daddy alone. Eventually, I fell asleep against mother's arm, and thankfully, slept the rest of the way home.

CHAPTER TEN

Andrew helped mother get daddy into the house, and into his bed, before taking off for home. We all waved at him, as he drove away. The boys were in from milking, and were full of questions, as well as hungry. Mother helped Eileen finish preparing the supper, and got it on the table, while answering their questions the best she knew.

She prepared a plate for dad, placed it on a serving tray, and took it in to him. We could hear them talking, as dad ate, but the words were muffled. We all finished our supper in silence, each one wondering just what lay ahead of us.

Not much changed for the first couple of weeks that dad was home. He managed to get out of bed, and sit in his over-stuffed chair, the second day he was home. Mother fussed at him about it, as she thought it was just too soon for him to exert himself that much. He said that he had to get his strength back. He had lain in bed long enough. When dad got something in his head, mother was helpless to change it. She insisted on bringing him his food though, and sat a small table beside his chair, to accommodate him. He passed the time by listening to his battery-powered radio, and reading the paper that Mr. Foss dropped off for him, each day. It was a day old and a bit wrinkled, but dad did not mind.

Neighbors dropped by, from time to time, to see how dad was doing, and to catch him up on the latest news of the area. They would always bring something to hand to mother, a fresh baked pie, a frosted

Country Splendor

cake or a plate of cookies. I especially liked it when the whole family came, because there would usually be someone for me to play with as well.

Canning was in full stride, as everything seemed to be coming ripe at the same time. Peas were done up first, and I remember sitting on the back stoop with mother and Eileen, shelling them. That was a special time, as we would exchange funny stories and thoughts to help pass the time.

Tomatoes were canned next. I loved to drop them into the boiling water and watch their skin crinkle and loosen up. Mother thought that dipping them from the boiling water was too dangerous for me. In fact, she would seldom allow Eileen to do it either. That was one job she insisted on doing herself. We would have the jars scrubbed and rinsed already, so she would drop the skinless tomatoes right into the clean jars. Eileen was allowed to finish filling them with boiling water, as long as she dipped it very carefully. The rings and lids were then screwed in place, and the jar placed in the large canner on the stove. The jars were covered with water, and allowed to boil for a specific amount of time. Then they were taken from the water, placed on towels, and allowed to cool. Lids were checked to make sure they sealed, and then the jars were carried to the cellar, and placed on shelves.

Green beans were picked and canned next. It was a lot of work, and Cora Espeseth came over, more than once, to spend a day, helping mother put away the vegetables.

The teenage daughter of the Foss's would come over to help often. At first mother was thankful for her help, but Arlene always seemed to find a reason to go into the front room, and spend more time than necessary, talking with dad. In fact, it began being more time spent with dad, than with the women in the kitchen. He seemed to enjoy her visits, so mother would bite her tongue, and not complain. I think it rankled mother sometimes though, because I would catch her listening at the door to the front room, as she heard dad's laughter ringing through the house. Sometimes she would send me in to 'see if there is anything your father needs.'

Helen Marie Fias

The end to this 'visiting' came suddenly, one day, after I walked in unexpectedly, and found Arlene sitting on daddy's lap. I went into the kitchen, just as mother was lifting the finished jars out of the hot water and sitting them on clothes, placed on the table, to soak up the water. I told mother what I had seen, and she didn't even stop to wipe the water from her hands on a towel, but used the corner of her apron to dry them, as she fled for the front room. Dad's chair was placed in the far corner of the room, behind the parlor stove, so mother had to approach that before she could verify the picture, my tale invoked in her mind. Sure enough, Arlene was perched on dad's knees, but his hands were on the arms of the chair he was sitting in. She was leaning towards him, and they were both laughing at some remark she had made. Mother's indignation could be heard clear in the kitchen, and that young lady was up, and out of there, in record time. I don't recall her ever coming to visit again.

If mother and dad ever discussed this event, the children never heard it. Mother and dad always kept their personal problems, private. Maybe they talked it over behind their bedroom door, but I never asked, nor was it ever mentioned in our presence.

The harvesting of the corn was completed in one day, just as Andrew had promised it would be. Right after milking, one morning, our driveway filled up with cars, men and boys. A large corn binder was pulled in behind a matched pair of Clydesdale horses, and set up close to the silo. Several men headed for the cornfield, some with long scythes and others armed with sickles. Each took on their own row of ripe corn, swinging their sharpened hand tools, with practiced procession, cutting the stalks off at the base. The boys would follow them, two or three to a row, depending on how big they were. It took one bigger guy, or two smaller boys, to put the stalks into shocks, and the other boy would cut off a length of twine from the roll he carried, and whip it around the stalks, catching the flying end of twine and tying it off. If everything went well, they would end up with a shock that would hold together, as it was piled onto the hay wagon.

The horse, drawn wagon, was slowly driven up a row of shocked corn, while another lad would walk along, throwing the shocks on the

Country Splendor

wagon. When the wagon was full, they would both hop on, and drive the horses back to the barn, where the shocks were unloaded, next to a corn binder. The stalks of corn were fed into the corn binder, where the ears of corn were separated from the stalks, and dropped into a pile. Several men would pick through the ears of corn, to make sure it was clean of husks and blight, and then toss the good ears into a shed, called a crib. It had walls made of slats that were several inches apart, allowing air to flow through the crib to dry out the corn. It had a good solid roof to keep out the rain and snow.

The corn binder, which was run by a gas engine, had great teeth inside that turned, chewing up the corn stalks, and blowing the pieces into a long pipe that extended from the top of the binder, into the top of the silo. This corn fodder would eventually turn into silage, which was fed to the cows during the winter months, while they were kept in the barn. It added nourishment to their diet, and helped keep them regular through their inactive period.

The fieldwork proceeded well, and while the men worked on the corn, the women worked with mother in the kitchen, preparing a large lunch for the men. At ten o'clock, I was given the privilege of ringing the triangle that hung outside the back door. I took the medal rod and hit the triangle, until I saw men coming in my direction. The sound carried to the fields as well, and soon the yard filled with hungry men and boys. A bench on the porch was provided with several washbasins, and buckets of clean water. The curved handled ladle, hanging in each bucket, was used for dipping the water into the basins. The men would wash the sweat and chaff off their hands, arms and faces, thereby refreshing themselves before sitting down to eat. Large towels were hung near by to dry one self on.

Large horsehair mats were just outside the kitchen door for the soles of their boots to be wiped on, before entering the kitchen. The table in the kitchen was pulled out to its full length, which sat at least fourteen men at one time. The over flow would carry their plates outside and sit on benches under the shade trees. The teenaged boys seemed to prefer eating outside. There they talked on the subjects that interested them the most. Usually about girls, I found out. The girls around Eileen's age and older would find some reason to stroll by from time to time, sneaking looks at the boys. The bolder ones would even stop and talk to them for a few moments, then turn to their shy friends and walk off, giggling behind their hands.

There were always girls close to my age to play with, so we would sneak around, eavesdropping on the boys, and giggling over what we could hear. Once the older girls had moved on, the comments we heard would send us into gales of laughter, smothered behind our hands, until we would have to run off before they noticed us.

Once the men finished off their second cup of coffee, they would be ready to get back to work, and the boys would be called together to go as well.

The women would clear the table, handing the children a sandwich and a glass of milk, and shooing them outside. Then they would sit down for a sandwich and a cup of coffee for themselves, sharing the experiences they had since the last time they were together. Then a couple of them would proceed with the washing and drying of the dishes, while another swept the floor. Some had babies and small children to feed, and diapers to change. With that done the preparing of the large meal would then proceed. Fresh vegetables would be brought in from the garden, and prepared for cooking or salad making. A large roast would be in the oven, having been prepared very early in the morning, allowing it to cook slowly, to a tender, dark brown, by dinnertime.

After dinner was served, and the men had eaten, the majority of them headed back to the barn for the remainder of the afternoon, working hard to get all of the corn in, and processed, so they could return home to their own chores. Dad had taken his place at the table for the noon meal, and then excused himself to return to his chair in the front room.

Andrew and Emil followed dad from the table, in hopes of having a few moments alone with him. Andrew sat in the rocker, close to dad, while Emil squatted in front of him. "How are you feeling Hubert?" he asked. "We've been worried about you."

Country Splendor

Dad shook his head and uncharacteristically answered, "Those doctor's cut me half in two, from my backbone all the way around to the middle of my stomach. You would think they could get to the kidney without opening me up that much. It hurts like hell, every time I move. I'm going crazy not being able to do more, and they told me it would take several weeks before I will be feeling better."

Andrew moved a few inches closer, to keep the conversation private, just between the three of them. "You sounded like the operation did not go as well as it should. You said you would tell us about it later. Just what happened, anyway?" he asked.

"They prepped me, you know, shaving my body and painting it with iodine, or some such stuff. Then put me to sleep, but they mustn't have given me enough stuff, or they took too long, I'm not sure what the problem was, but I came awake before they were through. I felt them sewing me back together, and I thought I had suffered pain before, but this was beyond anything I had ever felt. I thought I would die before they got through with me. I'll tell you this; I'll never let anyone, ever cut me open for anything, ever again. They are worse than butchers. At least the carcass we operate on is dead first." Dad stated, with a finality that left no room for argument.

Both men expressed how sorry they were for what he had endured. "But once you are healed, you should be as good as new, right?" Andrew asked.

"The way the doctors talked, I probably will have trouble the rest of my life. They took out the kidney, opened it up and removed the stones that were in it, but they can't promise that new ones won't form again. Verna boils potatoes with their jackets on, and I am supposed to drink the water off of it. They think that it will help me heal faster inside, and that it might help the stones from forming. Personally, I think they are all quacks and really don't know what they are doing! I was an experiment, they said, as they had never seen a kidney so badly damaged as mine."

"You mean they put back a bad kidney? Why didn't they just leave it out?" asked Emil

"They said that they weren't sure a person could live with only one kidney. I don't know if they know what they are doing or not, but this is what I will have to live with," Dad said, disgustedly.

"Well, listen, don't you worry yourself about the farm or the harvesting. We have discussed this, and we are all going to help out. You just take care of yourself, and let yourself heal, before you try to do anything," Andrew stated, accompanied by a nod from Emil. The two men shook hands with dad, and said they needed to get back to work, and see that the corn was attended to. They promised to see him as often as they could, to make sure all was going okay.

Dad thanked his friends, and choked back the anguish he felt, as he said goodbye to them as they retreated from the room. I had been listening from the stairway, and I almost gave myself away by rushing to him, as I saw him drop his face into his two big hands. 'My poor daddy, suffering so, and feeling so helpless.' I thought, as I cried a tear for him. I knew he would be mad if he knew I had been listening, so I headed out of the room instead, tiptoeing so he wouldn't know I had been on the stairs.

I hadn't planned on eaves dropping. I just wanted to show my friends a picture I had drawn, so I had run up to my room where I had left it. As I started back down the stairs I heard the men talking with daddy, and I just had to listen. Now I needed to find the girls, who must have gone outside by this time.

Some of the women had left for home already, asking their husbands and sons to catch a ride home with someone else. No one was left for me to play with. I headed back in to the front room to see if daddy was better. He wasn't there. I went to dad's bedroom, and listened at the half opened door. He was moaning as if he were in a lot of pain. I ran for the kitchen, found mother at the sink, and shook her skirt to get her attention. "What is it Helen, can't you see I'm busy?"

"Mama," I whispered, "Daddy is hurting real bad. He's in the bedroom."

"Okay Helen, you watch Bobby for me, and I will give him some medication to make him feel better. Thanks for letting me know." She wiped her hands on her apron, and headed for the cupboard where

Country Splendor

the medicine was kept. Finding what she wanted, she filled a glass with water and headed for the front room, crossing to their bedroom. I watched her as she opened the door, stepped quickly inside, and shut the door behind her.

She stayed in their bedroom a long time. The ladies finished up what they were doing, and told me to let mother know that they were leaving. Most of the work was done outside, so the men who needed to get to their own chores, rounded up their families and left. Eileen and I played with Bobby to keep him occupied, wondering what was wrong that mama was taking such a long time. We stayed where we could watch their bedroom door. It finally opened, with mother walking out, wiping her eyes with her apron. We wanted to know what was wrong, but mother wouldn't tell us anything that she thought we were too young to understand, so we remained silent. We followed her into the kitchen where she crossed to the stove, and poured herself a fresh cup of coffee, then sat down heavily on a kitchen chair. She placed her cup on the table beside her, and dropped her head into her cupped hands.

Eileen sat down on one side of mother and I sat on the other. "Mama, is dad alright?" Eileen asked, the worry evident in her voice.

She raised her head and wiped her eyes. She took a long drink of her coffee and then said, "He's hurting really badly. It took a long time for the painkiller to take effect. I think it bother's him that he can't help with the work. It goes against his grain to have to depend on other's to do his work for him. He's always been so independent. I'm really worried about him. He won't tell me anything about the operation itself, just says it was unpleasant and something he would never go through again. I can't help thinking that there is something more that he won't talk about," Mother finished on a worried note.

"Mama, I think I know what it is," I said. She turned to me, giving me a 'what are you talking about' look. "Well, when I was coming downstairs, I heard him talking to Andrew and Emil. He was telling them about the operation, so I sat down on the steps and listened too. Am I going to get into trouble again?" I asked.

"I will forgive you this time. Just tell me what you heard," she implored. I related all I had heard, as best I could, letting her know how bad the operation had gone, and why dad would never have another one. "He said he thought he was going to die from the pain, it was so bad. He thinks the doctors don't really know what they are doing," I ended my recitation with a shake of my head.

"That explains a lot," Mother said. "Thank you for telling me, Helen. Let's just keep this to ourselves for now, okay? Dad will talk about it when he is ready to share it with us. Until then, we will not tell anyone else, understand?"

I had no recourse but to promise, but it was not going to be easy to keep that promise.

CHAPTER ELEVEN

    With the corn harvesting behind them, Ron and Roy decided that they needed a day off. They had played in the creek on our place but it had been a long time since they had been anywhere where they could have a good long swim. Mentioning that to Herbert Zobel, as they worked on the corn harvesting together, he told them about a large lake located a few miles past Cameron. Cameron was only about eight miles away, so they figured that if they took off right after milking, rode their bikes to the lake, they could have a few hours of fun and be back in time for the evening milking. The more they thought about it, the better it sounded to them.
    At the supper table that night, they explained all this to mother and asked her if they could take some time off from work the next day. Dad had not come to the table to eat, so she took it upon herself to tell them that she thought they had earned it. Ron mentioned going to this lake they had heard about, just on the other side of Cameron. He assured mother that they would be back in time for evening chores. She gave her consent.
    When the boys came in from their morning chores, the next day, they washed up and grabbed their swimsuits. Mother handed them a packed bag of sandwiches and cookies to take along. They hopped on their bikes and took off, waving as they proceeded down the road.
    As Eileen and I waved back, we complained that we were not able to go along. "You can't swim anyway, Helen. And I don't have a bike,

Country Splendor

so how could we go? Maybe mom will let us play in the creek this afternoon. Should we ask her?"

"Yes, yes, yes," I agreed, already imagining the cool water up to my knees and the fun I would have looking for crawdad's among the rocks.

When we asked mother, she agreed that we could go to the creek for a while after dinner, as long as Eileen watched after me. Eileen promised she would and even crossed her heart. I thought, 'Wow, she really wants to go to make that kind of promise.'

By noon the heat was at its peak. We had little appetite, so mother settled for sandwiches and salad for dinner. It took a few minutes to wash, dry and put the few things away we ate with. "Can we go now, Eileen? Can we?" I could hardly contain my excitement, as we finished wiping off the table.

"Is there anything else you want us to do before we go, mom?" Eileen asked the question and I held my breath until mother answered.

"Go on and have fun."

We were out of the door and heading across the pasture before the screen door slammed shut behind us. We were finally on our way to the special spot in the creek we loved to play in. We had to cross the cornfield that was full of stubs and stray leaves, first. We were barefoot, so we walked between the rows of corn stubbles as far as we could, stepping carefully across the stubble as we headed for the place we wanted to play. The closer we got to the creek, the more excited and impatient I became. I was talking as fast as I could, telling Eileen all about what I wanted to do when we got there. She ignored me, as she did when she got tired of answering my endless questions, or responding to my unending wishes.

When we reached the grassy area leading to the creek, I began running down the slope; then suddenly, I stopped short and started screaming. Slithering through the grass in front of me was a long, green snake. The boys had always chased me with these things, telling me that they would bite me, and I believed them. Eileen came running up to me, to find out what I was making such a fuss about. I pointed in the direction of the retreating snake, and when she saw it, she began to laugh. "What are you making such a fuss about? That's just a garter snake. They won't hurt you!"

"But the boys said…" I started to explain.

"I know what the boys said, they tried to scare me too, but dad told me to ignore them. These snakes won't hurt anyone. Want me to catch it and show you?" she asked, as she took a step towards it.

"No, don't. I believe you. Just let it go away. It won't go into the water, will it?" I asked, thinking, I don't want to be in the same creek with a snake.

Eileen finally convinced me that there was nothing to worry about, and the sun was so hot, that I followed her into the cool, running water. The water was so clear that we could see the creek bed, the rocks, and everything that was among the rocks. We got so caught up in looking for fish, crawdad's and frogs that the time just flew. I managed to fall down, completely soaking my clothes. It felt so good that I sat there splashing it on my sister, laughing as she ducked and splashed me back. We were both dripping from head to foot when we heard the clanging of the triangle, calling us home.

Eileen looked up at the sky, studying where the sun was in relationship to the tall trees in the distance. "I wonder if something is wrong? It doesn't seem to be late enough to start supper yet. It sounds serious, we had better get back as fast as we can," she stated, as she stepped out of the water and tried to wring some of the water out of her skirt. "Come on Helen, we better hurry!"

"I'm coming, I'm coming!" I called back, as I stumbled out of the creek, with water running from my clothes like a fountain. It was hard to hurry with the wet skirts clinging and tangling around my legs. In desperation, I reached down and pulled my skirts up around my waist, and holding them thusly, I was able to run freely. Up the bank and across the corn stubbles I ran, but there was no catching my longer legged sister. The dirt clung like heavy mud to my wet feet, causing me to stumble forward, falling across the stubbles of corn stalks. I felt them pierce my skin as I landed heavily on them, my arms still wrapped up with my skirt. "Owe! Help Eileen," I cried loudly.

Country Splendor

She didn't respond, and as I tried pushing myself up and off the offending stalks, I realized that they had punctured my thighs, and blood was running down my legs. I cried harder, but to no avail. It was up to me to get myself home, and to someone who could help me. I dropped my skirts and used my arms for balance, as I hurried home as fast as I could. I winced with each step, as the motion of the clinging skirts, caused more pain.

Once I was back by the buildings, I crossed the back yard to the house, and again called out for attention. Mother came out onto the porch. When she saw me, bedraggled and muddy and crying profusely, she inquired, "What's the matter with you?"

"I fell and hurt myself and Eileen wouldn't help me," I said in an accusatory voice, between sobs. By this time I was close enough for mother to see the blood on my legs from the knees down. She came and bent down, pulling my skirts up so she could get a better look.

"My goodness! How did you manage to gash your thighs up so badly? Your skirt isn't torn."

"I was holding my skirt up so I could run faster, but then I stubbed my toe and fell on the corn stalks," I managed to explain between sobs.

"Okay, hold the crying down a bit, you will scare your baby brother and worry your father. We will take you into the kitchen and get you fixed up in no time," she said, as she grabbed me by my arm and lead me quickly to the porch, up the steps and into the kitchen.

"What took you so long, lazy bones?" my sister asked, as she came in from the front room and spied me standing by the washbasin.

"Now Eileen," mother said, as she came back from the cabinet where her medical supplies were kept, "If you would stop long enough to take a good look, you would know that Helen hurt herself. Bring the teakettle from the stove and pour some warm water into the basin. I'll need to wash her up good before I can properly take care of her cuts." By this time she had pulled my wet clothing off, leaving me standing with just my bloomers on.

When Eileen got a good look at my legs, she said, "Wow, you really did hurt yourself, didn't you?"

"Yes, and you wouldn't even stop and help me," I accused her.

"I didn't hear you, I was too far ahead. I thought you were just taking your time and I wanted to get home to see what mama wanted," she explained, justifying her actions.

"Okay, you two, it happened, now get over it. How is dad doing Eileen?" she asked, with a worry evident in her voice.

"He seems to be resting now, the pain killers have taken effect. Mama, are you sure he is going to be all right? He looks so pale and seems to be in so much pain all the time."

"And it doesn't help when he tries to do too much for himself. He is so independent that he doesn't want to ask for help. He claims I have enough to do without catering to his needs," she said, with a 'what am I going to do with him?' air.

"What happened to cause this last problem, mama?" Eileen asked.

"Well, I was busy preparing him and Bobby's lunch, and dad was sitting in his chair. Bobby went to him, wanting to sit in his lap, and dad bent over and tried picking him up. That's all it took. I thought he was going to pass out from the pain!"

"Ouch! Ouch! Ouch!" I squealed, as mother began applying Iodine to the open wounds

"I'll use this on the lesser scratches, but I'll use bag balm on the deepest punctures. That won't hurt as much. Now stop wiggling so I can get this done!" She ordered, with a pat to my rear. Although it was hard to keep still, I gritted my teeth and didn't move until she had finished attending to all my wounds. "Now, run up and put on a dry dress. Your panties are dry already. Now, git." She gave me a little push in the direction of the stairway. I walked a little stiffly, but made it up the stairs and into my sister and my bedroom. Hanging over the back of a chair was a dress I had worn the day before. I picked it up and looked it over. It had only a little stain on the bodice where I had dribbled a bit of my supper on it. It would do. Once I was dressed again, I made my way back down the stairs, walking softly to dad and mother's bedroom door. It was ajar, allowing me a peek inside.

Country Splendor

Dad lay on his back, spread out on the bed, and his eyes were shut. I started to turn away, when he said in a quiet and gentle voice, "What was all the commotion about, little one? Come here and tell me all about what happened." He patted the side of the bed, where there was room for me to perch, without making him uncomfortable.

I crawled up beside him and began relating the whole story to him. He kept me talking by asking me pointed questions about the creek, what I saw, what I did, and how badly were my hurts? I was happy to just sit beside him and tell him everything. My daddy was so special to me! He looked so big and capable of doing anything. I always thought of him as the person who would always protect me. From my earliest memory of him, holding me carefully in his big arms, to this day, even though I sensed that he was a little more vulnerable right now because of what the doctors did to him, he was still the one that I could always depend upon. He called me 'his angel' and I always felt special to him. I heard women remark about how handsome he was. I guessed that was a good thing, because of the wistfulness in their voices as they spoke of him. I just knew that when he looked at me with those clear blue eyes, so full of love, and the sound of his deep voice often filling with laughter, that he was the most wonderful person in my life.

Of course, Mother was special too. But she was always so busy, with so much to do all the time that she very seldom had time to spend with me. She would push me off on my brother's occasionally, or more often, on my sister, to keep me occupied. As I grew a bit bigger, I was given simple chores to do that would help keep me busy. I loved feeding the chickens, looking for eggs in their straw nests in the hen house, and carrying the eggs in a basket, provided for that purpose. A couple of times I would get so preoccupied by the baby chicks pecking around my feet, that I would reach down to touch them, tipping the basket and spilling an egg or two. When they hit the ground they would splatter in every direction. I would worry about another spanking from mother, for being careless. She surprised me those times, by just warning me to be more careful next time, and of course, I promised that I would.

Mother was the disciplinarian of us girls and the boys when they were small. As the boys grew big enough for certain responsibilities, dad took over disciplining them, but primarily left the girls for mother to handle. Therefore, I never looked at daddy as someone who might spank me. But I respected him and tried to never let him down.

The few times I remember him getting after Eileen; it frightened me. I couldn't understand why he would get so mad at her. Mother never seemed to have any trouble with her. It was years before I understood how much like my father, Eileen was. She could be strong willed and stubborn. Strengths, if used in the right way, but obstacles if abused.

I saw those same traits in Roy, and although dad realized how much like himself Roy was, he still insisted on strict obedience from him. When Roy became hardheaded and determined to have his own way, or have his say, dad would reprimand him. If Ron happened to be with Roy at the time, he would get the same punishment. I must admit that the punishment could be quite harsh at times, depending on how mad dad was. Mother called it dad's 'German temper.' Dad's mother and father were both Germans. I was to learn from my German grandmother, that my father's father was also a very harsh man at times, and that daddy was subjected to many severe beatings during his growing up years. Once a young man and at his full strength, dad stood up to his father and was never beaten again.

The time for milking arrived, but my brothers did not. Mother told me and Eileen to run out and round up the cows and get them in the barn. She had potatoes with their peelings on, in a pot on the stove. She needed to finish boiling the potatoes and pouring the water into a pitcher to cool for dad.

We found the cows in the far meadow and headed the lead cow towards the barn. Once she was on her way, with the bell that was hung on a rawhide strap around her neck, ringing, the others would follow. Once at the barn it was an easy job. One of us would open the door to their milking area, and they would walk in, stopping at the stanchion that they considered theirs. All we needed to do was walk up beside each one and fasten the stanchion closed. It was tight

Country Splendor

enough that they could not pull their heads out, but loose enough to allow them room to move a bit. They could lie down or stand up; they could eat from the food put before them or drink from the cup at one side of the stanchion.

Once we had them all secured and food put in front of them, we headed to the house to let mother know we were done. We entered the kitchen to find mother finished with dad's drink and the potatoes cooling in a bowl. She turned from her project asking, "Have you seen anything of the boys yet?" We both shook our heads no. She shook her head and said, "Where are they? They promised to be back by now."

We both understood her concern. Eileen broke the heavy silence with, "Shall we call the Zobel's to see if they know anything?"

"No, not yet. They may have misjudged the time and are on their way home now. If they aren't home soon, we will start the milking and they can finish when they get here."

"What about Bobby?" I asked.

"What about Bobby?" Mother answered. "You will take care of him while Eileen and I go out to work in the barn."

"Can't we take him out there with us and I can help too?"

"Helen, you're too little to be of any help to us, and you would have your hands full trying to keep him out of trouble. Better that you stay in here, so if dad needs anything you can help him too. Meanwhile, when the boys show up, you send them right out to the barn, understand?" Mother ended with a direct demand.

I nodded to let her know that I did understand. "Come on Bobby, we'll play in the front room."

Mother and Eileen ended up doing the milking all by themselves. It took much longer than it would have if the boys were doing it. The boys hands and forearms were so strong from milking the cows by hand, as well as all the other farm work they did, that it took them less than half the time that it took mother and Eileen. Actually Eileen was very slow, as she had done so little milking, that it was almost totally up to mother. She was good at emptying the pails into the milk cans, and mother had her doing that more than the actual milking. When they finally entered the house, it was all they could do to make it to a chair and sit themselves down.

"I'm so tired," Mother said with a sigh, "how about we just fry up some of these boiled potatoes and have some of the cold roast with it for supper? Maybe I will mix it all together, add some onion, and make a tasty hash. How does that sound?"

"Sounds good to me," Eileen stated.

"Can I help mama?" I asked, always willing to help out any way I could.

"Sure, you can peal the potatoes for me. Eileen, would you change Bobby and get him ready for bed? Give him a warm bottle tonight, he had some bread and peanut butter earlier."

Eileen left the kitchen to do mom's bidding, while I peeled the potatoes and mother put a frying pan on the stove. She placed a pat of home made butter in it, then took an onion from the basket in the pantry, peeled it and sliced it into the melted butter. While the onions sautéed, she chopped up some roast meat and added that. Then the peeled potatoes were cut into cubes and placed in the pan, adding salt and pepper, and then, mixing it all well, until it heated through. I watched every move she made and committed it to memory. I was to know how to prepare food and cook it in many ways, before I was big enough to do the work myself.

The evening meal was eaten, and the dishes put to soak in a pan of heated, soapy water. "We will leave this job for later," Mother said, as she joined dad in the front room, sitting next to him on their two favorite chairs. Dad had an overstuffed one and mother's was a padded rocker with a small table by hers, lit by a lovely kerosene lamp. The soft light enhanced mother's delicate features, giving her a younger look than her forty years.

Eileen and I sat down on the hard kitchen chairs, placed on the far side of the table. We listened to mother's worried tone as she asked, "Hubie, what do you think? The boys should have been home long ago. Should we contact one of the neighbors to check on them for us?"

"What could they do? You said the boys were headed for Lake Chetek, right? They could have taken any number of roads there or back. Who knows where they may be or what might have happened to them? It would be futile to look for them in the dark. Let's give them until tomorrow morning. If they haven't showed up by then, let's have Emil run in to town and alert the Sheriff for us. They can do more in a much shorter time than we can," Dad wisely stated.

Hearing dad's decision, Eileen and I knew that nothing more was going to be done that night. Both of us were so tired that our heads were nodding and my eyes wanted to close. We got up, said our goodnights to mom and dad, and headed up the stairs to our bed. It was all I could do to pull my dress off over my head, and drop it to the floor, before climbing into bed. My eyes shut before my head hit the pillow, and I wasn't aware of even covering myself up with the sheet.

Our big, red rooster with the long, black, tail feathers woke me with his morning serenade. He was sitting atop the hen house and crowing at the sun, which was just beginning to show itself above the trees. Without ever looking at him, I knew just what he was doing. He would stretch up to his full height, stretch his neck even further, crowing at that sun with all his lung power, while flapping his wide spread wings as if to hurry the sun in its rising.

Usually, I was up before he was, and looking across the bed, I realized that I was alone. Where was Eileen? I must have overslept, I decided. It sounded very quiet downstairs. The room was beginning to fill up with early morning light, sending shadows across the walls. The window was open to capture any breeze that might come our way, and a slight one moved the light, white curtain, ever so gently.

Feeling a strong urge to make a trip to the outhouse, I slipped from the bed; grabbed my dress from the floor, and began pulling it over my head as I headed for the stairs. Because I had the dress over my face, I couldn't see where the top step was. I stepped too far, missing it and tumbling head over heals, down the rest of the stairs. I lay at the bottom wondering if I had broken anything. No one came to see what the commotion was, so I guessed that I must be alone in the house. I gingerly picked myself up from the floor, testing my legs, ankles, and feet. I seemed to be all right. I was standing without anything hurting worse than the contusions I'd sustained, from hitting the steps in different places on my body. I straightened my dress and moved over to the baby crib, which was against the back wall of the front room, and not far from mother and dad's bedroom. Bobby was curled up, with a thumb in his mouth, breathing softly and regularly.

"Guess he will sleep for a while yet," I said to myself. I approached the opened bedroom door, and stood just before it, listening a moment. Hearing nothing, I looked in the door. There was no one in the bed, or behind the door, or in the closet. I continued on to the kitchen. The teakettle was placed at the back of the warm stove, hissing ever so slightly. No one was in the kitchen, no one in the pantry. I moved towards the porch and heard the old wooden swing slowly creaking, as it moved gently, back and forth. I stepped through the door and past it, so I could look behind it, towards the swing.

There was my daddy, looking out across the backfields, with a far away look on his face. One got the feeling that he really wasn't there at all, but somewhere out there in the fields, looking the crops over. Wondering how soon they would be ready for harvest, and pondering on just how that was going to be accomplished.

He must have felt my eyes on him, because he turned suddenly, as if just coming back to where his body was. "Hi angel," he said softly, as he moved himself to one side; patting the place he had just vacated as if to say, "here, come, sit."

"Just a minute daddy, I have to go wee-wee," I called, as I hurried down the path as fast as I could go, without making my body hurt anymore than I could help. I finished the job and hurried back to him, stepping up onto the porch with some effort. I pulled myself up beside him, hurting from my wounds from my fall the day before, and also from the bruises I sustained from my fall down the stairs, a short while ago. I was beginning to think that I had some kind of a problem, falling so much. 'Was that normal?' I questioned myself. Then I asked daddy, "Daddy, is it normal to fall so much?"

"What do you mean, fall so much? How many times have you fallen?" he asked, as he looked directly at me.

Country Splendor

"Well, I fell in the corn field yesterday, and this morning I fell down the stairs."

"You what? You fell down the stairs? How did that happen?" He asked one question upon the tail of the other.

"I was putting on my dress and wasn't watching where I was going, so I fell down the stairs."

"Are you okay? Do you hurt anywhere in particular?" he asked, sounding totally interested in my welfare.

I shook my head, and then, thinking about it, I explained, "I hurt in lots of places. Where the corn stub's dug into me yesterday and where the stairs hit me this morning."

"I think it is more like, where you hit the stairs, little one. But I mean can you walk all right? Do you hurt real badly in any special place?" he asked, as he tenderly felt around my ribs.

I let him examine me, but felt no sharp pains from his gentle probing. "No, daddy, I think I'm okay. Just sore, you know."

"Vell, that makes two of us then," he stated flatly. "But would you please watch your step on those stairs? I remember you falling down that steep flight of stairs at the place we lived when you were born. Do you remember that?" he asked.

"Yes, I do remember. I was upstairs with Eileen and the big boys. Bobby was a tiny baby then, right? I think we had company too, because I remember other kids up there as well. As I looked down that sharp flight of stairs, I remember thinking that I wanted to be down stairs with you, and I suddenly felt myself falling. I remember screaming, but then I don't remember much after that. I think someone picked me up, but I don't remember whom. I fell head first down that stairs, didn't I?"

"Yes, you did. I was the first to reach you, as I had jumped, hoping to catch you before you hit the floor. I saw you looking at me, from the hole above the stairs, and I had a feeling that something bad was going to happen, and just then it did. It all happened so fast, and I was so sure that you would break your neck, I can't remember being so scared, not even when I fell from that haymow myself. Guess that happened so fast that I hardly knew what happened until I tried to pick myself up. See, you are not the only one that falls sometimes." He stated, with a gentle hug, and a kiss on the top of my head.

"Daddy, where is mama and Eileen?" I asked.

"They went to Zobels' to see if Emil would drive into Barron and let the Sheriff know about our missing boys. They should be back any minute now. Guess they will have to do the milking by them selves again this morning. I feel so helpless." A sob in his throat choked back his next words, but I knew what he meant. I put my hand over his, hoping to comfort him a little.

Just then, we heard the front door open, and mother's footsteps heading into the kitchen. Then another set of footsteps, much lighter, started across the floor, following the front door slamming. "We are out here, Verna," Dad called.

"There you are," she said, as she rounded the door and continued in our direction. Following close behind her was my sister, with eyes that were sad, but excited at the same time. The same look she would get when she knew the boys were in trouble with dad. I wondered about that. How could one feel bad about something and feel excited about it at the same time? Older people were certainly hard to figure out, sometimes.

"Hubie, you won't believe what is happening. Emil had a phone put in, because his wife is ill, and he wants to be able to get help as soon as it's needed. He put a call into the Sheriff and told him about the boys. They said they would start looking for them right away. Then Emil called some of the neighbors and asked if they could help with the chores while you are laid up. They said that they would help for as long as you need it. Now Hubie, understand that your pride is not the most important thing right now," she stated, as she recognized the embarrassed look that crossed dad's face.

"You know I hate to be beholden to anyone," Dad said.

"Yes, pride can be a powerful motivator, but too much pride can be a hindrance, sometimes. We know that you have never been one to shirk a job that needed doing, and you are the first one to offer help when you see the need. Well, sometimes it is important to let others help you," Mother said softly, as she patted his hand.

Country Splendor

"Now, Emil said that he and Herbert would be over as soon as they finish their own milking. He said that it wouldn't hurt the cows to be milked a little later this once. Then tonight, if the boys aren't home yet, the Foss boys will come over to do the milking. Instead of being upset, we should be thankful for such wonderful neighbors and friends," Mother continued, with that no-nonsense way she had. "If this is the Lord's way of blessing us, we should be grateful, not unhappy." She patted dads' hands once more, to reassure him that this was something he should consider carefully.

Dad actually nodded his head and said, resignedly, "Yes, you are right mama. It just goes against my grain to have to accept help from other's, who already have so much to do themselves. But I am grateful that all this work isn't going to be all on your shoulders, hon." He reached up and pressed his hand against her soft cheek.

She smiled down at him and said, "It's so pleasant out here this morning, why don't you stay here where this breeze will blow your cares away. Don't you worry about anything. The boys are capable of taking care of themselves. I'm sure it isn't serious trouble they are in. Now I will go in and make us a nice breakfast. Good food always makes one feel better. Okay?" She did not wait for, or expect an answer, as she turned and headed back into the house.

Eileen squeezed in next to me, as daddy moved over as far as he could. "What do you suppose those boys are up to?" Eileen asked, more as a question to herself that one she expected an answer to. Then she turned to me, asking, "Remember how Roy was talking about running away sometime? You don't suppose that he talked Ron into going too, do you?"

"When did this happen?" Dad asked in a very interested tone.

"I think I have heard him say that more than once, haven't you, Helen?" she asked, drawing me into the discussion.

"Well, actually, I have heard Roy talk about that. Several times in fact," I answered, with much importance.

"When, and what did you hear? Exactly," he asked, in a no-nonsense voice that sounded like mothers, when she was after the facts.

He directed that question at me and I was afraid not to answer him honestly. "I was in the barn one day, actually in the haymow. I heard the boys talking and Roy was trying to convince Ron to run away. I guess he has said that more than once, huh Eileen?" I asked, trying to draw her back into this conversation.

"Did he say why he wanted to run away?" dad asked. I looked to see whom he was directing his question to. I didn't want to tell the real reason. I thought it would make daddy unhappy if he knew it was his own fault.

I looked at Eileen, and she kept her eyes on her knees as she moved her legs back and forth, trying to avoid dad's eyes. I could tell that she was thinking the same thing I was, although she didn't want to tell the real reason, because she didn't want to make dad mad, not sad. "Vell?" Dad asked, more forcefully this time, as he looked directly at me.

"Will you get mad if I tell you what he said?" I asked daddy, not wanting to be the one to answer.

"No, I just need to understand what is going on here," he answered, a bit more gently.

"He said that they had too much work to do all the time. He wished he could live in town where there wouldn't be so many chores to do all day long," I hedged.

"Is that all? Or is there something else you haven't told me? Come on now, I want you to tell me everything."

I took a deep breath and tried to get it all out, fast, before I lost my nerve. "He said he wasn't going to take any more of your beatings. He said you are mean and unreas…eh, unreason …"

"Unreasonable?" he finished for me.

"Yes, that's it. What does that mean?"

"Vell, don't vorry about what that means. He probably has reason to feel that way. I have been rather hard on them, I guess." He said it with real regret in his voice. He really did not seem surprised at what he heard. He dropped his head back against the backboard of the swing, shut his eyes and remained very quiet.

"Eileen, Helen," Mother called. "Come in here and help me with Bobby, and with breakfast now."

Country Splendor

"Coming," we called back, as we both got up at the same time, leaving the swing, swinging rather erratically, with the weight only on one side. "Whoops, daddy, are you all right?" I asked.

He stopped the motion of the swing and slid into the middle again. "Yes, it's all right. Go help your mother now."

Eileen and I left together, looking at each other, conveying by the looks in our eyes that we were grateful to have a reason to leave daddy alone.

CHAPTER TWELVE

That day turned into another long, hot day, but towards evening, some storm clouds began appearing on the horizon. Neighbors had been over to help with the milking and other outside chores. Others stopped by to check on how dad was doing, and left behind some prepared food as an offering of their support. I was delighted to have some children to talk to. The main topic was of the missing boys, of course.

Everyone was gone by late afternoon, and we had just settled around the kitchen table for our evening meal, when someone knocked on the door. "Eileen, would you get the door?" Mom asked, as she was putting the last of the filled bowls of food on the table.

Eileen hurried to the door, opened it and stepped aside to usher Emil Zobel into our home. He took his warn, felt hat off as he entered, almost stooping to get through the door. "Hello there, Hubert, Mrs.," he said as he neared the table, walking to dad's side. "Hubert, the sheriff called me on our telephone. He said the police from Madison called to let him know that he found your two boys. He's sending them home now, they should be here in a few hours."

"What were they doing down there? And how did the police come across them?" Dad asked, looking over at mother to include her in his puzzled inquiry. Mother returned his look with raised eyebrows and a shrug of her shoulders.

Country Splendor

"Well, Hubert, I think the boys were confused as to where they were, or where they were going, or something. I understand that they stopped by a policeman and asked him directions to some place. He thought they looked awfully young to be traveling by themselves, and asked them where they were from. He had someone from his station call the sheriff here in Barron, found out they were run-a-ways and told the Sheriff that he would be bringing them home."

Dad uttered an expletive under his breath. Mother reached a hand across to him, laying it on his arm, "Now Hubie, we must be grateful that they have been found and that they are alright and will be home soon. Isn't that an answer to prayer?"

I looked carefully at my daddy's face and it seemed like some dark clouds had entered it. His jaw was working as if he was having difficulty holding back what he wanted to say. He sighed heavily as he came to terms with his inner anger. He looked up at his friend and neighbor and held out his hand to shake Emil's. "Thanks, Emil. I appreciate your taking the time to come tell us. That new telephone of yours comes in handy doesn't it? Oh, that reminds me, how is your Mrs. doing?" Dad asked, understanding how worried Emil was about his wife.

"She's a bit frail, is in bed more than not now. The doctor can't seem to help her much. I would appreciate your prayers, Mrs.," he said as he nodded his head at mother.

"Emil, if there is anything I can do for her, or to help out, please let me know," Mother replied.

"I'll be getting back now," he said, as he turned and went to the door, opened it and started out, "Well, looks like we might be in for a storm, Hubert. Just saw some mighty bright lightening our there!" He stopped just outside the door, and turned one more time to dad. "I'll check in the morning to see if you need any more help with the milking or the like, okay?" Then he shut the door and was gone.

"Vell I'll be damned!" dad said, "They were all the way to Madison! What do you think they were up to so far from home?"

"I can't imagine what was in their minds, guess we'll just have to wait until they are home to find out," Mother offered as a way of stating the obvious. "But, Hubie, let's not jump to conclusions or go off half cocked. We need to find out just what happened before we begin getting ourselves worked up over this. Let's eat, so I can clean up and get these children to bed. I'll save some supper at the back of the stove, just in case the boys are hungry. Lord knows when they ate last."

Dad reached out for a bowl of food, placing a helping on his plate and passing it on to Eileen, who was sitting on his left. As the passing of the food and the filling of our plates continued in silence, I kept sneaking glances at mother and daddy, then at Eileen. She seemed to be avoiding looking at anything, except the plate she was filling, but I could sense an excitement in her. The muscles at the side of her mouth seemed to want to pull it into a smile. I could not help but wonder what was going to take place once the boys were home. I only knew for sure that I was glad that it was not me, having to face my father's anger.

We all ate in silence, until a loud thunder clap, rolled across the sky, and continued as if it was never going to stop. Directly on the first ones tail, another one crashed heavily over head, splitting the heavens apart. Then a third. Suddenly, the rain could be heard, hitting the roof and the ground outside the window, as if a dam in heaven just burst.

"Listen to that dad, hope they will not have any trouble driving in that down pour," Mother said, in a worried tone.

" If they stick to the main roads they should be all right. It's black top all the way to Barron. Then if they take the Poor Farm road out of Barron, they'll only have the one bridge to cross just outside of town, and if the road doesn't get too muddy before they get here, they should make it," Dad stated, as he reached for a second slice of mother's freshly baked bread.

"Hubie, you know how muddy these roads get in this kind of rain. They could get stuck. I don't think we should expect the boys home tonight, " Mother warned.

"Vell, it is not going to do any good vorrying about it now," Dad said, giving his anxiety away by how much heavier his accent became. "Ve'll just have to vait and see vat happens." With that, he laid the last

Country Splendor

bite of bread he had held in his left hand, on the edge of his plate, pushed away from the table and walked heavily into the front room, to his chair.

"Girls, finish eating and help me get these dishes done. I want to have everything in order before the boys get here. I will get Bobby settled in bed and then be back to help you finish up." She left the table, pulled Bobby from his wooden high chair and carried him through the door into the front room.

"I want to wash the dishes this time," I said, as I began picking up dishes and moving them to the wash pan. Just then, another thunderbolt hit, slightly shaking the house. It was so loud that it startled me, and I dropped one of the plates I was carrying. The sound of it's hitting the floor was drowned out by the loud noise just above our heads, but the pieces of china flying all over the floor, was easily noticed. I placed the other plate I was carrying into the wash water. Then, turning towards the door, I went for the broom and dustpan to sweep up the broken plate.

Of course, Eileen saw what had happened and used that as her excuse not to let me wash the dishes.

Rather than tempt fate, and the possibility of getting into trouble over the broken plate, I resignedly reached for the dishtowel. Another loud thunder role crashed, directly overhead, making me duck as if I were going to be hit.

"What you ducking for? Such a scaredy cat!" Eileen said, as she began the washing and rinsing of the plates, placing them in the drainer. For once, I had no smart retort ready. It really did scare me. Lightening kept flashing around the house, lighting up the windows, with hard cracks of thunder following them. The rain fell even harder, until it seemed to be coming down in sheets. It made me so nervous that I dropped a cup, but thankfully, it only bounced.

"Helen, if you drop any more I will tell mother, and she will spank you for sure!"

"I'm not doing it on purpose! That lightening and thunder scares me!" I cried.

"You're such a baby! You just want to get out of helping do the dishes," she accused.

"Do not! It does scare me! You don't know how I feel!" I yelled at her, trying to talk over the loud outside noise.

"I don't know who is louder, the rain storm or you girls! What's all this yelling about?" Mother asked, as she came through the kitchen door and around the table to where we were working. "How do you expect Bobby to sleep if you are going to keep up this shouting?"

"Helen's afraid of the storm and keeps dropping dishes. She broke a plate," Eileen told mother.

Mother walked over to me and pulled the towel from my hands. "Helen, go on into the front room with dad and I will finish up here." She gave me a push in the direction of the front room, and I gratefully fled to a seemingly, safer place.

As I approached dad, I saw that he was holding a book in one hand, and a cup of coffee in the other, but he was not reading, nor drinking from his cup. He seemed to be staring at the window, watching the light show just outside. I decided not to bother him.

Instead, I turned and made my way to Bobby's crib, to check on him. I reached in and pulled his blanket up over his sweetly, curled up body. His thumb was in his mouth again, but he did not seem to be bothered by the storm, thundering down around us. I left the front room, feeling my way up the stairs to our bedroom. The lightening flashes brightened up the room, making it easier to see where I was going, and helping me find what I was after. I pulled a blanket off the bed, along with my pillow, and pulled it behind me, as I made my way back down the stairs. I picked out a spot on the floor, close to Bobby's crib. It was as far away from the windows that I could get, and I felt safer there. I spread my blanket out, laying my pillow at one end. Curling up on the blanket, with my head on my pillow, I pulled the edges of the blanket around me, covering my head to shut out some of the noise. I lay there for some time, listening to the storm, and finally, drifted blissfully off to sleep.

'Noise!' "Voices! Loud voices!" 'What? Where?' I sat up, rubbed my eyes and pulled something off my head. 'The storm.' I remembered

Country Splendor

the storm, but it was not that noise I heard. The rain was still beating on the roof and all around, but the noise was very loud voices. 'Coming from where? Where was I?' Oh, yes, now I remembered. I was on the front room floor in my makeshift bed. The loud voices were coming from the kitchen. That was dad speaking, now Roy's raised voice, loud and accusing. Ron's joined Roy's making it impossible to understand what was being said. Then mother was talking, and the other voices became softer. 'They are home, the boys have made it home!' I thought to myself, happy that they were home and safe. I wondered at what was being said, but I was afraid to venture out of my cozy nest, and besides, I was far too sleepy. I cuddled back down on my feather pillow, pulled the blanket up over my ears, and drifted back into the comfort of unconscious bliss.

I was creeping across the yard, trying to be small and quiet. I heard a loud commotion coming from the area of the haymow. Yelling, cries of anguish and loud swearing. Different voices intermingled, sounding harsh, full of anger and full of pain. I was afraid to get too close, but I needed to know what was happening. Closer and closer to that mélange of voices, that sound of desperation, that sound of rage, all intermingled. Now I could differentiate from the sounds, dad's voice, loud and harsh, Roy's' voice filled with pain and outrage, Ron's voice pleading and desperate. I could not go any further. It hurt me to listen, to what? I could only imagine what was happening, what was causing this furor. NO! NO! I wanted to yell, to put a stop to this; I wanted it to go away.

I woke up with a start. 'Where am I?' I looked around me, 'oh yes; I am on the floor of the front room. No noise now. No voices. It was only a dream. A dream.' I rubbed the sleep from my eyes and rose slowly to my feet. The house was very quiet. The rain had stopped; the sun was shining through the uncovered window, casting long rays of warm, golden, sunshine across the linoleum floor. I could see dust particles dancing in the rays. A fly bussed just out of reach, over my head, sounding loud in the stillness.

I left my blanket, and stood looking into Bobby's crib. He was still sleeping, on his tummy now, with his little behind in the air, and that comforting thumb still in his mouth. His golden hair was damp, and curled tightly against his head. I imagined that angels must look like this. So sweet, so innocent, so peaceful.

I tiptoed to the partially opened door of my parents' bedroom. Dad was lying on the bed, on his back. His mouth was slightly opened, and his breathing was deep and peaceful. I thought again of how much I loved this father of mine. Of how gentle he was when he held me close to his chest, or when he reached out a hand to lay it on my head, gently tousling my hair. How could this be the same man of my dreams, that nightmare? Impossible!

I headed for the kitchen, still wondering at the stillness. No sounds of anyone else moving in the house. The coffee pot was pushed to the back of the warm stove, with a small wisp of steam emanating from the spout. The odor of fresh coffee smelled inviting, but a more pressing need had to be filled, before I could think of anything else. Out of the door I ran, and up the path to that faithful little building. It's door swung open on rusted hinges, and squeaked a little, as I pushed it open even further, to enter. I ignored the feel of damp wood against my legs, as I perched over my spot. The catalog hung from it's nail, dripping water from its pages.

Once that business was taken care of, I lit out for the barn. Coming towards me was my mother. "Good morning mama," I called as I ran to meet her.

She put out a hand to steady me, as I ran up to her, and threw my arms around her waist. She gave me a quick hug and pushed past me, as she said, "Go say hello to your brothers, they are doing the milking."

"Okay!" I answered, over my shoulder. I ran towards the barn hitting the open doorway in a full out run. I skidded across the floor to slow my pace. "Roy, Ron!" I shouted, as I pushed myself off the wall and continued down the walkway, looking for my older brothers.

"Here," "Here," I heard from two different areas between the cows. I continued my search until I spotted Ron squatting on his three-legged milking stool, beside Black Bess. I rushed to embrace him, nearly knocking over the pail he was balancing between his legs.

Country Splendor

"Whoa, Helen, take it easy," he warned, as he reached out to wrap his arms around me, and hugged me close. "How are you peanut?" he asked, using his pet name for me. "Did you miss me?"

"Yes, I missed you, and we were all worried about you. Where did you go? How come you did not come home?"

"Hey, whoa. You need to slow down and take a deep breath," he said. "We just went for a ride, looking for a lake to swim in. When we couldn't find it, we kept on going, and pretty soon we were so far from home that we just decided to keep on going. But I guess that wasn't a very smart thing to do. Dad was really mad at us."

I pulled myself out of his arms and looked at him real closely. He seemed to have sad eyes, they looked red rimmed and wet. It made me think of the dream I had, and I felt a hurt around my heart. "I am glad you are home. You won't run away again will you?" I asked.

"No, peanut. I won't run away again," Ron said, with a wistful sound to his voice.

"Promise?" I begged.

"I promise," he said. "Now git and let me finish my chores. I'm really hungry, and we can't eat until we have this done. I will see you at breakfast, okay?"

"Okay," I conceded, then scrambled out from between the cows and onto the walkway behind them.

"Hey, pumpkin," Roy called from the doorway. I turned towards his voice, and noticed that he was pouring the milk from his bucket into the tall, milk can, by the door.

"Hey!" I shouted, as I raced to him.

"Don't bump me! I'll spill this milk and I don't need any more grief!" He stated. I stood back and watched the foamy milk pour into the can, making almost a drumming sound as it hit the bottom and splashed up the insides of the can. When the last of the milk dripped from his bucket, he sat the bucket down on the walkway, and put the milk can cover back into place. Then turning to me, he scooped me up in his arms, and gave me a big bear hug.

"Ugh!" I said, as the air was forced from my lungs.

"You squeeze too hard!" I complained as I continued to struggle for release from his strong arms.

"Aren't you glad to see me too?" He asked, laughing as I kept struggling helplessly in his arms. "Didn't you miss me?"

"Yes, I missed you, and I am glad you are home, but you are squishing me!" I said, as I continued to struggle for freedom. He sat me down then and turned to pick up the bucket.

"How about you go to the house and wake up that lazy sister of yours, and help her get breakfast ready for us? We'll be in as soon as we get these chores done." His voice sounded much like dads, when he gave an order.

"Okay, I'll see you then. Don't take too long." I said. I turned and headed out of the door, almost tripping over Chaser, as he walked quickly along with his nose to the ground, in pursuit of some interesting smell. "That dang dog!" I exclaimed, as I managed to right myself. Then I continued across the yard, hopped up onto the porch, and stepped through the kitchen door.

Mother was at the cutting board, slicing long strips of bacon off of the thick slab that lay in front of her. Then turning slightly to her left, she reached out and placed each piece into a large black wrought iron pan, that sat over an open flame on the stove. As the bacon hit the hot pan, it complained with a hissing sound. Already the room was filling with a wonderful hickory smoked, bacon smell

Eileen sat at the table, peeling potatoes for frying. I could hear Bobby complaining from his crib. "Shall I go get Bobby?" I asked mother.

"Can you take him out without dropping him?" Mother asked.

"Sure I can. Do it all the time," I answered.

"Well, I should do it I guess, as he needs his diapers changed anyway. That's enough bacon for now. Eileen, do you suppose you could watch the bacon and turn it over before it burns?" Mother asked. She hurried from the kitchen not waiting for an answer.

"I will be so glad when you are big enough to do more around here," Eileen said. "I am tired of having to do everything myself."

Country Splendor

I watched her get up from the chair, putting her knife down by the bowl of potatoes she had been peeling, and cross over to the stove. "Well, I would do more if people would let me. Everybody thinks I am too small or too young to do much of anything. I can take care of the bacon," I said.

"How can you? You can't see above the stove well enough to take care of it," Eileen argued.

"But I could if I could stand on a chair," I argued back.

"Well pull one over here and lets see how good you can do it then," Eileen dared, with that know-it-all superior air of the older sister.

I grabbed the back of a chair and pulled it from the table, moving it across the floor to the stove. I hopped upon it, and showed Eileen that I was taller than her now, and could easily reach the bacon. "All right, smarty pants," she jeered, "here is the long handled fork to turn the bacon with, just don't drop it on the floor!"

"I won't," I promised. I took the fork and poked at the bacon importantly, like I knew just what I was doing.

Just then dad walked into the kitchen, saw me standing on the chair and leaning over that hot, wood-burning, cook stove, with a long handled fork in my hand. He walked around the table, moving as quickly as he could, to my side. "Just what do you think you are doing, Little One? Give me that fork and get down."

"But Daddy," I began to wail.

"Don't 'but daddy' me! That is too dangerous for someone as small as you are. There are other things you can do to help, but hanging over this hot stove is not something you are to do, until you are older and bigger. Do you understand?" He stated his demand in his 'no-nonsense,' and 'that is final' voice.

"Yes, dad," I replied. I slipped off the chair and started to pull it away from the stove.

"No, leave the chair here. I will use it to lean on while I watch the bacon. You could get that deep pan over there," he indicated by pointing his finger at it, "and bring it here to me. Get me some of mom's lard and I'll get the potatoes frying. Eileen, wash those peeled potatoes, and bring them to me, along with your knife." It seemed like no time at all until dad had the potatoes sliced, and frying away in that hot lard. He reached for the salt and peppershakers and seasoned the potatoes. The bacon was turned and sizzling away in the other pan. I was surprised to see how well dad could handle the cooking. I thought only women could do that, but I was to find out in the days ahead, that daddy knew a great deal about cooking and baking. He might not be able to do the heavy farm work yet, but he could help in the kitchen.

"Helen, grab mother's egg basket and see if you can find enough for breakfast. Eileen, get the table set" The screen door slammed on dad's last words. I was on my way to the hen house. My favorite chore was gathering the eggs, next to actually feeding the chickens. When I entered the chicken yard, I noticed feathers floating on the breezes, much more than usual. I wondered if the storm the night before, created some problems with the chickens some how. Then I went through the swinging door into the coop, and found a hen hanging dead from the roost, with feathers everywhere. I hurried back to the kitchen to let dad know that something had been in the hen house during the night.

He told Eileen to watch the food on the stove, and then followed me back to the coop. He shook his head as he looked around, and pointed out some very distinct footprints around the muddy yard. Then dad sniffed the air, "Aw, skunk!"

I sniffed the air and wrinkled my nose at the strong, acidic, lingering smell that clearly identified our middle of the night caller. "Did it get many chickens, daddy?" I asked.

"Well, he must have hurt this big white leghorn," he stated, as he pointed to a chicken hanging from an upper perch. "But she had enough fight in her to fly high enough that he couldn't reach her. She must have died after he left. You can be sure that he caught one before he was through though. In that storm last night, we couldn't hear anything, so no telling how long the skunk was in here. Go ahead and see if he left any eggs for us, and I will have Ron take care of this dead hen after breakfast."

I went among the nests checking for eggs. Some hens had returned to their nests, and I slipped my hand under each one, feeling for eggs. I found six eggs in all. Usually, there were from twelve to sixteen eggs

Country Splendor

a day. "Either that was one hungry skunk, or there was more than one visitor last night," I said as I looked around to show dad the amount of eggs I had found. He was nowhere in sight. I stepped out of the hen house, walked through their muddy yard and stepped out of the gate, shutting it firmly behind me.

While crossing the yard to the house, I noticed the boys carrying the milk-cans into the milk house. 'It won't be long before they will be in for breakfast,' I reasoned. I hurried in to inform dad. Mother was at the stove instead, with Dad sitting at the table sipping on a mug of steaming coffee. Eileen was nowhere to be seen. "Mom, the boys are on their way in."

"Okay, Helen. Dad told me what happened. How many eggs did you find?" Mother asked.

"I only found six. I wonder how many hens were lost last night?"

"Until the chickens settle back down and come out of the trees, we won't be able to take a count. Dad, do you think you should send the boys out with their twenty-twos to try to find the skunks? Once a skunk has raided a coop, won't they try again? It was so muddy last night that the tracks should be easy to follow." Mother concluded her argument with one last thought. "Just think about it before you make up your mind."

Dad ran a big hand through his curly hair as he contemplated her suggestion. "With that rain last night the fields are too muddy to work in. The boys might enjoy a chance to chase after those thieves. Couldn't hurt to give it a try," he said.

"I'll scramble what eggs we have here. With the potatoes, bacon and fresh bread, we should have enough for everyone to eat their fill." Mother turned back to the stove, with the basket of fresh eggs, and another skillet in her hand.

Once the boys were in, we all sat down to eat. The atmosphere was cool and quiet, as the plates of hot food were passed around, and everyone took their share. We ate in silence, which was not unusual, as we seemed to take the eating of our food quite seriously. It is usually after we have eaten our fill that the conversation really gets going. I had hoped that we would hear about the boys' bicycle adventure, and learn what happened to them that kept them away two days. However, for some reason, the topic was never brought up. Instead, dad cleared his throat and addressed his attention to Roy and Ron, who had not looked his way since they entered the kitchen.

"Boys, because of the storm last night, we won't be able to do anything out in the fields until the ground dries up, but I do have something for you to do instead," Dad paused, as he noticed the 'so what's new?' look that passed between Roy and Ron. Then he continued. "We had visitors to the hen house during the night. Some hens are missing and most of the eggs." At this news, the boys looked at dad with renewed interest. Dad noticed that he had their undivided attention. "Guess they knew that they wouldn't be heard with that storm roaring around our ears. Anyway, I thought you might like to take your twenty-twos and see if you could track them down."

Roy was the first to respond with a questioning look and asked, "Do you have an idea of what got after them?"

"Looks to me like skunks. However, I would like the two of you to go look at the tracks yourselves. The havoc we saw inside, sure suggests that its more than one critter, but you two look for yourselves and see what you think." Again, silence, as the boys digested this information.

Ron addressed dad next. "You think we should track it, or them, whatever the case may be, and wipe out the den?"

"Once a skunk eats eggs and kills chickens, they will come back for more. There is only one way to protect our hens and that is to get rid of them," Dad stated with finality.

"Have you got bullets for our guns?" Roy asked. Dad nodded.

"How soon can we start?" Ron asked.

"The sooner the better, you don't want the trail to get too cold. If you think it might take a while, mother can wrap up a couple of sandwiches for the two of you. Herbert might want to tag along for the fun of the chase," Dad suggested.

"Okay, lets go!" Roy said, as excitement settled in at the prospect of some new adventure. "Ron, you want to run over to Zobel's to see if Herbert would like to come with us while I get the guns and ammunition ready?"

Ron nodded his head, rose from his chair and headed for the door, paused and looked at mother, "Would you mind putting some sandwiches together for us, please?"

He smiled, as mother nodded her answer, and then left on his errand. Mother signaled for me to get some more bread from the pantry shelf. Dad and Roy were already heading back to our parents bedroom where dad kept the firearms and ammunition stored.

Eileen had been drawn to the kitchen by the sound of excitement, but had remained quiet all through this exchange. Now she turned to mother and asked, "Mom, do you think this is a good idea? Just a couple of days ago you let them go off by themselves with a bag of food along, and look what happened? What if they just decide to keep going again?"

"Look, Eileen. I think that was just a fluke. I don't think it was planned or they would not have been caught. Anyway, they have learned their lesson. Now we need to show that we trust them and give them a chance to prove themselves."

Eileen looked doubtful, as I am sure she was remembering the conversation she overheard when Roy was bragging about running away. She did not want to cause any more trouble though, so she just remarked, "I hope you are right."

"At least, with Herbert along, I don't think they will do anything foolish," Mother concluded.

As soon as Ronald and Herbert were there, the boys headed out to thoroughly survey the site of the crime. I followed, hanging around as close as I could, listening to their theories. They smelled the culprits' scent that still lingered in the air. "One of the skunks must have sprayed in the excitement of the chase," Ron said. "Where's our dog?"

Herbert and Roy looked around as Herbert remarked, "Funny that dog didn't hear anything last night. What kind of a hound dog is he anyway?"

"The kind that doesn't like storms!" Roy stated, as he left to hunt him down. He found Chaser curled up in the haymow, and took him to the hen house where he could get a good whiff of the scent. The tracks were all over the place and many were very distinguishable in that fresh mud. Roy released Chaser and said, "Go get 'em!"

I watched Chaser take off across the fields, following his nose, which was also following the tracks, with all three boys in hot pursuit. They were headed for the neighbors' woods behind our property. Once they crossed the last fence, they disappeared into the woods. I turned and went back to the house, wishing I could have gone with them.

"However, I could never have kept up with them in the first place, and wouldn't have enjoyed watching the kill in the second place," I conceded with a shake of my head.

I wandered back to the house thinking about life as I had seen it on this farm. I came to the conclusion that female animals were on earth to give life to the babies and the males were on earth to kill them, for one reason or another.

CHAPTER THIRTEEN

We spent the day doing a few chores that needed to be done. Mother took advantage of the lull to catch up on some household chores that were left for those more leisurely times. Patching up the knees on pants, repairing seams on dresses, mending worn socks, and talking to dad while he helped with what he could do. I found that dad also knew how to use a needle. His mother believed in the boys being self sufficient in all things. I remembered one of her favorite saying. "You never know when being able to cook and sew may come in handy."

Eileen and I sprawled out on the front room floor playing a game of marbles while we listened to the relaxed conversation between mother and dad. The crunch of tires on our graveled driveway alerted us to the possibility of company coming. Eileen and I both sprang up and ran to the kitchen window, watching for the car to make its way around the circular driveway between the barn and the house. It stopped close to the kitchen porch. We could see that it was a single man in the car, but not anyone we recognized. He seemed to be taking a few minutes to round up what he wanted to bring with him, or at least in our impatience it seemed like he was taking his time.

"If it's a salesman, he's new. I don't recognize him." Eileen continued to observe him through the window.

"You mean like that man who was by about a month ago? He was trying to sell mother on a new mop and nice hairbrushes?" I asked.

"Yah, like him."

Country Splendor

"He's getting out mama. Should we let him in?"

"Oh bother! It's probably that Fuller Brush Man again. I don't need anything that he has to offer. Maybe you could tell him we are not interested," Mother replied.

I was already at the door, so I opened it and said, "Hi." Eileen was behind me but since she towered over me, the young man directed his response to her.

"Hello, my name is Richard Hughes and I am a Watkins Dealer. I have a line of spices, flavorings, medicines, and more that every home can use. It is the best products available today, and offered at the best prices. Is the lady of the house home?" He finished his recitation with the whitest, most engaging smile I had ever seen. It must have fluttered Eileen's heart as well as she ran into the front room to tell mother who this fellow was, and to ask her to please come to the kitchen. I stood in the doorway; smiling shyly, and waiting to see what I was supposed to do next. The young man waited patiently, passing the time by trying to find out what my name was. I had finally found my voice enough to whisper, "Helen," when mother came up behind me.

"Come in." She brushed me aside and made way for the salesman to enter. She ushered him to a chair beside the table, and asked if she could get him a cup of coffee or a cold glass of water. He opted for the water.

Eileen got a glass from the cupboard, and filled it from the pitcher of water kept cooling in the icebox. "It's not very cold," she said as she handed the glass to him. "The iceman hasn't delivered our ice to us, yet, today."

The young man smiled at Eileen. "He may be delayed, because of the muddy roads. I had some trouble myself. I only turn up the driveways that have a solid rock base. Some of these farms have long, dirt driveways, and they are nothing but soft mud this morning. What days does he usually deliver?"

"Tuesdays and Fridays, usually. Aren't the roads muddy as well?" It was evident that she was wondering how he made it around without getting stuck somewhere.

Mr. Hughes drank deeply from the cool water. "You can get around if you are careful where you drive. I keep my wheels centered on the most heavily graveled area of the road." He smiled at her again, noticing how her cheeks colored slightly, and her eyes dropped away from his gaze.

He placed the glass on the table, leaving room to display the goods from his leather cases. He turned to mother, and began to show her all of the items he offered for sale. Spices, seasonings, and flavor enhancers of every kind. Puddings and jellies, flavored Jello, candies and condiments. Elixirs, salves, shampoos and soaps. So many things. Mother seemed impressed by the display and found many things she could use. She asked prices and seemed pleased with the answers. She worked out the items she would purchase that day, and then asked him how often he would be by.

"Ordinarily I try to set up my routes so I can be by once a month," he replied.

"That will work out fine as we get paid by the creamery once a month," Mother stated.

The whole procedure was boring me. I left the kitchen and went to talk to dad. Eileen stayed to listen. I told dad about the things that mother was buying. He nodded and said, "It is handy to have someone bring things out to us. Especially when it is hard getting into town as often as we need to, sometimes."

"But Eileen isn't buying anything, so why is she so interested?"

"Life on a farm can be confining and slow at times, with so little to entertain us after the chores are done. Just to sit and listen in on a conversation can be refreshing. Especially when it is someone new to listen to."

" And he is cute!" I said, eliciting a deep chuckle from dad.

After the salesman left, we started preparing the evening meal. Mother commented on the fact that the boys had not showed up yet, and she wondered if they would be back in time for the evening milking. She asked Eileen and I to run to the far pastor and bring in the cows.

Country Splendor

We had barely gone past the barn when we heard the sound of voices coming from the direction of the woods. We stopped to listen, realizing that the voices were coming towards us. "Do you think it's the boys?" I asked. Just then Chaser jumped over the far fence and headed towards us, with his tongue lolling out as if he had been running for some distance. He looked rather shaggy, like he had been through a rough time.

"There's the dog, the boys must be right behind," Eileen said.

"Wonder if they got the skunks?"

"We will soon find out, there they are now, and what a muddy bunch they are! Wonder how far they had to go? They've been gone all day." Eileen commented.

"Hey there!" I shouted, as I jumped up and down waving my hands.

"Hey yourself!" they called back. They carried their guns over one shoulder as if they were very pleased with themselves. I couldn't wait for them to come to us, so I took off running to meet up with them. Eileen stood by the barn, patiently waiting.

"Did you get them, did you?" I shouted, as I ran up to them.

"Well, iffen we did or iffen we didn't, you're not going to find out until we tell the folks. You can wait till then to find out. We are not going to tell it twice," Roy said.

"Awe, come on. I want to know. All you have to say is yes or no. Why do I have to wait to hear that? Why can't you tell me now?" I badgered, but it only brought laughs from all three, and they ignored my pleas all the way to the barn.

"Helen, come on, " Eileen said. "Mom said for us to get the cows in from pasture and we had better do it before we go in. It won't take but a few minutes if we get right to it, so come on."

"Okay," I said with a shrug of my shoulders. "These mean old boys won't tell me anything anyway."

Off we ran to fetch the cows. Ten minutes later, we had the cows in their stanchions and we were running to the house. We heard laughter and loud talk, coming from the kitchen. We hurried through the door, letting the screen door slam behind us. All talk stopped with the slamming of the door, and all eyes were on us as Eileen and I found seats at the table with the rest of the group.

I was anxious to find out what happened and asked, "Well, did they kill the skunks?" My question was directed at mother, who happened to be next to me.

"Hey, brat, we said we were only going to tell the story once. Sorry, you already missed it," Roy teased.

"No fair! You're the brat!" I shouted, standing to make myself taller. "We had to get the cows, cause you boys took so long getting home!"

"It's alright, Helen. They are still telling us the adventures they had just trying to track the scoundrels down. Sit down and listen, you haven't missed much," Mother assured me.

Ron took up the story where they had left off. "After searching through our woods we found the tracks continued on into Emit Johnson's place. He has not done much to keep the undergrowth down, making the going much harder. Those skunks don't mind going right through the middle of those big, black berry, patches. We found their tracks going into one that seemed to go on forever. We couldn't follow through it, so we had to start searching around the patch, to see if we could find where they came out."

"Old Chaser could not follow them either," Roy cut in, "but he tried and got so tangled up in the bushes that we had to stop our search, to get him out. But he did not want to get out; the more we pulled on him, the harder he pulled to get further into the thicket. He seemed to think they were inside and he wasn't going to give up until he had them." Roy began laughing as he thought of their predicament.

Ron grinned as he continued the narrative. "That stupid dog got so tangled up in those bushes that he couldn't go forward, and he was so far in by that time, that we couldn't get him out. Herbert had to go to Emits' place and ask for something to cut the bushes with, while we waited with Chaser, trying to keep him from getting further into that thicket. It seemed to take forever, but, finally, Herbert came back with a pair of clippers. He had a time getting them to us, and then it still took us quite some time to cut the briars back, to where we could untangle that dog."

"Yah, Dad, you won't believe what happened next!" Roy's voice was high with amusement as he told of their next predicament. "We had him loose and was about to get him backed out of the patch, when something went skittering through the undergrowth and off Chaser took again, straight back in, deeper than before, and just as badly tangled up. He'd try to rare up to loosen the thorns hold only to get tangled tighter!" Roy was laughing so hard by this time that he couldn't go on.

He had us all laughing with him as well, and yet we were anxious to hear what happened next. Ron choked down his laughter first, and continued, "We started hacking away at those briars again, and making a wider swath this time. We knew it was going to take at least two of us to get him untangled again. Chaser was thrashing and crying, trying to get loose, and we were working as fast as we could. Those briars have nasty thorns and we kept getting stuck ourselves, but we kept on until we were up to him. I was trying to calm him down, while Roy worked at pulling Chaser's fur free from the brambles. We finally got him backed out of the mess, had a good hold of his collar, and was leading him back out the way we came in."

"Dad, you really won't believe this!" Roy interrupted Ron. He was holding his sides and trying to control himself, as he continued. "We were just clearing the last of the briars when we heard movement somewhere in back of us, and old Chaser pulled back so suddenly that we lost our hold. He turned so quickly that it was all I could do to grab his tail, but that didn't even slow him down. Back into the briar patch he went, and down I went trying to hang onto his tail. I hung on as long as I could, but those briars were cutting into my chest, so I said, ' to hell with it' and let him go!" Roy dissolved into helpless laughter once again. By this time he had us all laughing so hard that tears were coursing down our cheeks, and dad was holding his hand over his mouth trying to control himself.

"Not back into the thicket?" Mom exclaimed, as she held her throbbing sides.

"By this time I would have shot that old hound," Dad laughed, only half convincingly.

"Well, we were thinking about it!" Herbert chimed in, as he choked up again, remembering how frustrated they were with that dog.

"I suppose you had to hack some more at the briar patch to get to him again?" Dad asked.

"We hacked on that patch until there was hardly a briar standing. We figured that by this time, if there had been anything in there, we would have spooked it out. With no more briars to get tangled in, old Chaser took off running some more. Took us clean out of the Johnson place, across the road and into that next farmers woods and you wouldn't believe where he headed for again!"

"Not another briar patch!" we chorused.

"As a matter of fact, yes. I think we cleaned at least three farmers' woods of its briars today. I wonder if we went back and asked them for wages if they would pay us?" Ron laughed and shook his head. Roy and Herbert grinned and nodded in agreement, with weary sighs.

"Vell, lets just hope that they weren't saving those patches for a berry pie!" Dad chuckled. "But what I want to know is, did you clean out that family of chicken snatchers or not?"

"To tell you the truth, Mr. Ruprecht, we never did catch up with them. I don't know where their lair is, but I bet we scared them clean out of this county!" Herbert stated emphatically. "Now I had better get home and help dad with the chores. He's probably wondering what happened to me. See you guys tomorrow?" he asked, as he stood to his feet and headed for the door.

"Yes, see ya," the boys answered, as the screen door slammed once again.

"I know you are tired," Dad said, turning back to his sons, "but those cows are going to think we have deserted them. Think you could wash some of the grime off your faces and hands, and get the milking done? Supper will be ready by then."

Both boys looked beat, and if they had a choice they would have left the cows go dry. But they knew it had to be done. They, reluctantly, got to their feet and took turns at the washbasin, then headed out to

Country Splendor

the barn. Mother watched them go, and turning to Eileen she said, "Everything is cooking, do you think you could watch it so it doesn't burn? Put it to the back of the stove to keep warm until we get in. I am going to help the boys tonight."

"Verna, I'll come and help too," Dad offered. "I don't think a little udder pulling would hurt me. I need to get my strength back, anyway."

"No Hubie! We can't take a chance on you opening up those stitches. You help here in the kitchen. These girls are too small to handle this stove by themselves. I would feel better if you would stay here and see that everything's okay. Please?" He turned and looked at her, ready to argue. He could see that mother was not going to relent, so, reluctantly, he agreed with a nod. Satisfied that she had won this round, she caressed his cheek, and smiled at him, as she turned and followed the boys to the barn.

CHAPTER FOURTEEN

A week of hot sunny days followed. The ground dried out and the grain turned golden. The heads on the oats filled out and all was ready to be harvested. The boys had helped harvest some of the neighbors fields the day before, and this day was to be our turn.

We were up earlier than usual that morning, as there were always so many things to prepare for on harvest day. The boys finished the milking, and the cows were let out to pasture. Breakfast was on the stove when Roy and Ronny came bounding through the kitchen door, letting the screen door bang shut behind them.

"You boys would wake the dead from their graves! We were hoping to let dad and Bobby sleep in a little this morning, but that's not going to happen now. Eileen, will you go get Bobby up and put him in his chair? Helen, you might as well let dad know that breakfast is on. Oh, Hubie! There you are!" Mother acknowledged, as dad entered the kitchen.

"Don't fuss at the boys, Verna, I was already awake. The threshing crew should be arriving shortly. Got plenty of coffee and biscuits ready?" He asked, as he walked to his chair, pulled it out from the table and sat down stiffly.

"You've been doing too much lately, Hubie, you are hurting again. What am I going to do with you?" Mother asked, as she walked over to dad and gave him a hug from behind and planted a kiss on his forehead.

Country Splendor

"I've got to be up and about if I'm ever going to get my strength back. There's too much work around here for you and the children to do alone," he argued, as he stroked her arms.

She straightened up, removing her arms from his neck, saying, "Be that as it may, you are not going to help anyone if you get yourself torn open. Promise me that you will only supervise today." It was more of a command than a question, and dad answered with a shrug of his shoulders. Mother turned away with a shake of her head, as if to say, 'What am I going to do with you!'

She returned to the stove, and began dishing up the hash and eggs she had prepared for breakfast, sitting the bowls in front of dad. Dad took his portion and passed the bowls on.

The boys had finished their bowls of hot cooked oatmeal, and dove into the hash, eggs and fresh baked biscuits as if they hadn't eaten for days. Eileen gave them each a glass of cooled milk, and mother poured dad a steaming cup of coffee. Then Eileen brought him a small pitcher of fresh cream and the sugar bowl. I watched as he put a spoon of sugar in the coffee and topped it off with thick cream. He gave the coffee a quick swirl of the spoon, and began sipping at it as if it were the elixir of the Gods. I could hardly wait until I was old enough to have my coffee like daddy's. I wanted to learn to drink it hot off the stove, without burning my lips, as he did. I had watched other men with hot coffee, and they poured a small amount into the saucer that the cup had sat on. They would swish it around a few times to cool it off and then raising the saucer to their lips, they sipped the cooled coffee. I liked dads' way the best.

Before we had all pushed ourselves away from the breakfast table, horse drawn wagons full of men, women and children pulled into the back yard. Next, came horse drawn mowers and thrashing machines. Men walked into the kitchen accepting the already full cup of coffee that mother handed each of them. They made their way to the now empty table, and sat down to talk to dad. The younger ones met on the porch and began exchanging hellos. The women filed into the kitchen next, laden with baskets full of food. It would take a healthy amount of food to feed the hungry men a lunch about ten o'clock, and then a large dinner, about one.

Mother had the food placed in the pantry, to keep it cool, and then ushered the women into the front room to visit, until the men folk were out of the way.

A couple of babies were deposited on blankets laid on the floor, and Bobby toddled over to inspect them. He dropped the ball he was carrying at one of the little boys feet, as if to entice him to play with him.

The baby picked up the ball and began chewing on it. That was not what Bobby had in mind, and he grabbed the ball back, setting the younger boy to howling. The mother of the child hurried over to protect her charge, but Bobby toddled off with his ball, ignoring the baby. He came to where I was and threw the ball in my direction.

I was disappointed that no children my age had shown up yet. I played toss with Bobby to pass the time. I laughed when he let the ball bounce off his tummy, and then ran after it on those short, solid legs of his. He was a chunky little guy, and so determined to grow up fast. "Ball go bounce!" he would say, as he ran across the room in pursuit of the ball, having to wait for it to roll to a stop before picking it up again. Then stooping over, he would pick it up in both hands and turn to me, trying to throw it. It would go off at some weird angle, and I would have to cross the room to get it.

Mother seemed worried that Bobby might break something, or worse, hit one of the babies with it, so she ordered me to take Bobby and his ball, out to the front yard to play.

I opened the door to usher Bobby through, when I heard familiar voices shouting greetings to me. Looking up and in the direction of the road, I saw the Olson girls running my way. There was Carol in the lead, with Lillian right behind. Behind her, Betty was keeping time with her mother. "Mom," I yelled back through the door, "the Olson's are here!" and then turning back to the welcome sight, I yelled, "Hi!" as I waved my hand in greeting. Forgetting all about Bobby, I ran to meet them, as they climbed upon our front lawn from the road.

Behind me, I heard Bobby let out a wail. Turning to tell him to wait for me on the porch, I saw him tumble off and land on his face and tummy on the grass. I ran back to him, reaching him just as he was trying to right himself. I bent down and helped him up, brushing the grass from his face, and checking him over to see if he was all right. Carol and Lillian joined me, crouching down and looking Bobby over as well. They had no boys in their family, and they loved my baby brother.

Mother stepped out onto the porch, saw that Bobby was fine, then walked down the steps and across the lawn to meet Mrs. Olson. Mother took the basket that Betty was carrying, and greeted them both. Betty, free from her burden, took off on a run to find Eileen. She was part way to the porch when Eileen stepped out onto the porch, drawn by the excited voices she heard. Betty bounded up beside her, and both girls disappeared around the house, holding hands as they went. They were laughing and talking just loud enough for each other to hear, but not loud enough to let others know what they were up to.

I knew they were headed to the back porch where the boys would have gathered, talking among themselves, and waiting for the men to come out. That's the first place girls' their age went. I had watched them many times. I knew just how they would stop running, just before they reached the boys, and then they would walk, slowly, past the boys, acting as if the boys weren't there. It was a mystery to me why they wanted the boys to see them, when they acted as if they did not see the boys. Some kind of a game I had not figured out yet.

I took Bobby by the hand and led him into the house, following behind mother and Mrs. Olson. Carol and Lillian followed me. Once I had Bobby deposited on the floor, with a small car to play with, I led the way to the back porch. As we passed through the kitchen, one of the men made a remark and the others started laughing. I looked to see if they were laughing at us, but they were engrossed in something dad had been telling them. I had an idea it was about the boys' adventure, of trailing the dog that was trailing the skunks.

Once out on the back porch, I noticed Roy, Ron and Herbert, entertaining the other boys, with many gestures and laughing. I was certain that the same subject was being discussed there. We did not stop to listen; however, as we were more interested in playing with the kittens in the haymow.

Before long, we heard men's voices shouting orders, as horses and machinery were put in place. We stepped to the door and watched as the mowers were being pulled to the fields by teams of horses, driven by the men. Following behind them, were more men and boys. Soon the action of threshing the wheat and grain would be under way. The wheat and oats would be mowed down and stacked into stalks, much as the corn had been. Then others would heave the bundles upon a wagon and bring them to where the threshing machine was set up. The wheat stalks were then fed unto a conveyor belt that would pull the stalks into the machine, where the grains would be separated from the stalks and sent down a chute. Men with gunnysacks caught the grain in their sacks, filling them almost to the top, and then moving so another man with an empty sack could take his place. The filled sacks were then carried to the granary, where they were emptied into bins. Once the wheat was done then the oats were put through the threshing machine.

The machine shredded the stalks into straw, which was then blown through a large tube, forming a stack over the pigsty. The chaff filled the air around the machine, settling on the men's hair and shoulders. Those who were prone to having allergies or asthma were not allowed to work in the area. They were given the job of driving the wagons or the mowers.

The threshing machine made so much noise that no one could hear another unless he shouted, so everyone had to know what was expected of him, before the chore began.

It was amazing to see how quickly the work was accomplished. The men took an hour break for lunch, to eat and freshen up, and then they would work at least three more hours before taking their dinner break. By mid to late afternoon, the work was finished, and the men took their families and machinery, and left for home.

Once the last family was gone, we all relaxed in the kitchen, talking over the day's events. Dad and the boys were pleased how

Country Splendor

smoothly the work had gone. Mother placed the leftovers on the table for a snack. "This should help you regain enough strength to get the evening chores done," she said.

She sat down beside dad again, and began asking him how he was really feeling. I could tell that she was anxious about his health, and hoped he hadn't over done it. She worried more about him than she did about her self. He seemed to be in high spirits though, and very pleased at having that big job done. The boys were almost too tired to eat. I was glad that they would have a couple of hours to rest before the milking had to be done.

Small talk ensued between mother and dad with the boys interjecting a tidbit here and there. The boys finished eating and took off to lay in the shade of the large oak tree to rest. I remained on the floor, rolling the ball to Bobby, unnoticed by my parents. Mother asked if dad knew how Mrs. Zoble was doing. "Emil talked to me a little before he left. He says she is getting thinner every day, and weaker. He is afraid that he is going to loose her. I just don't know what to tell him." Dad's voice was touched with sadness, for his friend.

"I don't think there is really anything one can say to make it better. All anyone can do now is to listen and sympathize. I was over there just a couple of days ago, and she was looking very pale and weak. The doctor mentioned cancer, when he examined her some time ago, but you know how people hate to talk about that. She will not discuss it so I don't mention it either, but I guess we all know that it is just a matter of time."

"Your dad died of cancer of the jaw just a few months ago, didn't he? When we were down there at Christmas time last year, I thought then that he wouldn't last much longer. How long did he have it before they knew?" Dad asked.

"Remember when mother wrote that dad had his jaw operated on in September? They suspected cancer then. They had hoped that they had gotten it all, but remember how he never recovered from that? I appreciate your taking me down there at Christmas, so I could see him, 'just-in-case.' I will always be grateful that I had that time with him, even though it was a difficult time. He was only in his sixties."

Mother paused, blinking back a tear. "And look at Audrey, she's only in her forties. So young to be so sick."

"What will Emil do if he looses her? They have been so devoted to one another."

"Now you know why I worry about you! We aren't any older and I don't want to loose you either," Mother said, with a sob in her throat.

"Now Verna, you know I'm too ornery to die. You are going to have me around for a long time yet," Dad said, with a certainty that belied mother's arguments.

"Let's go lie down for an hour," Mother suggested. "A rest would do us both good." As she rose from her chair, she spotted Bobby and me on the floor across the table from her. "How long have you been there, Helen?"

"Since everyone left. I've been keeping Bobby quiet so you and daddy could talk. He's rubbing his eyes so I think he is ready for a nap too. Shall I lay him in his crib?" I asked, hoping that I could appease mother, as I knew how she hated having us children listen in on her and daddy's conversations.

"I'll take him," Mother said, as she walked around the table and picked Bobby up. "It wouldn't hurt you to take a nap too young lady. By the way, Helen, I don't want you saying anything about Audrey to anyone. You understand? We don't want to spread rumors."

"What's 'rumor's' mama?" I asked, as I watched her change Bobby's diaper.

"A rumor is something someone may think he knows, but it is not a for-sure thing. We really do not know for sure if Audrey is going to die. We hope that she will get well and live a long time yet. It might make her children and her husband unhappy, if they heard that we think she might not live long. Do you understand?"

"I think so mama. I won't tell anyone what you and daddy said. I hope she doesn't die. I really like her a lot. Why do people die before they are old? I heard Eileen say that the baby you had before you had me, died. Why? Where do people go when they die?"

"You are too full of questions. Right now, I want to lie down for a nap. One day when you are older, I will tell you all about it. Right now, I want you to lie down and rest for a while too. Now scoot. Before you know it, it will be time to start supper."

I was so full of questions that I knew I would never be able to sleep, unless I had some answers. I decided that I would go look for my sister, and see if she would answer some of them for me. I walked around the house, then out on to the front porch. She wasn't in any of her usual spots. Then I realized I had not seen her since everyone went home.

I thought about asking mother where she was, but she had gone into her bedroom with dad, and shut their door. No one bothered them when their door was shut. The house was very quiet. I supposed that the boys were still out doors, resting beneath the shade trees. I walked by the crib and noticed that Bobby had rolled over on his tummy, and that his eyes were closed. I knew he was sleeping. I went slowly up the stairs, not knowing what else to do. I plopped on the bed and thought on all that had gone on that day. It really had been a nice day. I rolled onto my side and slipped into unconscious slumber.

CHAPTER FIFTEEN

I awoke to a gentle shaking of my shoulder. Looking up from my pillow, I saw my mother's large, dark brown eyes, smiling at me. "Honey, I need you to watch Bobby for me. I have to get some vegetables from the garden for supper. You sleep any longer, you won't sleep tonight." My eyes wanted to close again, but mother insisted that I get up.

"Okay, mama. I'm coming," I said, as I raised myself up and rolled from the bed. "But where's Eileen? Why can't she get the vegetables?" I inquired, as I followed mother down the stairs.

"She's gone home with the Olson's. Dorothy wanted her to stay with the girls while she and Kelly went to town," she answered.

"But how come I couldn't go too? I never get to go anywhere," I complained.

"Now Helen, you know that I need at least one of you here to help out." She stepped from the last riser and headed towards the kitchen.

"But …"

"No buts, Helen. Bobby is already in his highchair eating on some cookies, which were left by one of the families that had been here. You just mind him so he won't wake your dad, and I'll be back in before you know it."

I knew that it was hopeless to argue any more with mother, so I sat down at the table, close by the baby, and reached for a cookie for myself. "Now don't eat more than one, you'll spoil your appetite,"

Country Splendor

Mother stated, as she reached for her vegetable basket, and headed out of the kitchen door.

"What's appetite?" I asked, but she was out of hearing by this time, and my question hung in the air, unanswered. I turned to Bobby and remarked, "Well, she mustn't be worried about your appetite, you have a cookie in each hand!"

He grinned at me as if to say, "I'm special, that's why!" and beat his tray with one cookie while he chewed on the other.

'Yes, you are special,' I answered my own thoughts. 'If I had all those golden curls and pretty big, greenish blue eyes, I would be special too!' But my hair was fine and straight, and brown. It always seemed to be tangled when my mother brushed it, and I would squirm and fuss as she worked the tangles out. Eileen on the other hand, had a heavy head of hair, just a little darker than blond, but naturally curly, and I heard people remark on what a pretty girl she was. No one said that about me. I did hear one lady remark to another, while mother was out of the room, about what a good-looking family the Ruprecht children were. All of them that is, except for that scrawny little one. She wondered why that was. I looked at her as she was talking, and noticed the way she looked at me as she made that remark, and I knew it was me she was talking about. It was not the first time I heard that kind of remark, and I wondered just what scrawny meant?

When I asked mother about it, she said that I was small and thin. I asked her why, and she said that I had been a sickly baby. I had almost died of pneumonia when I was about one year old. I had climbed out of my baby bed and managed to get out of the door, and half way to the barn before she caught me. I was barefoot and with only my nighty and diaper on. It was in the winter and I caught a chill that went into my chest, I was very sick for a long time. Ever since then, and even though I eat well, I never seem to put on weight.

When I asked mother what I was doing out doors, she said that I had been on my way to find my daddy. She said that I walked from the time I was ten months old, and I climbed like a monkey. I was daddy's little girl, and I was always running to find him.

Just then I heard movement from the front room, and turning to look, I saw my daddy walking towards the kitchen. He was moving stiffly, and holding his side. I ran to him and asked him how he was. "I'm alright kitten. Just did a little more today than I should have, I guess. I'll be alright though, once I have a cup of coffee to clear the cobwebs." He chuckled as if remembering my inquiry of what that meant. Then he asked, "Have you seen the boys since you've been up?"

"No daddy, I've just been watching Bobby. Mama went to the garden for some fresh vegetables to fix for supper."

He reached for a kitchen chair and gently sat himself down. "Can I get you some coffee?" I asked.

"I don't think you can handle that big pot, Helen, and I don't want you scalding yourself. Just give me a minute and I will get one."

Just then, mother entered through the kitchen door, looking rather upset. She looked over at dad and shook her head, went to the drain board and sat the vegetables down. I could tell by the droop of her shoulders that there was some bad news coming. Dad noticed also, and he asked, "What is it now, Verna?"

I could tell that she hated telling him, but she finally turned towards us and said, "Hubie, I might be wrong, but, the boys seem to be gone and their bicycles are missing. Did they say anything to you about going anywhere?"

"No, the last I saw them, was after everyone had left, and they headed for the shade trees in the front yard to rest. Maybe they've just gone for a bike ride, and will be home in time for the milking."

"Let's hope you are right. Helen, would you like to scrub some vegetables for me while I get dad his coffee?" She asked, as she turned and started towards the stove. I got up and headed towards the drain board, to get a pan of water to clean the vegetables in. "Oh, and before you start the vegetables, run and get me an arm load of wood for this stove."

I stopped in mid flight, and turned instead towards the kitchen door. I stepped through it and headed for the woodbin, almost colliding with Herbert Zoble, who had just stepped upon the porch. "Whoa, where

Country Splendor

are you going in such a hurry?" He asked, as he grabbed me to keep me from falling.

"To the wood bin for some wood, where you headed?" I asked, as I pulled away from him.

"Just need to talk with your folks. Here let me carry that wood in for you," he said, as he crossed to the bin and pulled an armful from the stack. He turned towards the door and stepped through it, greeting mother and dad. "Where would you like this?" He asked mother as he crossed to the stove.

"In that box by the stove, and thanks." Mother had just poured dad his coffee and the coffee pot was still in her hand. She held it up to Herbert and asked, "Would you like a cup, too?"

"No thanks, "he said, as he dropped the wood into the wooden box by the stove, and brushed his sleeves of any wooden fibers that clung to his shirt. Then turning to the table, he asked dad how he was doing.

"A little tired, but okay," dad replied. "Sit down. How's your mom?"

"About the same, I think. She was up when we got home today. She's helping sis with supper. I need to get back and help dad with the chores, but dad said I should tell you something," He faltered, looking down at his hands, now clenched before him on the table.

"What is it, Herbert?" Dad asked. Mother looked at him, and I could tell by the look on her face that she had a good idea of what was coming.

"It's about our boys, isn't it?" she asked gently, trying not to intimidate him.

"Well, yes. I really don't think I should be telling you this, but my dad said I need to," he began again, and again went silent with his eyes looking down at his hands.

"Herbert, if it's that important, we need to know. Just come out with it," Dad stated, with that authoritative air that broached no argument.

"We were talking today, you know, after the work was done and all, and well, Roy was saying that he was wanting to take off, now that the harvesting was done with here at your place. He was trying to talk Ronny and me into going off with him. He said that if we stayed around here, we would be doing nothing but harvesting for everybody in the area, and he was tired of working all the time. He said he wanted to have some fun before the summer weather was over. But I can't go off and leave my folks, you know, with mom so sick and all," he said.

"You're right Herbert, you are needed at home, but so are our boys. Did Roy say where he wanted to go? Did he have a destination in mind?" Mother asked.

"Well, yes," he said, as if that was all he wanted to say about that. There followed a few moments of silence before dad spoke up again.

"I know you think you are telling something that was told you in confidence, Herb, but we really need to know what is going on. You can see that, can't you? We won't think any less of you for telling us just what you know," Dad urged.

"My dad said the same thing, that he would want to know if it were me that had taken off. And I know that too, and they really didn't tell me not to tell," he faltered and hesitated again. "I can't believe that he would really do this, but he said he wanted to go to his grandma's place in Missouri. He said that you all went last winter, in fact for Christmas, and he and Ronny and Eileen, couldn't go along. He thought it was only fair that they get to go, too."

"What? To Missouri? That's three states away! That crazy kid, he surely wouldn't really do that, would he?" Mother asked, as she turned to dad.

"I wouldn't think so," Dad said, as he leaned back in his chair and brushed the hair back from his forehead as if to clarify his thoughts. "I know he can get some crazy thoughts in his head, and he talks of adventures he would like to take. I can't see Ron going along with that, though. What makes you think that they might have done this?" Dad directed his question right at Herbert's bowed head.

"I watched them ride by some time ago, and they each had a small bundle tied on their bikes. They were traveling fast, like they wanted to make good time, going somewhere," he stated.

"How long ago?" Mother asked.

Country Splendor

"Wasn't too long after we got home. I had just finished washing up and was going out to the mail box for mom, when I saw them heading East as fast as they could go."

"That would have been about the time we laid down for a nap. They could be a good ways away by now. Should we notify the sheriff again, Hubie?" Mother directed the question to dad. He looked at her, not answering right away, as if he were giving the whole matter a lot of thought.

He rubbed a large calloused hand across the back of his neck, and then shook his head. "No. If they are that determined to leave, they will just keep trying until they make it. I know it won't be easy, getting along without them, but we can't keep them prisoner here either."

Mother started to protest, but dad reached out a hand and laid it on hers. "I don't like it either, but think about it. This is the second time they have taken off. If we have them caught and returned to us, what good will that do? They need to find out for themselves that life out there isn't that easy. Let them find out for themselves," he repeated, as if to convince himself as well. "I'll wager that they will only be gone long enough to get really hungry. If they come back on their own, then they will settle down and be glad to have a warm bed to sleep in, and food on the table."

I could tell that mother was really thinking this over, as she looked from dad, across the table at the young teen aged boy sitting quietly, waiting to see what the final decision would be, and then back to dad again. "They are so young, Hubie," she stated.

"My point exactly," Dad said. "They are old enough to have all kinds of ideas about life on their own, but too young to know what that entails. They need a reality check. They need to find out how rough life can be out on their own. You'll see, mother," he said softly, using 'mother' as a reality check for her. She looked at him sharply, at first, and then with a look that said, 'okay, you made your point.'

Then she turned to Herbert, reaching her hand across the table and laying it on his, she said, "Thanks for coming over and telling us, Herbert. You were right in doing this, and we are very grateful to you. You can go home and thank your dad for us as well. Let him know that we won't be calling the sheriff this time. You can explain to him our decision, okay? And give your mother our love. We will be over to see her soon."

Herbert looked at mother with evident relief on his face, and rising from the table, he said his goodbyes, and began to head for the door. He paused, as if just remembering something, turned back to face my parents, and said, "Oh, by the way. Dad said that we would come over after our chores are done and help you with yours."

"We can't expect you and your dad to help us after all the work you've done today. We will manage somehow," Mother said, with her voice trailing off, then remembering that Eileen was not home to help either, she turned to dad. "Oh, Hubie, I forgot. Eileen is staying at the Olson's tonight, babysitting."

"That's alright, Mrs. Ruprecht, we will be over." Herbert headed for the door again, and this time he made it, with dad's thanks and mother's words of appreciation following him through the door. "Bye now, I'll see you later," he called, as he stepped from the porch and headed for home.

The rest of the day went by in a flurry of activity. I cleaned vegetables, as mother took care of Bobby and put him on the floor to play. She stoked up the stove with more wood and put the vegetables on to cook. There was some chicken left from the noon meal, as well as other leftovers that she decided would do us for our evening meal. She asked dad to keep an eye on Bobby, as she went to help me get the cows from the far pasture, and herd them to the barn for their evening milking. Old Chaser went along to keep us company, but took off about half way to where the cows were, following some scent that interested him. "He sure is a no-account dog!" I stated, repeating what I had heard dad say once, as I watched him lope off towards the woods, with his nose sniffing the ground.

"He's just a hunting dog, honey. He is just doing what comes naturally to him."

"But why doesn't he help herd the cows like Blacky use to?" I asked, referring to the smaller black and white spotted dog we use to have.

Country Splendor

"Blacky was bred for herding cows, that is what came naturally to him. This dog is a different breed entirely."

"Well, how come dad didn't bring us home another cow herding dog then?" I asked.

"When Blacky died, dad wanted a dog that wouldn't remind him of Blacky. When the neighbors' dog had pups, the boys fell in love with this one, so dad let them have him. Besides, a dog like Blacky is hard to find."

"Why did they go?"

"Why did who go?" Mother asked, being thrown off by the change of my questioning.

"The boys, why did they go?"

"Some people like working on farms, like Blacky did. He was a dog that liked to chase the cows. But not everybody is like that. Chaser now, he likes to take off after other things. He likes hunting and roaming the woods. People have different ideas about what they want to do, too." Mother explained.

"Will they ever come back?"

"I hope so. Hey, there's Black Bess, you get on the other side of her and get her started towards the barn. The other's will follow, now hurry, we have a lot of work ahead of us yet tonight," She said.

I hurried towards our big black cow, but she was more interested in the green grass she had found to eat, than she was of me. I went up to her and tried to get her attention, but she just kept her head down and moved further into that patch of sweet, grass. Even my shouting at her did not distract her from her quest. I ran over to a large hazelnut tree that grew on the edge of the woods, picked up a small branch that had fallen off during our last storm, and headed back to Black Bess with it. Mother was still standing where I had left her, watching to see how successful I was going to be. I thought about Blacky and how he would snap at a cow's heel to let them know that they needed to move. Once they were moving he would run around to their head and bark at them, to get them to move in the direction he wanted them to go. I went to the back of Black Bess and hit her legs with the stick. At first she ignored me, but when I hit her right above her hoof, she picked it up and moved it forward, and then took another step. I ran to her head, and tapped her on the neck, saying, "Go to the barn, go on, move!" But she ignored me, as if I were one of the pesky flies that she would shoo away with the flick of her tail, and just kept pulling large mouths full of grass from the ground.

Mother came from the other side of Black Bess, walked around to her head, and said, "Okay old girl, head out now!" Black Bess pulled up the last mouth full of grass she had reached for, and ambled off towards the barn. As the bell that hung from around her neck, swung on its leather thong, the ringing sound alerted the other cows that it was milking time again. One by one they raised their heads, and followed in formation, behind Black Bess.

"Don't walk too closely behind her, Helen, she's raising her tail," Mother warned.

I saw it coming and quickly dashed over to mother's side, just as the steamy mass fell to the ground in a round heap.

"That was close!" I said, and mother laughed in agreement. "How come they call that a cow pie?"

Mother answered, "Because of the shape. Doesn't it look a little like a pie?"

"I don't think anything would want to eat it. Ugh!" I exclaimed.

"No, I don't suppose they would," she said, with a chuckle.

We were almost to the barn when Chaser came out of the woods, bounding across the barnyard, and to the barn door. He was clawing at the door when suddenly it opened. There in the doorway stood Ronny. He grinned and waved at us, as we followed behind the lead cow. Ron stepped aside as Chaser jumped up on him, and he pulled the dog to one side, so the cows could get past. I took off at a run as soon as I recognized my big brother. I dashed through the door ahead of Black Bess and jumped at Ron. "Your home, your home!" I yelled, as he grabbed me and gave me a hug. Mother followed Black Bess in, and stopped beside Ron, who put me down, while still holding Chaser's head so he wouldn't scare the cows and make them bolt.

"Where've you been?" Mother asked, as she came to Ron's' side. "And where is Roy?"

"I just got back a few minutes ago. Dad told me that you were after the cows and that I should help you. Roy is on his way to Missouri," he said.

"I heard that was where you both were headed. What changed your mind?"

"I thought I wanted to go, had planned on it at first, but the further we got from home, the more I thought about what a hardship that would work on you and the girls, not having us to help with the chores. Especially with dad still unable to do much. I decided that I was needed here, and that there would be time enough to make a trip to Missouri, after dad is back on his feet," Ron said.

"How come you did not talk Roy into coming back too?" Mother asked.

"I tried, but he was so determined that there wasn't any way to change his mind. I'm sorry, mom, it's just that Roy has never cared about farming, and you know how dad can be some times. He can be so hard on us. When I think about that temper of his, and how mean he can be when he gets really mad, that I don't really want to be around him, when he's like that either. But I thought of you mom, and I knew I had to come back and help out, at least until dad is well again." Mother reached out her arms and wrapped them around Ron. He was already a head taller than her, so he bent over a bit to hug her back.

"Thanks, son," Mother said, against his chest before stepping back, and letting me get close enough to give him another hug.

"I'm glad you came back too, Ronny."

"How about you going to the house and helping dad with Bobby, while mom and I get to this milking? Okay?" He released me once more and gave me a shove in the direction of the barns front door.

"Mama, do you want me to set the table for supper?" I asked, as I headed towards the door.

"Yes, do that and how about taking Chaser with you? We don't need him spooking the cows," Mother said.

"Okay, come on Chaser," I told him, as I grabbed his collar and led him out of the barn. Once we were in the yard, Chaser took off for the house and his food dish. He gobbled up the dinner leftovers mother had placed there hours earlier. "How can you eat that? It's covered with flies! Ugh!" I would never understand dogs I thought, as I pushed through the screen door and into the kitchen. Dad was at the stove, stirring something, and Bobby was on the floor at his feet, playing with a little truck. "Can I help you fix supper, daddy?" I asked, as I crossed the room and stood beside him.

"No, little one, I have it all ready. Actually, mother prepared it before you went for the cows; I'm just making sure it isn't burning down. You could set the table. Can you reach the dishes all right?"

"If I stand on the kitchen stool I can," I answered, as I crawled up the steps of the stool and stood on the top.

"Wait a minute. Let me hand the dishes to you." Dad walked across the room and stood beside me. "Get down now and I'll hand them to you."

"Okay," I replied, as he held my arm, helping me retreat back to the floor. "Did you see Ronny? Isn't it wonderful that he came home? I hope Roy comes home soon, too."

"Yes, vonderful." I noticed the sigh that slipped out with his words, as he turned and handed me four plates. "Are you sure you can handle these okay? This many at one time I mean?" he asked, with a bit of a worried note in his voice.

"Oh sure, I'm getting bigger now. I can do all sorts of stuff. See, it's not too heavy for me," I said, as I struggled to the table, not wanting him to notice how hard it was to lift them onto the table by myself. I usually took only two at a time, but I was always trying to do more, like my big sister did. Having placed the plates around the table, I crossed to the cupboard to get the silverware. "It seems funny to be setting only four places," I said.

"Can you get the cups and saucers by yourself?" Dad asked.

"Sure I can daddy, and I can get the bread and butter and salt and pepper and everything," I said, as I continued moving things onto the table.

"It sure is nice having a good worker to help me," Daddy said. I took that as high praise and promised myself that I would always be a good worker. I loved the farm, because daddy loved the farm.

Country Splendor

I enjoyed doing things to help out, and never considered it a chore. I thought about what mother had said, about how some people liked working a farm and others would rather do other things. I had no idea of what other things were, the farm is all I knew. But I knew I loved all the animals, and there was always something to do. It was never boring to me. In fact 'boring' was a word I just did not understand at all. Life was so full of so many interesting things. There was never enough time to do, to touch, and to explore, all the things I wanted to.

By this time, dad had sat down in his chair at the head of the table, and watched me move around the room, reaching for what I could reach, and using the kitchen stool when it was out of my reach. "You really need to grow some more, Helen, you are too small to do everything you want to do. But you have more energy than other's twice your size," He said, with a shake of his head, as he reached for the hot cup of coffee he had taken to the table with him. He picked it up and started drinking it, carefully, as the steam curled past his lips.

"How come that doesn't burn you, daddy?" I asked fascinated at how he could drink something that hot. I had learned the hard way what hot was, especially when it took me a long time to heal from the wounds.

He laughed at me, at the worried expression I must have had on my face, as I watched him with that hot cup of coffee. "I learned from my dad how to drink hot coffee," he said, explaining it to me. "There was always a lot of work to do so we rarely had the time to let the coffee cool down first. He taught me how to bubble it across my lips in a way that cools it enough that it doesn't burn my lips or tongue. When you are older, I will teach you. For now you don't need any coffee, it would stunt your growth."

"What does 'stunt your growth' mean?" I asked.

"That means that you would stay as little as you are right now." His answer was accompanied with a grin that softened up his face, and made me feel good all over.

"Will I be pretty if I grow bigger?" I asked, looking at him with a hopeful heart.

"What makes you think that you are not pretty now?" he asked, as he saw I was serious.

"People call me plain, and they say Eileen is pretty. Plain is not good, is it?"

"Come here my little princess. You are pretty to me, and yes, when you grow up you will be a beauty. Do you know what beauty is?" I shook my head no, as he sat me on his lap. "Vell, beauty is more than pretty, and it comes from the inside of a person. When you are happy with what you have, when you like to do things for other people, when you like to make others happy, that is real beauty. Do you understand? You, my little one, will never be plain. You bubble over with beauty." He gave me a kiss on the head and patted my back. "Now would you like to bring me the cream pitcher from the ice box?"

"Sure daddy," I smiled, as I slid down from his lap, and ran around the table to the icebox, which was located close to the kitchen door. The handle was heavy and high enough that it was a stretch for me to work it up and over its latch, allowing the door to swing open.

"Do you need help with that?" he asked.

"No, I can do it. See?" I grunted, as I pushed it high enough that it would fall on over on its own weight. The door swung on its iron hinges, and I moved back so it would open wide enough to allow me to reach inside its cool interior, for the pitcher of cream. It was hard to shut the door and fasten back the latch though, with the pitcher in one hand. I tried pushing the latch up with my left hand, but the pitcher, held precariously in my right hand, began to tip and poured some of its liquid onto the floor.

"Okay, now you do need help," Dad said, as he raised himself carefully from the chair and came over to assist me.

"I'm sorry daddy, I didn't mean to," I said, as I looked at the white milky mess on the floor. I wondered if he was going to hit me on the head, as my sister did, when I made a mess like this.

He came up to me and patted my head gently instead, and said, "Go put the pitcher on the table and get the wash cloth to clean up the mess. I'll shut this door for you."

Country Splendor

"Thank you, daddy," I sighed, as I hurried off in relief, not to have him mad at me. I placed the pitcher by his coffee cup, and went to the dishpan for the washcloth. I swabbed at the milky mess on the floor, wiping most of it up before taking the cloth back, and dropping it into the dishpan.

"There, all done," I said, as I dried my hands on the skirt of my dress. Daddy was sitting at the table again. He looked at the smear of white left on the linoleum and smiled behind his coffee cup, taking another drink instead of correcting me.

Mother and Ron came into the kitchen and headed for the washbasin to clean up. Mother was in the lead, and when her feet hit the milky residue, still damp on the floor, her feet slipped, and she would have fallen, if Ron had not grabbed her under her arms, and steadied her back to her feet. "What's this?" Mother wanted to know, as she looked towards the offending, slippery patch.

"Now, mama," Dad said carefully "It's just a little spilled cream. Helen did her best to clean it up." I was glad that I was behind dad at this time, keeping Bobby occupied on the floor. I started to get up, and then decided that it might be wiser to stay hidden until she 'cooled off,' as my big sister would put it

Mother grabbed the mop that was hanging on the back porch, wet it in the mop bucket sitting behind the door, and proceeded to mop up the slippery residue. Ron stepped gingerly around the spot mother was working on, and washed his hands at the basin. Drying them on the small hand towel that hung near by, he turned to dad. "How are you feeling, dad? Is the pain letting up any?"

"I am doing better, some better every day," Dad said.

"Yes, just enough better to try and do more than he should," Mother added, with a note of frustration sounding in her voice.

"Now Verna, you know that the doctor said I was to begin doing a little more each day, until I get my strength back. If I followed your orders I would still be lying on the bed."

"Well, I can see it does me no good to worry about you. You will do what you will do, regardless of what I say," she said, sounding a bit aggravated.

"How about we feed these kids before they die of starvation?" Dad said, hoping to change the subject.

"Just let me hang this mop up and I'll get it on the table." Mother headed for the back door with the mop in her hand. She had just stepped through the screen door when we heard; "Well, hello there," from mother, and a couple of "hello's" from the Zoble men who had just stepped upon the porch.

"Oh, dear. We forgot to let you know that Ron is home, and we just finished with the milking. But, come on in and have a cup of coffee. In fact, we were just going to have a bite to eat and we would love to have you join us."

"Yes, come on in and join us," Dad called to them.

They agreed to come in for a bit, and stood back, holding the door for mother to walk through first.

As they entered the room, Mr. Zobel walked to the table and offered dad a hand. "How you doing, Hubert?"

Herbert had sat down beside Ron and slapped his hand as if to say, "Hi, good to see you back." Ron responded with a knowing nod and a smile.

Dad smiled at Emil, shaking his hand and saying, "Better every day, thank you. And you?"

"Just fine. Wife's a bit better today. We will finish up the thrashing at our place tomorrow and then we move on to Thompson's. It will be good to get all the grain in for everyone," Emil replied. Mother poured each man and both of the boys, a cup of coffee, scooting the cream and sugar towards our guests. I loved to watch Emil pour his coffee into his saucer, let it breathe a few seconds, and then carefully tip it to his mouth. He never lost a drop. Herbert, on the other hand, wasn't quite so adept with his, and a little trickled out of the corner of his mouth, which he caught with his tongue, and used the back of his hand to wipe off the remainder.

"Mighty fine coffee, Mrs.," Emil said. Mother nodded her thanks, and went about placing cold salads from the icebox on the table, and then the warmed vegetables and roast beef. I got two more plates and sets of silverware for our guests, placing a set before each one.

Country Splendor

"Hi there, Helen, thank you," Herbert responded, as I sat his plate before him. "See any signs of those skunks around the chicken coop again?"

"Not a sign. Guess you guys must have scared them plumb to death. They won't dare come around here again," I said.

"Hope you're right," Ron chimed in, "because next time we won't let them get away, right Herbert?"

"Right!" Herbert agreed. "Next time we'll have them for supper!"

"You can't eat skunks, can they mom?" I asked, mortified at the thought. The men all began to laugh at my consternation.

"No, I do not believe that we will be eating them, but it would be a relief to know that they wouldn't be attacking the chickens again," Mother added.

The food was dished out on each plate, and the proceeding next fifteen minutes was given over to enjoying our food. Bobby broke the silence with a yell for attention.

"Helen, would you put Bobby in his highchair so I can feed him?" Mother asked.

"Sure, coming Bobby," I called. He was already trying to climb up the side of his chair. "Just a minute, until I lift up the tray." I barely raised it when Bobby pushed his way into the seat, and moved his head so I could pull the tray into place. Mother turned to Bobby and began spooning mashed vegetables into his hungry bird mouth. She placed a piece of bread into his hand so he would have something to chew on between bites, while mother grabbed a mouthful as well.

"That was mighty fine eating, Mrs.," Emil said, as he pushed his plate back and took up his coffee cup.

"Ronny, would you fill Emil's cup again for him, and get the pies from the ice box, please?" Mother asked.

"Sure," he said, as he rose to obey, Herbert offered to help. "You take care of the coffee refills and I'll get the pies," Ron responded.

Over fresh coffee and bites of the delicious pies, the conversation resumed. Emil directed his next question to Ron, "Roy kept going?" he asked.

"Fraid so. I tried to talk him out of it, once I decided to come back, but he would not relent. He was bent on getting to grandma Vaughan's place in Webb City, Missouri, and nothing I could say would change his mind."

"Mr. Ruprecht, how long do you think it will take him to bicycle there?" Herbert asked.

"I've been thinking on that. By car we have made it in a couple of days. By bicycle? In good weather and no breakdowns, he might be able to make it inside of a week, I should think. Maybe less. Course he will have to find places to sleep at night, and I don't know what he is going to do about eating. If he has to work for his victuals it may take longer. Just depends," Dad said, thinking of all that could happen to a young boy barely thirteen years old and on his own.

"Mama," I whispered, "what's victall's? Why would Roy need that?"

"Victuals is food, honey," Mother answered.

"Food?" I echoed, wondering why anyone needed a word like that to mean food. Maybe it was a certain kind of food that one needed while riding a bike. I looked at mother, planning on asking her that question, when she anticipated it and shushed me with a look. 'Oh fine, now I will never know,' I thought to myself, as I turned back to my pie.

Emil finished his pie and coffee, looked across at his son, giving him a 'lets go look,' and pushed himself away from the table, rising to his feet. "Thank you kindly, Mrs. and Hubert. We will be getting home now. Let us know if there is anything you need, and let us know when you hear anything about Roy." Emil turned to the door and left, with Herbert following close behind. Herbert gave everyone a final wave, and let the screen door slam behind him.

It had been a long, busy day for me, and I said my goodnights and headed off to bed. "Take a trip to the outhouse first," Mother called after me, and with a nod of my head I slipped out through the door, and headed for the end of the path. With that job taken care of, I was about to leave the little building, when I heard a hoot owl give a hoot, and then all kinds of noise began at the hen house. I ran for the

Country Splendor

kitchen, slamming the screen door as I burst through. "The hen house! The hen house!" was all I could say.

Ron made it to the door first, with mother and dad right behind. "Listen to that! Something's at the chickens again. I'll get the gun, dad can you light a lantern?"

"Right behind you son. Hurry!" Dad urged. Mother ran for the broom handle that she kept for emergencies, and hurried to the porch behind Ron. Dad was already outside with the lantern burning brightly, held aloft in his hand, lighting the way.

"Helen, you stay with Bobby," Mother ordered. I was always being left out of the excitement, but I knew better than disobey. I helped Bobby down to the floor, and with his stubby hand in mine, we crossed to the porch, standing in the shadows. The kerosene lamplight from the kitchen table, created a path of light across the porch in front of us. Listening to the ruckus in the chicken coop, I could only imagine what was taking place. It lasted for several minutes, until a shotgun blast split the night air. Chickens were still complaining as the trio headed back to the house, with a very proud brother holding up his prize. A very abused looking owl hung from his upraised hand, and for sure, would never chase another chicken.

"Bird, bird," Bobby said, as he pointed one finger at the hanging owl.

"A dead bird, Bobby," I said.

"Dead bird, dead bird," he said, following Ron into the house.

CHAPTER SIXTEEN

It was hard to get to sleep, after all the excitement of that night, but it was even harder to get up the next morning. Mother called up the stairway before dawn, letting us know that the chores needed to be done early, as we were expected over at the Zoble's that morning to help with the harvesting. I rolled over, half aware of a voice calling to me, requesting that I get up. Ignoring it, I rolled back over and lay quietly. I peeked through half raised lids and saw only black. I listened for my oldest brother's feet to hit the floor in preparation for dressing. Nothing. My eyes were so heavy; I relaxed back into my feather pillow.

I was running across a green meadow, the sun was warm and bright, and the butterflies were flitting from one wild flower to another. I chased an especially big one, brightly colored and just hovering outside of my reaching fingers. I wanted to catch that butterfly; I wanted to show it to my mother and daddy. I kept following its flighty path, drawing closer to it, almost reaching it, almost, almost....

"Kids, get up, now!" Mother's insistent voice came ever closer as I left the meadow and opened my eyes. I squinted against the yellow light glowing in my room. "I know it's early, but we have a lot to do. Now get up and get dressed. Eileen will meet us at Zobel's. You can bring the lantern down when you have finished dressing," Mother said, as she sat the lantern on a chair. "I've got to rouse Ron. He's sleeping pretty hard this morning too." She left my room and turned to

Country Splendor

the right to go to the boys' room. I heard his door creak as she opened it, and then I heard her calling his name.

"I'm awake, mom," he answered.

"I'll have some coffee ready for you in the kitchen."

"Thanks, mom. I'll be right down." The door creaked again and mother's footsteps retreated down the hall making soft creaking sounds as she moved down the stairs.

"The one morning I would like to sleep late and I have to get up early," I complained to my pillow. But I pulled myself up, climbed out of bed and began to dress.

Ron stopped at my door on the way to the stairs and said, "Good morning, sleepy head. How are you doing this morning?"

"Good morning, Ronny. What are you going to do with that owl you shot last night?" I asked.

"Dad said I should have it stuffed, but I think he was just pulling my leg. I'll probably end up feeding it to the pigs," Ron said.

"To the pigs? Do they even eat owls? I heard dad call them our garbage disposals once, but what's that?"

"Well, garbage is all the food we have left over that we don't eat. Even all the parts of the vegetables that we would throw away, the pigs will eat. You know that. You've seen us take the garbage pail down and dump it into their troughs," he said.

"But birds? They would eat birds?" I asked incredulously.

"I'll bet they would. They ate that chicken that died from that skunk attack. It's just what they do," Ron stated.

"Kids, are you going to take all morning? Hurry up now, I need your help." Mother sounded agitated.

"Coming," we called in unison, as I headed for the open doorway with the lantern in my hand, while Ron hurried down the stairs ahead of me, touching every other step.

The time flew in the frenzied activities of completing the chores and eating a hasty breakfast, as well as preparing some food to take over to the Zoble's. I dressed Bobby, and then I helped mother finish up in the kitchen. "Is daddy coming over with us?" I asked mother, as she packed the last pie into a large basket.

"He wouldn't stay away. I made him promise that he would only supervise," she said.

"What does supervise mean?" I asked.

I heard an exasperated sigh slip from mother's lips at another of my questions, but she answered anyway, "It's when someone just watches to make sure everything is done right, but doesn't do any of the work themselves, understand? And that is the last question I want to hear out of you this morning. It's time to go now. Let's put the last of this food in your red wagon to pull across to Zoble's. Will you see if Ronald is ready to go?"

"Yes, I am ready mom," Ronald answered, as he entered the kitchen from the front room. "Dad told me to tell you that he's heading over and will see you over there. Is there anything else you need me to do right now?"

"Yes, I want you to help Helen pull this wagon of food over, being careful with it. You will have to take it down the driveway, down the road to their driveway and up to their house that way. I'll grab Bobby and follow dad across the yard. We shall see the two of you when you get over there. Okay?" She didn't wait, nor expect an answer from us, as she crossed the front room to where Bobby waited on the floor. She scooped him up in her arms and left by way of the front door, stepping off the front stoop unto our yard. "Hubie!" she called to him, as he was crossing the road. Hearing her, he stopped and waited for her to catch up. They crossed the ditch to the neighbors yard, together.

"Come on, Ron, let's go," I urged, as I maneuvered the wagon through the kitchen door and onto the back porch by myself, anxious to get underway.

"Wait!" Ronald yelled from the kitchen, where he had been washing his hands at the basin. "Don't you try to handle that wagon by yourself! You'll tip it over, and then we will be in big trouble."

I realized that he had a point. It was piled high and there were several steps to take it down. But as I waited, I was overcome by a sense of urgency to get on my way. I had the wagon pulled right to the edge of the porch just as Ron came through the doorway and yelled, "Wait right there, Helen, I will take that off the porch." He handled the

Country Splendor

wagon carefully; working it off the porch, and down the steps. A sigh of relief escaped my lips when we were finally on our way.

The sun was up, and one could feel that it was going to be a hot day. I was barefoot, as usual, and the road felt extra warm beneath my feet. We were almost to the point of pulling the wagon into the Zobel's driveway, when I noticed movement further down the road. As I focused my eyes on the movement of the tall grass in the ditch, I saw the raised black and white stripped tail of a skunk. "Look, Ronny, look," I shouted, as I pointed to where the skunk was just passing beneath the barbed wire fence, heading into Olson's woods. Ron looked in the direction I was pointing, and saw it just as it disappeared into some bushes.

"Bet that's the one that we tracked all over the country a while back. Guess we didn't scare it off, after all. Helen, can you take this wagon on up to the house by yourself? I'm going to tell dad, and see if Herbert and I can try to get that critter," Ron said, as he started towards the barnyard area where the men would be gathering together, waiting for the others to arrive.

"This should be fun," I said. "Those two take off they'll be gone all day. Wish I could follow and watch them get it."

I was almost to the kitchen door when I heard girls' voices behind me. I stopped and looked around. Coming up the driveway were my sister Eileen and Betty Olson.

"Hey!" I yelled.

"Hey, yourself," they called back, quickly catching up to me

"Did you come through the woods?" I asked

"Yes, why?" Eileen asked.

"I was wondering if you saw the skunk?"

"What skunk?" Betty asked.

"When Ron and I were at the edge of the road, I saw a skunk crossing the road and going into your woods. Ronny went to ask dad if he and Herbert could try to catch up to it and kill it. He thinks it's the same one that got our chicken and eggs the night of the storm," I answered.

"What you want to bet that if dad lets them go, they will be gone all day!" Eileen exclaimed.

"Funny, that's what I said," I said. "But he did kill an owl last night that was after the chickens."

"He did? Really?" Eileen asked, as I nodded my head. "What did he do with it?"

"He said that they were going to feed it to the pigs," I answered.

"Too bad he couldn't have it stuffed and mounted, so he would have proof that he finally killed a chicken killer," Betty laughed.

"Yes, a good idea," Eileen said.

"Dad said that too, but Ron said he thought dad was just pulling his leg," I said. "Anyway, Pigs don't eat birds, do they?"

"Of course they would. They eat anything," Eileen replied.

"Wish we could follow the boys though, I would love to see a skunk hunt," I said.

"You don't know if dad and Mr. Zobel will allow the boys to even go hunting now. They will probably want them to stay and help with the harvesting. Anyway, that's not something girls get to do, that's for sure," Eileen said, as we pulled up to the kitchen stoop. I left Eileen and Betty with the wagon, as I darted up the steps and into the kitchen looking for mother.

The kitchen was empty. I stopped a moment to look around. It was a smaller kitchen than most of the farm houses had. Instead of a large kitchen used for eating, as well as cooking and canning, Mr. Zobel had built a separate room to eat in, which was just past the kitchen.

I admired this kitchen that was decorated so prettily. To the left of the door, leading into the kitchen, was a cupboard that held a white sink that actually drained into a large pail that sat underneath, behind green trimmed, white doors. A small, hand pump was installed to one side of the sink, allowing water to be pumped right into the kitchen, from the well. Above the sink, was a window that could be opened outward, by a hand crank at the side. Lovely, flower, printed curtains, framed the window. Past that cupboard stood the stove.

The kitchen stove was much fancier than ours, with white, porcelain warming ovens, above the cooking area, and a covered, porcelain basin,

Country Splendor

at one end, which held water that was heated by the stove. The oven door was of that same white porcelain. Pretty, colored, flowers with intertwining stems and leaves decorated all of the white porcelain.

Built in cupboards painted white with green trimming, ran along the back wall, with a pantry door at the end. A long, low, worktable stood along the far wall, just past the door of the pantry, with built-in shelves above it, that held an assortment of jars in different shapes, sizes, and colors. An arched doorway leading into the eating parlor finished that side of the room.

To the right of the outside door, stood an icebox, and past that were bookshelves that held cookbooks and miscellaneous knick-knacks.

I walked into the eating parlor, taking in the lovely sight. The attractive, oval, dark wood dining table, with eight matching chairs around it, sat in the center of the room. In the middle of the table was a vase of artfully arranged, fresh flowers, as well as a fancy, kerosene lamp with a flowered shade.

Along the wall to the left was a tall, china cupboard with glass-enclosed doors that held an array of beautiful, fine china and crystal. The tall windows on the back wall were framed with white Priscilla curtains, held back with matching sashes, to let the light in.

On into the front room I stepped, following the sound of female voices in deep conversation. Mother was sitting on the deep, green, horsehair sofa, straight ahead of me, holding Bobby on her lap. To her right was a dark, wooden, round table with an elegant, Aladdin lamp sitting on it, along with a crystal, candy dish of a deep, burgundy color. On the other side of the table was a matching deep, green, over stuffed armchair where Mrs. Zobel sat, holding a teddy bear out towards Bobby's out stretched hands. A handsome, round, parlor stove, a baby grand piano and a white, wicker, rocking chair completed the furnishings on mother's left side. In the middle of the floor was a hooked rug of a variation of colors, with the greens and burgundy's being the dominant colors. White, Priscilla curtains also framed the double, front room, window that was behind the chair where Mrs. Zoble sat, as well as the single window behind where mother sat.

A dark, wooden door to the left took one out onto a rather large, covered, front porch, where a hanging swing and several more wicker chairs, and a table, made a comfortable setting. Just passed the doorway from the eating parlor, to ones right, was a doorway that led into the master bedroom. Just past that, a stairway wound its way up to the second floor and to two more bedrooms.

I imagined myself walking into a Queen's home each time I entered this house. Not even our wealthy, German grandparents lovely, two-story home in Rice Lake, seemed as grand as this one. I always felt a little like the poor Cinderella in her stepmother's fine house, that Eileen read to me about. Except that Mrs. Zoble was very kind and always had something special to offer me. She was a small woman, fair-haired and blue eyed, and was always dressed in crisp, soft colored, dresses. She wore a frilly apron over her dress whenever she worked in the kitchen.

As I crossed to where the lady's sat, Mrs. Zoble looked at me with a smile that made me feel welcomed to her home. I said hello to her, and then turning to mother, I said, "Eileen and Betty are waiting outside the kitchen with the wagon. They would like to know where you would like the food put, and Ronny is hoping that dad will let him hunt down the skunk."

Mother looked at me rather strangely and asked, "What skunk?"

"The one I saw crossing into Olson's woods. He thinks it the same one that got our chickens," I said in one breath.

Mrs. Zobel said, "Helen, Gertrude is upstairs. Will you ask her to come down and help the girls with the food? She'll know where to put it."

"Okay," I answered, as I headed for the stairway and proceeded to go to Gertrude's room with the message from her mother. I never knew how Gertrude would react. Sometimes she was friendly to me and other times she treated me like a pest. But I rapped on her door and delivered her mother's message.

She answered without opening the door, "I'll be there in a minute."

Country Splendor

I turned around and headed back down the stairs. At the bottom, I turned to go to the kitchen doorway, where the girls waited, but mother called me back into the room where she was. "Helen, stay here with Bobby for a few minutes. I will help the girls with the food, and then I would like a word with your dad. I won't be long. Will you be alright, Audrey?" Mother directed the last inquiry to Mrs. Zobel. She was always worrying about her health.

"Of course, I'll be fine. In fact, I'll go with you to the kitchen. Your pies will fit into the icebox, I think. Here, Helen, Bobby can play with this bear. Why don't you let him play on the rug with it, and just watch him, to make sure he doesn't try to go up the stairs?" Audrey rose and followed mother out of the room. Gertrude came bounding down the stairs, following her mother through the eating parlor and into the kitchen. I noticed that she was wearing one of her prettier dresses and had her hair combed in a fluff around her face.

"Wonder who she's all dolled up for?" I whispered to Bobby. He gave me a big grin and sat down on the bear, rolling over on his side with a laugh.

I moved over to the windows where I could watch for the arrival of the others. Vehicles of various sizes and makes began turning into the driveway, and it looked as if everyone had arrived at the same time. I wanted to see if any children my age would be here, so to get a better look at the ones arriving, I stepped out onto the porch. I was so engrossed in what I was looking for that I totally forgot Bobby, playing on the floor in the parlor. I watched until everyone had driven in and out of my range of vision. I turned back into the parlor and looked for Bobby, who was nowhere in sight. "Oh, no," I said to myself. I crossed to the stairs, and seeing the bear that had been discarded on the landing, I knew he must have climbed them. Sure enough, I found him in Gertrude's room. She had left her door open, and he had crossed to the little dresser, and was busy pulling bottles and hair ribbons and other girls' things, off onto the floor.

"Bobby, no!" I shouted at him. He looked around at me and dropped a container of hairpins that he had managed to reach, the contents now spilling all over the floor. "Look at what you've done!

Bad boy!" I said, as I started picking up the items that were strewn all over. He mustn't have taken me seriously, because he kept reaching for other things, until I grabbed him and pulled him down beside me. I was frantically working at replacing all the stuff from the floor, back to the dresser, when I heard a gasp from the doorway.

Gertrude came storming into her room, shouting at me, "What are you doing in my room, with my things!" She was noticeably upset, and I understood why. I tried to explain, but she just grabbed me by my arms, lifted me up to my feet, and told me to take my brat of a brother out of there.

I did as I was told, took Bobby by the hand and led him out of her room and toward the stairs. He said, "Bear, bear," as he pulled free of my hand, and dashed down the hall, with me in hot pursuit. Just as I reached him and grabbed for his collar, he fell, head first, down the stairs, tumbling until he lay at the bottom in a heap.

I raced down the stairs after him, and reached him, just as Eileen and Betty came in through the parlor doors to see what created all the noise. Seeing Bobby lying there, elicited an "Oh no!" from them, as they bent down and began to examine him. He must have picked up on their frightened voices, because he began to wail and fuss, where before he just looked bewildered.

Mother had gone out to talk to dad, so it was Mrs. Zobel who looked him over for signs of injury. She found a red bump forming on his forehead. Eileen picked him up and took him to the kitchen, where Mrs. Zobel placed a cold cloth filled with ice, on his bump. He made more of a fuss about that cold cloth than he had the roll down the stairs. I hung around the edges of the activity, wondering what mother was going to do to me when she found out what had happened. Other women were in the kitchen as well, and they were all making a fuss over Bobby. I think that bothered him more than his bumpy roll down the stairs. He did not know some of them, and being a shy little guy, he wanted only people he knew around him. He whimpered and reached out to Eileen, who put a comforting arm around him. I wanted to take him out of there, but I knew that was impossible. I went out looking for mother instead. Maybe, if I explained to her how this accident

Country Splendor

happened, before she came in and heard the other ladies versions, I could save myself from a spanking. It was worth a try.

Beyond the back porch, I noticed several boys and girls about my size, in a game of catch the butterflies. Remembering my early morning dream, my attention became focused on the gaily-colored, winged creatures, and all thoughts of finding my mother was forgotten. I ran with the other children around the flowered bushes, delighting in the sight of so many wonderful butterflies. We shouted and laughed, while dancing and jumping in our attempts to catch a colorful prize.

The day was over before I was ready for it to end. It had been a delightful day, after all. Full of fun, good food, and new friends. Mothers began rounding up their children and piling them, along with empty food containers, into the travel conveyance they had arrived in. The men shook hands, and wished each other well, climbed in with their family and took their leave. As quickly as the yard had filled up in the morning, it emptied even quicker in the late afternoon.

Returning to the kitchen, I found our red wagon waiting outside the door, already loaded with empty containers. I had not talked to mother through out the day and the earlier worries suddenly came flooding back. Because she had not come looking for me, I guessed that Bobby must have had no lingering effects from his tumble down the stairs. Hope rose in my chest, as the thought materialized that perhaps nothing more would come from that incident. Or was she just waiting to get me home?

The ladies had cleaned the kitchen of all evidence of food and food containers. Even the floor was swept clean. Friendly voices of light banter could be heard coming from the front porch. I walked in that direction, mindful not to make any noise. I wanted to assess the situation before drawing attention to myself. I was half way across the front room, when I heard an upstairs door open and Eileen's voice exclaiming, "I can hardly believe they got away with that! I told you we should have followed them to see what they were up to."

"And if we did, would we have been able to see anything? Those are thick woods with heavy underbrush. I doubt if we could have followed closely enough to have seen anything anyway," Gertrude said indignantly. "Sometimes I almost wish I would have been a boy. They seem to have all the fun!"

The girls were on the stairs and heading my way. I wanted to remain unseen so I could continue to overhear their conversation. They talked more freely if they did not know I was around. I ducked down and stepped as far behind the piano as I could. Eileen continued the conversation with a laugh, "Did you get a whiff of how they smelled when they came in? Even if they did not get that skunk, it sure as shooting got them! And did you notice how quickly the women got them out of the house? You can almost smell them yet."

As they headed for the kitchen Gertrude asked, "What was that your mother said they were to wash themselves and their clothes in? I thought she said tomato juice. Can you imagine taking a bath in tomato juice? I wonder what your house smelled like by the time they were finished?"

"And what it stills smells like. Knowing them, their clothes are probably piled in the middle of the kitchen floor. I just hope no one expects me to wash them! Seems like that's all we do, clean up after men," Eileen complained, as the screen door slammed shut behind their departing figures.

I crept out from my hiding place and began to follow them, but the gales of laughter coming from the front porch sounded much more interesting. I turned and headed in that direction instead. Peering through the opened doorway, I could see mother and Audrey, with Bobby between them, relaxing in the bench swing, facing out towards the yard. Dad and Emil were sitting at the edge of the porch in front of them, with their backs against porch posts, facing each other. They each held a tall glass of water in one hand while the other rested on a bent knee. Emil looked hot and sweaty, his Scandinavian tall, lean body a contrast to dad's German stocky and somewhat shorter frame. They both were handsome men in their own way. Emil had Vikings leaner features, high cheekbones with a full mouth, and darker blue-green eyes, where dad's face was square jawed, with a wider mouth and larger sky blue eyes.

Country Splendor

"I was surprised you two let the boys go after that skunk, with all the work there was to do today," Mother said. As my attention was drawn to them, I noticed the contrast between the two ladies on the swing. Mother was five foot one, with a slender top and wider hips. Her hair was dark, almost black, thick and curled around her face. Her large dark brown eyes looked as if they were always smiling. Her cupid bow lips added to her attractiveness. Her face was almost heart shaped, ending in a gently pointed chin. People remarked on how much I resembled mother. Why then, did I feel so plain?

Audrey, Mrs. Zobel to us children, was even more petite than mother. With her golden hair pulled back in a bun, she looked pale and delicate.

"Well," Emil said, addressing his remarks to the ladies. "We had a good amount of men here today and I don't think those two boys were even missed. They wanted to finish what they had tried to do the other day, and Hubert and I decided to let them go for it. The chase that wily skunk gave them will be something they will talk about for a long time. Especially since it managed to get away from them again. Even if it left a strong impression of itself behind!" He exclaimed with renewed laughter, with the other's joining in.

"Vell, mother, guess it's time we headed for home," Dad said, looking up at mother with a warm smile accentuating his dimples.

"Yes, we need to get over there and see how those boys are doing. I can imagine what we will find when we get there."

Eileen and Gertrude rounded the corner of the house just then, coming up to where the folks were. "Eileen, round up Helen, and the two of you get the wagon and start for home. Dad, Bobby and I will be along shortly."

"I don't know where she is, I haven't seen her for quite some time," Eileen said.

"I'm right here," I said, as I stepped into view.

"Well, come on then, let's get the wagon," she ordered, in that big sisterly way of hers.

As we pulled the wagon up to our kitchen porch, we heard the boys talking between bouts of laughter. Eileen opened the door, with me at her back. The smell that assailed us was almost over-whelming. The boys were in clean clothes, but the skunk scented ones were lying in a heap on the floor, just as Eileen predicted.

"Ron, you had better get these clothes out to the back porch, and open up the doors and windows to air this place out before mom and dad get home. They will be here shortly," Eileen informed him. He looked over at her and then at the clothes at her feet.

"What's wrong with you taking them out? I've just managed to clean enough of the smell off of myself to stand being near myself!" He laughed, as he slapped his friend on his shoulder.

"Okay, I'll do it this once, but you owe me," she said, as she picked up the offensive smelling clothes and held them away from herself, as far as she could, while carrying them out to the porch, and depositing them in a heap to one side of the doorway. "I can't imagine ever making them smell good enough to wear again!" she stated, as she returned to the kitchen.

The boys had the kitchen windows opened and were whipping towels around, trying to direct the offensive smelling air out of the windows.

"So what happened?" I asked them.

"What do you mean, what happened? You can surely smell what happened," Ron said.

"We know you were sprayed, but how did you get close enough to get sprayed, but not able to kill it?" Eileen asked.

Herbert turned from his fanning and directed his answer to Eileen, who was standing with one hand on her hip, and looking at them with that 'I can't believe you guys' look on her face. "We found the skunks tracks and followed him through the bushes, right along the creek. We had no idea of how far ahead of us it was, and we were so intent on not loosing the trail that we didn't look far enough ahead of our selves," he explained.

Ron clarified the story with his version. "We must have tracked it for hours through underbrush and briars, sometimes having to skirt around the briar patches and picking up the trail on the far side. We were clawing our way through some heavy undergrowth, bent over to

Country Splendor

avoid low hanging branches, when suddenly; there it was directly in front of us and primed for war. Its tail was up and we were sprayed before we could react. It was all we could do to hold our breath and head for the creek to wash our faces, trying to clear the stuff from our eyes." He choked with the memory.

Eileen and I were nearly bent over double, laughing at our imagined sight of them, and she remarked, between sobs and giggles, "So, ha, ha, the skunk, ha, ha, had the last laugh, hee, hee, once again! Ha, ha, ha."

Herbert's grin lit up his face as he watched Eileen, doubled over with glee. Ron tried hard to remain serious, even though his eyes twinkled as he replied, "Sure, you can laugh, you weren't the ones suffocating in skunk perfume!" And with that remark we laughed even harder.

"Skunk perfume! Ha, ha, ha," I echoed, continuing to enjoy the merriment.

"By the time we could function again, it was gone and we decided to head for home," Herbert finished with a chuckle.

Eileen couldn't help snickering, as she asked, "So, are you guys ready to agree that the skunk is too smart for you?"

"Never!" They said as one, as they threw an arm around each other's shoulder. "Never say die! That's our motto!"

"Vell! Looks like you two survived your initiation into the battle of man versus skunk," Dad said, as he entered the room with mother and Bobby following. He fanned the air as if to ward off the lingering odor. "A bit strong smelling in here yet."

We laughed at Bobby's reaction to the odor, as he put both dimpled hands over his nose and mouth and said, "Bad dog!"

"That wasn't the dog, Bobbie, that was a skunk!"

"Bad skunk!" he said, running from the room.

Dad chuckled deeply as he walked over to the boys and gave them each a handshake. "You may have been bested but you're not beaten. That's real courage."

Following that kind of praise from dad you could see both boys backs straighten a little more and their heads held up a bit higher.

CHAPTER SEVENTEEN

Summer was fast coming to a close and school would soon begin. I had heard Eileen and the other girls talking about it the last day of harvesting. They were discussing the issues involved, the new clothes they hoped to get, and if there would be any new boys at school that year. I envied them, as I wanted to go to school too.

This was the subject that was on my mind as I entered the kitchen one morning; a couple of weeks after the harvesting of the grains were completed. I heard the folks talking about Roy. Mother was sitting at the table, with a cup of coffee in one hand and a hanky in the other, which she would dab against her eyes every few minutes.

"Listen, Verna," Dad said, "there is no use worrying about him. He is doing what he wants to do and he will have to face the consequences of his decisions. Hopefully he is smart enough to keep himself out of trouble. I've been listening to the news everyday on the radio. There has been no mention of a lost boy or anyone in trouble. Surely, your mother will let us know when he reaches her place."

"Shouldn't he be there by now? I expected a letter by now. How long will it take for a letter to reach us, anyway? She must have received my letter alerting her to the fact that he was headed down that way," Mother said, dabbing at her eyes again and taking a long drink from her cup.

"We may hear today. I'll have the girls watch for the mailman. In the meantime, we should make a trip to town for supplies. School

Country Splendor

will start soon, shouldn't we be getting some things for the kids?" Dad asked. My ears perked up at the thought that maybe I would get something new. I loved presents and new things.

"The kids will need new shoes for sure," Mother answered, sounding relieved to have other things to concentrate on. "Ron has filled out this last summer and grown a few inches, his pants are above his ankles. He needs a couple of new shirts, and a heavy winter coat, too. Eileen will need a couple of dresses, a coat and a pair of shoes. They will all need some new winter underwear. Probably should get them each a pair of galoshes to wear when it rains or snows, as well. Eileen will be walking a good mile each day, to the Langlade School. Ron, and Roy if he comes home, will be catching the school bus into Barron at the corner. It's hard to believe that they will be starting their freshman year of high school already. I wonder if they will need some school supplies as well?" Mother reached for her tablet and pencil that was on the table beside her. She turned to a clean page and began writing down a list.

I had been wondering why my two brothers' were in the same grade. I knew there were two years differences in their ages. I decided that this might be a good time to find out why, so I asked, "Mama, how come Roy and Ron are in the same grade?"

She gave me a long look, as if she was upset for being interrupted, but then she softened, as she saw that I was seriously curious about this. "Well, it did not start that way," she said. "You see, Ron is two years older, so he started school when he was six and Roy was four. Roy was always the curious one, so when Ron would bring his school books home, to practice reading, Roy would be right beside him, listening to him and asking question. Ron would show him the words and pronounce them out loud, and Roy would repeat them. The same when it came to math, you know, counting and take-away, like Eileen teaches you?"

"Oh, you mean, Ron taught Roy like Eileen teaches me?"

"Yes, exactly like that. Roy remembered everything, so when he was old enough to start school, the teacher noticed that he already could read all the books she taught from. She gave him a test, and when she saw that he was already at the high end of the second grade level in his skills, she put him in the same grade as Ron. They have been in the same grade ever since."

"So if I learn everything that Eileen knows, can I be in the same grade as her?"

"I'm afraid that is too much of a stretch. After all, Eileen is five years older than you. But you keep working at it, and you will always be one of the top ones of your class."

Dad sat listening to us, and he said, "You know, I'm not sure that was the best thing that happened with Roy, his head has always been ahead of his years. Probably one reason he thinks he can take on the world now, and do as he likes." He took another sip of his coffee before continuing, "I've been thinking about taking that yearling bull calf into town and selling him. He should bring enough to pay for the things the kids need. How about Helen? She's not in school yet, but she has grown some over the summer. Shouldn't she have some new clothes too?"

Mother looked at me, listening hopefully by her side. "I need to go through Eileen's old dresses and see what will fit Helen now. I've saved the best of them. Probably will have to alter them some, as Helen is much thinner than Eileen was, but that won't be hard to do." I sighed, and turned away. I didn't need to hear more. It was rare to get something new to wear. Either Eileen's old clothes were made over to fit me, or a neighbors' child's clothing, that they had outgrown, was given to mother for me. After suffering through the last depression, mother was very careful not to 'squander' any money, on anything that we could do without. Her favorite saying was, 'we will make do, or do without.' As a result, she rarely threw anything away. If there was a way to recycle it, it was used in a new way, or it was saved until a use was found for it.

I made my morning jaunt to the little house outside, and while sitting there in the early morning light, I thought to myself, 'What if I pray for some new clothes? Maybe just one new dress that was bought just for me, that no one else had worn first?' But I wasn't sure how to pray. I had been taught one prayer, 'Now I lay me down to sleep,

Country Splendor

I pray the Lord my soul to keep, if I should die before I wake, I pray the Lord my soul to take.' It bothered me even saying that prayer, because I thought, 'I don't want to die in my sleep. Why should I pray like that? If I just talk to Him, would He hear me?' I decided to try it. "Lord, if I try really hard to be a good girl, every day, and do what my mommy and daddy say I should do, could I please have a new dress? One bought at a store? Please?"

A meadowlark could be heard, singing to the rising sun. I listened, and wondered if God spoke to people through his creatures? Mama told me that God made every living thing. I wondered who God was? I equated Him to someone like Santa Claus, who could see everything I did, and if I were bad, he wouldn't give me any presents.

'But can God talk to me through a bird?' I wondered. I liked to think He had.

I had lots of questions and I wanted answers. Eileen would read to me, and tried to teach me the words, and I would repeat them after her. Maybe, if I tried very hard to read, I could find some of the answers in books. Mama had this real big book that sat on a table in the front room. Eileen called a Bible, God's book, and she showed me the names of all of our relatives that mama had written down in it. She wrote our names, as well, and the dates we were born. It was just squiggly lines to me, but if other people could figure out what it meant, surely I could. It was hard being so little and so young.

Heading back to the house, I met Ron as he came from finishing the chores at the barn. "Ronny, do you think I could go to school, too?"

"You will go to school one day, but you are too young yet," he said.

"But I want to go now," I said, stomping my foot for emphasis.

"There are rules and one rule is you have to be six years old before you go to school. Don't be in such a hurry to grow up. Getting bigger means you will have to work harder. Right now, you can play and enjoy yourself." I thought he sounded wishful, like he wished he had never grown up. I followed him into the kitchen, wondering about many things.

"Breakfast is on the table. Wash up and sit down, and eat before it gets cold," Mother said.

I dashed to the washbasin, but Ron beat me to it, so I had to wait for him to wash first. 'Getting bigger means I won't have to always be last,' I thought to myself.

Breakfast was over, the kitchen chores were done, and dad and Ron had rounded up the bull calf to take to town. Mother was dressing Bobby, as I walked up to her and asked, "Can I go to town with you and dad?"

"Not this time, Helen. Dad has to remove the back seat of the car, so the calf can ride to town in that space. Ron needs to go too, and there is just enough room for him to sit in the front with dad and me. You and Eileen need to take care of Bobby for me," she said.

"But it's been years since I got to go to town," I fussed.

"Last month you got to go with dad, remember? Anyway, there is no room for you this trip. You be good and help your sister, and we will bring you back a surprise, okay?"

"What kind of a surprise?" I asked.

"If I told you, it wouldn't be a surprise, would it?" she answered. "I promise it will be something you will really like. I need you to watch for the mailman today. As soon as he comes by, you check on the mail for me. Bring it in and leave it on the table where I can find it. I am expecting a letter from my mother. Maybe, we will find out something about Roy, whether he has made it there or not."

Eileen entered the kitchen and approached mother. "Mom, I heard you and dad talking about our school supplies and clothing. Should I make a pattern of my foot, so you can buy me some new shoes?"

"Yes, that's a good idea. Would you like black or brown ones?" Mother asked.

"Wish I could have white ones, but I know they are hard to keep nice. Maybe, one day I could have a white pair," Eileen said softly, to no one in particular. She turned her face to mother and said, "Black ones are okay. It really doesn't matter."

"Do I get shoes, mama?" I asked, hopefully.

"Yes. Eileen, make a pattern of Helen's foot, too," she said.

Country Splendor

"Come here, Helen. We will take a piece of mother's letter paper, it's big enough for your foot." She tore a piece of paper from the pad mother had been writing on. She laid it on the floor and told me to put my right foot on it. I did as she asked, but she wasn't satisfied with the angle.

"Not that way, turn your foot so it is completely on the paper. We need paper sticking away from your foot on all sides. Here, let me move your foot into the proper place," she said, as she lifted my foot up, and turned it, trying to get it into the position she wanted it. I almost fell down, as she twisted it around.

"You are breaking my foot off!" I shouted.

"Then let me move it, here turn your body so your foot will be in the right direction."

When she finally had it on the paper to her satisfaction, she took the pencil and ran it around my foot, touching the side of my foot as she went. When she was done, she had me pick up my foot, and there was a print of my foot on the paper. I was delighted. "That looks like the prints I make in the mud after it rains," I exclaimed.

"That's right. Now we will get the shears and cut it out. Mother can use it to measure the new shoes by, so they will fit your feet. Once I have yours done, I will do one of my foot."

"Can I draw the line around your foot?" I asked.

"No, you don't know how to do it right, and I want to be sure it will be a good pattern. I will use the newspaper to make my footprint pattern," she said.

I watched her carefully, so I would know how to make good patterns. It looked very simple to me. I couldn't understand why she made such a big thing of it. "Can I make more patterns of my feet from the extra paper?" I asked.

"Go ahead, Helen," Mother said. "It will give her something to do, Eileen." Eileen looked doubtful, but she passed the remaining paper to me, along with the pencil and scissors. I was excited with a new project to do. I drew around my foot as best I could, although it wanted to move, as I traced around it. When I lifted up my foot, my pattern looked a little strange, but I cut it out anyway, very proud of my creation. I took it to daddy and showed him my footprint. He had just came in from helping Ron with the bull calf and sat down heavily in a kitchen chair. He reached for my piece of paper and proceeded to look it over. "What's this?" dad asked.

"My footprint," I said, as if that should be obvious.

"Vell, vell, that would take one funny shoe to fit that foot," he chuckled. I wasn't sure what he found so funny, but I loved to make him laugh, so if he thought my footprints were something to laugh about, I would make more. Once I got tired of cutting out prints of my feet I tried making prints of my hands. They made daddy laugh even harder. Working on another print, I found that I was sitting right in the middle of another sheet of newspaper. I traced around my bottom and showed daddy my seat pattern. He laughed so hard at that one that he held his hand over his mouth, until he had himself under control once again.

"Hubert, it's time we left," Mother said, as she picked up her purse, along with the footprint patterns Eileen had laid beside it, and headed for the door. Dad eased himself up from his chair, and followed her out. I ran behind, watching them from the back porch, as they climbed into dads Chevy, beside Ron. The calf moved restlessly in the back, and seemed to fall down as the car lurched forward and headed out of the driveway. I ran back through the kitchen and front room, stepping out onto the front porch, where I watched the car as it headed up the hill, to the corner, turned and disappeared from sight. I was filled with longing to be with them, and filled with excitement at the same time, for the promised surprise I would receive when they returned home. Turning back into the house, I headed for the kitchen to resume making patterns.

There, on the floor, in the middle of my paper and cut outs, was my little brother, Bobby, having a great time tearing up my paper. "Hey, what are you doing?" I yelled, as I headed towards my startled, baby brother. As I tried to pull him away from my things, he grabbed at the paper with two determined hands, and made squeals of distress. Eileen came running in from the front room, where she had been reading another one of her books, checking to see what the problem was.

"What's wrong with Bobby?" Eileen demanded to know.

"He got into my paper and ripped it up. What's left is all crinkled into a mess," I complained, as Bobby continued to fuss and reach for more paper.

"Why don't you let him play with it? It's ruined now anyway. I will see you get some of tomorrow's paper before it's used as fire-starter paper." She placated me with that promise, and I acquiesced, turning and heading out to the barn to look for my cats.

Some time later, hunger pangs directed my attention back to mother's kitchen, for something to eat. I entered the kitchen, noticing the mess of paper still laying all over the floor. Then, I noticed how quiet the house was. Entering the front room, I saw Bobby lying in his bed, with a bottle held firmly against his chest, and his head turned to one side. His gentle breathing told me that he was fast asleep. I tiptoed around him, looking for my sister. She was curled up in dad's armchair, with a book in her hands, completely engrossed in the story she was reading. When I touched her arm to get her attention, her startled yell woke Bobby.

"What are you doing?" she asked, greatly agitated.

"I'm hungry. I was trying to get your attention so I wouldn't wake Bobby up," I answered.

"Well, it did not work did it? You scared me half to death!"

"It's not my fault you weren't paying attention," I reasoned. "Can I make myself a sandwich?"

"Go ahead and make me one too, while you are at it."

"But I'm not suppose to use a knife. How will I cut the bread?" I asked.

"Oh shoot! All right, I'll be right there to cut the bread for you. Go ahead and get the butter and peanut butter ready," she said, as she turned back to her book, looking for the place where she was interrupted.

I went to the kitchen and retrieved the butter from the icebox, then went into the pantry for the peanut butter. When both were placed on the table, along with the loaf of mother's freshly, baked bread, a sharp knife, and a butter knife, I went to the door of the kitchen to see where

Eileen was. Evidently, she was back into her book, so I headed across the room once more. Sure enough, there she was, as deeply engrossed in her book as before. Should I touch her again, or just talk to her? Bobby had settled back down, and I did not want to disturb him a second time. I looked at her intensely, thinking that maybe I could get her attention subconsciously. I thought real hard, 'Look at me, I am here, Eileen, I am here.' After several minutes I realized that would not work, so I whispered close to her ear. She jumped even more than the first time, and shrieked even louder than before. I jumped back, expecting to get hit, making sure I was out of her reach.

"Darn you, Helen!" she said, as she turned an angry face towards my retreating figure.

"You aren't coming!" I said. "I'm going to tell mom you said a bad word!"

"Darn's not that bad and besides, you made me say it. Now get back to the kitchen, and pick up the paper you left on the floor. I'll be right there."

"You said that last time, and you never came. Come with me this time so I can have my sandwich, and then I'll clean up the mess on the floor," I said, "and it shouldn't be my mess cause you told me to let Bobby play with it."

"Okay, okay. Let's get this over with, so I can be rid of you," she said, as she put her book down on the side table, and rose to her feet to follow me. This time Bobby was sitting up in his bed, rubbing his eyes as if they were still full of sleep. As she passed his crib, Eileen laid him back down, putting his half empty bottle back into his mouth. He sucked at it greedily, relaxing back into a prone position. His eyes closed once again, as we continued into the kitchen.

Eileen proceeded to cut large pieces of bread, while I began slathering them liberally with butter and covering that with peanut butter. "I'll get us some milk to go with it," Eileen said, as she headed towards the icebox, slipping on the loose paper on the floor. She almost fell, just barely catching the back of a chair to stop her fall. "Will you get this mess picked up right now, before I break my neck!" Her yelling upset me.

Country Splendor

"You don't have to yell. I can hear you. And anyway, you will wake Bobby up again," I said, as I knelt down on the floor and started pulling all the paper pieces towards myself. Once I had it in a pile, I managed to pick it up, and put it in the kindling bin beside the kitchen stove. Having accomplished that chore, I sat down by the peanut buttered bread, and picking up a piece by its crust, I took a big bite and began to chew. "Mmm, this tastes so good!"

Eileen placed a glass of milk close to my place at the table, and I gratefully took a swallow to help wash the sticky mass down. She sat in the next chair, reached for a piece of the prepared bread, and proceeded to wash bites of it down with the milk, as well. We continued in silence until we were both satiated, then she broke the silence with, "How about running down to the mailbox and seeing if the mail man has been by yet?"

"Okay," I agreed. I licked the last of the peanut butter from my fingers as I headed out the door, running down the driveway to where the mailbox stood beside the road. I opened the door and peeked inside. One lone envelope lay there. I reached inside, closing my fingers around it, pulling it out. I studied it for a minute, wishing I could understand the writing on it. I gave up, shut the door of the mailbox, and started across the lawn to the front porch. The grass was getting high, making walking through it a chore. I realized that it had not been cut since Roy left home. It was his job to keep the front lawn cut, with dad's push mower, and Ron usually kept the area between the back of the house and the barn cut. Both had been neglected with Roy gone. There was just too much work that demanded attention first.

I hurried into the house, and to the chair where Eileen was once again ensconced; throwing the letter on the opened page she was staring at. It took a second for her to realize what dropped in her line of vision, but then she gave a little delighted sound, as she picked up the letter, and studied the return address on it. "It's from grandma Vaughan, all right. Mama is going to be so happy to see this. I wish I dared open it and read it right now," she stated wishfully.

"When will they be home?" I asked.

"Probably not until supper time. They had to sell that calf, and then shop for groceries, as well as for clothing, and shoes for us kids. That's quite a bit to do in one day."

"Would you read a story to me?" I begged.

"Not now. You can see I am interested in this one, and besides, I've read too far to start over," she stated flatly.

"What one is it?" I asked.

"Tom Sawyer and Huckleberry Finn," she answered.

"You have read that to me before. Just read to me from where you are and I'll remember the beginning."

"Well, okay. Sit there in mother's rocker and I'll read to you. This is where they have run off to take a trip on the Mississippi River, remember?" Eileen asked.

"Yes, I remember, they meet up with that black guy, right?"

"Yes, right," and she began reading where she had left off. I listened carefully to every word, pretending that I was right there with them on that raft.

The rest of the afternoon went quickly. Bobby had to be changed, fed, and given some toys to occupy his time on the floor, and then Eileen read again. How I loved to hear the stories in her books. 'When I'm big I am going to have lots of books,' I thought to myself.

Eileen had just finished the last page and laid the book down, when we heard the car coming down the road. I jumped up to see if it was the folks returning, and went dashing towards the back porch when I realized it was them. Eileen caught up with me, and practically pushed me off the porch, so she could get a look as well.

Dads blue Chevy pulled up to the garage, and stopped short of entering it. Ron stepped out first, and reached in to take mother's hand to help her out. Dad moved carefully out of the driver's side. They opened the back doors and began extracting the packages, each carrying their share. Even dad had a bundle in his arms. Eileen and I rushed out to help them. Once all the purchases were in on the kitchen table, and the folks had sat themselves down with fresh cups of coffee, the opening of packages began. Ron was aware of which packages

Country Splendor

held his things, and he had already grabbed them and was headed for the stairs.

Mother pulled a cotton dress, with a blue background, decorated with tiny pink, white, and rose-colored, flowers from the package. She shook it out for Eileen to see. Eileen grabbed it, holding it against herself. "It's just like the one I saw in the Sears and Roebuck Catalog!" she cried, as she began to dance around the floor with it. "You got it, you got it," she said, as if she just could not believe anything that wonderful could happen to her.

"I'm glad you like it Eileen. How about this one?" Mother asked, as she held up a second dress of a heavier weight material that was long sleeved. It was of a soft brown color, with yellow collar and cuffs.

Eileen reached out and felt of the material. "It's so soft," she said. She traded mother dresses, and held the second one against her to see how it would fit. "Can I try them on?"

"Let's look at the rest first, and then you can try them all on," Mother suggested, as she pulled a two-pieced snow suit of a warm, heavy, chocolate brown material from another package. A cap and mittens of the same color and material came with it.

"Oh, momma," Eileen breathed deeply, "it's just too pretty!" Then mother showed her the black shoes she had gotten for her, as well as the black goulashes to wear over them, when it rained or snowed. The shoes were of the best leather, built strong to withstand the harshest weather. They would last until she outgrew them. They came with black laces. A slip of heavy cotton, and half a dozen cotton panties followed. Then several pair of long white cotton stockings, and a pair of garters to hold them up with, was placed on her pile. She was busy looking everything over, as mother finally turned to me.

I had been standing quietly by, knowing that because I wasn't going to school yet, there would be nothing for me. I tried to be happy for my sister though, as I knew she worked hard all year, and she deserved some pretty things.

"Come here, Helen." Mother motioned with her hand for me to come to her. I slowly walked around the table to her side. "Guess what's in this package." she said, as she held it up to me.

"I don't know," I answered. I hadn't noticed the package that had been placed on a chair next to mother.

"Open it," she urged.

I reached out and pulled the top open. Reaching inside I felt soft warm material. I pulled it out and discovered a two-pieced snowsuit, of a dark blue color. It had a jacket with an attached hood that was trimmed with white fur like material, which was made to fit snuggly around the face. The long pants ended with snug cuffs around the ankles to keep the cold out, as did the sleeves of the jacket. A pair of lighter blue mittens finished the outfit. I "oohed" and "aawed!" at the loveliness of my new snowsuit, as I rubbed my face against the warm material.

Mother chuckled softly, as she handed me a box. I recognized it right away as a shoebox. I put my snowsuit on the chair, and then grabbed the box and lifted the lid, exposing a pair of black shoes, high topped and made to last. I was so excited and surprised that I could hardly believe my eyes. I sat right down to try the new shoes on. "Wait," Mother said, "put these on first." In her hands was several pair of new, long, white, stockings. I took one pair and pulled them on my legs, then pushed my feet into the shoes that mother had loosened for me. I asked her to tighten the laces and to tie them for me. As soon as she was done, I stood up and danced around the room. It felt funny to have something on my feet again, after going bare-foot all summer.

I thanked mother and daddy, as I hugged each article to me, and then gave them each a hug and a kiss.

"Your are welcome," Mother said, as she smiled at my delight. Daddy gave me a big hug and kissed my cheek, as I had kissed his.

Then, I remembered the letter. I ran for it, but Eileen had remembered first, and she was on her way back to the kitchen with it in her hands. "Let me give it to mom," I said. "I'm the one who got it from the mailbox."

Country Splendor

"I'm the one who thought of it first, and I have it, so I am going to give it to her," Eileen insisted. I trailed behind, knowing I was defeated and not happy about it.

"What's going on, girls?" Mother asked, as she heard the exchange.

"Here's the letter you have been waiting for, mom," Eileen said, as she thrust the envelope towards mother's eager hands.

"It's here, Hubie! A letter from mother, at last!" She quickly tore it open and unfolded the contents.

We all crowded around mother, anxious to hear what her letter from her mother had to say. Ronny walked into the kitchen just then, as if he had been drawn by the excitement the letter created. "What's up?" he asked.

Mother held the pages of grandmother's letter up for him to see, as she said, "A letter from my mother. Sit down all of you, and I will read it to you."

Once we were all settled around the table, she began to read. "Dear ones," she read, "I know you are anxious to hear the news about Roy. He arrived here almost one week to the day of when he took off from home. He arrived here before your letter did, Verna. When he knocked on the door, I recognized him, as someone I should know, but that it was your son, was the furthest thing from my mind. He said, "Hello Grandma, I'm Verna and Hubert's son, Roy. It's been years since I saw you last, but I've come to visit you for awhile, if you will have me."

Well, you could have knocked me over with a feather. All I could say was, "You came all the way from Wisconsin? By yourself?"

He said, "Yes, on my bike." I noticed a bike up against the porch post and assumed it was his.

He said, "I sure am tired and a bit hungry. Can I come in?" Of course I took him in and fixed him up some victuals and fed the boy. I didn't think I would ever be able to fill him up. He's as thin as a rail fence.

You mentioned that you would be willing to send money to pay for his way home, iffen he decides he wants to come home. If it's alright with you, I am willing to let him stay here for a spell, which it seems, that's what he wants to do right now. But I reckon it won't be long before he rethinks everything, and asks to go home. In the meantime, know that he is fine and we will keep in touch."

Mother stopped reading, wiped at a tear that slipped down her cheek and said, "Well, that's the gist of it. The rest is personal to me. Thank God that he is all right, and safe."

The next few minutes were filled with silence, as we all sat thinking our own thoughts. I noticed the word grandma used for food, victuals, now I understood where that word came from. And she used 'iffen' instead of 'if and when.' When I asked mother about it, she told me that people in the south, have a slightly different way of expressing themselves.

I looked at dad. He had a far-away look on his face, and ran his hand through his hair, as if it was too much to comprehend. "Vell, I'll be damned!" He stated, almost too quietly to be heard. I could tell that his mind was on his son, Roy, and not how grandma expressed herself.

Ron had a smile on his face and looking from mom to dad, shaking his head, he said, "He did it. He said he could do it, and he did it!" I wondered if he was wishing he hadn't changed his mind, and that he would like to have been with Roy, instead.

Eileen rose from her chair, left the kitchen, and gathered up her things from where she had laid them when she had remembered mom's letter. She crossed the room, and fled up the stairs, with them clutched tightly against her bosom. Her eyes glistened suspiciously, but I knew she would never admit that she missed Roy, or that she was as relieved as the rest of us were, to know that he was all right.

I returned to my new things, and gathering them up in my arms, I proceeded to carry them up the stairs. One leg of the snow pants hung down from the wad of clothes in my arms, and I stepped on it, causing myself to stumble, falling to my knees against the steps. I cried out, as my elbows connected with the edge of another step, and I sprawled out, full length, slipping backwards a step or two.

Country Splendor

"Hey there, clumsy," Ron said; as he came up behind me, and reached down to help me to my feet. "Did you hurt yourself?'

"I think I broke my bones!" I whimpered.

"Let me look," he said, as he felt my arms and then my knees. "No, no broken bones. Here, let me carry your things for you." He reached around me and gathered up my clothing. "Okay, now get on up the stairs, I'll leave these things on your bed."

I ran on up the stairs, and turned into Eileen and my bedroom. Eileen had just hung her new dresses on hangers, and the hangers on a large nail on the wall. She turned to watch us enter the room. True to his word, Ron deposited my new things on our bed, and turned to leave.

"Ronny, do you miss Roy?" I asked, before he could get out the door.

He stopped, hesitated a minute, and turned to say, "Sure I do, don't you?"

"Yes, I do. Do you think he will ever come home?"

"Not for a while. He was pretty determined to get away. As long as grandma is willing to have him, he'll likely stay."

"Do you wish you went with him?" I asked.

"Sometimes I do, but you know that I am needed here on the farm right now. Dads getting stronger everyday, and even helps with the milking now, as long as I do the heavy lifting. But, it will still be a while before he can handle the chores by himself. Schools starting too, and I've decided to go on to high school this year." Ron turned and sat down on the edge of the bed.

"Do you have to go? I heard that some kids don't," Eileen asked. "The government says you have to finish the eighth grade, but it's up to you whether you go on to high school or not, isn't it?"

"Yes, but I've decided I want to. Maybe I can learn enough to get a job in town someday. I know dad would like us to be farmers, but I would rather find other work to do."

"Like what?"

"Like factory work, or something. I really don't know yet, but something where you have a certain number of hours to work, and the rest of the time you have off. On a farm, your work is never done. You know that Eileen, and its hard work for little pay. You have to like this kind of life to do it all your life. Me, I would rather do something else."

She nodded her head in agreement.

"Ron, what's war?" I asked.

He looked at me, with a funny expression on his face, and asked, "Where did that come from? We were talking about school."

"I was listening to the radio with daddy, and it said that there is a war going on. Dad was wondering if men from our country were going to go. He said they might make our young men fight, and if they did many would die. What's war?" I asked again, as he looked at me and shook his head.

"War is where men from different countries, fight each other," he said.

"What are countries?" I asked.

"We live in America. America is a country. There are many countries in this world. Like Germany is the country that dad's father came from, when he was a young boy. That is the country that is making war against other countries right now."

"Why?" I asked, as I scooted up closer to him, all eyes and ears. I was always asking questions and trying to understand the answers. I wanted to know everything, and it was hard being so young, and not knowing what others were talking about.

Ron looked at me, as if he were trying to decide how much to tell me. Sometimes he called me a pest, when I asked him so many questions, but this time he seemed to understand that I really wanted to understand, too. "You know that there are men who run the country? Like the president, Mr. Roosevelt? You have heard about him on the radio, right? Its like dad is the leader of our family, see, and he tells us what to do, and we do it. Well, the president is the leader of our country, and he tells all the people in our country what to do. The leader of Germany has decided that he wants to be the leader of many countries, so he is telling his men to take over other countries, so he can lead them. The other countries fight to keep the men from

Country Splendor

Germany from taking their country away from them. That is what war is. I know this is hard for you to understand, but when you get bigger you will."

"Will I understand if I go to school?"

"Going to school will help you understand, yes. You learn about things like this. Also, you will learn to read books and the newspaper, and then you will be able to understand even more about many things."

"I want to go to school now. I am four years old. I'm big enough, but Eileen says I have to be six. Why?"

Eileen answered for him. "Because most children are not ready for school until they are six years old."

"Helen, you may think you are old enough, but other children your age may not be old enough. The people who make up these rules are thinking about all of the children, not just busy minded ones like you," Ron explained, as he ruffled my hair.

"But it's not fair!" I argued, as I hopped off the bed and stomped my foot for emphasis.

Ron laughed at me, as he rose from the bed, and turned to leave. "You'll get to go to school soon enough, and then you'll be wishing you didn't have to go all the time."

"Yes, that's exactly right," Eileen interjected.

"Will not!" I shouted at both of them.

Ron laugh again, as he left our bedroom and entered his own.

I flung myself back onto the bed, and buried my face into the soft snowsuit, breathing in its new smell. I remembered my prayer for a new dress. I told Eileen about my prayer, and wondered why I didn't get it.

She looked thoughtful, as she looked over at me and said,

"I guess that God must be like mother; He knew that you needed this snow suit more than you needed a new dress."

I thought about that. She was probably right. I took my shoes off and tried on the new snowsuit. It was so warm and cuddly that I hated taking it off, and suddenly I was in a hurry for winter to arrive. Everything always took so long!

CHAPTER EIGHTEEN

The next couple of weeks passed in a flurry of putting up the last of the vegetables. I watched as mother and dad chopped up several heads of cabbage, and placed them in a big crock, to which they added salt, pressing it all down until the crock was full. The crock was placed into the cool pantry, where the cabbage would be left to ferment into sauerkraut.

Next, came the pickling of the cucumbers. Eileen, mother and I, picked them from the vines, and brought them into the house. My hands were a little sore, from the cucumbers bristly skin. I washed my hands in warm water, and then mother rubbed some ointment on them. "That feels better!" I said, as I held them in the air to dry.

The larger cucumbers that were turning color were put to one side to feed the pigs, while the others were washed and dropped into a large wooden barrel. While Eileen and I worked on this procedure, mother placed one of her large, metal, washtubs on the hot stove, filling it with water, vinegar, and spices. As it warmed up to bubbling, the kitchen filled with the rather sharp, aroma. Once the wooden barrel was filled with the cucumbers, as well as the fresh dill and garlic cloves that were put in between the layers of cucumbers, the barrel was moved to the basement. This job took Ron, dad, and mother, to get it down the stairs, and set in its place. Next, the hot vinegar and spice mixture, bubbling on the stove, had to be dipped into stainless steel buckets, and transferred to the cellar, where it was poured into the wooden

Country Splendor

barrel. Once the cucumbers were covered with the brine, the wooden cover was put in place. Now the pickling process would begin. By Thanksgiving, the cucumbers would be ready to eat.

The cellar shelves along the sidewalls, were already lined with colorful jars of various fruits, vegetables, and jellies. Carrots were dug up and put in a basket of sand, to stay crisp throughout the winter. Pumpkins and squash were placed on shelves, along the back wall of the cool cellar. A large back corner, enclosed with short wooden sides, was filled with the freshly dug potatoes.

The slaughtering and preparing of our winter meat came next. Not one of my favorite times. I hated the thought of killing anything that we had raised on the farm. Mother kept Bobby and me in the house, while the men accomplished the killing, and the skinning of the animals. However, when the carcass had to be cut up, it was brought into the kitchen, and placed on the large kitchen table. Once in that state, the sight of it didn't bother me. In fact, I made a nuisance of myself, wanting to stand on a chair, in order to watch the whole procedure. Mother would tolerate me for only so long, and when my endless questions became tiresome, she would shoo me off to the other room. Smoking it preserved some of the meat; while some of it was salted down and placed in a cool area of the attic. Much of it mother canned. The best cuts of the beef were wrapped in brown butcher paper, and taken into the refrigerated cooler in town. Dad rented a small section of the cooler, to store the meat in, bringing some home to use each time he went to town.

School started the first Monday of September, right after Labor Day. It was a hectic time, as the chores needed to be done, breakfast served, and lunches packed, in time for Ronald and Eileen to leave. They had to walk to the end of the road, where Ron would catch the bus that would take him into Barron, and Eileen would continue down the road to the schoolhouse. With dad helping with the milking again, Ron managed to change his clothes, and eat breakfast with time to spare. Eileen, on the other hand, had trouble with her hair, couldn't make up her mind which dress she wanted to wear, her first day back to school, and was almost in tears when mother ordered her down to the kitchen to eat some breakfast.

"I just can't eat this morning, my stomachs in knots," she complained, with a plaintiff note.

Mother insisted that she try to eat a small bowl of hot, cooked, oatmeal, with milk and sugar, at least. "I'll throw up," Eileen insisted.

"Just eat a few bites," Mother said, as she sat the bowl, along with a spoon, in front of Eileen. A knock on the door saved Eileen from further argument, as she jumped up from the table, and ran to the door to open it. There stood Gertrude and Herbert, wreathed in smiles, dressed in their new clothes, and carrying lunch pails and books.

"Are you and Ronny ready?" They asked.

Ronny jumped up from his place at the table, grabbed his lunch bag and books, and headed for the door. "Bye mom," he called over his shoulder, as he went through the door, and started a conversation with Herbert, as they headed across the yard.

"Hurry, Eileen," Gertrude said, as she watched the boys hurrying ahead.

Eileen ran for her lunch bag, grabbed it from mother's outstretched hand, and said a quick "Thank you, mom," as she turned and ran across the front room, and through the door. I stood in the doorway, watching the girls run to catch up with the boys, laughing and talking all the way. The boys ignored them and kept up their pace, anxious to reach the spot where the school bus would pick them up. I sighed, stepped back inside, and shut the door.

"It's just not fair!" I said to no one in particular, as I went to the kitchen to have some hot oatmeal for breakfast.

"Here, Helen, you might as well eat Eileen's breakfast. No sense in letting it go to waste."

"I'd rather be going to school," I said.

"Now, Helen, you know you are too young yet," Mother said. "Tell you what, the teacher usually has a day or two during the school year, where a student can bring a younger brother or sister to school, to visit for the day. Maybe Eileen can take you, would you like that?"

Country Splendor

"Oh yes, how soon?" I said, with a great deal of excitement mounting in my breast.

"We will have to wait and see. It is usually close to a holiday, and then again, at the end of the school year."

"That sounds so far away," I sighed, as I felt the excitement dwindle down to disappointment. I picked up my spoon and slowly ate my bowl of cereal, already missing my big sister.

Mother left the kitchen to change Bobby, and to bring him into the kitchen for his breakfast. "I have an idea," Mother said to me, as she placed Bobby in his highchair, and began feeding him some cooled oatmeal. "How about you go on outside, and see how many different, colored, leaves you can find? If you can gather enough of them, we could make a pretty bouquet of them for Audrey. I was planning on taking her some of that blueberry cobbler I made yesterday, and you could give her the bouquet of leaves."

"Okay, I know just where to go. The woods just past the pasture is full of trees with leaves turning all shades of gold, and reds, and oranges. I can get lots and lots!" I said, warming to the idea. I loved Mrs. Zobel, and she always had something special for me. I ate the last spoonful of oatmeal, drank the last of my milk, and ran for the door.

"Wait, Helen. I think you should take something to carry the leaves in," she said, as she crossed the room to the pantry and brought out a basket with handles. "This should do." She handed the basket to me. It was a little large for me, but I wasn't going to admit it. I hoisted it up, and ran for the door, before she could change her mind. Out the back door of the kitchen I flew, crossed the porch, and jumped to the ground, clearing the steps by inches. The basket was so heavy that it pulled me off balance, and I fell forward, onto the graveled driveway. I dropped the basket, trying to break my fall with my hands. Dad was just coming from the barn when he saw me take my flying leap, and landing in the gravel. I pushed myself to my knees, taking stock of my scraped hands, where blood was beginning to show under the gravel. I brushed the gravel off my hands, against my skirt, just as dad lifted me to my feet.

"Just what do you think you were doing? You know you can't fly yet," he stated with a laugh, as he assessed my wounds. My knees were beginning to hurt, but I didn't want to open my mouth to complain, for fear I would start crying. I did reach down and press my hand against my dress though. "Here, let me see those knees," Dad said, as he carefully lifted my dress, exposing them. "Ouch, you did skin them up some, didn't you? Come back in the house and let mother put some iodine on those scrapes." He folded one large hand around my wrist, and led me up the steps, across the porch, and into the kitchen.

I was trying not to cry, but just the thought of iodine on my wounds brought tears streaming down my cheeks. "Mother, we have a little problem here," Dad said, causing mother to looked up from her dishwashing.

"Now what?"

"Just a little scraped knees and hands. Our fledgling bird hasn't learned to fly yet."

Mother reached for a towel to dry her hands on, and motioned for dad to sit me down on a chair, as she went for the medicine.

"Now, Helen, you know it's not that bad," Dad said soothingly, as he wiped the tears from my cheeks with a gentle finger. "I'll clean the dirt and gravel out of those scrapes, while mother fetches the medicine." He pulled a hand towel from a shelf, and wet it in the warm, soapy, dishwater. Coming back to me, he gently took one hand and cleaned it, then reached for the other. Once that was done, he carefully lifted my dress, just enough to expose my knees, and began cleaning them.

Mother returned with an ointment, some bandages, and the hated iodine. "Let's see how bad it is," she said, as she turned one hand to look at the palm, and then the other. "I've seen worse. You'll live," she said, as if it were all a joke. The lid was unscrewed on the iodine bottle, and then lifted up, revealing the glass applicator covered with red liquid. I shut my eyes to avoid seeing the fiery, red, stuff, being applied to my wounds.

"Owe, owe, owe!" I said, through clenched teeth, as the medication burned the germs from the raw places on my hands. As soon as mother

Country Splendor

released my hands, I whipped them around in the air, hoping to help put out the fire. In a matter of seconds the burning stopped, but it seemed a lot longer than that to me. Then came the anointing of my knees, and once again, I whimpered and complained, until the fire went out.

"Now, that wasn't too bad, was it?" Mother asked.

I wondered out loud, "Compared to what?"

That hit dad real funny, and he burst forth with a real guffaw, and said between laughs, "Where did you ever pick that up?"

Mother started laughing with him, and then it all seemed worthwhile. What were a few scrapes, and a little pain, if it brought so much joy to my parents? I laughed along with them and dad gave me another hug, saying, "That's my brave girl!"

Just before lunchtime, I arrived back at the house, with my basket brimming with multi colored leaves. I lugged the basket into the house to show mother. She was preparing lunch for us. "Well there you are. I was just about to call for you to come in. My, that is a lovely bunch of leaves. The colors are beautiful. Put the basket on the porch swing, and call your daddy in for lunch. Right after we eat, we will take the fall bouquet, and the blueberry cobbler over to Audrey."

I carried my basket back to the porch, but I had trouble balancing the basket on the porch swing, so I ended up sitting it on the washstand by the door. Once that was done, I ran towards the barn in search of dad. The milking area was empty. I headed into the haymow, but it appeared to be empty also. I called daddy's name, and then I heard it, a moaning sound of someone in pain, coming from the direction of the calf barn. I hurried into that area, searching everywhere. I heard another moan coming from the bull's pen. It was to the right of the calf barn, and just outside the building. As I rounded the corner, I saw Dad. He was curled up on the ground, just outside the pen. The bull was inside its pen, and moving around as if it was greatly agitated.

"Dad, Dad, what's the matter?" I cried; as I touched his shoulder and leaned down to see his face.

"Uh, I'm hurt. Get your mother," he whispered, in a pain filled voice.

"I'll get her, I'll be right back," I promised, as I took off running for the house, shouting for mother. As I hit the porch, she met me at the door.

"What's all the yelling about?" she asked, sounding annoyed.

"It's dad. I found him. He's on the ground outside the bullpen. He's moaning," I explained, as mother hurried across the porch, rushing down the steps, and across the yard to the barn. I couldn't keep up with her, and she was already on her knees by dad, trying to lift him up, when I got there.

"Helen, run and get Emil. Tell him we need him right away." When mother said 'run' I was already on my way, and her voice rose higher and higher as she continued shouting orders, as I ran for the Zobel's place. "Tell him to bring his car. We need to get Hubie to the doctor," was the last orders I heard, as I plunged on toward my goal.

I ran as hard as I could, ignoring the pain in my knees first, and then the pain in my side, as I hopped up onto their porch, and knocked, loudly, on their door. Emil opened the door, and seeing my worried face, he asked me what was wrong.

"It's daddy," I croaked out, trying to get my breath. "He's laying by the bull pen. He can't get up. Mama says come right away and bring your car." I started to turn away and run back, but he called to me and told me to get in the car.

"You can ride with me," he said. I turned in mid stride and headed around the house and to his car. He must have stopped in the house long enough to explain to Audrey what was going on, as it seemed that several minutes had passed before he came out of the kitchen door, and to the car.

"Get in," he said, as he opened his door and quickly slid behind the wheel. His keys were in his hands and he had the car running and backing up, by the time I had shut the door behind myself. His tires squealed, as he put the car into drive, and headed quickly out of the drive, up the road and into our driveway, pulling up close to the barn before coming to a stop. "Come on, show me," he said, as he slid out of the car and headed for the barn.

Country Splendor

"He's around here," I said, as I led Emil around to the bullpen. Mother was on the ground, holding daddy against her breast. She looked up with relief showing in her eyes, as she saw Emil arrive.

"He's hurt himself again. The bull got loose when he was putting fresh straw in for him, and he strained himself getting the bull back in his pen."

"Okay, let's get him into the car and head for town. You can tell me the details on the way. Will Helen and Bobby be all right here by themselves? Or, how about Helen taking Bobby over to my place, and waiting there for us to get back? Would that be okay?" Emil asked.

"Helen, can you handle that okay?" I nodded yes. "Remember to take a bottle for him, and a change of diapers as well. Okay? We will be back as soon as we can. If the kids get home before I do, Eileen and Ronny can take care of you both. Now do you understand what you need to do?"

"Yes mama, I will do just what you said. You know I can. I will take Bobby over right away, with his bottle and diaper. Don't worry," I said, feeling very important. I ran for the house to do just what I was told. Behind me I heard daddy groaning, as Emil and mother helped him up from the ground, and into Emil's car. I stopped on the porch just long enough to see that dad was in the back seat, lying down, as Emil closed the back door, and then climbed into the front seat. At the same time, mother was entering the other side of the car. Emil started the engine, and moved the car slowly and carefully, out of the driveway. I proceeded into the house in answer to Bobby's distress signals.

"I'm coming Bobby, I'm here," I said, as I stooped down and lifted him to his feet. "Oh, you are wet. No wonder you were fussing. I guess it is time I figure out how to change your diaper. Lie down here and I will be right back." I turned and headed for the chest where Bobby's diapers and pants were kept. I found what I needed to change him, and took a second diaper to take with me.

Bobby waited dutifully for me to return. I stooped down beside him, trying to sit on my knees, but they hurt too much to put that much pressure on them. I ended up sitting down, with my legs extended in

Helen Marie Fias

front of me, but spread out so I could lay Bobby down between them. Once I had him in the right position, I undid his trouser buttons, and pulled them off of him, laying them in a heap on the floor to my right. I reached for the diaper pin on the right side, and unfastened it, pulling it out and free from the cloth. I laid it on the floor beside me, as I went for the second diaper pin. He started to roll towards the pin I was reaching for, causing the diaper to fall open. I grabbed at his arm and pulled him back on his back. "You hold still now!" I demanded.

He gave me a grin and started to roll again. "Bobby! This is not a game. Now lay still!" I finally got hold of the second pin, and wrestled it open and free of the other half of the diaper, just as Bobby rolled the other way and scrambled to his feet, taking off across the floor with his bare butt shining.

"You come back here!" I shouted after him. He just laughed and ran faster. "Oh brother! You little devil!" I said, as I lay the second pin by the first one. I put the wet diaper on top of his wet pants, and tried to fold the clean diaper the way I had seen Eileen fold them. I decided that I had better get everything ready, before going after Bobby, and trying to re diaper him. After several tries at folding it, it looked about right. I lay it on the floor. I reached for the dry pants and lay it within my reach. I then got up from the floor and proceeded to catch my little brother, as he ran past me the second time.

I wrestled him back to the place on the floor I had just vacated, and preceded to lay him down on the diaper. Then I held him down, as I sat back down, again spreading my legs on each side of him. He wasn't through playing though, and struggled to roll away from me. I gave him a slap on his bare butt, and rolled him back into position. He whimpered as he realized that I meant business, but at least he lay quietly, as I worked the diaper around him, and proceeded to pin it in place. It was a lot harder than it had looked when Eileen did it. Getting the pin to go through all that material, and then fastening it, was no small chore. I finally got one done and then reached for the other pin. It had slid out of my reach when I struggled with Bobby, and as I sprawled out to reach it, he took that opportunity to roll over and up, and once again was running through the house, only this time

Country Splendor

the diaper was riding down one leg. "Oh no," I groaned, as I got to my feet and played 'catch the kid' one more time.

I rounded him up and laid him back down on the floor. The diaper was still hanging on his leg but it wasn't folded neatly anymore. I decided that I was going to get it around him regardless of how it looked. Once he was covered I could hold it on with his britches. I pulled the diaper around him, gathered two sides together and proceeded to pin it in place. After pricking my fingers until I had two of them bleeding, I finally had the diaper secured. I grabbed up the pants, putting first one leg in and then the other. Once that was done, I stood him to his feet and pulled the pants up to where I could slip the straps over his shoulders, and buttoned them in place. There! He looked okay to me. I felt that I had won the war, but wore out myself in the process. When I turned him loose, he took off running again, giggling as he went. "Fine! Just behave until I get your bottle and clean diaper together, then we are off to Audrey's place and she can change you next time."

Less than ten minutes later we were sitting in Audrey's living room, telling her about my day. She sympathized over my skinned knees and hands, reassured me that it was okay that I forgot to bring the blueberry cobbler and fall bouquet over. After all, I had my hands full, just getting Bobby there safely. She asked me how badly I thought my dad was. I told her how I had found him and how much pain he seemed to be in. She assured me that he would be all right, once the doctor took care of him. I hoped she was right, because we needed him. She understood and agreed. Then she laughed heartedly, as I told her about my experience of changing my little brother's diaper. She then told me of a funny experience she had, while learning to put the diaper on her own baby, in a way that it wouldn't fall off when she picked him up. She had me laughing, then.

The afternoon went quickly, and soon the sounds of two giggling girls could be heard, coming up to the house. Audrey went to the door and called to the girls, asking them to come inside.

Eileen was surprised to see Bobby and me there. Audrey explained the situation to her, and a frown puckered Eileen's brow, as she heard the news about dad. You could see that she worried about loosing him, too. She came over to me and asked me if I knew what happened, exactly. "I don't know, exactly," I said, "but what I heard was that Dad was cleaning out the bulls pen when the bull got out. Dad had a hard time getting him back in. I found dad collapsed on the ground, and moaning in pain. It took Emil and mom to get him up, and into the car. Mom told me to bring Bobby over here, and to wait here for you and Ron to get home. She would be back as soon as possible."

"Do I take you on home and wait for Ron there, or do we wait for him here?" she asked.

"I guess that's up to you. Either way we should help with tonight's chores and fixing something for us to eat," I replied feeling quite grown up.

Audrey offered her opinion as she said, "Why don't you wait here for Ron? Herbert and Ron should be home within the next half hour, I should think. Then you all can go home together. There should be plenty of time to start the chores after you have something to eat. In fact, I'll bet that one of the Foss boys would come over tonight and help Ron with the milking, if you asked them."

"That's a good idea," Eileen conceded. "In fact they should all be coming home together, as they are all in high school now. We could watch for them and ask them."

"Yes, in fact, lets wait on the porch for them so we won't miss them," Gertrude said, as she led the way to the front porch, and took a place on the swing. Eileen followed her out, and sat down beside her. That left me in the house to watch Bobby, as usual, I thought. He's too fast for me to watch him on the porch, and the girls are too busy watching for the boys, to be of any help.

Audrey noticed the aggravated look on my face and must have understood my thoughts, because she came up to me and said, "You need a break. Leave Bobby with me and go out to the porch with the girls."

"Thank you," I said gratefully, as I turned on my heel and hurried out to the porch. The sun was low in the sky, and the heat of the day had passed. The air was comfortably warm, and a gentle breeze brought a

Country Splendor

hint of honeysuckle with it. I didn't want to bother the girls and their whispered giggles, so I sat on the far end of the porch, and hung my legs over the side. I suddenly felt very tired. I lay back against a post and stretched my legs out on the porch, along the railing. It felt so good to relax.

"Hey little one, it's time to go home." I heard my brother's voice, and felt him gently shaking me awake.

"I guess I must have fallen asleep," I said, as I sat up and rubbed the sleep from my eyes.

"You sure did. You must be worn out from all that's happened today. Eileen told me some of it, and Mrs. Zobel filled me in on the rest. How about we go home, have a bite to eat, and then you and Bobby can go to bed early? Roger and Bill Foss are coming over to help with the chores. Eileen can handle cleaning the kitchen. Okay?" he asked, as he grabbed my arm and helped me to my feet. "Eileen, get Bobby and lets head for home."

For once, Eileen didn't argue with Ron. She reached over and picked Bobby up, said goodbye to Audrey and Gertrude, and headed out the door, and across the yard behind us.

We had just reached our front porch, when we saw a car headed down our road. "That looks like Emil's car," Ron stated. We watched as it passed Emil's driveway and slowed down to turn into ours. We went into the house then, passing through the front room and kitchen, to wait on the back porch. Emil stopped the car close to the back porch, turned off the motor, and got out to open the back door. Before he could reach in for dad, Ron was beside the car, helping Emil get him out of the car and into the house.

"How do you feel, dad?" Ron asked.

"I've felt better. That fool bull just about did me in. The doctor says I have to have bed rest for a couple of weeks, until I heal. Guess it tore something loose inside. It hurts like hell, that's for sure."

I knew by the words I heard dad using, that he must feel awful. He usually never used those words in our hearing. 'He must be in a lot of pain to admit it,' I thought to myself. As I turned to follow the men into the house, Eileen came up to me and said, "Dad must be in a bad way to admit how bad he feels."

"That's just what I thought," I said.

"Girls," Mother said from behind us. We jumped and then turned to see her coming in behind us. She looked very tired and worried. "Could you warm up some of that soup I made for lunch? Cut a few slices of bread to go with it. Have you had something to eat?"

"Not yet, we just got home too," Eileen, answered.

"Then we will open up some fruit too, so there is enough for all of us. Helen, can you go down to the cellar and pick out a quart of peaches?" Mother asked.

I thought of how late it was, and of how dark the cellar would be. I thought of the scary story Eileen told me, about 'the bloody rag' that waits down in people's cellars to grab them when they come down in the dark, and I shivered. "Can't Eileen get it?" I begged. "I can put the soup on to heat."

Eileen heard me and teased, "She's afraid to go down in the dark. Spooky things will get her." And she laughed knowing the reason for my fear.

"How about I light a lantern for you to take down with you. Would that be okay then?"

"I guess," I said, not wanting to be called a scaredy-cat. Mother lit the lantern and handed it to me. I turned on trembling legs, towards the cellar door. As I opened the door, cool air brushed against my skin. I thought of spider webs touching my face, and almost backed out. I stood for a moment, regaining my nerve, and slowly proceeded down the stairs, one careful step at a time. The lantern glowed brightly against my face, but it created shadows in the dark room. I moved it ahead of me, using it as a shield, as I looked along the row of jars, searching out the peaches. I hadn't realized I was holding my breath, until I suddenly let it out, and it sounded soft, like a haunted voice talking to me. I turned around, searching out the dark corners, for anything that might be there to grab me. My heart was beating in my breast, so hard, that I was afraid it would burst. Nothing moved in the dark recesses, and I turned once again to the shelves of fruit. There!

Country Splendor

There are the peaches. I grabbed a jar off the shelf, almost dropping it, in my haste to draw my hand back close to my body. I backed towards the stairs, and then thought of how dark it was under them, and of how anything hiding there could reach between the treads of the open stairs and grab me. I turned the lantern towards the steps, and hurried up them, while all the time I was waiting for something to grab my ankles, or come up the stairs behind me. I made it through the door, and into the security of the kitchen, without dropping the lantern, the peaches, or my composure. I breathed a sigh of relief, moved to the table, and placed the jar of peaches on it. I returned to the cellar door, and shut it with more force than necessary. Lifting the globe of the lantern, I blew out the flame, and dropped the globe back into place. I sat the lantern on the shelf by the door, walked to the table, and sat down.

Eileen turned from the stove, where she had been stirring the soup. "The bloody rag didn't get you? Wait until you go to bed tonight!" she said in her spookiest voice. Then she laughed and turned back to the stove.

I sat at the table, with my head in my hands, remembering the line the bloody rag used, as it made its way up out of the cellar, and up the stairs to our bedroom, "I'm on the first step, I'm on the second step, I'm on the third step, I'm on the fourth step, I'm on the fifth step, I'm at the door, I'm in the kitchen, I'm in the front room, I'm at the second set of stairs, I'm on the first step, I'm on the second step, I'm on the third step, I'm on the fourth step, I'm on the fifth step, I'm on the sixth step, I'm on the seventh step, I'm on the eighth step, I'm on the ninth step, I'm in the hall, I'm at your door, I'm in your room, I'm at the foot of your bed, I've gotcha!" I jumped inside, just as I always did, every time Eileen told me that story.

Mother entered the kitchen and patted my back as she passed me. That was her way of saying 'good job' and I felt rewarded for facing my fears, and accomplishing the task given me. She opened the jar, and poured the peaches into a bowl from the cupboard. They sat on the table in front of me, like a special treat. "Mama, can I eat and go to bed? I'm really tired," I said.

"Eileen, ladle a small bowl of soup for Helen. She needs to eat."

Eileen looked over at me, with a smirk on her face. She leaned close and said in a quiet, low voice, "want a bowl of soup, so you can go to bed?" I knew what she was saying, without saying it, but I had faced my fears, and I knew it was just a story, after all.

"Yes, I do," I answered, with a smirk of a smile right back at her. I ate my soup with a slice of mom's fresh bread, and finished my supper, with a couple of peaches for dessert. I left the table saying goodnight to mom; went to the door of the folk's bedroom and said goodnight to dad. He smiled at me, and waved a hand to say goodnight. I turned toward the stairs and said, "God, please don't let anything get me," as I placed my foot on the first step. I stepped on the second step, and felt a peace flow through me, as I made my way up the stairs, and into the darkness of the upper hallway. I felt my way through the doorway of my bedroom and to the bed. I was so tired that I dropped my dress on the floor and crawled into the bed. I pulled the blanket up around my head, curled my body into my feather pillow, and fell into a totally, peaceful sleep.

CHAPTER NINETEEN

Now that school was in full swing there was no sleeping late in the morning. Everyone was up earlier than usual, doing chores, preparing breakfast and lunches, and getting the two oldest out the door. Roger Foss came over to help with the milking, which was a big relief. Mother invited him in for breakfast with Ron, and he proceeded to eat a huge amount of food, but then he was a pretty big guy. Six foot at least, with broad chest and shoulders, and only sixteen years old. After he left for home, mother commented on how it was worth the food it took to fill him up for the amount of work he did. She appreciated his help and so did we all.

Once Ron and Eileen left for school, the mundane work was left on mother's shoulders. The pigs had to be slopped, the chickens fed and the eggs gathered. Thank goodness there were no young calves to feed, they were all old enough to be out in the pasture with their mothers. I offered to feed the pigs, but mother said the slop bucket was too heavy for me. She told me to watch Bobby so dad could rest, and when she got the pigs fed I could take care of the chickens for her. Being given some responsibilities gave me a feeling of being needed, and it made me feel special.

I had Bobby in his highchair when mother came in from taking care of the pigs. I had just finished feeding him his oatmeal. "Would you mind putting Bobby on the floor now and taking care of the chickens?" she asked.

Country Splendor

"Yes, mama," I answered. It was a struggle getting his tray over his head, and freeing him from the chair, as he was getting to be quite a chunk. But between him and me working together, we finally freed him and got him to the floor.

"Me go too," he said, as he followed me to the door.

"No, Bobbie." I began to say when mother overruled me.

"Go ahead and let him go with you. You know how much fun he has going along, and you can let him have a handful of seeds to throw on the ground for the chickens too." Mother seemed to know the right things to say to convince me to do as she wished. In fact, she could make it sound like an adventure, and I thrived on adventure.

"Oh, alright. Come on Bobby, we'll feed the chickens."

"Feed chicks, feed chicks," he repeated, as we headed out of the door and in the direction of the granary. There was a definite chill in the air. I shivered and wished I had put on a sweater.

"I think winter is going to be here soon, Bobby. Feel how cold it is this morning? We should hurry with our job."

"Our job!" he repeated. It was a relief to reach the granary and step inside. Here, at least we were out of the wind.

"Here Bobby, you can fill this little can with feed, while I fill the bucket, okay?" I said, as I handed him a small soup can that was lying nearby.

"Fill can, fill can," he said, as I held him up so he could reach into the bin. Once he had some seeds in it, I stood him down on the floor and filled my bucket. We hurried across to the hen house, opened the gate, and entered the chicken yard. Numerous, hungry chickens met us. Bobby dumped his can at his feet, and quicker than you could say, "Jumping cat-fish!" he had a swarm of chickens pecking around his bare toes. He yelled and did a little dance, sending some of them squawking, while others crowded in closer.

"I guess we should wear shoes to do this job," I laughed, as I watched him trying to avoid hungry beaks. Then I tossed my feed a bit further away, and they were running to take advantage of the pile I left for them. "Okay, Bobby, lets see about the eggs now." I took his hand and led him around the feeding frenzy going on.

"Eggs, get eggs," he nodded, as he followed my lead into the hen house. A basket for carrying the eggs was hanging just inside the door, so I exchanged it for my pail and proceeded around the nests. Most of the hens were outside by now, so collecting the eggs was a breeze. It took just a few minutes and the nests were emptied. My basket was over half full of eggs as we left the henhouse and started across the chicken yard. Just then, Chaser saw us, and thought he would have some fun. I always knew what that ornery dog was thinking, and I was always right, because just then he came charging for the open door of the hen yard.

"Go way Chaser!" I yelled, as I ran to intercept him. I had the door almost closed when he hit it with his body, knocking me back onto my behind. Of course it sent my egg basket to rocking as well. Several fell to the ground, breaking as they hit. I got to my feet, placed the basket out side of the door, and returned inside to catch me a dog. "Bobby, get out of the pen. I've got to catch Chaser and get him out." For once he minded me and stepped outside. He spotted the basket of eggs right away, and headed right for it, picking it up. As he did, two more eggs fell out.

"No Bobby, not the basket," I yelled, but he was already on his way to the house with the egg basket swaying.

By this time, the hen yard was in a real frenzy, with that crazy dog having the time of his life, chasing the chickens around. I ran after him, to no avail. I knew he would turn at the fence and head back, so I tried running across the yard and grabbing him as he passed. It should have worked, except he was too fast and too strong for me. The next time he charged past me, I grabbed at him again and managed to latch onto his tail. He was in full gear, and it took some time to slow him down. Meantime, chickens were squawking and flying every which way, trying to avoid the two of us.

Mother came out onto the porch to see what all the fuss was about. There was Bobby trying to carry the basket of eggs to her, loosing another one every few steps. He stopped once; stooping to pick up one that had rolled from the basket. He clutched it too tightly and it broke in his hand, filling his hand with sticky egg stuff. He swiped at

Country Splendor

his pants trying to wipe off his hand, as he continued toward the porch with the basket swaying more with each step. Mother ran down to rescue the few eggs left in the basket. As she took it from him, Bobby objected by throwing himself down on the ground. Mother ignored him, looking to see what the commotion in the pen was about.

By then, I had Chaser by his collar and was struggling to get him out of the pen. Some of the hens had taken to the tree branches, and some had gone into the henhouse. A few truly hungry ones, or stupid, or both, were back at the seed on the ground, pecking away. I was red with rage at that dog, and wished I were capable of really teaching him a lesson. I did manage to get him out of the door, and the door secured behind us.

It was the first chance I had to see what Bobby was up to, but when I looked in that direction, I saw mother standing there instead. She had one hand on her hip and the almost empty basket in her other hand. I said to myself, "Oh, oh!" The look on her face was a mixture of fascination, exasperation and resignation. I stood looking at her, waiting to see which way she was going to go. Old Chaser was happily licking at broken eggs on the ground, and Bobby was sitting on the ground, trying to clean his hands on his pants. I looked at mother again, and just raised both shoulders, and my hands, and my eyebrows, and she burst out laughing. I breathed a sigh of relief and laughed with her.

"Come on Helen, let's get out of this cold breeze before we both catch our death," she said, as she turned back towards the house. I thought, 'Cold? I was sweating!'

She grabbed one of Bobby's arms as she passed him, and propelled him up onto the porch and into the kitchen. I came trailing along behind, relieved that at least this one time, I was granted a pardon.

Back in the kitchen, mother told me to wash Bobby's hands and take him into the front room to play. He struggled with me as I applied a wet washrag to his hands. "Why do boys hate to be cleaned?"

Mother paid no attention to me, or my question. She was seated at the table, drinking from her cup of cooled coffee, and staring at a sheet of paper on the table in front of her. 'She must be writing to someone'

I thought as I passed. Wonder if it's grandma Vaughan. I wanted to ask but thought better of it. 'Better to let well enough alone and keep her happy,' I decided. I followed Bobby to a spot in front of the windows where he had a small pile of playthings gathered together. I sat down with my back to the wall and watched him. He picked up a block and began to build a tower. He was very precise with each one, fitting it carefully on top of the one under it, so it would stay put and not fall over. "Wish you could have been that careful with the eggs this morning," I said to him. He paid no attention to me, but continued with his building.

Dad emerged from his bedroom just then, dressed and making his way to the kitchen. He was walking very slowly, with one hand trailing along the wall and the other holding his mid section.

"Daddy, can I help you?" I asked, as I jumped up and ran to him.

He looked down at me and smiled, "No angel, but thanks for offering."

"Hubert! What are you doing up!" Mother chided dad, as she watched him enter the kitchen door. When she used his formal name, he and I knew, she was talking business.

"I can't stay in bed any longer. Thought I'd come sit at the table a while. Got any more hot coffee and maybe a slice of that cake you made?" His voice sounded strained, as he gingerly sat himself down in a chair at the table.

"There is plenty of coffee, but let me check on the cake," Mother said as she rose from her chair, pushed away from the table, and went to the cupboard for a cup. She filled it from the large, blue enamel, coffee pot, simmering at the back of the stove, took it to dad and sat it at his right hand. "The cream is right here, as well as the sugar bowl. You can use my spoon. Now I'll go check on that cake."

She spun around and headed for the pantry. "You're in luck. There is one piece left." She came back in the kitchen and placed it in front of dad, then leaned over and kissed his forehead. He reached up and patted her cheek.

"How are you really feeling?" She asked softly, remaining close to his face a moment longer.

Country Splendor

"No use denying that I hurt like hell, but what good does it do to complain? I have only myself to blame for getting in with that stupid bull. Verna, would you be upset if we sell that beast? I know he's a highbred bull from excellent stock, but you know how I hate an animal that you can't trust. We could borrow Foss's fine bull for the time being, until we find another we would like to have." He finished with the question pending.

"Hubie, you know that, which animals we keep is entirely up to you. You are the expert in that area. If you want to sell that bull, I'll have Emil call the newspaper and put an ad in it for you."

"That's an excellent idea. Let's do it right away. We can use some of the money to buy a ticket for Roy, if and when he is willing to come home." Dad's voice held a wistful sound as he mentioned Roy's name.

I knew he missed the boy very much. Roy was another pair of capable hands to help with the work, but Roy was more than that. He was the one who could entertain us on those quiet evenings when we would gather in the front room and just talk together. Us children would get dad and mother talking about their experiences in the various places they had lived. Before the evening was over though, Roy would come up with a funny tale to relate. By the time he would get through, he would have us youngsters rolling on the floor with laughter. Dad would be throwing his head back, letting his deep-throated laughter roll through the house. If Roy's story didn't make us laugh, dad's laughter would.

Thinking about my brother made me unhappy. I realized that I missed him, too. His teasing, and the way he had of pulling my hair from behind to get my attention. The silly names he called me. And the good times we had. He would put me in the wheelbarrow sometimes, and run it around the circular driveway between the house and the barn. He loved to take the turns sharply, tipping the wheelbarrow precariously, making me scream.

When he hitched King to the manure spreader or cultivator, he would occasionally let me ride along. Roy would even lift me onto Kings back and let me ride him, as he drove him up one row and down the next. The more I thought about it, the more happy times I remembered with him, and the more I missed him.

I got up from my place on the floor and wandered into the kitchen. Dad and mother were still talking quietly to one another. Whenever I was in their presence, when they were like this, I felt like an intruder. They seemed to be so involved with each other that there was no room for anyone else in their lives at that moment. I hung around the peripheral boundary for several minutes, then realizing that they were so deeply involved with each other that I might as well vanish, I left the room. For the next few minutes I imagined that I was an orphan, completely alone, with no one to associate with. It made me feel sad. I turned back to Bobby, but he had fallen asleep on the floor, with his neatly piled blocks now forming a circle around him. I went to the chair where Eileen always sat to read her books, and picked up the latest one she was into. I crawled up into the chair with the book in my hand, and started turning pages. Words, words, words, but no pictures. How I wished I could read. This was boring. I put down the book, slipped back to the floor, and decided to find something outside to do.

I slipped my arms through the sleeves of a sweater and went out the front door. I headed to my favorite spot beneath the huge oak tree. A bushy tailed, gray squirrel ran across the yard, to the tree, and in one long bound was half way up the trunk. As I watched, it ran out on a limb, looked down at me and chattered. "Well, hello to you too, Mr. Squirrel," I said. "Would you be my friend today? I'm ever so lonesome." He studied me for a few moments more, and then satisfied that I was no threat, continued on up the tree. "Even he doesn't want to play with me!" I moaned.

As I sat beneath the tree, I realized that the day had turned much warmer. The huge leaves had turned to sharp shades of red and gold. Every once in a while, one would drift down towards me. I began gathering them in a heap. Acorns were all around the base of this great tree, and I gathered them as well. They were so cute, with their little oval faces topped with a cone shaped hat. I began to talk with them as if they were my friends. As I did, an imaginary friend developed in my mind. I thought about her until I could picture what she looked like. She had fiery red, curly hair, and pretty, green eyes. She smiled a lot and she liked me. She said only pleasant things to me, and me to her. We laughed and played, making the leaves and twigs into various pieces of furniture, and the acorns into our children. My red headed, friend's name, was Patty. I liked her name better than my own. Helen sounded so old and cold to me. I asked Patty if she would call me Lilly? It sounded like a flower and I so wanted to be pretty.

Before long Ringo and Blacky joined us. We played with our cats, talked to our acorn children, and watched for the squirrel. He would come down to where he could see us, chatter his displeasure at our being under his tree, and then disappear again. We laughed at him, while rolling over the leaf and stick furniture we had made. Ringo decided to go up the tree after the little critter. The squirrel watched the cat approach and then took off. He was too fast for her though, and Ringo stopped on the now empty limb. She meowed at the squirrels' retreating figure as he disappeared into the branches high above.

"Ha, ha," Patty and I laughed at her. "Now you have got to get yourself down." She answered us with a low, mournful, meow, and reached out a paw towards us as if to say, 'come get me.'

"Sorry Ringo, you got yourself into that mess, you'll have to get yourself down." We lay on our backs, watching the cat, and talking softly to each other.

"Helen, where are you!" Mother's voice finally cut through my reverie, and I realized that she was calling me. It had taken a few calls before I realized that I was Helen to her, and not Lilly.

"Here I am mama," I called, as I got to my feet. She looked in my direction and motioned for me to come to her.

"Bye Patty, I have to go now. Watch Ringo for me," I instructed my friend, as I turned and ran to the stoop where mother waited. She handed me an envelope, and asked me to put it in the mailbox for her.

"Be sure to put the flag up," she reminded me.

"I will, mama." It took only a few minutes to run to the mailbox, open the door, place the envelope inside, shut the door and raise the red flag. Before heading back to the house, I saw a large truck coming down the road in our direction. It slowed at Zobel's driveway and turned in, driving to the back of their house. I ran quickly to our house, calling to mother as I hit the stoop running, and sprang for the door. She opened it before I had a chance to, causing me to fall forward into the front room.

"Oops!" I said, as I hit the floor, landing hard on my hands and knees.

"Helen, for heavens sake, what's got into you? What's all the shouting about?"

"A big truck turned into Zobel's place! It was really big!" I said breathlessly, as I rolled over into a sitting position and began rubbing my knees with smarting hands.

"Well, for goodness sakes! Haven't you ever seen a truck before?" she asked.

"Yes, but not at Zobel's," I said. "What do you think it is there for?"

"Well, little miss curious, they probably have ordered something from town. If you really must know, I have to be going over there in a few minutes anyway, and you can come with me. Did you hurt yourself?"

I took a moment to think about it, and decided that my knees would stop smarting in a few minutes. More importantly, mother had told me I could go with her to the neighbors. I needed to be fine for that, so I said, "I'm all right."

"Get up from the floor and go wash your face and hands. Brush your hair too, it's full of leaves."

"Okay mama," I said, as I bounced to my feet and headed into the kitchen and to the washbasin. I dipped some water from the water pail and poured it into the basin. The bar of ivory soap was lying on a dish near by. My hand was wet, causing the soap to slip from my hands and fly into the basin. It took several tries before I could lather up my hands, and get the soap back into its dish. I ran my hands over my face, rubbed my hands together, and then dipped them into the basin to rinse them off. I grabbed the towel that hung from a rung at the side

Country Splendor

of the cupboard, rubbed it across my face and the palms of my hands, before hanging it back up. I reached for the brush that was at the back of the cupboard and brushed at my hair. I couldn't see my reflection so I had to go by feel, and my hair felt fine, so I put the brush down and turned to daddy asking, "Do I look fine?"

He glanced across the table at me and started to laugh. "I think we need to work on that hair a bit more. Bring me the brush."

I reached for the brush again, taking it to dad. He turned me around and began on the back of my hair. He pulled leaves from it, as he pulled the brush through it. "Ouch!" I complained, as I struggled to pull myself free.

"Hey, Little one, hold still. You must have been rolling around in the leaves. I'll try to be gentle, but I have to get them out of the tangles, and the tangles out of your hair." I tried to stand still as he worked, but every now and then the brush got caught in yet another tangle and pulled a little hard. I bit my lip to keep from crying out, and continued to stand close enough for him to reach my head, but I did move a few times when it really hurt.

Finally, he pushed me forward and said, "I think that will do. Put this brush away." I was so glad to have that torture over with that I jumped to oblige. Grabbing the brush, I put it away before he could change his mind. I wasn't about to ask him how I looked again, so I just hurried into the front room to find mother. She was bending over Bobby, pulling his pants back in place, after changing his diaper.

"Are you ready?" she asked me.

"Yes, I washed my self and daddy brushed my hair."

"Okay then, we will leave in just a few minutes."

Because of my enthusiasm to go see what that truck brought to the Zobel's, those 'few minutes' seemed to take forever. I asked mother a number of times, if she were ready yet. She finally answered back in a frustrated tone, "Ask me one more time, young lady, and you will stay home!" I knew that tone meant business, so I paced quietly, until she finally headed for the door, saying, "Come on."

She carried Bobby on one hip, with one arm around him, and a piece of paper in the other hand. Her strides were long, and I had to run to keep up with her. We were across the road and up to Audrey's door in record time. It took a second knock to illicit a response, when the door opened to a prettily smiling face.

"Hi, come on in," Audrey said, as she stepped back to make room for us to enter. She seemed to be in good spirits. She closed the door behind us. Turning back to us she ushered us into the kitchen. "Come, look at what Emil has bought," she said, with a touch of excitement in her voice.

I rushed ahead of the women, as that was exactly why I was there. To see 'it'! The kitchen door was standing ajar, allowing me a clear view, through the screen door, of the new investment. That's what Audrey called it, "the new investment," as she explained to mother, what they bought and why.

"Isn't that a beauty? Newest one they had in stock, and the biggest. Said it would do the work of four horses in half the time. Can you imagine?" Audrey exclaimed.

"That's the nicest one I've ever seen," Mother commented. "Must have cost a pretty penny!"

"But, what is it?" I asked. It certainly was huge, had monstrous sized wheels, and a seat that sat up so high that I wondered how anyone could manage to climb into it.

"That's a tractor," Audrey explained.

"What's it for?" I asked.

"It pulls machinery," she answered.

"But you have horses that do that," I reminded her.

"But you see, Helen, this tractor takes the place of horses. It is very powerful and can do the work faster and easier than with horses."

"What will you do with your horses?" I wanted to know.

"I think Emil has it in mind to sell them," she replied.

"Could we buy them, mama?" I asked. "Dad said we need another horse since Old Black Joe died."

"I don't think we could afford those horses, Helen. They are an expensive pair, not your ordinary working horses," Mother stated, matter-of-factly.

Country Splendor

"But I heard daddy say that he would give his right arm for a pair like them," I said.

"We can't always have what we want," Mother said resignedly.

Audrey said with a smile, "Don't be too sure about that, Verna. Sometimes miracles do happen."

I wondered about that. 'I asked for a miracle and got a snowsuit instead of a dress. Maybe grownups know how to talk to God better than I do,' I reasoned.

Mother was explaining to Audrey, dad's decision to have Emil call in an ad, to be placed in the paper, to sell dad's prize bull.

Audrey said, "That's too bad he has to sell that fine bull. It throws handsome calves. Really top of the line dairy cows."

I thought, 'throws calves? Why would anyone want a bull that throws calves?' That sounded mean to me. 'Maybe that's why dad wants to get rid of him.'

Audrey seemed to be deep in thought for several minutes, as we stood watching Emil move his new tractor around. The man, who came with the truck, seemed to be showing Emil how to operate the various handles and levers on the tractor. The tractor looked enormous to me, and Emil seemed small in comparison. The sight of one man, being able to handle such a massive machine, enthralled me.

Audrey offered mother a cup of coffee while they discussed the ad mother wanted placed in the paper. They left the doorway, went to the stove for their cups of coffee, and then carried them into the front room where they would be more comfortable.

Bobby was playing on the front room floor with the stuffed bear Audrey had handed him. He seemed to love rolling all over the floor with the bear. It was almost as tall as he was, and made a perfect toy to wrestle with.

Audrey came back to the kitchen and offered me a glass of juice. I accepted. She went to the icebox, took out a jar and poured me a glass of orange juice. She offered to let me bring it into the front room, where they were, but I declined. I explained to her that I wanted to remain sitting where I was, so that I could continue to watch the goings on outside, through the door. She said she understood, and returned to the front room where mother waited for her.

Emil put the tractor through its paces; going forward, backing up, turning in first one direction, then another. Lifting the snowplow that came with the tractor, dropping it down and lifting it again. The man, who brought the tractor, continued instructing him in its operations. They finally removed the snowplow from the front of the tractor and put it to one side. Then Emil drove the tractor up to a field plow, and watched, while the instructor attached the plow behind it. He climbed up on the tractor beside Emil, and showed him how to work some levers, and then got down again to work levers on the plow itself. Once they had that mastered, they proceeded to attach other farm implements to the tractor, and worked through the process of how to handle each one. It seemed like a lot of work to me.

The afternoon slipped quickly by, as Emil gained the knowledge he would need to be able to handle this new machine. He seemed satisfied at long last, and I watched as he shook the hand of the man who was tutoring him. The man pulled himself into his truck, started the engine and drove away. Emil stood still, watching the man leave, and then turned to take one last look at his new investment. He nodded his head as if to affirm that it was a good purchase, then turned and headed to the house.

I got down from the stool and moved it away from the door, allowing Emil the room to enter. "Hi there. I saw you watching me handle that monster out there. What do you think of it?" He asked.

"I think it's huge! How can you handle such a large machine?"

"It's really not as hard as you would think. Would you like me to give you a ride on it?"

"Oh no. I like horses better." He looked at me and laughed, causing his face to look soft and kind. His eyes always seemed to be twinkling, and dimples played at the sides of his mouth, when he was amused. I liked looking at him. He was such a kind man.

"Think it's time I have a cup of coffee. Did your mother have something to talk to me about?" he asked, as he saw her looking at him from the front room, as if she had something to discuss with him.

Country Splendor

"Yes. Dad wants to sell the bull because it throws calves and hurts him."

He turned and looked at me, with a puzzled look in his eyes, and suddenly realizing what I must have deciphered from adult talks I had over heard, he chuckled softly, shaking his head. He crossed the room to the stove and filled himself a cup of coffee, before heading into the living room. He was still grinning to himself, as he sat down on the chair beside mother, and spoke softly to her. She looked at me and started to grin, placing her hand in front of her mouth, to hide her mirth.

I watched to see if they were laughing at me, but they began talking about the ad for the paper. Emil listened to mother, nodding his head in understanding. He was quiet for some time, as if he were contemplating something. Finally, he answered mother, but they talked so softly that I couldn't make out what was being said. Something must have been decided, as mother rose from the couch, and motioned for me to join her in the front room.

"Get your brother, Helen, we must get home. Emil will be over later to talk with dad. Thank you for the coffee, Audrey. I'll check back with you soon. Emil, we will see you later then?"

He was on his feet, heading for the door, to open it for us, when he answered. "Yes, right after supper, if that's all right with you."

"Yes, of course. Hubert will be glad to see you. Time hangs heavy on his hands when he can't work. We'll see you then," she said, as she passed through the door and out onto the porch. "Come on kids, let's get home." I had Bobby by the hand, and we were right at her heels, all the way to the road and across to our yard. Once mother knew we were safely in our yard, she took off for the house, leaving us behind to follow as we could. By the time we made the house, and entered through the front room door, mother was sitting by dad at the kitchen table, filling him in on all that had happened at the Zobel's that day.

I slipped into the kitchen and sat down at the table, too. I had seen so much, and wanted to share it with daddy, but mother got to him first. I knew by past experience that I must never interrupt when the grown-ups were talking, so I sat quietly, waiting for an opening. I waited and waited, and struggled to keep my eyes open. My lids were getting heavier with each passing minute. I lay my head down on my arms, which were folded on the table in front of me. The quiet talking became a murmur, and then nothing.

CHAPTER TWENTY

The banging of the front door woke me. I raised my head from my arms to see Ron and Eileen enter the house. I tried to raise my arm to wave, but found it wouldn't work. "Mom, my arm won't move!" I cried at mother, as she moved around the kitchen, preparing some vegetables to drop into the soup kettle on the stove.

She looked at me, saying, "You've been sleeping on your arms. Now they are asleep. Just move them around and they will wake up."

"I've tried to move them, and it hurts!" I complained.

"That's because the blood has to run back into them, and that can hurt a bit. But, just keep moving them, and they will get better."

"Hi, mom," Ron said, as he walked into the kitchen. "We stopped by Zobel's on the way home and saw his new tractor. Boy! That is some mean machine!"

"We were over there shortly after it arrived, and Helen watched Emil working it. He's convinced that it will cut down on his work time. What did Herbert think of it?"

Ron shrugged his shoulders. "He knew his dad was getting it, so he didn't get too excited. I think he feels bad about the horses. He doesn't want his dad to get rid of them."

"What do you think? Horses or tractors?" I asked.

"Knowing you, it would be horses," he said. "But frankly, tractors are something of the future. I heard a couple of other kids at school

Country Splendor

say that their dads are getting tractors. They figure that the cost of gas is a small price to pay to replace all the care that horses take."

Mother looked thoughtful for a moment, and then responded. "You have a point. The only thing is, some people love their horses so much that the extra work is considered a labor of love. Take your dad for instance; watching a beautiful team of horses working is what convinced him into getting back into farming. He might break down and get a tractor one day, but I don't think he would ever give up his horses."

"Good! I just love horses!" I said.

"Hoses, hoses," Bobby repeated, as he came running up to my chair.

"That makes three of us, Bobby," I said, as I patted him on his golden curls.

Eileen entered the kitchen, wearing her everyday dress. "Good, I see you've changed out of your new school dress. How did the girls at school like it?" Mother asked her, as Eileen circled the table and came up beside mother's chair.

"They said it was pretty. Of course they were all wearing new clothes, too, all except this one new girl. Her name is Marge. I felt sorry for her. Her clothes were clean, but the colors were almost washed out of them. She kind of hung back and wouldn't talk to the other girls. At recess, I noticed her standing behind the school all by herself. I went over and talked to her, and found out that they moved here from Racine. They bought the old Hansen place. Isn't that in pretty sad shape?"

"Yes, that is, or was. They must have done some work on the house in order to live in it. As I recall, the windows were broken out and the door sagged on its hinges. The roof and walls were still solid, when we looked at it last. Dad and I looked it over pretty thoroughly before we decided to move here. It had a lovely pond on it and some good-looking fields. There was a very thick stand of timber behind it, as I recall. But it hasn't been worked in years. The barn needed replacing and the sheds were in sorry shape."

"I was thinking, mama, Marge is a little thinner and shorter than I am. That dark blue dress of mine, with the white collar and cuffs, you know the one, right? Could I give that to Marge? It would just fit her," Eileen said.

"But I was saving that for Helen. It's almost like new."

"Mama," I spoke up, trying to get mother's attention, "it's alright if you want to give Marge that dress. It is still way too big for me. She needs it more that I do."

Mother looked over at me. "Are you sure, Helen? That color blue looks very pretty on you."

"Eileen, you really want her to have it, don't you?" I asked.

"I just thought that it might be nice to give her something pretty to wear. It might make her feel more like the rest of us," she insisted.

"You know something, Eileen? You are right. Tell you what we will do. Since they are new to this area, we will make a day of going over there and welcoming them here. Let's do it on Saturday. I'll fix up a welcome basket of fresh baked cookies, cake and bread, and maybe a few of my jars of vegetables and fruits too. Then we'll slip in a couple of dresses for Marge as well. Are there any other children in their family?"

"I really don't know. She seems to be the only one coming to school. I will ask her tomorrow. Should I tell her that we want to come over on Saturday and welcome them here?" Eileen asked.

"Yes, I think that would be a good idea. It is better to set up a visit than to surprise them. Be sure and let them know that it is a tradition around here, to welcome the newcomers. Actually, what we usually do, is get several of the families together to go at one time, and everyone brings things to give to the new family. How would you like that?"

"Oh, yes! That would be so nice. It would be like the party everyone threw for us when we moved here, remember? There were so many people here; they had to take turns coming into the house. And remember all the wonderful stuff they left for us? We were eating on it for weeks, it seemed like," Eileen replied.

"You know what I liked about that best?" Ron chimed in, "how the men helped with things that needed to be repaired, and even brought extra bags of feed and such. Remember how they rehung that door to the haymow? And, they repaired the tract in the barn that the manure spreader rides on. It looked like it had not been used in a long time, they said. They even put a new glass window into the milk house. What they couldn't do to help us that day, they came back later, with the parts that were needed, and finished repairing the rest. They have been our close friends ever since."

"Yes, I remember that too," I said.

"You don't either!" Eileen said. "You were too young to remember that."

"Wasn't either. I do so remember. Don't I mom? I remember all the kids that came along, and we played in the front yard, after one of the big boys mowed it for us, first. We piled the grass up high, under the big oak tree, and played in it. Remember how I came into the house with grass in my hair, and you fussed at me about it, mama?" I asked.

"As a matter of fact, I do remember that Helen. You have always had a good memory. You were three years old then and Bobby was just a year old. Seems like yesterday, and yet it seems like a long time ago. Much has happened in this last year and a half," Mother stated reflectively.

"By the way, Eileen, do you know Marge's last name? That would be helpful when I send the notices out," Mother said.

"I think it was O'Leary, or something like that. The teacher mentioned that it was a good ole' Irish name. I will make sure tomorrow and let you know. Will that be soon enough?"

"Yes, that will do," Mother said, "I will be the whole day getting the notices written up, anyway. I can insert their name before I catch the mailman and ask him to leave a notice in each box. I think I will tell the milk carrier as well. He often talks to the farmers as he picks up their milk. "

"Mother, how about asking Emil to call some of the neighbors that have telephones. That would be quicker than sending notices, wouldn't it?" Eileen asked.

"That's an idea, but I don't know if he would want to take the time to do it, or not."

"If who would do what?" Dad asked, as he came in on the tail end of our conversation.

"Eileen just told us that a new family has moved into that old Hansen farm, on country road F, just west of here. Remember, the one we looked at before we decided on this one?"

"Are you talking about the one that had its windows broken out, and the poor excuses for out-buildings?" Dad asked.

"The very one. We were discussing about having a neighborhood welcome party for them, this coming Saturday. You know, like they did for us, when we moved in?" Mother reminded him.

"Oh yes, that was wonderful. They made us feel like one of them, and all the help they gave us sure made life easier. I think that is an excellent idea, Verna. Lord knows, anyone who tries to get that farm up and running, can use all the help they can get! What's their name?" Dad asked.

"I think its O'Leary, or something like that. I'm going to ask Marge tomorrow, to be sure. That's the new girl at school, the one who moved onto that farm," Eileen explained.

"Were you thinking of asking Emil to spread the word by telephone?" Dad asked.

"Yes, that's what we were talking about when you came in. What do you think? Should we ask him?" Mother asked.

"I think you should mention it to him. You know Emil; he would want to be in on something like this. In fact, when he comes over tonight, I'll talk to him about it then," Dad said.

"Speaking of that, we should be getting the chores done. Eileen, would you take Helen and bring the cows in for milking. Ron, was Roger going to help with the milking tonight?"

Old Chaser started barking just then, and Ron stood up to look out the window. "Well, in fact, here he is now," he said. "Mom, since he

Country Splendor

is already here, why don't we round up the cows and get the milking done? Eileen and Helen can help you with supper."

"Good idea, Ron. Eileen, would you stir the soup, make sure it isn't burning down. Helen, you bring some fruit up from the basement. How about a quart of rhubarb and strawberries mixed? I would like to sweep the floor before Emil gets here. Dad, would you keep Bobby busy in the front room, while we get everything ready for his visit?"

Dad laughed and said, "If I didn't know better, I would think that you had been a sergeant in the army, in a past life.

"Thanks," she said. He pushed back his chair to return to the front room, and stood up to leave. She reached out and touched his shoulder, with an affectionate caress, as he passed her on his way out of the kitchen. Dad turned and gave her one of his heart-felt grins, and continued on to where Bobby sat playing with his little truck.

The milking was done, and our supper was over with by seven thirty. Eileen and I were just finishing up the dishes, when we heard steps on the porch. Mother went to the door and welcomed Emil into the kitchen.

"Hello, Mrs., how is Hubert tonight?" Emil asked, in his polite Norwegian way.

"He's in the front room, and he's good as can be expected. Why don't you go on in and sit with him. I've just put some fresh coffee on. It will be ready in a few minutes. I will bring you each in a cup when it's ready."

"Much obliged," Emil said, as he turned and made his way to where dad sat, in the far corner of the front room. "Hi there, little lad," he said, as he passed Bobby playing on the floor.

Bobby grinned up at him, and dad said, "How are things? Heard you got yourself a new tractor. How do you like it?"

Emil sat down in the chair beside dad. "You know something Hubert? That is one son of a gun, big tractor! I spent the whole afternoon, learning how to operate it. It will take some getting use to, but I think it will save us some working time, and come in handy in many ways."

"You know, Emil, that I have thought on having one of those machines, myself. But then, I thought about not having an excuse to work with my horses, and I changed my mind. Course, I only have King right now, but I've been putting money aside, so if a horse comes available, I'll be able to get it."

"That's one reason I am here tonight, Hubert. I noticed that you have always admired my pair of fine workhorses. What would you say if I told you that they are for sale, if you would like them?" Emil asked, with a gleam in his eye.

"Queen and Prince? You'd sell them?" Dad asked Emil. In his minds eye, he was seeing again, Emil's team, moving gracefully down the road, pulling Emil in his two-seated cutter. They were sleek of body, their coat a shiny bronze color that gleamed with hints of red sunshine, as they pranced regally along. They held their heads and tails in a proud, tight arch, with their long mane and tail, blowing in the wind.

"You know that they have meant a great deal to me. They move out real smartly, and work like a welled oiled machine. Even though they are a smaller and more streamlined breed than the usual work horse, they still are hard workers."

"Emil, you don't have to sell me on that team of yours. I've never seen a more beautiful team or one with more heart. I've dreamed of owning a team like that, but I don't think I have enough money to pay you what they are worth."

"I've been thinking about this for some time," Emil said. "You have an expensive bull that you are wanting to sell. I have need for one and have admired that one of yours. He would be an asset to me, bring fresh good breeding to my stock. I would take him off your hands and together, with whatever you've saved up for another horse, will be good enough. What do you say?"

Dad sat, looking stunned. He rubbed one large work-worn hand across his forehead, smoothing his light curly hair back from his brow. Tears glistened in his eyes as he cleared his throat. "Vell, vell," his voice could hardly be heard. He blinked a couple of times and then turned his sky blue eyes on his friend. "I've never heard of a deal that would please me more. Are you sure you aren't getting the short end of the stick, though?"

"Hubert, you are the only man I would trust with my horses. I know that you would treat them right. I would feel privileged if you would agree to my offer."

"Emil, let's shake on it right now, before you come to your right mind!" Dad laughed, as he held out his right hand and took Emil's big hand in his, squeezing it to cement the deal.

Mother entered the scene just then, carrying a tray with three cups of coffee, a creamer, sugar bowl, and three spoons, on it. She sat it down on the table next to dads chair and took the vacant chair beside it. Then looking at the two men, she noticed that they were both wearing big grins, which were deepening the dimples in their cheeks. "Okay, you two. I know that neither my presence, nor my coffee, would put that kind of look on your faces. What's up?"

They started speaking at the same time, stopped, looked at each other, and started laughing. "You go first, Hubert," Emil conceded.

Dad grinned even wider as he said, "Verna, we are the proud owners of the most beautiful team of horses in this whole state."

"Really? How?" she said, almost speechless. Emil proceeded to tell her the deal that the two of them had shook on.

"Oh Hubert! I know how much you have coveted a team of horses like his. I can't believe that they are really yours! Emil, you will never know how much we appreciate your generosity and kindness. You are truly a friend in deed." She wished that she could reach over and give each of them a kiss, and a hug of gratitude and joy, but she knew that a lady did not behave in that way, so she just sat, smiling at first one of them, and then the other.

In her mind, she knew that this was like a fresh breeze of hope for her husband. Nothing would make him want to get well faster, than a new pair of extremely beautiful horses to play with. And she truly believed that working with horses that he loved, was like playing, to him.

Ron had walked Roger home, and Eileen and I had just finished the kitchen chores, when he entered the house. We all headed for the front room; curious to see what Emil's visit was all about. Eileen, Ronald and I, took chairs with us from the kitchen, and placed them into a circle, which included the folks and our visitor. Once seated, we looked at the three of them, sitting there with looks on their faces that suggested that something pleasing had just happened.

Ron broke the charged silence with a greeting to Emil, and with a "how are you?" thrown in.

Emil smiled a greeting back, and answered that he was better than okay.

"How so?" Ron inquired. "Guess you are really pleased with your new tractor then?"

Emil laughed softly, "Well, that, and the deal your dad and I just made."

"What was that?" We all wanted to know, but Ron asked the question first.

"I am now the owner of your prize bull, and your dad is the owner of my team of horses."

"What? Really?" Ron said, with an echo following from Eileen and I.

"Yah, that's right," Dad said. "Can you believe it? I'm still not sure that I'm not dreaming all this."

"Nope! You are very much hooked, Hubert, and you will not wake up from this one." Emil gave an evil chuckle as we all laughed at him.

"Isn't that the best news you have heard in a long time? Just think, Queen and Prince and King. We have royalty as work horses!" Mother stated.

"Grandfather Ruprecht said our ancestors were royalty, so now we have horses, fit for a king," Eileen responded. "Just think of that! Wait until I tell the kids at school tomorrow. Won't they be surprised?"

"Whoa, Eileen," Dad warned. "They may not believe you about our ancestors, even though it is true. Sometimes that kind of news is better kept just among family. About the royalty in our background, I mean. Which reminds me, Emil. There is a new family living on the Old Hansen place on country road F. Their daughter goes to school

Country Splendor

with Eileen. Eileen seems to think that they may be down on their luck a bit, and we were wondering about having a welcome party for them. What do you think?"

"The old Hansen place, you say? That was in bad shape the last time I saw it. Course that was some months back, but still, it seems to me that it would take a lot of hard work to bring it back to what it use to be. You know, at one time that was a very attractive farm. I had thought of buying it myself, when we first moved here. But the couple that owned it, the original owners, had died in an accident. The ones that stood to inherit it, couldn't, or wouldn't, come to an agreement on how to split the money. The property was tied up in litigation for so long that the land went fallow and the buildings began to deteriorate. Then no one wanted to buy it, until recently, I guess. But all that aside, I think that plenty of our neighbors would be glad to know that someone is finally on that piece of property. They would jump at the chance to welcome them, and to get to know them. When would you like to do this?" Emil inquired of mother.

"We were thinking of this coming Saturday. Do you think that would be too soon? If so, we could probably do it the following Saturday," Mother suggested. We all sat looking at Emil, watching his mind work, as thoughts played across his face.

"It is short notice, but we have put things together that fast before. Let me give some neighbors, with phones, a call and see what response I get. Then I will let you know. How would that be?"

I wanted to bring up a subject, but was a little unsure of how to do it. Finally, I decided I was just going to blurt it out, and let it fall where it may. "Mama is going to give one of Eileen's dresses to that new girl at school, because she needs some nice clothes," I said.

"Helen, we don't tell things like that." Mother's rebuke made me blush with shame.

"Is that true, Mrs.? That the new peoples daughter needs some nice clothes?" Emil kindly asked.

"Yes, she does," Eileen confessed. "And I asked mother to give one of the dresses that I've outgrown to her."

"That is a very noble thing you are doing for her. I will talk to my wife, and see if there aren't a few things of Gertrude's that we could give as well. Are there other children in that family?" he asked.

"I am going to find out, tomorrow," Eileen explained.

"We will let you know tomorrow for sure. Maybe by then, you will know when we can have the welcoming party?" Mother asked.

"Yes, I will call around and find out when to plan it. Ron, would you like to come by on your way home from school tomorrow, to bring your horses' home with you? Herbert and I will come over with you and take that ornery bull off your hands," He laughed.

"Good riddance to bad rubbish!" Dad said, with a groan, and then chuckled beneath his breath.

"I must be getting home now, tomorrow comes very early these days. I will be seeing you tomorrow afternoon then." Emil rose to his full height and stretched a bit. "I'm a bit sore from working that tractor," he admitted with a grin. "Hope you have a good nights rest, Hubert. Don't let those horses keep you awake."

"Don't you worry, I'll probably be grooming them all night," Dad said, with a wave of his hand.

Mother walked Emil to the door, opened it and stepped out onto the porch with him. "Emil, I don't know how to thank you for all you have done. I really think that with the gift of those horses to Hubert, you have given him a reason to live. I've not seen him look that happy for a very long time."

"I'm glad we could work out a deal. There is no one I would rather have that team, than your husband. I know they will get the best of treatment and care. He's a real horse lover. To tell you the truth, I've done this for myself, as well as for him. Those horses have become like family to me, and Hubert is like the brother I never had, so you can see how this has worked out for the best, for both of us. I must run now. I'll see you tomorrow afternoon." He stepped off the porch and waved, as he crossed the yard and headed across the road for home.

CHAPTER TWENTY-ONE

After school the next day, Eileen came home with her news. The information on the new family was confirmed, their name was O'Malley, not O'Leary, and there was a set of twin boys, four years of age, at home, besides the older girl, Margaret. The neighbors, whom Emil was able to reach by phone, voted unanimously for a welcoming party on the following Saturday. Notices were to be sent out to the others on our mail route, in case they wanted to take part in the welcoming party as well.

Mother, had just confirmed that she had the notices ready to be mailed, and she would post them in the mailbox the next morning, when Ron, Emil and Herbert came into the back yard. Chaser was barking up a storm, so we knew that the new team of horses must have arrived also. Dad hurried out to great them, filling his eyes with the beauty of his new pair of horses. The bull was exchanged for the horses, and all four of them, Emil, dad, and the two young men, seemed to have permanent smiles glued to their faces.

In the days ahead, dad became a bit of a problem for mother, though, as he kept sneaking out of the house whenever mother's back was turned. Mother would find him gone and guess his where-bouts, being right every time. He would be in the horse barn, with brushes and curry combs in his hands, working on one or the other of the horses. Mother finally gave up trying to control his movements by chastising him about doing more than she thought he should. Once she came to

Country Splendor

the conclusion that neither threatening, cajoling nor reasoning, would make dad adhere to her wishes, she gave up entirely, and told him that his health was in his hands and he'd better not come whining to her with his aches! Dad just grinned at her and turned back to his horse grooming.

Instead of the care of his horses causing him more pain though, just the opposite was true. Just as mother had prophesied the night that Emil had made that deal with dad, that beautiful team of horses had given dad a renewed reason for living. Miracles come in some amazing ways and we were grateful that dad received his. He was much more active, and complained little about his pain. His healing seemed to occur in an inordinate amount of time.

Saturday morning was wet from a heavy rain beating down, all the night before. But the sun broke out from behind the clouds by the time the milking was completed. As I walked across the grass to the hen house, I noticed a vapor rising from the wet grass as if being drawn by the sun's strong rays. The air had a fresh, washed smell to it, and I breathed it in deeply.

A puddle had formed in the driveway where the milk truck pulled up each morning and then pulled out again. The driver stepped on the gas, spinning his tires as he pulled away, creating an indentation in the gravel. After the rain, the ground was softer and the hole grew considerably that morning. It had become a nice sized hole, filling up from the run-off from the slightly higher ground around it.

I was on my way to take care of my morning chores, when I noticed the puddle. I walked bare-foot through it, savoring the cool, wet feel of the water as it rose to my ankles. I splashed in it playfully, wishing it were big enough to swim in. Not that I could swim yet, but how was I ever to learn if I never got in water deep enough to swim in? That definitely was a real conundrum.

I left my lovely puddle and made my way to the granary, only to reach there and remember that the bucket I used for carrying grain to the chickens, was left in the hen house. I proceeded to the hen house to retrieve my bucket and woke up the sleeping chickens. They stretched out their necks and beat their wings in the air for a moment, before settling back down on their perch. "Well, good morning to you, too," I said. "I'll be right back with your feed. You may want to eat indoors today, as the ground is very wet. Or maybe not, what do you think?" The trouble with talking to chickens; is, it is only a one-way conversation. Occasionally, one might cluck a bit, as she flew down from her perch, but other than that, they are not prone to be very vocal.

Back to the granary I went, just in time to frighten a couple of marauding mice into diving through a hole in the sidewall of the grain bin. "Ha, caught you at it! Guess I'll have to bring one of the cats in here to guard the grain," I said, as I filled my bucket. I knew that as soon as I left they would be right back, but in reality, there was grain enough for all the creatures on the farm. I just loved to threaten them a bit. 'Such timid creatures,' I thought to myself. 'And so cute, with their tiny round gray bodies, slender long tails and large round ears.'

I decided to leave most of the chicken feed in the troughs, inside the chicken coup, and threw just a small amount of it around the very wet yard. When the weather is severe they seem to prefer to dine inside anyway. I then proceeded to gather the eggs, shut the door that humans walked through, crossed the hen yard and passed through the gate, latching it securely behind me. Hen houses have a smaller open door, close to the floor, just to one side of the bigger door. This smaller hole was outfitted with a small wooden, slatted, slide that reaches from the hole, down to the ground on the outside of their house, for the hens to use. It was fun to watch them pass through that door, using their wings to fly from that height to the ground. They looked so silly, with their feathers all ruffled, their wings beating wildly, and squawking shrilly as they descended to the ground. The slide is really a ramp for them to go back up and into their house on.

"Everything is relevant to the action," Eileen told me when I asked her, why it was a 'slide' and a 'ramp.' "Look, silly one" she said to me, "When they come out, it is a slide, when they go in, it is a ramp, got it?"

Well, whether I did understand why it had two names or not, after she called me 'silly' I sure wasn't going to act 'stupid' as well, so I let

Country Splendor

the matter drop. I still couldn't see the point of having two names for one piece of board, but how do you fight adult logic?

With the basket of eggs in my hands, I headed back to the house, by way of the mud puddle, of course. How often did I have the chance to play in water, after all? The cool water felt so good, as I stepped gingerly into it. The bottom of the puddle was getting slippery, and when I wiggled my feet in the mud, it would squish up between my toes.

"Helen! Get in here with those eggs. I need to get this meal fixed, now!" Mother stated from the porch, sounding a little irritated by my procrastination.

"Coming, mom," I yelled, as I hurried to get across the puddle. I lifted my right foot to place it on dryer ground, just as my left foot slid out from under me, and I landed on my back with a big splash, covering every inch of myself with muddy water. I came out of that puddle, spluttering, and shaking the mud from myself. I still held the basket of eggs in my right hand, and had somehow managed to keep the eggs in the basket, fairly in tact.

Mother watched the whole fiasco, of course, and she told dad later that she likened me to the creature of the black lagoon coming out of the mire. My hair was matted to my head with rivulets of muddy water running down my face. My clothes clung to me as only wet, muddy, clothes can. I proceeded in the direction of the kitchen porch, hampered by my wet things clinging to my legs. "Well, will you hurry?" Mother asked. "I need the eggs."

"I'm coming as fast as I can," I answered, hoping she wouldn't take my remark as insolence. She didn't seem to bristle anymore than she already had, so I felt fairly safe coming within her reach.

"Child, when I send you out to do a job, I never know what will happen or what shape you will return in. It certainly makes my life a bit more fascinating!" She said, as she shook her head as if she just couldn't believe what had just happened. "Take that muddy dress off and leave it on the porch here. I've some water on the stove heating. It's a good thing I planned on bathing you kids before we left for the party."

As she preceded me into the kitchen, she motioned for me to sit on one of the wooden chairs. "Stay there until I have the bath water ready. Eileen can wash you off while I get Bobby ready."

Mother had brought in a washtub, earlier that morning, and sat it in the middle of the room, between the table and the stove. A sheet was hung across the doorway into the front room, affording some privacy to the one taking their turn at the tub of warm water. She poured some water from the large pan on the stove and then cooled it down with water from the water pail. "Eileen, bring Bobby here," she called.

Eileen must have undressed him for her already, as this thoroughly naked little boy came running into the kitchen, standing in front of mother, holding his fat butt cheeks with both hands. Mother laughed to see him standing thusly, and reached out, picked him up and deposited him into the warm bath water. He sat down with a plop and started splashing water, every which way.

"Bobby, stop that!" Mother told him, as she started rubbing the bar of ivory soap all over him. Next she took the washcloth she had lying on a chair, and wetting it in the water, she washed him with it. "There you are, all nice and pink and clean." She picked him out of the tub, sitting herself back into a chair; then wrapping a towel around him, she sat him on her lap.

"Okay Eileen. Will you help wash this mud child off, while I dress Bobby?" she said, turning her head towards the front room as she spoke.

Eileen came into the kitchen, took one look at me and said, "Mud child is right! Must have taken you several tries to get this covered."

"Actually not. One good fall and here I am," I said.

"I've got a good idea. Let's play a trick on dad. He hasn't seen you yet, has he?" She asked.

"No, I don't even know where he is."

"He's in the front room reading his paper. We'll leave your bloomers on for now. Stick only your left leg into the tub." She instructed me by touching, which leg was the left one.

I did as she said, and she proceeded to wash half of my face off with the washcloth and soap. Then she washed that side of my neck, that arm and half of the side of my chest and back. Then she washed the leg that was in the tub. "I can't do anything with your hair right now, but this will do." Then she wrapped a towel around my middle and carried me into where daddy sat.

"Dad," she got his attention from the paper he was reading. She stood me on the floor in front of him and whispered to me to ask him which side he liked best.

"Daddy, which side do you like best?" I grinned at him.

He looked me over very thoughtfully, rubbed his chin and said, "This side," pointing to the one that was still caked in mud.

Eileen and I started laughing, as she picked me back up and carried me back to my bath. I heard mother and dad chuckling to each other, as they watched us walk from the room.

This time Eileen pulled my bloomers off and sat me down in the tub and started pouring water from a pitcher, over my head. I had to close my eyes real tight and hold my breath. Once it was thoroughly wet, she used the soap to work up a good lather in my hair. She had me scoot down in the tub where she could lay me back, so my head was over the water in the tub. Then she poured clean water through my hair until the water ran free of soap. That done she sat me back up and washed the rest of the mud from my body. "Okay, stand up, step out onto this rug and I'll dry you off."

She rubbed me down with a coarse, thick, towel until I was dry. My skin was pink and tingly by the time she was through. She dressed me in the clean clothes that mother had laid out for me to wear that day. First came the fresh pair of bloomers, then a pair of the new white stockings that reached to the bottom of my bloomers, held up by garters. Next she pulled a white cotton slip over my head, followed by a dress. When I looked down at the dress she put on me, I gasped. "This isn't mine. I've never seen it before." It was a pink dress with tiny blue and white flowers on it. The collar was white lace and a blue sash tied around my waist.

Mother had been watching from the doorway, and now she walked in and stood before me. "How do you like it? I understand that you wanted a new dress of your very own, and one that no one else has worn. Will this do?"

I looked at mother, then I looked at Eileen, then I looked again at the pretty pink and white dress I had on. "How did you know?" I asked, as a bit of laughter caught in my throat, just as a sob followed some tears. I wasn't sure if I should laugh or cry, it was just so wonderful.

"Well, lets just say that a little bird told me. Do you like it?" Mother asked again. I twirled around the room and loved the way the skirt billowed out around me.

"Oh, mama, it is the most beautiful dress in the whole world!" I gave her a hug, with tears threatening to spill out of my eyes once again. She allowed me to hug her, and then she pushed me back, as if she wanted to get a better look at me. "I'm glad you like it. But no playing in mud puddles with it on," she said. "Now we must gather the things together that we are going to take to the O'Malley's today. She moved to the pantry and began to bring items out to place in a box.

Eileen was having me step into my new black shoes when I asked, "Eileen, aren't you going to take a bath?"

She began tying the laces. "Already did, before you came in. Ron got his over with as soon as he came in from milking. We should be leaving soon so we arrive before dinner time."

"Are they going to feed us?" I asked, as Eileen brushed my hair and braided it into two long pigtails with a small ribbon at each end.

"No, everyone that comes brings things to eat. It will be set up on picnic tables outside so everyone can help themselves. There is always enough for everyone, with a lot left over to leave for the O'Malley's to eat later."

"What if they don't have enough dishes for everybody to eat on?" I asked, as even the details were important to me.

"Everyone brings their own plates and silverware too. That way the O'Malley's won't have anything to do but relax and get acquainted with everyone, see? "

"This is going to be a great party, huh, Eileen?" I said as I did a little circle dance in my new finery.

Country Splendor

"I hope so. Marge sounded worried because her folks sounded a little doubtful about it. They don't believe in taking charity and Marge had a hard time convincing them that everyone was bringing welcoming gifts, because everyone is happy that they are living here. Not charity."

"Charity? I heard dad say once that he would never accept charity. He made it sound like a bad thing."

Mother heard our discussion and chimed in, "Charity can be a good thing, if people don't take advantage of it. There is no shame in accepting help when you really need it. But if you take it, just because you are too lazy to work for it yourself, then that can be a bad thing. Your dad is a proud man; he has always worked for everything he has. A few years ago, the country was in a bad depression, which means that there wasn't enough jobs or money for everybody. Your dad walked ten miles everyday, to work for only one dollar a day. True, we raised most of our food, and if it hadn't been for that, we would never have made it. But that one-dollar a day pulled us through. We had no store bought food, we had to patch our clothes, and we made our own soap out of pork lard and ashes. Dad put straw in the bottom of his shoes to keep his feet from freezing when he walked all that way in the snow. It was hard times, but we made it through it, and without having to take hand outs from anyone."

"But, if people bring you stuff because you moved here, that's not charity?" I asked, trying to understand this new concept.

"No, there is nothing wrong in giving or receiving gifts. In fact, it is a good thing. God says He gives good gifts to His people and He expects us to do the same. When we help out a neighbor that is having a hard time, that is a good thing," Mother answered. Dad had entered the kitchen and was listening to mother's explanations.

"But you shouldn't be beholden to anyone," Dad said.

"What does 'beholden' mean?" I asked.

"That means that if you accept a favor from a neighbor, then you should return that favor sometimes when he needs help. It says in the Bible, 'Do unto others as you would have others do unto you.' In other words, if you want people to be nice to you, you be nice to them first," Dad said.

"Does that mean that if the O'Malley's accept all the gifts that are brought to them today, that they should give each person a gift back sometime?"

"I think that it would be more correct to say that they should return the favor by helping out someone else, when they need it. Do you see what I mean? For instance, when we moved in here, all the neighbors brought us all kinds of gifts. Some of them were food; some of the gifts were jobs that needed to be done around here, like fixing things. We accepted everything we were given, and we thanked each one for their gifts. We return their gifts by doing things for others that could use some help. We helped put out the chimney fire at Emil's house that time. We took a load of hay over to Espeseth's after their haystack burned down. See? We might not do something for each person that brought us something, or did something for us, but we help others, as they need help. That way we are doing for others as others have done for us. Do you understand?" Dad asked.

"Is that like when Eileen gave me a bath today, does that mean I should give her a bath some day?"

"No way, little sister. You aren't ever going to give me a bath!" Eileen said indignantly.

Mother laughed and said, "I would say, since she did a favor for you by giving you a bath, that someday you could do something nice for her. You know, like doing one of her chores when she isn't feeling good. It could also be something you do nice for someone else, not necessarily back to the one who did something for you."

"I liked the first explanation best," Eileen laughed, "Do one of my chores for me. That's the one you should do. I'll remember that, you owe me one."

"Eileen, don't tease your sister. It is hard enough trying to get a point across without mudding up the waters," Mother stated. "And I think it is time we start loading this stuff in the car. We don't want to be late."

Country Splendor

Just before noon we pulled into the O'Malley's driveway. "Well, would you look at that?" Dad said, "the yard is mowed and the house is looking very nice. Besides doing the obvious repair work on it, they have painted it as well. Looks great."

"Looks like we are not the first ones here. There's Andrew's car, and the Zobel's are here too. I don't recognize that Model A though, do you dad?" Mother asked.

"Can't say that I do. Guess we will find out shortly." Dad wheeled the Chevy up beside Andrew's car, pulled on the brake and turned off the key. "You know, that Model A looks like the first car my dad ever bought. Remember how he had never driven one before, and when he drove it up to his garage, he didn't remember how to stop it, so he just yelled, "Whoa, whoa!" as it ran through the garage and out the back wall?"

Even though we had heard that story a number of times before, we all laughed as if it were the first time we had heard it. One had to admit it was a funny story. And even funnier when you knew it was true, and it had happened to someone you knew well. Poor grandfather had driven only a beautiful matched pair of chestnut colored horses. A motorized carriage was something completely new to him. We were still chuckling over grandfather's Model A as we exited the car and began unloading the food and packages we brought. Everyone carried something, as we made our way up to the porch. Dad was in front, and even with his hands full he managed to knock on the door.

Marge opened the door, and recognizing Eileen peeking around dad's back, she smiled, stepped back, and invited us in. The front room was painted a lovely, light yellow, and furnished with a dark green, horsehair sofa and matching great chair. A small table holding a lamp and a book, stood between the two. A round hooked rug of various colors graced the floor, and a round wood-burning parlor stove stood to one side. Other chairs were placed around the room, as if waiting for more occupants.

We passed through the front room and entered the big country kitchen. Even though it was a rather large room, it seemed to be filled with people, some sitting and a few standing. I couldn't get a good view past dad and mother, so I wasn't sure who was there. Mother and dad managed to walk into the kitchen and deposit the dishes of food they carried, onto a side table set up for that purpose. Ron and I stood in the doorway, waiting with the things we had carried in. Bobby was hanging onto my leg, trying not to be seen. Eileen had stayed behind in the front room with a girl I presumed to be Marge, and the two of them were whispering among themselves. Eileen came up to me, drawing the red haired girl, with the large, green eyes, with her. She said, "Helen, this is Margaret O'Malley, Marge for short."

I said, "hello," unable to take my eyes off this pretty girl with the red curls and green eyes. It was my friend Patty from under the oak tree. How could this be? Eileen had never mentioned Marge's coloring.

Marge noticed me staring at her and said, "You look like you've seen a ghost. Have you seen me somewhere before?"

I noticed an unusual lilt to her voice that sounded familiar and yet strange. "Not really, but you do look like someone I've played with before. Is there somewhere I can put this package?"

She pointed a delicate finger at a table, standing to one side of the stairway, which curved in an arc up to the second floor. I placed my package among the others already there, and went to Ron, shaking his arm to get his attention. I showed him where to put his package as well. He followed my lead to the table, and having deposited the package, he turned an inquiring eye to his sister, Eileen. She introduced him to Margaret, and Margaret said a bashful hello, as her eyes dropped from his, and a blush brightened her cheeks.

I took a good look at my eldest brother then, trying to see him, as she must have. He was taller than most boys his age, really quite handsome, with his dark hair combed back, his big, dark eyes shining, and a dimpled smile playing around his full lips. He turned his attention to Eileen. "Are the Espeseth boys here yet?"

Marge found enough courage to answer. "Yes, they are in the back yard."

"Thanks, think I'll go back out the way I came in and see if I can find them." I noticed Marge's eyes followed him out the door, and

Country Splendor

only when the door shut behind him did she turn back to Eileen and me.

Bobby kept pulling at my skirt for attention, and I turned to him, asking him, "What do you want?"

Marge looked down at Bobby. "And who might this wee one be?" She stooped down to be closer to his size, and he stared at her with his big, greenish blue, eyes, almost popping from his head.

"My, you are a fine lad. I have two brothers' that would like to play with you. Would you like that?"

He continued to stare at her, as he pushed himself further behind me. There wasn't much to me, so he couldn't hide himself, but he managed to hide his eyes in my skirt.

"A wee bit shy isn't he?" Marge stood back up to her full height, which was still a couple of inches shorter than my sister, Eileen. "My brothers are out back, give me a moment and I will round them up for you. I'll be right back," she said to Eileen, as she headed for the front door.

In a matter of minutes she was back, leading a couple of red headed, blue eyed, boys, about my size, into the front room. "Here is Patrick and Robby," she said. "Boys, why don't you bring a couple of your toys down here and play with this young man? His name is Bobby."

They both ran for the stairs and raced up them. A few minutes later they were running back down the stairs, and into the room to where I stood. I pulled Bobby around to stand in front of me and said, "Look, Bobby, someone to play with, and toys, look."

The twins sat down on the floor in front of Bobby and said, "Hi. Want to play with us?" One had a small colorful ball in his hand, and the other had a small red fire engine. Bobby stared at the boys, and then at the toys. He plopped himself down in front of them and reached for the ball. The one with the ball rolled it towards Bobby's out stretched hands. Bobby grabbed it and rolled it back to him, playing the game I had played with him so many times.

As I stared at the twins, I wondered which was which. They were so much alike, that I couldn't tell them apart. Their faces were full of freckles, even more so than mine. I had so many that people teased me about my freckles. I was very conscious of them, and wished many times, that I had the clear skin my sister and brothers had. I've stared in the mirror above the washstand, wondering what freckles were and how come I had them. When I broached mother with that question she said, "You have been blessed by your Irish ancestors. You have red highlights in your hair, green and gold in your eyes, and pretty reddish freckles across your nose. Don't ever be ashamed of how you look. God made you that way for a purpose."

I sat down on one of the chairs placed against the wall, and watched the boys play together. 'So these people may be my ancestors,' I thought. Not really understanding what ancestors meant, except that mother indicated that they were family, so I assumed that they were part of my family or I was part of theirs. That made me feel special, as I watched Margaret, nicknamed Marge, and thought, you are my special friend. The one God gave me to play with so I wouldn't be so lonely, the same way He gave me my beautiful dress.

More people arrived, burdened with gifts of all kinds. They deposited them on the chairs and in the kitchen. I had yet to meet the parents of my new family, but I knew it was only a matter of time before I would catch sight of them. The front room filled up with adults, and the children were encouraged to play outdoors, to make more room. The girls had escaped to the backyard some time ago, along with other girls that had arrived with their parents. But I felt responsible for Bobby, so I stayed with him and the twins. Now we were heading outdoors as well.

It was a warm fall day, and though the ground was still damp from last nights soaking rain, the porch was dry. I sat on the steps watching Patrick, Robby, and Bobby run around the bushes playing 'I Spy.' Several more of the younger children joined in, wanting to be part of the happy laughter that seemed to make this game so much fun.

As I watched from my place on the porch, I noticed a familiar looking car slowing down, as it approached the now, very full driveway. There was barely room enough for it to slip in among a couple of cars that had pulled slightly onto the grassy yard that bordered each side of the driveway. The car on my side of the driveway obscured my view

Country Splendor

of the passengers in the newly arrived car. I watched as a couple of girls emerged from around that car. "Carol and Lillian!" I called out. I was so excited to see that the Olson's had arrived that I ran to greet them, and the two girls each grabbed a hand, trying to pull me in two directions at once, telling me hello.

"Hey, don't pull me in two," I laughed.

Betty came around into view next, loaded down with packages. Her parents followed, with their arms full as well.

"Helen, where is Eileen?" Betty asked.

"Around in back, somewhere. I haven't seen her or Marge for a while. Why don't you leave your packages inside and I will help you find them?" She nodded, and continued up the steps and into the front room. Her parents said hello to me and followed Betty inside. Moments later she was back out. We joined up with her and ran for the backyard, anxious to find the older kids that were there.

There were quite a number of children formed into two long lines, facing each other in a game of 'Rover, Rover.' They were so caught up in the game that they didn't acknowledge us at first. We stood to one side, watching the game, feeling a little left out.

"Rover, Rover, send Eileen right over!" the one side shouted.

If Eileen could get past the line opposite her, breaking through their outstretched and clasped hands, then she would return to her team. But, if she could not break through, she would become one of the opposing team's members. The strategy was to run as fast as you could, towards the weakest looking link, throwing yourself at that pair of hands, and breaking through their line.

Eileen picked up as much speed as she could in that short distance, hurling her body against two clasped hands, she broke through the opposing teams line. We cheered for her and she looked over, spotting us as she slowed down.

"Oh, hi!" She said. "Do you want to play?" We all nodded and she called to the others. "Hey guys, we have some more players. How should we divide them up?"

They usually banned the smaller kids from playing this particular game, because they usually formed the weaker link, but since there were four of us; they could divide us up equally. "How about Helen and Carol on one side and Lillian and Betty on the other?" The team leaders agreed, and everyone else agreed also, so we were in the game.

Eileen returned to her team with Betty and Lillian in tow. Carol and I fell in with the other team. Now it was Eileen's team's turn to call one of our team members over. Each team had a leader who would strategize on whom to call to come over, hoping to build their team up. The team with the most players when they quit playing, would be the winner.

Herbert Zobel was Eileen's team captain. My big brother, Ron, was our team captain.

Herbert yelled, "Rover, Rover, send Helen right over!"

"Oh no!" I said under my breath. I didn't want to fail my new team so soon. I looked carefully at the team line opposite us, where was the weakest link? Even if there was a smaller person than me there, if his hand was held by a strong enough person, they could prevent me from breaking through. I usually looked for someone who was not paying very close attention, hoping to surprise them. We weren't allowed much time to debate our choices, so I had to decide quickly and move out. I charged full out for a couple that had been talking to each other, instead of paying attention. I threw my body full force at their clasped hands, but my small body hung suspended on their arms, with their hands still clasped, and I was captured.

There was a lot of good-natured teasing and laughing as the two parted, making me join their line. Now it was Ron's turn to pick an opposing member to run, and he shouted, "Rover, Rover, send Betty right over!"

She took off, heading to her right and half way over, quickly diverted to her left, taking that couple completely by surprise, breaking their hold. She headed back to Herbert's team with 'oh no's' from the loosing team, and 'hoorahs' by the team she returned to.

For the next hour or so, we continued the game, gaining and loosing team members, until a call for lunch was heralded among us. The team captains quickly took a count, with Herbert's team the victor,

Country Splendor

and we dispersed in the direction of the picnic tables, set up outside the kitchen door.

Casseroles, salads, fried chicken and buns were piled high on the first table. The second table held a colorful and mouth-watering array of pies, cookies, cake and watermelon slices. Each family doled out plates and silverware to their own members, and the eating began. If there was one observation I could make in all truthfulness, the farm ladies in Wisconsin were all wonderful cooks, every one of them. The only problem I encountered, was that ones stomach just could not hold enough, to try everything set out for us to eat.

With our filled plates in hand, we would group together under tall trees, sitting in the shade, trading small talk and laughter, while enjoying our food. The bigger boys finished their plates first, unfolding from their prone positions to a more or less, upright one. After stretching out the kinks from sitting on their folded legs, they would proceed to the food-laden tables for refills. I was amazed at the amount of food some of them could put away.

The time flew by and families began gathering up their things, calling farewells to others, and departing in their traveling conveyances. Some left in their horse drawn carriages, pulled by handsome teams. A couple of families piled into small wagons filled with hay, with only one farm pony to pull it. A few boys took off on bicycles, and others had cars of different vintages and models.

The old black Model A caught my interest. I wanted to see who owned that old Ford. A rather lanky man, with thinning hair, approached the car. I couldn't identify him as anyone I had seen before. He walked around to the drivers' side and reached in, turning something. Then with a tool of some kind in his hand, he walked to the front of the car. Dad stepped out of the house and stopped beside me, watching the man insert the tool into an opening in the grill area of the car.

"Watch this," he said to me softly, as the man began cranking that tool with all his might. The car's motor sputtered a few times and then stopped. The man rose up and headed back to the drivers side, and reached in again. He came back to the tool and began cranking it once more. Suddenly, the motor took hold, wrenching his arm violently, as the crank whipped around with him still holding it. The words that came out of his mouth, as he grabbed his hand, were ones I automatically knew never to repeat. Dad muttered close to me, "Damn fool should know better than to hold that crank with his thumb wrapped around it. He's lucky it didn't rip it off completely." Shaking his head, dad took my arm and turned me back in the direction of the house. "Come on, we need to help gather up our stuff and head for home."

The house was almost empty of people, as the ones who had not left yet, were in the back, helping gather up the food. Women kept coming in with hands full of bowls, pans and platters. A group of older girls were in the kitchen, busily washing, rinsing and drying dishes, cups, glasses, silverware and utensils. I followed dad out the back and to mothers' side. "Are you about ready to go, Verna?" Dad asked.

"Just about. Have you asked Michael when it would be a good time to get together for the barn raising?" Mother asked.

"We discussed it at length, actually," Dad said. "He needs some time to gather all the material together. He would like some help in preparing the rafters ahead of time. A group of the young men and older boys will come over to help with that in a couple of weeks. He has the lumber for that already. He's been cutting down timber in the wooded area, and has enough for rafters, cross beams, and poles. He has ordered the lumber for the walls and roof, and hopes it will be here within the month. We have agreed to bring as large a work force together as possible, as soon as all the lumber is in place. We want to get the barn up before winter sets in."

"That's good. I told Katherine that a group of us women would bring the food to help feed the crew. Think it can be finished on one weekend?"

"Oh yes, if everything is here and we have enough men to help, you will be surprised at how quickly it will go up."

Just then an attractive lady with long, dark red, hair, and dancing, blue eyes, came up to mother and dad saying, "I've been listening to your conversation. Forgive me for eaves dropping, but I must tell you of how very pleased I am. I never imagined in my wildest dreams that there were people like you here. In Ireland, our neighbors would

Country Splendor

help each other out, but in America, we found people to be more standoffish. But here, you all have made us feel so welcome and I am truly beholden to all of you."

I realized that this was Mrs. O'Malley. I loved the way her voice sounded and the slight lilting accent to her words. When she smiled, which is what she was doing just then, large dimples appeared in both cheeks. Just then a tall, black haired, good-looking man appeared and dropped an arm around Mrs. O'Malley. He had kind eyes that seemed to be smiling as he spoke. "Well now, and what do we have here?" He said with the same accent that Mrs. O'Malley had. "Can I interrupt or is this a private party?" ending his words with a deep chuckle.

"Oh, go on with ye, ye know well and good that we are having a friendly chat and nothing more," she said to him.

Dad laughed and turned to Mr. O'Malley. "Vell, Michael, we were just discussing the barn raising we are planning for the end of the month. I think that there will be enough manpower to get that barn of yours up and ready to use over one weekend. The men will bring their own tools, and the women will bring the food. If the material is all here, you'll have your barn before the snow flies."

"A mighty fine thing, that!" He replied. "I do believe the Gods are smiling on us after all."

"And well He might. We've been doing a bit of praying lately. It is a big step we've taken, coming here and buying this poor wee place. But we felt a peace settle on us as we walked this land. It felt right. After today, we know that God Himself led us here and gave us the go-ahead and wherewithal to put it in our name. We have stretched our budget a bit, buying the stock, putting the house in order and all, and there have been moments when we've had to go without a bit, to make it to the end of each month. But glory be, we have hope now, we can see the good Lord's hand in everything. You folks have been a God's send and we are grateful." Mrs. O'Malley finished with a swipe at suddenly wet eyes.

Mother, being the kind-hearted woman that she was, approached Mrs. O'Malley and put her arm around her shoulder. "We were glad to be able to do something to welcome you here. You are a wonderful addition to our neighborhood. Drop over whenever you can. Coffee is always on. Is there anything else we can do before we head home?"

Mrs. O'Malley pulled herself free from mother arms and said, "Thank you kindly but you've done enough. We will be by to visit a bit one of these days though. Thank you for inviting us, and you be sure and drop by too. I will need to return your bowls and such, as soon as we eat all the food left for us. You've all been too kind."

Mother noticed me standing near by, all eyes and ears, taking in the conversation. "Helen, round up your sister and your brothers. We need to get on home." She started to turn me towards the house when Mrs. O'Malley said, "You are the little sister that Eileen has been telling my Margaret about. Well now, you are a pretty little thing."

I must have blushed, as I felt a warmth flood my face. I ducked my head and mumbled, "Thank you." Then being a little embarrassed, I turned and ran to the house to round up my siblings, as mother had instructed. A few minutes later we were all tucked in the car and headed for home.

As I sat reflecting on the interesting day I'd had, I remembered Mrs. O'Malley's kind words to me. I wondered at her calling me a 'pretty little thing.' I looked down at my pretty new dress and as I caressed it with my hand I thought, 'thank you God, for answering my prayer and helping me feel prettier for one day.'

CHAPTER TWENTY-TWO

Two weeks later, two wonderful things took place. The first thing was Ron, Herbert, the Foss boys and several other young men, whom they were able to coerce into helping, spent the weekend working with Michael O'Malley, building the rafters for his barn. Ron came home Sunday in a very good mood. They had completed the work and Michael praised the young men for doing a superb job and paid each one two dollars. They tried to refuse but Mr. O'Malley 'would have none of that now' he told them.

"I asked for the help and I pay what's due and we won't have no more discussion about it," he said.

Then to show how he felt about the boys, he gave each one a sip of Irish whiskey. "You work like a man, you get treated like a man," he said. "If we were in Killarney I would have taken you to a pub and showed you how we treat a man there, but being we are in America, I wouldn't be getting your folks mad at me, so this wee taste will have to do."

It might not have been much, but coming to them the way Michael presented it to them, the boys were elated. They laughed and talked all the way home, about finding a way to go to Ireland where they would be treated like the men they were. It boosted their ego, and put them on a high that lasted for days.

The second wonderful thing to take place was the letter that arrived in Monday's mail. A letter from grandma Vaughan, letting the folks

Country Splendor

know that Roy would be arriving on a bus the evening of Sept.21, which was that very evening. A letter from Roy was included in her envelope. He wrote that he heard that dad had been injured again and he realized that he was needed at home. He said that grandmother had assured him that he would be treated with appreciation, and he was willing to give it a try. He sent his love and said he hoped he could make it home by dad's birthday. Dad's birthday was September 21.

I had delivered the letter to mom and dad as they were having a cup of coffee in the kitchen. When mother saw whom the letter was from, she hurriedly opened it, with trembling fingers. As she read the letter to dad, I noticed him blinking his eyes, and trying to cover his emotions by drinking great gulps of coffee. When mother finished reading both letters, she wiped the tears from her eyes; leaned over to dad, kissing him squarely on his lips and said, "Happy birthday, Hubie!"

Dad grinned at mother and asked, "Did you plan this Verna? No, don't tell me. I know that you had something to do with it, but this time, all I can say is, thanks. I couldn't have been given a nicer gift."

"Mama, are we going to have birthday cake tonight?" I asked, already knowing the answer to that question. I had seen mother whipping something up and guessed it was in the oven right then. "Never mind, I can smell it baking right now, right?"

"Yes, right. We are going to have an angel food cake with chocolate frosting, and since we will be making a trip into Barron to meet a certain bus this evening, we will stop by the drugstore and buy a carton of ice cream to have with it."

"Wow, wait until Ron and Eileen hear! Won't they be surprised?" I danced around the room, super-charged with all the excitement.

"Helen, let's have some fun. Don't tell Eileen or Ronny about Roy's coming home. I'll let them think that mom and I are going to the movies as my birthday present, and then we will bring Roy and the ice cream home as a surprise. Do you think you could keep a secret that long?" Dad asked me, accompanied by a nod of approval from mother.

"I can try, but if I went with you it would be easier." I tried to bargain with them, hoping I could go.

"To make it believable, you have to stay home with them, but don't let on you know anything or it will spoil the surprise," Mother said.

"But that's so hard when I'm so excited. They will see something's up for sure. I know, I'll say I'm not feeling good and I'll stay in bed until I hear the car come in the driveway."

"That's an excellent idea, Helen. If you can keep the secret until we get home, I'll see that you get an extra scoop of ice cream," Mother promised.

"Is it alright if I tell Bobby?" I asked.

"Sure, you go tell Bobby right now. That will help you keep from exploding and he won't tell." Dad laughed, as mother just shook her head. "Sometimes I wonder where that little one came from," I heard dad say to mother, as I exited the kitchen in search of Bobby.

The afternoon went quickly and yet it seemed to last forever. I played with Bobby. He wasn't terribly interested in the secret I told him, and I was not placated. I wanted to share this secret with someone who would care. 'Patty, she would care,' I thought to myself. I hurried out to my tree in search of my invisible playmate. The weather was pleasantly warm. We were having an 'Indian summer,' I had heard mother say.

When I asked mother what that meant, she replied, "It had something to do with the Indians having to live outdoors and hunt buffalo and deer for food and clothing. They would pray to their earth mother to keep the cold away, until they were totally prepared with plenty of food stored away, and warm robes ready for the winter. So whenever we have warm, summer like weather, late into the fall, people call it an Indian summer."

I lay beneath the tree, staring up at the branches in search of my squirrel. I thought about the stories Eileen had read to me, about the Indians and how they had lived, a long time ago. Sleeping in a type of tent called a tepee, I think she called it. That sounded fun to my young ears. Moving from place to place in search of food and fresh water. I thought it might be a pleasant way to live, so free, like a picnic that never ended. New adventures all the time. But when I remembered how harsh our winters were, I decided that I liked living in houses better.

I thought of my friend Patty. After having met Margaret, I could picture Patty's face as clearly as I had pictured the color of her hair and eyes. I talked to her, telling her all of my secrets, starting out with the one about my brother coming home. "We mustn't let Eileen and Ron know, so I think I'll just stay out here with you until the folks come home." She agreed to help me keep it a secret.

Then I told her my most secret of secrets. The one about me being an orphan like the Little Orphan Annie in the story that Eileen had read to me. She wanted to know why I thought that. I said that I was different than my sister and brothers. I had freckles and red in my hair like Patty, and mother said I got that from my Irish ancestors. If I have Irish ancestors and the others don't, then I must be an orphan that mother and dad took in.

Patty interrupted my thoughts by asking, "How do you know your sister and brothers' don't have a little Irish in them as well? Did your mother actually say that?"

"Well, no. I guess I must ask her about that. But I did hear daddy say just this day that he wondered where I came from."

Patty agreed that it all sounded possible, but warned me that things weren't always like they seemed. Patty was so wise.

Then I told her about the Indians. "Let's pretend that we are Indians, living here beneath this big oak tree," I suggested. She was all for it, so we gathered some longer limbs and twigs and leaned them up against the tree. When we had enough to make a small place for us to crawl into, we covered the outside with the leaves that carpeted the grass. I told Patty that no one would know it was a hideout. They would just think it was a pile of leaves piled against the tree. A blanket of leaves inside made a comfortable bed. We curled up on the leaves and pretended to be sleeping.

"Hey, what are you doing in here? Hiding from someone?" The voice was my sister's.

'She's home from school already, on no,' I thought to myself. 'She's not suppose to find me.'

"Has something happened?" she asked, as she peered into my hideout. "Are you in trouble again?" She sounded genuinely concerned for me. She knew how I had a tendency to hide myself after getting spanked, or even a good scolding.

"No. I'm just playing Indian. This is my tepee."

"Oh, alright. I've brought a new book from school to read to you. I think you will like it. It's called Girl of the Limberlost."

"Oh good! You can read it to me when the folks go to town tonight." 'Oops, that slipped out without me thinking first.'

"Why are they going to town? Today is dad's birthday, we always have a cake and celebrate it together," she said, with disappointment evident in her voice.

'Now be careful of what you say,' Patty reminded me.

"I think there is a show that daddy and mother want to see," I said, remembering the story they decided to use to explain their going to town.

"Then I should get to go along because I was promised a movie for staying home when you went with mother to pick up dad from the hospital, remember?"

'Oh dear, that's right. Now what do I say?' I thought, while putting one hand over my mouth to keep from blurting out anything that would give the surprise away.

Patty always knew what I was thinking and she said, "Just don't say anything more. Let your mother handle it." Patty was so much wiser than I was, so I took her advice.

"Guess you will have to ask mother about that," I said and drew myself further into my tepee.

"I will!" she said, as I heard her kicking at the dry leaves on her way towards the house. I waited in my hideout a few minutes longer, wondering what was being said inside. The suspense was too much; I had to know what was being said. I crawled out and ran quickly to the porch. I stepped up to the door and opened it very slowly, hoping no one would hear. Stepping inside, I could hear voices in the kitchen.

Country Splendor

I had expected to hear some angry sounds, or at least someone upset, but there was only quiet talk. I had to get closer to hear, but I didn't want to be seen, so I sidled up to the doorway, staying just out of sight, yet close enough to hear.

Mothers voice was soft and conspiratorial, as she said, "We did mention to Helen that we might go to the movies, but actually, we have a surprise planned for you and Ron instead. We were hoping we could manage it without you having any idea of a surprise at all. You know, just spring it on you, with you totally unaware that anything was going on. But it will still be fun, because now you will be anticipating it, and sometimes that can be the most fun of all."

To confirm what mother said, Eileen asked, "But you are not going to the movies tonight, right?"

"Right. I promised you that you would be going to the movies the very next time dad goes, and a promise is a promise. Now I would like to get supper out of the way so dad and I can run into town real soon. I will leave it up to you what you tell Ron," Mother said, as I heard her chair scrap against the floor. Everything seemed to be fine, so I chanced an entry. Mother was at the stove, stirring the soup kettle. Eileen was sitting at the table with her back to me.

"Can I set the table, mama?" I asked, as I moved around the table in the direction of the stove.

Mother looked over and gave me a smile, "That would be very nice. Get the soup bowls and some spoons. We are having soup and biscuits for supper."

I was relieved to see mother smiling. My slip up must have been okay. I went around the table and started pulling one of the heavy, oak, chairs, towards the cupboard. "Wait, Helen," Eileen said, "I'll help you get the bowls." She got up and moved over to the cupboard, reached inside for the bowls and handed a couple to me. "These are too heavy for you to take them all at once. Set those on the table and I will hand you the rest."

I did, as I was told, happy that no one was mad at me. Once the bowls were arranged around the table, I went for the spoons and knives. Eileen was placing a glass at each place, as I returned with the silverware. I tried to figure out what kind of a mood she was in. She wasn't giving anything away. She kept her face devoid of any expression. That made me nervous. I knew her well enough to know that she was just waiting until the folks left, to pounce on me for more information, but she didn't want mother to know what she intended to do. She glanced over at me and caught me looking at her. She read my face, and confirmed my suspicions, with an ever so slight rising of the eyebrows. I ducked my head and began to strategize. She mustn't know what I intended on doing. If she grilled me I might just let something slip. She knew just how to make that happen too.

I wished that I could talk mother into letting me go with them. That was my only hope, but she had already said no to that. I could run away and hide until the folks got home, but where would I go that she wouldn't find me? I was still giving the problem a lot of thought when my brother came in the door.

"Having an early supper, mom? Something going on tonight?" He asked.

"As a matter of fact, dad and I have to run into town for a few minutes. Thought we would eat and get back here in time to have some birthday cake, before you go to bed," Mother explained.

"Got a special package to pick up?" He asked, with a smile working it's way into a full grin.

"What ever do you mean?" Mother asked, trying to sound innocent.

"Well, I figure the timing is just about right for the prodigal to come home. Am I right?"

Eileen's eyes widened and she gave mother a questioning look. She could see the answer written in her smile. "So that's the big surprise! I might have known. You're right Ron, that's got to be it. It is, isn't it mom?" She insisted.

"What can I say, the cat's out of the bag. Yes, we got the message today that he will be arriving on the six o'clock bus. We were hoping to surprise you with it, but Ron, you know you're brother too well," Mother confirmed. "Helen, go get your father and tell him supper is on the table and the surprise is on us!"

The talk around the table was charged with anticipation. What would Roy be like? Would he be glad to be home, or would he be looking for more adventure in a short while? Had he grown much in the two months or so that he had been gone? Everyone seemed glad that he would be home soon, but a little skeptical of why he was coming home. Did he really miss the family enough to come back to the farm that he hated? Or maybe it wasn't the farm and the work that he ran away from. That statement hung in the air for some minutes while each person chewed on the implications, according to what they thought, he thought or felt. The silence was broken when dad looked at the clock hanging on the wall.

"Look at the time! We had better be getting to town, Verna. We don't want to miss that bus," Dad stated, as he rose to his feet and headed for the door.

Mother followed him across the room, but at the door she stopped and turned back to us. "Girls, get the dishes done and feed Bobby. Ron, is Roger going to help with the milking tonight?" Ron nodded in answer. "Okay then, we shouldn't be long. Dad wants to pick up some ice cream to have with his cake. See you in a little while."

I was so relieved! No inquisition. No need to worry about spilling the beans. I could relax and enjoy the thought of my brother coming home. I was excited, and I asked Eileen how she felt.

"I'm glad. I know that it will make dad's birthday extra special for him. He missed Roy more than he would let any of us know, but I knew. Roy's his favorite. Always has been. Isn't that right, Ron?"

He remained silent for a few minutes, contemplating his own thoughts on the matter. He was the thinker of the family, the deep one. Finally he shifted in his chair, pushing it away from the table. "There is some truth to that, but dad loves all of us. He doesn't always show it, but he does. It's just that Roy is so much like dad, and even though it frustrates dad sometimes, still he understands him and admires his guts. Well, this isn't getting the work done." He rose from his chair and headed for the door.

"Helen, bring Bobby in and feed him while I get at these dishes. Let's have everything done and set up for dad when he gets back," Eileen ordered and I rose to obey.

How long is an hour? A short time to some, a lifetime to someone who is impatient, and anxious about what is coming. The minutes seemed to drag. I tried to keep busy. I fed Bobby his soup, or most of it, and headed for a washcloth to clean his face with, before putting him down on the floor to play. When I headed back toward him, I gave a little scream and then started laughing. Eileen turned to see what that was all about, took one look at Bobby, and burst into laughter as well. There he sat at the table with his bowl balanced upside down on his head like a hat, with strings of egg noodles dangling down around his ears and eyes. At first he looked at us with big eyes, as if to ask, 'what's so funny?' but then he started to grin and said, "Bobby go bye, bye."

"He thinks he has a hat on like dad puts on before going somewhere," I laughed, stating the obvious.

"Bobby go nowhere, you little imp!" Eileen said, as she took the bowl before it fell. "Are you going to be a clown when you grow up?'

"Clown," Bobby said, nodding his head with some of the noodles still dangling from his hair. It cracked us both up and we laughed so hard, we could hardly clean him up.

"He doesn't even know what a clown is, but he sure could be one." I giggled, as he grabbed a noodle that had fallen on his tray and put it in his mouth.

We finally got the noodles washed out of his hair, the soup washed off his face, and the last of the noodles off his hands. We placed him on the floor and he started doing a little sideways kick and dance. "Now where did he ever see anything like that?" Eileen exclaimed, with a grin and a shake of her head.

"He doesn't need to see anything, he's a natural clown! Clowns could learn from him!" I laughed.

Finally we had the table, chair, and floor cleaned, and the dishes washed, dried, and put away. Then we set the table again, with small

Country Splendor

plates, forks, and spoons. "Wish we had some flowers to put on the table to make it pretty," I sighed.

"I've got an idea," Eileen said. "Let's make dad a birthday card. I have some paper we could use and we could draw something nice on it, color it and everything."

"Yes, yes, let's. But we better hurry so we can get it finished before they get here," I said, as she left to run up stairs after her paper and colors. "Bring two sheets of paper down, Eileen," I shouted after her, "Let's make a card for Roy too, that says 'welcome home.'"

"Good idea," she shouted back. She hurried back down the stairs and handed me a piece of paper. "Here, you take this piece and figure out what you want on it for Roy, while I make dad's card."

We took our papers to the kitchen table, clearing the dishes to one side to make room to work. I decided to draw a picture of each member of the family with one hand raised saying 'hi.' I drew stick figures with big heads, each one a little different to represent a member of the family. I colored black hair on Ron, yellow hair on Eileen and red hair on me. Mama and dad were bigger stick people, mother with black hair and dad with yellow. Then I drew a little stick boy with yellow curls. "Eileen, will you put the words on for me?"

She turned from her project and looked at my paper. "What is that suppose to be?"

"Our family, can't you see? There is mama, there's dad, that's Ron and that's you. This is me, and that little one is Bobby. We are all saying hi to Roy. Can you write 'Welcome home Roy' for me?"

"Well, okay. But I have a lot of work to do on mine yet, so don't bother me anymore." She drew some letters on mine and shoved it at me. I took it and laid it at the place Roy usually sat when he was home, and put his plate on it, so it wouldn't blow away.

Then I went to the front room window and watched for the car. "It surely should be coming down the road any minute now," I told myself. "They have been gone a long time!" It was so black out, not even a star yet, I thought. 'Hope they can see to get home. Of course they can, the car has headlights. How stupid, Helen!'

"Mama come now?" Bobby asked, as he pulled on my leg for attention.

"Not yet. They should be here pretty soon." I turned my attention back to what Eileen was creating. I crossed to the kitchen again and stood by her side, trying to see over her shoulder. I had to stand on my tippy toes to see, and as I did, I bumped her arm.

"Darn you Helen! You made me mess up my picture. It's ruined now!" She turned on me in her fury.

"Wait, no it isn't. Look, you were coloring in one of the flowers, but this extra mark could become a small bud," I suggested, trying to placate her.

She turned back to the picture, studying it. It was very lovely. A large bouquet of flowers in a tall lovely vase made the background for a tall and yummy looking chocolate cake. It was on a pedestal plate of a delicate blue. The flowers were a fall variety of yellows, gold's and oranges. Their leaves were shades of dark yellow greens. As I watched, she took the orange color she had been using, and with quick strokes, she changed the slip of color into a lovely bud. She highlighted it with a bit of yellow, and placed a half furled leaf just below it.

"See, isn't that pretty!" I exclaimed.

"I must confess, that does add a special touch to it. Now I will add a little poem I remember from one of the books I read. Let's see, how does it go?" She sat with her hand to her head as she tried to recall the exact words. "Oh yes, it goes like this. 'Birthdays are a special time, to demonstrate one's love. It marks the blessings of the years that come from God above. Today we say, "I love you dad!" and here's a poem to prove it. We thank you God, for your great gift of a father who deserves it. Happy Birthday dad.' How's that?"

"It's beautiful, Eileen. Hurry and finish it, they should be here soon."

"You hope. You know the folks; they go for one thing and think of several things to do before coming home. I just hope they get here before we have to go to bed!" Eileen sighed, as she completed the card, and laid it at dad's place at the head of the table. Then we straightened up the plates and utensils again. "There, that looks nice."

"What looks nice?" Ron asked, as he came through the kitchen door, followed by Roger Foss. "Oh, I see, you've been fixing the table for dad's birthday. Wonder what's taking them so long? Thought they would have been here by now."

"Me too! I just looked out the window again and still no lights coming down the road. I wonder if something has gone wrong?" Eileen seemed to have a sixth sense about unexpected happenings and we looked at each other with a sense of dread. We all fell quiet, thinking our own thoughts..

CHAPTER TWENTY-THREE

As the other's tried to make small talk around the kitchen table, I kept watch by the kitchen window. Turning once more into the room and addressing my oldest brother, I said, "Is there anyway you can go look for them?"

"No, not really, and there is no use worrying about it. It won't make them come any faster." Then turning to his friend as Roger rose from his chair, Ron asked, "Roger, don't you want to stay and see Roy before going home?"

"I smell like a barn. Think I'll head on home and clean up. Haven't had supper yet, and mom keeps it warm for me so I should go." He stood up to leave; turned and concluded with, "Tell Roy I said hi and I'll see him tomorrow." He reached for the door and opened it. Just as he stepped out onto the porch a car engine could be heard, slowing down to turn into the driveway, and then gunning it to make it up the slight incline. As it swung in, the headlights brightened up the back porch.

"They're here! They're here!" I shouted, as I did a little bouncing aerobics in delight.

Bobby came running from the front room and made a beeline right past tall legs and out the kitchen door. "Mama, mama!" he shouted. Roger grabbed him just as he would have fallen down the steps.

"Whoa there young fella. You almost flew right off the porch." By this time the rest of us had crowded onto the porch, trying to see who

Country Splendor

was getting out of the car that had driven right around the circle, and came to a stop right in front of the porch. The passenger side door flew open, and out stepped a very delighted brother, Roy.

He made the porch in one bound and grabbed Roger with both hands. "Hi there, didn't expect to see you waiting here for me! How are you doing?"

"You almost didn't see me, I was just headed home. I must say you are looking well, and you've grown some, haven't you?" Roger asked.

"Guess I have, some. My pants are a little short on me now. Hey, brother!" He stepped past Roger and into Ron's out-stretched arms. Ron grabbed him in a bear hug like he would never let go again.

"Oomph! Hey, you've gotten stronger, you're about to squeeze the life right out of me," Roy said, with a voice struggling to take a deep breath. Ron released him with a grin stretching clear across his face.

"You try running without me again, and you won't live to have a life to squeeze out," he jokingly remarked.

"I'm done running. It's good to be home again. Hey, there sissies," referring to his two sisters that awaited him in the doorway. "How are you?"

Eileen and I grabbed out and each took a hand, pulling him into the light of the kitchen. "It's about time you came home!" I said, and Eileen seconded that statement. He hugged me first, and then released me to hug Eileen.

"You've grown some, too," he said to her. "You are becoming a young lady. Everyone treating you alright?"

"Good as it gets around here. Sure glad you are home. Now I have someone closer to my own size to pick on again," she said with a laugh.

"Hold the bus! Think I'd better run for it!" He laughed at her, whirling her around before letting her go.

Mother came into the kitchen, pulling Bobbie along behind her. She went to the icebox and laid a container of ice cream directly on the ice. "That should hold it until we eat." Then looking at the table she said, "Wonderful! I see you girls have been busy. Nice job!"

Eileen and I looked at each other with a 'good, she noticed, expression on our faces. I grinned and nodded to my sister, raising an eyebrow to suggest that mother's pleased with us. She grinned and nodded back.

"Where's dad?" Eileen asked, turning back to mother.

"He's getting the car put away. We had a bit of bad luck. First the bus was late, and then we got to the drugstore just as it was about to close, so we had to talk the owner into letting us in to purchase the ice cream. We told him it was Hubert's birthday, so he relented and let us get it. I guess he had a date to be somewhere early and was trying to make it. But anyway, we got the ice cream. Then we headed home and had barely made the Turkey Farm Road when a tire blew, almost putting us into a ditch. Thank goodness for another motorist coming towards us just then. He stopped his car and left the lights burning so we could see how to change the tire." She paused, as she thought about the car, dad, and the suitcase. "Roy, go help dad with your suitcase. He really shouldn't be lifting anything yet."

Roy had just picked Bobby up and was nuzzling his neck, making him laugh. "Oh, okay mom." He put Bobby back on his feet and dashed out of the house. Roger had just said goodbye to dad and was turning to head home as Roy descended on the car.

"Where's the suitcase, dad?" Roy asked, as he met dad by the back door, just as he was opening it.

"I think mom put it here in the back seat while we were changing that tire," Dad said.

Roy reached into the back seat area. It was too dark to see anything, so he felt around for it. "It's not here, dad. I've felt everywhere. You sure it got put in here after we took it from the trunk, when we got the tire out?"

"Vell, lets check the trunk again. Maybe it was pushed way back in there." He rounded the car to the trunk, lifted its lid and felt around in it. "Nope, don't feel it. You don't suppose we left it by the side of the road by mistake? It was so dark out, that if it had been in the shadows, we might not have seen it."

Country Splendor

"Now what do we do?" Roy sounded disappointed at this turn of events.

"What's holding you two up?" Ron called from the vicinity of the back porch. "Mom sent me out to get you. The cakes on the table."

Dad was saying to Roy, "Vell, we have to go get it. It's only about three miles away. Shouldn't take that long to find it." Turning towards the porch he said, "You want to come with us Ron, to look for it?"

"Look for what, dad? What did you loose?" Ron asked sounding puzzled.

"My suitcase, the one that grandma Vaughan gave me to carry the new clothes she bought for me, while I was there. When we were changing the tire, we had to take it out of the trunk to get to the tire. It must have been left at the side of the road," Roy explained.

"Okay, yes, I'll come with you. Let me tell mom what's going on, and I'll grab the lantern as well. Be right with you," he said, as he headed back through the kitchen door. Voices could be heard as Ron filled mother in on the latest development and "oh, no's" echoed from everyone's lips.

He returned to the porch, slamming the door behind him, and proceeded quickly to the car. Dad and Roy were waiting in the front seat for him, but he crawled into the back and said, "Okay, let's go!" It sounded like an order right out of a Tom Mix, cowboy, western movie; only they were heading out in a car, not on horses. Dad gunned the motor in response, and almost killed it, as it struggled to move the car in reverse. A shudder or two, and the motor caught again, purring nicely at last, as dad put the car in first gear and turned down the driveway.

"Can anything else go wrong?" Eileen asked in a plaintiff voice, as we watched the taillights of the car disappear down the road.

"Go wong?" Bobby repeated, while trying to see what we were looking at.

"Come on, Bobby." Mother reached for him and pulled him into her arms. She cradled him to her as she turned from the window to reenter the kitchen. "We are going to give you a little cake and some ice cream, since it's so close to your bedtime. Then off to bed with you." She placed him in his highchair and reached for the chocolate birthday cake.

"Mom, isn't it bad luck to cut the cake before the birthday person has had a chance to blow out the candles?" Eileen asked.

"Bad luck you say? What more could go wrong? I think we have seen the last of that, now let's concentrate on the positive." Her voice held a finality that belied any further argument. She cut a sliver of the cake and laid it on a saucer. "There, you can hardly tell that there has been any removed at all." She crossed to the icebox and lifted out the container of ice cream. She opened it up, remarking, "Well, shouldn't have any trouble scooping this up. It has softened very nicely."

"Any softer and it will be soup," Eileen said, as she watched mother spoon a small helping onto the saucer, next to the cake.

"Eileen, what did I say?"

"Do you know how hard it is to have a positive attitude, when so many things have gone wrong?" Eileen asked, being very truthful.

"You don't have to tell me, I've been witness to it. Sometimes I think God lets us have a taste of some hard times so we will more fully enjoy the good times."

I had been listening to this exchange, and I found myself feeling suddenly, very tired. I went into the front room, and crossed the dimly lit room to dad's favorite chair. I noticed that the wick was burning low in the Aladdin, oil lamp, sitting on the table near by. 'It needs its wick trimmed,' I thought as I curled up in dad's chair, trying to feel dad's reassuring arms around me. 'I'll just wait here for them to get back,' I thought, as I lay my head down on the armrest and shut my eyes.

"Helen, Helen, they are back," Eileen said, as she shook my shoulder to wake me.

I jumped out of dad's chair and followed my sister to the kitchen, where a lot of happy verbalism was going on. I entered just as Roy said, "and there it was, on the side of the road."

Dad interjected with, "Being it was this late you don't find many cars on the roads this time of night. Just the same it was a relief to find it right where we left it."

Country Splendor

"Well, alls well that ends well," Mother stated. "Now let's sit down to the table and have Dad's cake and ice cream while we can still dish it up." Everyone moved to the chair they were accustomed to sitting on, pulled it away from the table and sat down, all except mother who went to the icebox to retrieve the ice cream. "Thank goodness for ice, the ice cream is still firm enough to dish up." She moved back to the table to where dad was seated. "Do you want candles on your cake?"

"Forty one candles? It would take all night just to put them on. Let's just skip the preliminaries and get down to the basics here," Dad said, as he reached for the cake. "Looks like a mouse has been at it already," he laughed.

"Wait, we have got to sing happy birthday at least," Eileen said.

Murmurs went up around the table in agreement and to oblige everyone, mother led the singing in her sweet soprano voice. We all chimed in, and I thought the singing sounded like a lovely choir, with all the different levels of voices harmonizing. As the last "Happy birthday to you," ended, Roy's voice carried on with, "And many more!" with the rest of us echoing the sentiment.

"Now, Verna?" dad asked, as he patted mom's backside.

"Yes, cut yourself a piece of the cake and I'll dish the ice cream." She dug her spoon into the delightfully cold dessert and began spooning it onto his plate.

Light banter continued around the table, as first one and then another, helped themselves to a piece of cake, and mother continued to ply the ice cream to each plate in turn. Quiet descended as mouths were filled, and everyone experienced the joy of tasting and swallowing.

Dad finished his cake and ice cream, and asked mother if there was any coffee left. She nodded, and then rose from the table to get it for him. He noticed the two pieces of folded paper lying in the middle of the table, and sensing they were for him, he reached out and took them. Eileen and I watched as he unfolded and read them. "Mother, look at the vonderful birthday card our daughters made me! And Roy, I think this one is for you," he said, as he handed the one I had made, to Roy. "Thank you girls!"

Roy looked at his piece of paper, and turning to me he said, with as straight a face as he could keep, "You are quite an artist Helen, I recognize every person here. Thank you."

He handed it to mother who stifled a grin, as she looked my masterpiece over. "Very nicely done, Helen."

My smile must have lit up the room I was so pleased. "I'm so glad you're home!" I said, going to Roy and giving him a hug and kiss that he returned with a hug that squeezed the breath out of me.

"It's good to be home." He released me to return to my cake and ice cream.

Dad then turned his attention to Roy and said, "We are all wondering just how your trip went. That's quite a distance for a bike ride."

Roy finished his last bite of cake before looking across the table at dad and grinning. "Yes, it was quite a trip. I knew my way to Madison, having already made that part of the trip once. I got there late on the second day out, and I wasn't going to get picked up by the police again," he said with a wink at his brother, "so I stopped at a café where truckers eat. I sat down at the counter beside a friendly looking guy and ordered a hamburger. He watched me wolf it down; I was pretty hungry by then."

"He said, "Looks like you haven't eaten for a while.""

"I told him that I had been spending the summer in Barron, but that I was needed at home and this was the first chance I had to eat since leaving. He asked me where I was headed and I told him, Webb City, Missouri. He asked me if I was hitch hiking and I told him 'no, I had my own wheels, my bicycle.' He said that he was headed in that general direction and could give me a lift for a ways. I took the ride. I was pretty tired and didn't know where I would spend the night, so I figured that I could sleep as I rode with him. He put my bike in the back of his truck and off we went.

"We chatted a bit, but he could tell I was really tired, so he told me to catch a nap, and he would wake me up when we got to the road he would have to drop me off at. He didn't have to tell me twice! I fell right to sleep and two or three hours later, he was shaking me awake.

Country Splendor

"He said, "Here we are young man. This is Bloomington, Illinois. I have to catch hiway 74 to Cincinnati here, so you head southwest on hiway 55. It will take you all the way into St. Louis. Here's five bucks, rent you a room for the night at that little cabin place there," he was pointing at a group of cabins to my left. "Get a good nights sleep and then head out at first break of dawn. Get through the town before people notice you. Just a word of caution, don't trust every trucker you meet. Try to spend the night at a farmers place, ask them for a room in the haymow. If you have to do some work to pay for it, that's better than getting caught after dark, in town. Act like you know where you are going, but when asked; make it sound like a short way. That way they won't get suspicious and call the sheriff. I've written the best route for you to take, to get to where you are going. Your bike is waiting just outside, now be careful and play it smart."

"I thanked him, took the paper with the directions written on it, and the five-dollar bill, and put it all in my pocket, then opened the door. He reached across and grabbed my arm, stopping me for a moment as he said, "God be with you son," then he patted my shoulder and I slipped out of the truck and shut the door. I went to the office and paid for a cabin for the night."

Mother spoke up then, asking, "You mean to tell me, they didn't question a young person like you, wanting a cabin for the night?"

"It was an elderly man who waited on me, nobody else was around. I told him that my uncle Jack told me to stay the night there and he would pick me up in the morning. He just took my money and gave me a key to the cabin next door. I was able to wash up and sleep in a nice warm bed. I got up real early, just like that trucker told me to, and rode through town, watching to follow the signs to be sure I was taking the right road. I rode to Lawndale, a real small town, and stopped there for a hamburger and coke. Got to talk to a farmer that was on his way to Springfield, and asked him if I could ride that far with him. Turns out that he lived just outside of Springfield, so not only did he give me a ride, he had me stay for supper with him and his family and they let me sleep, that night, with their young son. They even fed me breakfast before I left the next morning, and packed me a lunch to take along."

"I hope you thanked them for their kindness," Mother interjected.

"Well, of course, Mom. I let them know how grateful I was, and they even gave me a slip of paper with their name and address on it, and asked me to let them know when I arrived at my destination. Of course I hadn't told them how far I was really going. But I did send them a note from grandma's."

"So how far did you make it the day you left them?" Ron asked.

"I rode pretty hard, trying to make as good time as I could. I knew it was a long way to St. Louis, but about half way I came to a lake, Lake Lou something. Anyway, it was late in the afternoon, so I decided to take a swim to refresh myself. I ran into these boys that lived close by. We had a good time diving from a high bank, and playing around there. When it was time for them to leave, I asked them if they knew of a warm barn I might sleep in for the night. They invited me home with them. I had supper with them and all four of us slept in their haymow that night. Course I helped them with their chores first.

"Then at daybreak, after their rooster woke me, I slipped out and headed on down to St. Louis. Stopped for breakfast at Litchfield, and talked another trucker into letting me ride with him to St Louis. That is one big city! It's so spread out it took me some time to work my way through there. I found hiway 44, as the first trucker told me to, and headed out of town to find a place to spend that night. That was quite a thrill, riding over the Mississippi River, that's a big river. I thought of Tom Sawyer and Huckleberry Finn and their adventure on that river. If it had been flowing in the right direction, I might have tried floating down it myself." He finished with a laugh.

"That might sound exciting son, but I've heard it's a pretty dangerous river, even has crocodiles and such in parts of it. Where did you spend the next night?" Dad asked.

"I actually rode a lot further that night than I had planned on. Just couldn't spot a good place to sleep and I wasn't too tired as I hadn't rode my bike that much that day. The twilight was real pretty, the skies were a bright orange as the sun went down, and it didn't get real dark for some time.

"Did you know there is a Mark Twain National Park? Close to a place called 'Devil's Elbow.' I searched around there for a place to spend the night and found a picnic table that looked good. At first I thought about making a bed on the ground, under the table, but then I remembered that they have poisonous snakes in that part of the country, so I fell asleep on top of the table. I woke up at dawn and found I was covered with an army blanket. Then I noticed a big truck pulled to one side of the picnic area. I left the blanket folded on the table, and took off. I would like to have thanked the truck driver, but I didn't want to wake him, and I was anxious to get to grandmas.

"By the time I got to Lebanon I was pretty hungry. I pulled into a truck stop café there, for some pancakes and eggs. I was just about through eating when a big guy came in and took the seat next to me. "Hi, young feller," he said. "Have a good nights sleep?" I was so surprised that I didn't know what to say. I just nodded and kept eating. He asked, "Going far?" I told him that I was headed for Webb City. He said, "Well, if you don't mind waiting while I have a meal you can ride on into Joplin with me." I of course said, "Sure!" So we talked and ate, and I rode with him into Joplin. He even insisted on paying for my meal. Course you know that it isn't that far on to grandma's house from Joplin, so I made it before suppertime."

"Was mother surprised when you showed up?" Mother asked.

"Was she ever surprised to see me! I wasn't sure if she was going to faint or hug me to death!" he finished with a laugh, as he remembered that meeting.

"Well, all I can say is the good Lord must have been watching over you, son. By the way, how was mother? I worry about her being alone there, on her little farm, all by herself."

"Actually, she isn't alone now. Just before I left, Uncle Earl and his son Billy came to spend some time with her. Seems he's having some family problems or something. But grandma is doing really well. She has her milk cow and chickens to take care of. I did her milking for her and carried in the buckets of water from her well each day. Even helped her finish canning the last of her garden vegetables. She seemed to enjoy having me there, and I enjoyed getting to know her again. We talked a lot. When I told her about my trip down to her place, she said that the good Lord must have been watching over me, just like you said, Mom."

"And I agree with that," Dad said. "Think you've got the wanderlust out of you now and can settle down here at home? We've a new team of horses you might like. Remember the team that Emil Zobel had?"

"Not them?" He exclaimed, as dad nodded his head. "How, how did you get Emil to part with them? They were his prize possessions!"

"Actually, he has bought himself a tractor now and he insisted on dad having his team of horses," Ron explained.

"That's terrific! Can I go see them now?"

"Can't you wait until morning, Roy? They will still be there," Mother said.

"Oh, let him go see them mother, he won't sleep until he does," Dad said, understanding that, at least in this way, Roy was like him.

"Well, if you must. But don't be long. Tomorrow will be here before you know it and you should be going to school."

"Do I have to mom, on my first day home? How about I stay home tomorrow and start on Wednesday?"

"Actually, son, I do think you need to start school right away. You have already missed some time and will have to make that up," Dad said.

"All right, but come on Ron and show me those horses. I won't be able to sleep until I see them for myself." With that the boys got up from the table, lit the lantern that hung by the door and headed out to the barn.

"What do you bet that they won't be in for a while, Hubie? They will have so much to talk about. We might as well clear up these dishes and head for bed. Eileen, you take Helen on up, and the two of you go to bed. Morning comes early around here."

I was tired, and I suspected Eileen was too, as she rose from her seat, said her goodnights, and headed for the stairs. I gave mother a kiss, then dad a big hug and kiss, telling him once again, "Happy birthday daddy, and goodnight."

He gave me a hug and then patted my head as I pulled away, and headed after my sister. "Goodnight angel, sleep tight. Don't let the bedbugs bite!" he said, with a grin.

"I won't," I giggled. I rounded the bend and headed up the stairs, following my sister.

Once we were in bed and just huddling down into a comfortable position, Eileen turned to me and said, "If it takes running away and coming home months later to be treated like a hero, maybe I should try it."

"No way, Eileen. Girls can't do that!"

"Oh, I know that. I just wish things could be better between dad and me. Sometimes I don't think he likes me at all."

"He does too like you. He loves all of us. Remember what Ron said? Dad just doesn't know how to show it some-times."

"What do you know? You are his little angel!" she stated it in a way that made me feel sad for her. She sounded mad at me, and I wondered what I had done to make her so unhappy.

Then I thought about my brother being home, and I smiled as I pulled my pillow closer around myself, settling down in it like a chicken in its feather nest.

'He must be so brave, to go all that way by himself,' I thought to myself as a picture of him riding down the road, mile after mile, further and further from home, played in my head. 'I could never do that, not all by myself. Maybe an angel was with him, yes, maybe that was it,' I thought, as I pictured an angel smiling down on me. Then I said my prayer, "Now I lay me down to sleep,
  Protect me Father, while I sleep,
  Provide our bread for one more day,
  Watch over us in work and play."
(I made the last part up myself.)

The End?